PENGUIN BOOKS

# About The Author

Hannah is a twenty-something-year-old indie author, mom, and wife from Western Canada. Obsessed with swoon-worthy romance, she decided to take a leap and try her hand at creating stories that will have you fanning your face and giggling in the most embarrassing way possible. Hopefully, that's exactly what her stories have done!

Hannah loves to hear from her readers and can be reached on any of her social media accounts.

Instagram : @hannahcowanauthor
Facebook : @hannahdcowan
Facebook Group : Hannah's Hotties
Website: www.hannahcowanauthor.com

SWIFT HAT-TRICK TRILOGY

*Lucky Hit*

BOOK ONE

HANNAH COWAN

PENGUIN BOOKS

PENGUIN BOOKS

UK | USA | Canada | Ireland | Australia
India | New Zealand | South Africa

Penguin Books is part of the Penguin Random House group of companies
whose addresses can be found at global.penguinrandomhouse.com

First published in the United States of America by Hannah Cowan, 2020
First published in Great Britain by Penguin Books, 2024
004

Copyright © Hannah Cowan, 2020

The moral right of the author has been asserted

Edited by Sandra @oneloveediting
Cover design by Booksandmoods @booksnmoods

Printed and bound in Great Britain by Clays Ltd, Elcograf S.p.A.

The authorized representative in the EEA is Penguin Random House Ireland,
Morrison Chambers, 32 Nassau Street, Dublin D02 YH68

A CIP catalogue record for this book is available from the British Library

ISBN: 978–1–405–96624–5

www.greenpenguin.co.uk

MIX
Paper | Supporting
responsible forestry
FSC® C018179

Penguin Random House is committed to a
sustainable future for our business, our readers
and our planet. This book is made from Forest
Stewardship Council® certified paper.

# Reading Order

Even though all of my books can be read on their own, they all exist in the same world—regardless of series—so for reader clarity, I have included a recommended reading order to give you the ultimate experience possible.
This is also a timeline-accurate list.

**Lucky Hit** (Oakley and Ava) Swift Hat-Trick trilogy #1

**Between Periods** (5 POV Novella) Swift Hat-Trick trilogy #1.5

**Blissful Hook** (Tyler and Gracie) Swift Hat-Trick trilogy #2

**Craving the Player** (Braden and Sierra) Amateurs in Love series #1

**Taming the Player** (Braden and Sierra) Amateurs in Love series #2

**Overtime** (Matt and Morgan) Swift Hat-Trick trilogy #2.5

**Vital Blindside** (Adam and Scarlett) Swift Hat-Trick trilogy #3

# Disclaimer

The WHL and NHL team names have been altered in this story for both copyright and creative reasons.

# Playlist

**If I Know Me** — Morgan Wallen ♥ 3:08

**Younger** — Jonas Blue, HRVY ♥ 4:39

**Nervous** — Jake Miller, TOMOS ♥ 3:16

**You Belong** — Shawn Austin ♥ 3:32

**Look After You** — The Fray ♥ 2:33

**I'll Be** — Edwin McCain ♥ 4:29

**Never Gonna Be Alone** — Nickelback ♥ 3:38

**Don't Give Up On Me** — Andy Grammer ♥ 3:44

**She** — Jake Scott ♥ 4:18

**The House That Built Me** — Miranda Lambert ♥ 3:56

**Slow Dance In A Parking Lot** — Jordan Davis ♥ 5:39

**You Make Me** — Chelsea Cutler ♥ 3:42

**I Believe** — The Jonas Brothers ♥ 3:38

**Roots** — The Reklaws ♥ 4:20

**Mommas House** — Dustin Lynch ♥ 3:51

**To Be Young** — Anne-Marie, Doja Cat ♥ 3:13

**Heaven** — Bazzi ♥ 2:51

**All I Want For Christmas Is You** — Mariah Carey ♥ 3:24

**To The Man Who Let Her Go** — Tyler Shaw ♥ 3:53

**King Of My Heart** — Taylor Swift ♥ 3:33

**My Own Worst Enemy** — Lit ♥ 2:49

*Every reader, friend, and fellow author, this one's for you.*

# 1

# Oakley

I NEED A SHOWER. DESPERATELY. BEFORE I PASS OUT FROM A MIX OF overexertion and dehydration and end up needing my ass carried to the dressing room.

But right now, that's the last thing I want to do.

Instead of ridding myself of the stench that's wafting up from beneath my gear when I should have, I hung back to do another lap around the ice. A victory lap, if you will.

For most of my teammates, this is just the end of another winning season. For me, this is the last time I will ever skate in this arena, as not only a player but the captain of my hometown team, the Penticton Storm. I'm allowed to feel a little nostalgic. This arena has been my second home for the past three years.

The familiar cold of the ice nips at my skin through my jersey as I stare at the empty stadium like a wounded puppy. This old, outdated arena helped me rediscover my passion for hockey when the last thing I wanted was to slip on a pair of skates.

It's where I watched my mom and sister scream at the top of their lungs, waving around their cheesy signs at every game.

And where I realized I could be a leader—a genuine force to be reckoned with.

Lines of fluffy snow trail behind me as I skate slowly around the rink, my breaths ragged as I push myself along the boards. It's peaceful. The silence is unusual compared to the screaming crowds during a game or Coach's colourful words after a loss.

By the time I haul myself off the ice and down the hallway leading to the locker room, my chest is tight, tense with nerves and a sense of loss that I wish I wasn't already familiar with.

With a hard yank, the locker room door rips open, and I narrowly avoid smacking chests with my best friend.

The walking brick wall otherwise known as Andre Spetza flashes me a wide grin and clasps a hand over my shoulder. "I was starting to think I needed to go out there and pull you off the ice."

"Any longer and you would have."

He adjusts his grip on his hockey bag before simply tossing it to the side of the room and following me to my cubby. I arch a brow but don't say anything. Collapsing on a bench, I start untying my skates.

"What? I'm going to wait with you. I need as much time in your superstar presence as I can get."

"You make it sound like you'll never see me again. This isn't a breakup." Despite my attempted joke, the hurt in his auburn-coloured eyes is obvious. He isn't the only one hurting. "You guys can carry your own. With or without me."

He forces a laugh. "Humility looks good on you."

"Soak it up, big boy. Maybe you could learn a thing or two."

This time, his laugh is genuine. "Nah. Me and humility aren't meant to be."

"You'll have to force it, then, if you want to take my spot next season."

His eyes widen. "Not happening."

"I've nearly convinced Coach." I shrug. "The team is going to need a new captain, and you're the only one I trust to step up." If he can manage to keep his dick in his pants long enough to actually focus on something other than sex.

He sits stiffly beside me. "I told you not to do that. The only thing I'm good at is throwing my fists around and snapping at the other D-men to focus. I can't lead an entire team."

"Just think about it, man. That's all."

"Yeah, okay. I'll think about it. But no promises."

I nod. "No promises."

The silence is heavy as I finish untying my skates and grab my bag from my cubby, stuffing them inside. I remove my jersey and gear, putting everything away before throwing on a T-shirt and sweatpants.

By the time I have my bag over my shoulder, Andre is typing away on his phone, a scrunch between his brows.

"You good?" I ask.

His eyes snap to mine. "Yeah. Just last-minute party prep. Friday night, remember? If you stand me up at your own going-away party, I'll never forgive you."

I swallow a groan. "I'll be there." Even if going to a party is the last way I want to spend my final night in town.

"I wouldn't dream of it. You know how much I love to party."

"Your sarcasm is unbecoming," he scolds.

I laugh. "Just try to keep the invites to a minimum. I'm not going to be in much of a party mood."

There's a devious look in his eye that has me fighting back a scowl. If it weren't for the fact I know he just wants me to have a good time before I leave, I would have told him to call the entire thing off. But if it makes everyone else happy to get drunk in my name, I'll suck it up and drag my ass to a house party for a couple of hours.

He stands and clasps his hands together. "That's nothing a platter of Jell-O shots can't fix, Lee. But you have my word I'll be stingy with the invites. Now, let me walk you out of here for the final time. Wouldn't want you to get lost."

"Unlikely. You just don't want to say goodbye," I tease, standing and bumping his shoulder with mine.

"Damn right I don't." He shakes his head and collects his bag from the corner of the room before following me out the door.

The lights in the arena have already been dimmed, and our shoes echo through the halls as we walk. Silently, we pass the equipment room and the wall of team photos, from the first Storm team to ours this season, before coming up to Coach's office. My feet falter, and Andre pats my back.

"You want to talk to Coach?" he asks.

I exhale a loud breath and debate walking through the door. It should be an easy decision. I should go in and say goodbye. But it won't be that easy. There's a lot more I owe that man besides a simple goodbye.

"What are you two talking about out there? Spetza, you better not be here to tell me you're leaving too!"

Andre and I spin on each other, our eyes wide before Coach's brash laugh fills the hallway. I swallow and steel my spine. "Go home, Dre. I gotta do this. Friday night. I'll be there."

He nods, and we throw our arms around each other in a tight hug. After a minute, I pat his back, and we break apart.

"Text me later. See ya Friday." With that, he walks away, leaving me alone.

It takes me four steps to reach Coach's office. Banner Yaras is sitting behind a large mahogany desk with one hand around a massive cup of coffee—regardless of the time—while the other scratches his overgrown salt-and-pepper beard. He grins when he spots me in the doorway.

"Hey, Coach."

He motions toward the grey two-seater couch resting against the opposing wall and relaxes in his chair. "I was beginning to wonder if you snuck out of here without saying goodbye."

I flop down on the couch and lace my fingers behind my head, kicking my legs out. "I was debating it. Goodbye doesn't seem fitting. Not after everything you've done for me and my family."

"That was all you, kid. I just lit the fire under your ass that got you out of a slump."

"It was more than a slump, and you know it. But thank you. You have no idea how much it means to us. My mom especially. I owe you."

He swipes a hand through the air. "You can thank me by kicking ass in Vancouver. They need the help."

"Not you too. Please don't give me the 'why are you doing this' speech. My mom has laid into me enough for it."

Nobody is happy with my decision to join the Vancouver Saints and not the Ontario Rebels like I was expected to. They don't understand why I would turn down an offer to play for a more successful WHL team instead, but I don't need them to. Ontario is too far from my mother and sister, and that's that. No discussion needed on the matter.

Vancouver is going to be my home until I get drafted into the NHL. It would be easier if everyone just accepted that now instead of trying to change my mind.

"Your mom wants you to have the best chance possible. She doesn't think that's the Saints."

I narrow my eyes. "She doesn't, or you don't?"

Coach meets my stare with one of similar intensity. He's the closest thing to a father figure I've had since I was young, and I know his heart is in the right place, but that only makes his doubt more hurtful.

He releases a tight breath. "You just turned nineteen. It's this year or nothing. You wanted to wait to enter the draft until you were sure your mother could handle it, and I've always supported that idea. But we're past that now. The teams know you're eligible this draft, and I'm scared you could be throwing away your shot at the NHL with this team because you don't want to leave your family."

My stomach sinks and twists. "You're not telling me anything I don't already know. But I'm not changing my mind. I need your support here, Banner." I push a hand through my hair. "Please."

He rolls his lips, looking torn. This is a man I've had shout at me for messing up my footing during drills but also bring left-overs his wife had wrapped in tinfoil containers to my house on nights my mom had had to work late. Sure, it helped that his wife is good friends with my mom, but they didn't have to do half of the shit they've done for my family over the years.

Disappointing Banner is almost as bad as disappointing Mom.

After a few long moments, he relents. "I will always support you, Oakley. Always."

A weight lifts from my shoulders. Suddenly, I can breathe again.

THE SUN HAS JUST ABOUT SET by the time I park outside our small two-story home in my dad's old, beat-up white Ford.

My childhood home is not grand by any means, but it's home. A small porch with scuffed wooden steps sits in the centre, in front of a bright red door that Mom painted with Dad shortly after buying the home. It's chipped and peeling now, but Mom refuses to repaint it.

A bay window sits on the right side of the house, in the middle of the living room, along with a wooden flower box that lies underneath, filled with yellow daisies.

Tilting my head back, I stare at the water pelting down from the grey, puff-filled sky and groan. It has been pouring rain ever since I left the arena, which isn't that much of a surprise. April in British Columbia is nothing but goddamn rain.

I grab my hockey bag from the passenger seat, throw it over my shoulder, and run inside. "I'm home, Ma!"

I kick my shoes off and haul ass upstairs to deposit my bag in my room before Mom catches a whiff of the smell.

After I've disposed of it, I shut my door and plop myself down on my twin bed, sinking into the worn-in shape of my body on the mattress. My long frame makes it nearly impossible to keep my feet on the narrow bed as they dangle almost comically off the edge.

I look up at my open door when my mom knocks, catching her as she leans against the frame, her arms folded and her lips tugged up.

"Hey, sweetheart. How was your day?"

My mom looks exceptionally young for her age. Maybe it has something to do with how she always has her short blonde hair done up or how her crystal-blue eyes haven't lost their sparkle over the years.

I got most of my features from my dad. Dark brown hair that swoops at the back of my neck, evergreen-coloured eyes, and long legs.

"It was alright. Hard to say goodbye, but I'll be okay."

"I would be worried if you weren't the least bit sad, honey. Goodbyes are never easy." Her eyes shine with tears before she blinks them away. "But you should also let yourself be excited. You're so close to your dreams."

She sits down on the edge of my bed and gives me one of her famous Anne Hutton smiles, her blue eyes bright. "I am so proud of you. I know your father would be too."

Mom always has a way of smiling and lifting people's spirits. Dad always called it her superpower. I didn't understand how a smile could be someone's superpower until after the crash.

Her smile was one of the few things that got me through it all. So, in my eyes, that does make her a damn superhero.

I sit up to look at her properly. "I am excited. What about you? Will you be okay? I'll try to come home as often as I can."

My promise is clear in my words, and I'll do everything in my power to keep it. My new schedule is going to be crazy, but I would do anything for my family. Even driving four hours each way just to see that damn smile on my mom's face.

She clucks her tongue against the roof of her mouth and shakes her head. "You need to stop worrying about your sister and me. You're going to get grey hairs before you make it to your twentieth birthday. We will be fine. I promise."

I frown. "Gracie is going to push you without me here. Have you seen the piece-of-shit car that's been bringing her to and from school lately? It looks like it could catch on fire if the air conditioning and the radio are on at the same time."

Mom just laughs. "It's not that bad."

"Not that bad? Mom, the exhaust is black."

She stifles her laugh behind her hand, and her eyes crinkle at the corners. "Yes, I suppose that could be an issue. Maybe you should talk to her about it."

I snort a laugh. "Right. She won't listen to me. That's a guys car. Have you noticed the tinted front windows? It screams troubled teen. Is she dating this guy? You're not going to let that happen, right? There's no way my baby sister is going to be dating a guy who can't even take care of his own car. Actually, there's no way she's ever dating. Period."

"Oakley, relax, sweetheart. You're going to blow a blood vessel. Your sister is a teenage girl who's spent her entire life under your protective wing. Let her breathe while you're gone. I promise she'll be okay. I might be small, but I'm mighty when it comes to my babies."

Some of the anger leaches from my veins, and I nod. "I'll try. But no promises. I would appreciate weekly updates regarding that boy and his . . . car. I don't think it's safe for her to be on the road in that thing."

She smiles sadly and places a hand on my forearm, squeezing it. "I will. I'll get it figured out. You're right, she shouldn't be on the road in a dangerous vehicle."

I cover her hand with mine, not liking how cold it feels. "I love you, Mom. You know that, yeah?"

"I know. There are leftover burgers in the fridge if you're hungry. I'll leave you to relax. Good night, I love you." She gives me one final squeeze before standing and heading for the door.

"Night, Mom," I mumble as she leaves.

# 2

# Oakley

I don't drink alcohol. Ever. But that doesn't stop the drunken idiots from shoving their cups full of who knows what in my face or trying to drag me toward the keg planted in the middle of the kitchen, encouraging me to do a keg stand.

It took me far too long to ditch the overambitious drink sharers and find a quiet corner to sulk in. And now that I'm here, it's taking everything in me not to go home.

Life of the party, right?

Andre ran off a few minutes ago, chasing the heels of a girl up the stairs and abandoning me at my own going-away party.

It's really not a big deal. Or that's what I tell myself, anyway. That's just how Andre is. I never planned to be here long, so it's not like it matters much.

I suck back the rest of my water before dumping my empty red cup in one of the trash bins and making a beeline for the back door. If I'm going to be stuck here for at least another hour, I will not spend it stuck inside this hotbox.

The night air is tight and muggy, but I embrace it. Anything is better than the second-hand smoke and booze from inside. Several voices float from the pool deck, so I take off in the opposite direction and park myself in a camping chair that I find tucked beneath two trees. It's not the most private spot, but it could be a lot worse.

A heavy silence surrounds me despite the music coming from the house. My thoughts are a scattered mess. I don't think it's fully hit me yet that tonight is the last time I'll see most of the guys inside. It's sad as hell to think about playing hockey without them.

When I first joined the team, I used to act like I single-handedly hung the moon. And yeah, I had the skill to back it up, but my attitude cost us way too many games.

Maybe it was the need to prove myself after falling behind and slacking on my prior team, or maybe it was simply that I wanted to be the best. Either way, it was Coach Yaras who knocked me down a few pegs.

I learned the hard way that being the best on the ice means nothing if you don't have your team's respect. They won't follow you otherwise. That realization was why I worked my ass off in the second half of my first season to do exactly that. Then, during my second season, I earned the privilege of having the beloved C on my jersey.

I can happily admit that all the work was worth it, considering I just came out of this season as the number one goal scorer in the minor league.

Someone flops down beside me, grumbling lightly. The smell of weed takes me by surprise before I notice the lit joint between Andre's fingers. "Tell me you're not hiding from your own party."

Meeting Andre's disappointed stare, I lift a shoulder. "Did you not have fun upstairs? You're back quick."

"Changing the subject. Noted," he says before taking a drink from his cup and setting it back down on the ground beside him. "When do you leave tomorrow?"

"Early." Too fucking early.

Andre hums. "Tough. I guess you'll be leaving the party soon, then, hey?"

A heavy silence falls between us when I nod. The knowledge of what's coming is painful. Andre and I have been friends and teammates since our peewee days. I feel guilty as hell for ruining that.

"Get out of your head, Oakley. You're destined for the pros. Don't think twice about taking your shot. We'll survive."

"It just seems wrong to be playing for a team without you."

Andre scoffs a laugh before taking a hit from the joint and letting it out in puffs. "You know that hockey isn't my end game. But it's always been yours. This new team will lead you there. Don't be a pussy about it, eh?"

I drop my head back and laugh. "There it is. I was wondering how long it would take for you to lose the sweetness."

He grins wickedly. "Just don't forget about us when you're making millions."

"Like I ever could." Or want to.

A loud crash comes from inside the house, and Andre jumps off the ground. Raised voices leak through the open windows and the screen door.

I wave at the house. "Go. I'm good here. Make sure nobody's dead."

He offers me an apologetic smile. "I'll be back. I swear if anything's broken, I'm going to kick some serious ass."

"Good luck," I say before he spins and heads back inside.

I lean back in the chair and stare at the sky. It's a cloudy night, but I search for the stars anyway. Constellations are not my thing—hell, I don't even remember my star sign or whatever they're called, but there's something about a clear, white-flecked sky that calms me.

"Pisces? Gemini?" God, Gracie would chastise me for not remembering.

The rustling of grass grabs my attention before the gentle voice does. "Pisces is for end of February or March birthdays. Gemini is end of May and June."

I double blink.

A tall brunette is walking my way, her arms wrapped nervously around her front. The closer she gets, the easier it is to make her out in the dark.

Piercing green eyes are locked on me where I sit, but there's a red ring around them that's too obvious to ignore. Her slim cheeks are flushed, and I know it isn't from the weather. It's too warm.

I clear my throat. "Pisces, then. What about you?"

She stops a few feet from me and drags the toe of her white sneaker in the grass. I have to swallow to keep my throat from drying out. She's beautiful, even with the smeared black lines beneath her tired eyes.

"Aries. Early March birthday," she replies, tearing her eyes away and darting them around the yard. "My best friend loves star signs."

"So does my sister."

She nods but makes no move to sit down. For some reason, that bothers me. I want this stranger to sit with me, even for just a few minutes.

"Care to join me?" I ask. She hesitates, eyeing the ground. "You can tell me why you were just crying, or we can sit in silence. I have a sixteen-year-old sister, though, and I've been told I'm a great listener."

She chews on that for a minute. "Why are you outside alone?"

"Honestly?"

"Honestly."

"I'm not much of a partier."

"Yeah, me neither."

I wring my hands together and chew on my lip. "Want my chair? I can sit on the ground."

She answers me by closing the distance between us and sitting on the grass, holding her legs to her chest. I slowly turn to face her and find her already looking at me. My heart thumps —*hard*.

"You're a hockey player." It's not a question.

I swallow. "Is that bad?"

"My *ex*-boyfriend is a hockey player." Her words are venomous, and my curiosity grows.

"Is he here?"

"Oh, he's here. I found him in the bathroom with his dick down a random girl's throat."

"Shit." I wince.

She laughs, but it's dark, humourless. "Have you ever done something like that? Taken a girl in the bathroom and let her suck you off even though you have someone who already loves you waiting for you in the other room?"

My palms tingle with the urge to reach out and hug this girl, but I wipe them along my thighs instead. "No. It's not something any guy should do."

"You're right. It's not."

"Is that why you were crying? That prick?"

"Pathetic, right? If Morgan were here, she would be shaking some sense into me."

"Is that your best friend?" I ask. She nods. "Sounds like a good friend. I could shake some sense into you, but I don't think it would be the same," I say, keeping my voice light.

When she cracks a smile, I grin. A swirling feeling ignites in my stomach as she holds my gaze, her curiosity unwavering.

"I think it would look terrifying if someone were to see that. You're much bigger than me."

My brain is immediately flooded with images of the different ways we could explore that size difference, and my dick stirs. With a shake of my head, I'm flinging those thoughts away.

"You're what? Five six? That's not small," I say.

"Close enough. I'm five six and a *half*."

I chuckle. "Can't forget that half."

She rolls her eyes. "Not all of us have feet to spare. Let me keep my half in peace. Let me guess, six three?"

"Six three and a *half*," I reply slyly.

"Liar."

"Nope. If we had a way, you could have measured me right now."

Her cheeks flush a deep red, and I break out in a fit of loud laughter. I'm surprised I don't draw out a crowd.

"Not what I meant," I assure her.

"Riiight," she sings. A smile pulls at her mouth.

There's a splash in the pool across the yard, and we both turn to find a shirtless guy with spiky blond hair doing drunken laps in the red-cup-filled water. He's bellowing out the lyrics to a song I vaguely recognize. It sounds terrible.

"Is that . . . a song from *Moana*?" Ava mutters.

"Like, the movie with the Rock?"

"That's the one."

I narrow my eyes on who I know recognize as Bradley Caplan, a power forward on the Storm, and bark a laugh. "That's Brad for you. He has twin younger sisters. They're four years old."

"Makes sense. Me and my friends have movie nights every Saturday night. *Moana* was the pick a few weeks ago."

A spark of jealousy flares before I stomp it out. "Are you all close?"

She hums. "Yes. I'm lucky to have them."

"Have you told them what happened tonight?"

If I were one of her friends, I would have already been on my way here to beat the shit out of this guy. Hell, if I thought she would tell me who the prick is, I would march inside and break his nose for her.

"God no." She chokes on a laugh. "That would be a disaster."

I arch a brow. "They're protective of you?"

"Very."

I offer her a smile. "Good. They'll take care of you, then."

My sincere words must surprise her because she doesn't say anything in return. Her emerald eyes watch me intensely, like she's trying to get inside my head. They shine even in the dark.

I tap my knuckles against the arm of the chair. "What's your name?" I blurt out.

Her mouth twists to one side. "I barely know you."

"My friends call me Lee," I offer, surprising myself.

"And mine call me Ava."

I grin. "So, Ava. Does this mean we're friends now?"

Our eyes lock and hold. Her mascara-clumped lashes brush the skin beneath, and I fight to keep from wiping away the black mess with my thumb.

My stomach erupts in a fluttery sensation that has my head running laps, trying to figure out what's happening right now.

"Yeah, Lee. I guess it does," she whispers.

Her smile short-circuits my brain, leaving me with only a single thought.

I've never liked having a friend as much as I do right now.

# 3

## THREE MONTHS LATER

*Ava*

"Ava, get your ass moving! The game starts in an hour!" Morgan yells, pounding on my bedroom door.

"Relax, you nutcase," I retort, earning a grumble from my best friend/roommate as she stomps away.

After giving myself a quick once-over in my full-length mirror, I spin on my heels and leave my bedroom.

I can't say that my black hoodie plastered with the Vancouver Saints logo and ripped skinny jeans are going to drop jaws, but I know I won't be freezing to the death in the arena tonight.

When I enter the living room, Morgan's already waiting for me on the couch. The two of us live together in a small two-bedroom apartment about fifteen minutes away from the University of Vancouver. It isn't anything special, but it's more than enough for us.

The kitchen has a small island with light granite countertops to go with the light wood cabinets and stainless-steel appliances. The living room is on the opposite side of the room, lit up by the sunlight that barrels through our floor-to-ceiling windows.

Morgan's platinum-blonde hair is curled loosely like always, sitting just below her shoulders, and her long, thick eyelashes flutter when she catches sight of me and smiles.

Her boyfriend, Matthew, is the starting goalie for the Vancouver Saints WHL hockey team—one of the highest-level junior teams in western Canada—which means as her certified best friend, I'm obligated to join her at every game, including the season opener tonight.

"Ready to go?" I ask when I pass by the couch.

She hops up and trails after me. "I have been for the past half-hour, Octavia. You're lucky I didn't break down your door and drag your perky ass out ten minutes ago."

I wince at her use of my full name but shake it off and open the door. She joins me a breath later, and we head downstairs.

Once we get inside her new Jeep—a gift from her OB/GYN parents—she looks over at me and starts the engine. Whatever frustration she was feeling has washed away and been replaced with excitement.

"You're coming with us for dinner after the game, right? I'll be suffocated with testosterone if you don't."

I inwardly groan. "I have homework."

"Already? Jesus, they couldn't even wait until the second week of classes to start piling it on?"

I look at her as we pull onto the road. "You don't have any yet?"

"Nope." She pops the *p*. "I only have three classes this semester, though. I didn't want to overload myself like last year. I told you that you should have done the same."

Morgan is majoring in English literature. It makes complete sense, considering she's a serious book nerd, although a closeted one.

"I just want to graduate as soon as possible. It'll be worth it in the end," I defend. "Plus, five classes a semester is quite normal."

She sighs. "I just want you to live a little, that's all. I can't imagine spending all day, every day hearing about social-work nightmares is very joyful."

I shrug. "It's better than actually being in the system and living it. I would take this over going back there any day."

"I'm sorry. That was insensitive."

I reach across the seats and cover the hand she has gripping the steering wheel. "It's fine. I'm long over being offended by the past."

She smiles. "So, does that mean you'll come with me tonight?"

I place my hand back in my lap with a laugh. "You're relentless."

"Pretty please?"

"Who's going?"

When her fingers start tapping on the wheel, I lean forward in my seat and pin her with a narrowed gaze. "Morgan?"

"It'll be us and the guys," she squeaks.

"Elaborate."

Her tapping increases in speed. "Matt, Tyler, Adam, and Oakley Hutton."

Well, I can't say I didn't see that coming. Shutting my eyes, I exhale slowly.

The infamous Oakley Hutton. Rumours have been flying around about the city's new hockey god since he moved here a few months ago. I wonder how we got lucky enough to be granted a dinner in his presence.

"No, thank you" is my reply.

"No, thank you?" she echoes, incredulous.

I nod. "Yep. Glad we got that cleared up."

"You've never even met him!" Her voice is a higher pitch than usual. "Come on. He's been living with Matt and Braden since he got here, and there hasn't been any problems yet. I've met him in passing and he's a looker. He came from some small town a few hours away or something."

"If Oakley's anything like the other guys on the team, then I don't need to meet him to know I'm not interested."

"That's not fair, Ava. You get along great with a lot of the guys on the team."

"Yeah, I get along with them. As friends. I wouldn't date any of them, and I have a feeling that is where your mind is going."

She grinds her teeth and inhales sharply. "Okay. You don't have to talk to anyone but me tonight. Just please come."

My gaze finds hers and holds. "Fine. But I'm not staying long."

With a beaming smile, she's smacking the steering wheel with excitement. "Thank you, babes. It'll be fun, I swear it."

I settle into my seat and push the thought of dinner out of my head. Instead, I spend the twenty minutes it takes to get to the arena preparing myself for what I'll find when we walk through the front doors.

The screaming crowds of fans, sudden drop in temperature, and the groups of girls that are going to be lingering in the halls, looking for a player who will hopefully take them home and give them a story to blab about tomorrow morning.

Having spent the past few years being hauled to game after game, tournament after tournament, you learn to keep away from the locker rooms directly afterward. The smell of lust and clouds of expensive perfumes is enough to do your head in.

As soon as we park and go inside the arena, I can barely hear anything Morgan says past all the "Let's go, Saints!" chants and other screams that I try to tune out. After struggling to keep up with her, I end up just ducking my head and letting her pull me through the crowds to our seats.

The game has a slow start, but that changes quickly after the second intermission. There are ten minutes to go in the third period, and the Saints are up by a score of three to two.

Tonight should have been an easy win with the long list of missing players from the Eagles roster, but we've been sloppy. Careless and arrogant.

Maybe it's just new-season nerves or the false confidence that comes with adding a future NHL franchise prospect to our team, but whatever it is, they have to nip it in the bud before it spreads like a virus. Last season ended rough for the Saints, and I know how badly they want to bring home a trophy this year.

There's an obvious shift in the air when Braden Lowry, one of the Saints' best defensemen, takes an illegal check from behind. Braden's massive frame crumples on the ice, and he stays down for a few seconds too long before shakily pulling himself up with the help of a few other players.

The crowd erupts in a fit of angry voices while some fans take to clacking those stupid plastic clappers. My brows furrow before I realize what—or *who*—they're shouting at.

The player responsible for sending a guy as big as Braden flat on his ass is currency dancing in circles across from our newest star player, Oakley Hutton.

The dance doesn't go on long before Oakley's rushing forward like an unhinged bull and grabbing the front of the player's jersey, forcefully bringing him closer. In a blink, Oakley drops his gloves and sends a hard right hook straight to the defenseman's face. Before the other guy can get a hit in, his lips part on words I wish I could hear, and Oakley is throwing another punch, this time at his abdomen.

Our new player continues his brutal beat down, his lips moving as he says something to the losing instigator. I can't help but notice just how tall Oakley is as he towers over his opponent on the ice. I can't get a good view with all of his hockey gear in the way, but by the strength of the hits and the fact the Eagles' player is now being helped off the ice toward the dressing room, I feel as if he's not lacking in the muscle department either.

There's a jab in my side as Morgan leans toward my ear. "That's Oakley. He knows how to fight." She stares at me with a playful glimmer in her eyes before looking away. Her features tighten up. "Oh, hell no! He's being ejected from the game!"

I jerk my head forward and am immediately met with a pair of raging green eyes. Oakley is on his way to the dressing room.

To the hallway that will take him there. The same hallway I'm sitting flush up against.

His eyebrows are deeply furrowed, mouth in a tight line as he holds my stare, not showing a sign of letting it go. White noise bubbles in my ears as I grip my knees, squeezing as if doing so will somehow pull me out of this brain fog.

My heart stops when he gets closer. Close enough for me to notice the scar above the corner of his mouth and the depth of his evergreen-coloured eyes. The same eyes I spent hours looking into that night three months ago.

*Oh my God.* When recognition flickers across his face, his eyes go wide, his steps faltering. He places a palm on the hallway wall to steady himself and swallows so hard his throat strains.

My knees shake when I push forward in my seat, unable to look away from him as he moves further down the hall. It's not until we have no other choice but to break eye contact that I force myself to sit back.

I close my eyes and touch my cheeks, not surprised to find them burning hot and beating with their own pulse.

"Do you two know each other or something?" Glancing over at Morgan, I watch with discomfort as she wiggles her eyebrows suggestively.

"He'll be lucky not to get suspended for that," I mumble, trying to shake the last few minutes out of my memory. But just like that night, Oakley is impossible to forget. "Can you go without me tonight?"

*Please say yes.*

Morgan scoffs. "You're joking, right? The Eagles deserved that. And no way. You're coming. It's been too long since you've gone out with everyone."

I stiffen at her words. The hair on my arms rises.

"I gave you some leeway after you and David broke up, but he's been out of the picture for three months now. You can't let what happened keep you from enjoying yourself from time to time," she says. I hate the way she's looking at me—like I'm a ticking bomb that could go off with the brush of the slightest breeze.

I know she just wants to help, but it's not as easy as she thinks it is. David was my high school boyfriend, but our relationship carried over into university. We dated for two years, and our breakup was a disaster of epic proportions.

"Do you ever think maybe it isn't even David keeping me from putting myself out there in the way you want me to?" I snap. "What if I just want to focus on school? Would that really be so bad?"

She flinches. "No, of course that wouldn't be bad, Ava. I'm not saying that. I just hate seeing you hold yourself up in your room like a hermit when you have people who would love to spend time with you."

"So it has nothing to do with your unhealthy obsession with matchmaking?" She's silent for a beat too long. "That's what I thought." I blow out a breath. "I'll still come tonight, but I'm serious, Morgan. Let me do things my own way."

"Fine," she agrees.

Thankfully, she leaves it alone, and we spend the remaining few minutes of the game in silence.

With neither team scoring another goal, the Saints take the win.

# 4

# Ava

MORGAN AND I ARE THE FIRST TO ARRIVE AT LUCY'S DINER AFTER the game. I'm bombarded by the strong, familiar aroma of greasy burgers and coffee, and my stomach growls, reminding me that I haven't eaten since breakfast.

Lucy's has been a staple in my life for years. My foster parents brought me here the day we finalized my adoption, and it's been one of my favourite places since.

We would sit in a booth for hours, talking about everything from what homework I had to what the new drama was in school. I miss how simple things were back then. Before school and friends swallowed up all my time and energy.

Morgan links her arm with mine as we start our search for a table. It doesn't take long before we find a teal-coloured booth in front of a window and sit down to wait for everyone else— Morgan on one side of the table, me on the other.

"Matthew texted. He just pulled up outside with Adam and Tyler," Morgan says a couple of minutes later.

My excitement grows as I glance around the diner. It's not busy for a Saturday night, a revelation that I make a note of. The quieter the diner, the fewer people that will come up to our table trying to talk to the three starring Saints players.

Matt and Tyler aren't ones to encourage the interruptions, but Adam—being the flirt that he is—doesn't mind them nearly as much. Before I had let myself become friends with the three guys, I would have assumed that they were all attention-seeking assholes, but they surprised me in the best way the more I got to know them.

I'm not best friends with either Matt or Tyler, but Adam and I are as very close, almost as close as I am with Morgan. All three guys have been there for me when it matters, though, and that's all that I can ask for.

Just as I open my mouth to reply to Morgan, the bell on the diner door rings, and the three guys walk in.

Confidence oozes off them as they make their way to our table. All three are sporting damp hair and casual clothes, as opposed to the suits they wear to their games. Adam stands the tallest, at his six-foot-two height, followed by Tyler and then Matt.

When they reach our table, I slide across the bench, making room for them to sit. "At least you guys showered for us this time. I forgot to bring something to shove up my nostrils."

Adam slides in beside me, flashing a grin in my direction while slinging his left arm around my shoulders, pulling me close. He smells good. Like a cologne that costs way too much.

"Funny, O. Do you want a round of applause for that one?" he asks, still smiling.

Tyler sits beside Adam and clasps his hands on the table. "Have you guys ordered yet? I'm starving."

"No. Morgan waved the waitress away when we got here, but she should be back soon," I say.

My attention falls to Matthew as he cozies up beside Morgan and kisses her head. His arm is slung across the back of the booth. "Hey, babe."

She grins, locking her bright blue eyes with his darker ones. "Hey, Matt." Her attention moves to the other two guys. "You guys regrouped well after that fight."

"We played like shit, Mo. It doesn't matter how we finished," Adam grunts.

"A shitty win is still a win," I say, pinching his side.

"Try telling that to Coach," Tyler laughs darkly. "He would have paddled our asses in the locker room if he had the chance."

"How's Braden doing? Is he okay?" I ask.

All three guys nod, but it's Adam that speaks. "Good as new. That fucker is too stubborn to let someone half his size earn him a seat on the bench."

"Ava is adamant that your fighter is going to get suspended for that fight," Morgan puts in, a twinkle in her eyes. "So, is he?"

I glare at her as Tyler turns around and jerks his head toward the door. "You can ask him yourself."

His eyes catch my attention first, the depth of them sending me reeling backward. An unfamiliar emotion pours out from behind them, settling like a stack of bricks in my stomach. When he blinks, whatever it was disappears.

The sudden change in his demeanour has me far more curious than I would like. I force a cough and divert my eyes, only to find them stuck on the sharp lines of his jaw.

I'm stricken by the rough, strong carve of his features. From his crooked nose that's definitely been broken a handful of times and a matching set of jutted cheekbones to his plump lips I know must taste like one hundred percent man, it's clear he's one of God's favourite creations.

The endless sleeves of black tattoos covering his veiny fore-arms catch my attention next as he grabs the baseball cap covering his ashy-brown hair. He removes it only to run his fingers through the messy locks before slapping it back on, his biceps flexing. The simple act shouldn't be as hot as it is, but my panties grow wet despite that fact.

He wasn't wearing a hat that night, and I'm grateful for that. It would have been even harder to avoid climbing him like a tree than it already was.

Forcing myself to stop gawking at him, I glance around the

room and try to focus on anything but the guy who is now staring at me with a playful grin.

"Sorry I'm late." His voice is straight sin. Smooth yet rough. Both bright and dark. I fight off a shiver and fail.

"All good, man," Adam says.

"Oh, hi!" Morgan smiles. "You don't mind having the window seat, do you, Oakley?"

I slide my stare to the innocent smile she's sporting and swallow back my growing suspicions. The window seat will leave him directly across from me.

"Morgan doesn't enjoy being trapped against the window," Matt adds with a shrug. Oh yeah, he's in on it.

"Yeah, sure. Doesn't matter to me," Oakley says.

Not even a second later, Morgan is shoving Matthew out of their booth, getting out after him and motioning for Oakley to slide into her previous seat. I plaster a tight smile on my face and plan her slow and painful death as she slips back into the booth.

"Do you always check out guys like that, or was that just for me?" Oakley whispers a beat later. His words caress my skin in ways I should hate.

I meet his gaze head-on, refusing to back down once I'm met with a playful stare. My heartbeat trips over itself when I realize he's talking to me.

"I would say it was just for you, but that would be a lie," I say with as much fake confidence as I can muster up.

He chuckles softly. "Hello again, Ava." His voice is quiet, a whisper meant only for me, before he sits back and asks, "What's your name, beautiful?"

I blink, surprised. Is he hiding the fact we already know each other for his benefit or mine? Was his compliment just for show too?

"Octavia!" Morgan shrieks. "Her name is Octavia."

"It's Ava," I correct her, slanting a dirty look her way before looking back at Oakley. I relax. "I already know yours. You seem to have a special way of introducing yourself to everyone, Oakley."

"It needed to be done. I was just the guy that took care of it." He shrugs—as if beating the crap out of a total stranger is normal. For him, maybe it is.

He drops the topic and turns his attention to the menu in front of him. I take the hint and do the same, even though I have the menu memorized.

It's clear his openness at that party was a rare occasion.

"I can't believe you got ejected, bro. That team was playing dirty all night. Even Coach agreed they had it coming. How are the knuckles?" Matthew puts in, grinning like the little shit disturber he is.

Looking at the hands holding his menu, I notice a white bandage wrapped around his right hand.

"Hurt like a bitch," Oakley says before Matt speaks again.

"I am curious about what that guy said to you out there. None of us could hear, but you looked pissed."

Oakley sits silent for a few seconds before saying, "Just some bullshit about the team." He clears his throat and changes the subject. "Who's hungry? I know I am."

As if on cue, the waitress wanders over to our table. She looks to be around our age, with shoulder-length brassy hair that hangs over the sides of her face. Eyeing us warily, she fiddles with her notepad and flushes a deep pink.

It's easy to tell she's nervous—presumably because of the gorgeous male specimens waiting to order. Can I blame her? No. If I were in her shoes, I would be shitting bricks right about now.

"Hi! I'm Jenny, and I'll be taking care of you tonight. What can I get you?" she asks, her pen floating over her notepad.

"I'll have a vanilla milkshake, a cheeseburger, and an order of curly fries, please." Oakley speaks so kindly to her, catching on to her nerves. I don't bother hiding my small smile of approval.

The waitress raises her eyebrows at me expectantly, but

Adam orders for me before I can string together a coherent sentence.

"A strawberry milkshake and a double cheeseburger with onion rings for me, and another order of the same, but with fries instead of the rings for the lady. Thank you."

I roll my eyes at him. "I could have ordered for myself."

"I know, but I wanted to flex my best friend muscles. Sue me." He winds his arm around my shoulders again.

Morgan snorts, and I level her with a glare, my brows raised. Her eyes bounce between Adam and me. I tilt my head and mouth a silent "What?" in her direction. She rolls her eyes, nodding in the direction of the window.

Slowly, I sneak a look across the table and catch Oakley watching me curiously—or rather, the arm slung around my shoulder—but he looks away as soon as I catch him.

I slip my lip between my teeth and drop my gaze, focusing way too hard on a set of initials that are carved into the tabletop as the surrounding conversations grow. Everyone catches up on their week and when the next game is, as if Morgan doesn't have the entire season scribbled on our shared calendar.

We chat for what seems like hours, and by the time our wait-ress rushes over with our food, I'm starving.

I'm stealing one of Adam's onion rings and bringing it to my mouth when Oakley says, "I don't know how you can eat those. Onions taste like dirty socks."

"Dirty socks?" I echo, blinking. He nods. "And you've tasted a lot of dirty socks in your lifetime?"

His lips part with a smile. "Are you saying that you haven't?"

"That's exactly what I'm saying."

"I haven't tasted dirty socks before, but if I had to guess what they taste like, I would say onion rings."

My shoulders shake with laughter. "You're an idiot."

"I'd rather be an idiot than someone who likes the taste of dirty socks," he tosses back, smirking now.

Holding eye contact with him, I toss the onion ring into my mouth and chew, moaning obnoxiously before I swallow. "Yum."

"Jesus, Ava. Do you want some privacy there?" Tyler snickers.

My cheeks go hot with embarrassment. Oakley's eyes are bright as they pierce mine, but I don't spend too much time reading into that before I'm looking down at my basket of fries and wishing that I could disappear.

Adam's fingers stroke my arm in a comforting motion that I sink into as I dig into my fries.

MORGAN LINKS her arm in mine as we leave the diner an hour later.

After my ultra-awkward sexual experience with an onion ring, Adam was quick to change the subject of conversation to one that was sure to capture everyone's attention: what movie we're watching for movie night tomorrow—the one Oakley has now been invited to. The group spent a solid fifteen minutes debating between *The Benchwarmers* and *The Mighty Ducks* before settling on the latter.

Morgan pulls me close to her body, whispering, "You seem to get along just fine with Oakley."

"Don't start."

The four guys are walking ahead of us, their combined laughter echoing across the parking lot. The sun is long gone, leaving the sky speckled with stars that the surrounding buildings do a good job of hiding.

"Oh, relax. I'm just stating the obvious."

"He seems nice enough." It's an unfair downplay, but I'm not ready to explain anything to Morgan yet. Not when I'm still confused myself.

An ache blooms in my chest as I let myself accept the fact that he's been here for three months and I've never once seen him. Three months wasted wondering where Lee was and what he was doing while I was spending my summer working at an animal shelter and tanning at the beach.

It feels like a loss. Like wasted time.

We barely know each other, but after spending five hours sitting in the dark with him, talking about absolutely anything and everything, we bonded. Grew a connection. One that hurt to let go of when we had to say goodbye.

"It doesn't suck that he looks like a model either."

I pinch the underside of her bicep and jump out of her grasp when she shrieks, swatting at me.

The guys spin around and stare at us curiously. I throw my hands up in the air and nod toward Morgan. "She saw a spider."

Matt's the one to crack a laugh first, holding his hand out for her to take. "Come here, babe. I'll keep you safe."

With a glare in my direction, she abandons my side and scurries over to her boyfriend, throwing her arms around him and sighing like a damsel in distress. "My hero."

"Damn right. Don't forget it, sweetheart."

My heart warms at the sight of Matt pulling her into his side and wrapping a possessive arm around her shoulders. If anyone deserves the love Matt gives so freely, it's Morgan.

I quicken my steps and join the group, falling between the towering figures of Oakley and Adam.

"Is Morgan still driving you home, or do you need a ride, O?" Adam asks. He pulls the keys to his Genesis G90 from his pocket and dangles them in front of him.

The fancy car was a gift from his lawyer parents after they bailed at the last minute and didn't show up to the Saints' final playoff game last season. Yeah, the team lost. But his family should have been there. I know firsthand how much their absence hurt him.

I smile up at him. "Morgan's got it covered. Thanks, though."

He looks reluctant but doesn't push the subject, opting for a quick goodbye hug before walking to his car and getting in.

Morgan's Jeep sits between Adam's car and an old, lifted white truck with a serious patch of rust on the back left wheel well.

I turn to Oakley and meet his already waiting eyes. "Is that yours?"

"It is."

His expression is cautious, like he's scared I'm about to tell him I hate it. The thought has me scoffing in my head.

"My dad has one just like it. A 1994 Ford. He has a thing for old vehicles," I say.

He blinks in surprise.

"Yours is what? A '96?" I ask with a confident smile.

"You know trucks," he replies simply.

I lift a shoulder. "Enough to know you should take off that rust before it spreads."

He barks a laugh that I feel all the way to my toes. "That's the plan. I've been too busy to get to it lately."

"The life of a future professional hockey player, right?"

Morgan yells from the driver's side of her Jeep before Oakley has a chance to reply. "You ready to go, Ava?"

"Coming!" I yell back.

Oakley's stare is hot on my back as I rush toward her before she leaves without me. "I'll see you tomorrow night, right?" he calls after me.

I swallow my surprise at his interest and yell without looking back, "Yep!"

As soon as I reach the Jeep, I slip inside and heave a sigh.

Now what?

# 5

*Ava*

"GET YOUR DICK OFF MY LEG, YOU JACKASS," TYLER GROWLS.

I choke on a laugh when I peel my eyes from the movie to find Adam leaning over Tyler from where they sit on the floor, trying to snatch a piece of pizza from the box on the coffee table.

"I can't help that I'm so well-endowed you can feel it with the slightest brush against your leg," Adam retorts. He releases a small noise of relief when he grabs a slice and sits back down, shoving it in his mouth.

"You're both disgusting," Morgan says.

"News flash, Mo, your boyfriend is just as nasty," Adam snickers.

Matt reaches forward and tugs on Adam's hair. "Don't throw me under the bus, you prick."

Tyler follows Matt's lead but grabs a thicker clump of Adam's hair before pulling. "Shut up and eat your pizza."

I give my head a shake and fold my hands in my lap, turning back to the movie.

"Are they always like this?" Oakley asks, his voice low and way too sultry for my liking. He's so close I can hear and feel each steady breath he releases against my skin.

I swallow and try to ignore the heat from his body beating

into my side. We're sitting as close as we can be without fully touching, with Morgan and Matt on the other side of the couch and Tyler and Adam in front of us. There have been a few times during the first few minutes of the movie where Oakley's thigh brushed mine—all of that hard, warm muscle pressed up against me—but I turned as rigid as a damn statue each time. He's kept his limbs to himself after the last time I froze up.

I wasn't expecting him to show up tonight. Shamefully, I expected a guy like him to have more important things to do than spend his Sunday night vegging out with a bunch of people he barely knows. I was both shocked and nervous when he was already waiting in Adam's living room when Morgan and I got here with the pizza.

Oakley has a way of sending a weird rush through my system when he's close by. I noticed it when we first met, and it's only managed to get stronger since. It scares me.

Loud music blaring from the TV's surround sound yanks me out of my head.

"Yeah. You learn to ignore it, though," I answer him.

He hums low in his throat. "I didn't hang out with my old teammates like this. Only my best friend."

I brush my hair behind my ear and glance over at him. He's staring at the TV, his jaw set and long fingers tapping away on the armrest. This guy is incredibly hard to read.

"Why didn't you hang out with them?" I ask, unable to help myself. He turns his head, and I'm met with a pair of deep green eyes, the colour of a lush forest after a long rainfall.

"That's a good question. I've never considered it before now. I guess I just wasn't into the same things they were."

"Parties, booze, weed, and sex? You guys don't make it hard to label you."

His mouth twists into a grimace. "It might be hard to believe, but we're not all the same."

"Enough of you are to make a general assumption."

"You're not wrong," he says.

There's a break in our conversation, one that has me forced to turn back to the movie to avoid holding eye contact for a creepy amount of time. We don't speak again for a while, a fact that has me thinking that I've offended him with my comments.

His next question comes from left field, leaving me slack-jawed. "Can I drive you home after this?"

"Like . . . tonight?" I ask slowly.

He chuckles. "Yes, Ava. Tonight. After the movie. I was hoping that I could convince you to take a detour as well. There's a place I've found that I think I want to show you."

Morgan's breath hitches, meaning she most likely heard everything we've been saying throughout the entire movie. *Great.* I tense up and slant a curious look at Oakley.

"You're not going to take me to your kill spot, are you? I'm pretty sure Morgan would hunt you down if anything happened to me," I say.

Oakley's smile stretches into a full-on grin. "No kill spot. I promise."

"Why the sudden interest?" I can't help myself from asking.

There's no hesitation before he says, "We have more to talk about. It seems you went home that night before I could get my fill of you."

For a reason I can't, nor want to understand, his honesty seems to be good enough to convince me. That and the goose-bumps his words bring to my skin.

"Okay. You can bring me home."

❄

# *Oakley*

THERE'S something about Ava that has my mind running laps like a mouse on a wheel.

She's honest, bluntly so. There's a bravery in her that I can't help but be envious of. In a fucked-up way, I think that's what drew me to her in the first place.

But there's also a wall guarding her. One I can't help but want to put a dent in. Something is telling me that what I would find behind all that steel is well worth the effort.

The girl I met in Andre's backyard, the one with splotchy makeup and tear-stained cheeks is a far cry from the one I slowly started to unravel later that night and an even further one from the woman I've known in Vancouver.

But there's more there. So much more. And I *need* to be the one to dig my claws in and explore.

"So, do you prefer to drive in silence, or is it okay if we listen to some music?" Ava asks, the warm tenor in her voice causing a shiver to climb up my spine.

I fight back a wince when I realize we've been sitting in silence for the past few minutes. Straightening my back, I pass her the aux cord. "Here, sorry. You choose."

She nods and connects her phone, choosing a cheery pop song that I've heard my sister play around the house on numerous occasions.

"I'm surprised. I didn't take you for a boy band fan." Risking a quick glance beside me, I watch her turn her body and shoot me an icy glare.

"If you have a problem with the Jonas Brothers, I'm going to need you to pull over and let me out right now."

A loud laugh shakes my shoulders. "Relax, killer. I'm very

well-rounded in the world of boy bands, thank you. My sister has had posters of Harry Styles on her wall since she was seven."

"She has good taste."

"I guess. There are worse things for a soon-to-be seventeen-year-old to obsess over." Like boys and drugs, to name a couple.

Ava hums in agreement, turning back in her seat. She's a little less rigid than she was moments ago. I can't imagine the awkward silence was very relaxing.

"Do you have any other siblings?" she asks.

I take the highway exit leading to our destination. Lush green trees flood the sides of the road now, the stars hidden behind them.

"No. Gracie's more than enough trouble by herself, anyway."

She stays silent for a few beats before saying, "For the longest time, I wished I had a sister. My foster brother is great, but there are certain things you just don't talk about with a brother."

My brows tug together. "Foster brother?"

"Yeah. My parents adopted me when I was fifteen," she replies, keeping it vague before changing the subject altogether. "Have you always been a physical hockey player? I don't think any of us were expecting such a show so early in the season."

I flip on my blinker and pull the truck off the road toward a break in the trees and the side road that feeds all the way through them. Gravel crunches beneath the tires, the sound almost comforting.

"I don't like to fight like I did at yesterday's game. If my mom finds out about what happened, I'll never hear the end of it. Coach already let me have it for risking myself so early in the season, but that was nothing compared to my mother's wrath."

"So why do it, then?"

It's a fair question, but I stiffen regardless. "I was only going to shove that guy around for a bit for the hit on Braden, but the asshole had a lot to say. Particularly about my sister." She sucks in a sharp breath. I laugh. "Yeah. It seemed they did their research before the game. Knew exactly how to push my buttons."

"God, what a prick!"

My eyes widen at her anger. I pull over to the side of the gravel road and shift the truck into park. Ava doesn't meet my stare when it falls on her. She's too busy staring out the window, her curiosity taking over.

"They hit my soft spot, and I did a shit job of hiding it," I admit.

She faces me again, the corner of her mouth lifted. "At least the team won. Got in the last word, so to speak."

I chuckle. "Yeah, I'm not sure I could show my face again if we didn't."

"It wouldn't have been that bad."

"Don't try to make me feel better, Ava. Yes, it would have."

Her small smile stretches into a grin that makes the corners of her eyes crinkle. "Fine. It would have absolutely destroyed your street cred."

With a playful shake of my head, I reach into the back seat and grab the heavy wool blanket I have stashed there. It's not cold out, but the wind can be sharp.

I lay the blanket on my lap and grab her headrest, nodding at her window. "Ready?"

She squints at the trees and the darkness behind them, as if they'll tell her whether it's safe to enter their home or if she should make a run for it. Her nerves are warranted. If she tells me to take her home right now, I would, no questions asked. I don't expect her to trust me yet, but I hope that she'll try. Just for tonight.

"If I were planning on murdering you and wearing your skin as clothes, I wouldn't have shown up to watch a movie with all of your friends and let them know I was taking you somewhere alone. You're safe with me. Scout's honour." I offer her a two-finger salute.

She rolls her bottom lip between her fingers before nodding, albeit a bit reluctantly. "Lead the way, then, Boy Scout."

# 6

# Oakley

I ALWAYS KNEW MOVING AWAY FROM MY FAMILY WASN'T SOMETHING I could avoid. Even so, the idea of something and the reality of it are two different things.

Winding up in Vancouver was always the plan, but I didn't expect it to become a reality so soon. My father was a huge Vancouver Warriors fan. There's still a room in the basement of Ma's house filled to the brim with his collection of signed NHL merchandise and jerseys. I'm pretty sure that nothing has been touched since before he passed away, nor do I think that it ever will be.

Despite having ten years to grieve him, I've never gotten to that point. The point where I feel okay enough to enter that room and be bombarded by the things he loved almost as much as he did us. I've accepted that he's gone—how could I not after ten years?—but I'm not naive to the fact that entering that room and packing his stuff away will break the last connection I have with him.

Even though I can't get myself to go inside that room, I could decide to do everything in my power to play for his favourite team. A ridiculous idea, in hindsight, considering you don't get to choose which team you get drafted to in the professional hockey league, nor is even getting drafted guaranteed. But success is in my blood. I won't stop until I get there. And while my dream is to play for the Warriors, I know my dad would have smacked me upside the head if I complained about being drafted anywhere else.

With so many thoughts and pressures stacking up since moving here, this clearing in the woods has become a safe haven of sorts. A quiet place where I can be alone, with nothing else to focus on but the lapping of the lake on the rocky beach and the wildlife trotting through the trees.

Finding this place after driving aimlessly with a head clogged with unwanted thoughts was a complete accident but a welcome one.

The *hoot-hoot* of an owl somewhere in the trees pulls me out of the sandpit in my mind. Ava shifts beside me, her arm brushing mine when she leans back on her hands and tips her head back, staring at the black sky. The stars are out in clusters, no longer blocked by the city's towers.

"Are you cold?" I ask Ava, my voice gruffer than I expected. With the blanket beneath us keeping the damp grass from wetting our pants, we're left with nothing but our clothes. It's not too cold, but I have no intention of letting her freeze in the wind.

She turns her head enough for our eyes to meet. "I'm good."

"Okay."

"Are you cold?"

"I'm flattered by your worry, but I'm fine. My temperature usually runs hot."

"I'm the opposite. Although, I can't say that I take my temperature often. Not unless I'm so sick I'm on my deathbed."

My brow twitches. "What kind of sick person are you? Whiny or stubborn?"

"Stubborn for sure. I'll wait until I'm so sick I can't get out of bed before I'll admit to not being fine."

"That was my guess. You don't seem like the whining type," I admit. A flicker of humour travels across her face.

"What kind of sick person are you?"

I pretend to think about it before saying, "Neither. I can count on one hand the number of times I've gotten sick, but I'm definitely the sleepy type. Until I get better, I sleep day and night."

"That easy, huh?" Ava asks, and I nod. With a small smile, she looks back at the sky and sighs. "I'm happy you took me here. It's peaceful."

"And a great place to clear your head."

"Do you do that often? Need to clear your head?"

Her question comes off innocent, but I know better than that. She's digging, which means she's curious about me. At least a little. But I'm not up for cracking myself open and letting my secrets fertilize the forest floor tonight.

I slide my knees in toward my chest and sling my arms over them. We're sitting in front of the small lake, a few feet from the rocky shore. Lush trees blanket us on both sides, almost like they're hiding the lake from intruders. I almost feel bad for disrespecting their privacy before I remember they're fucking *trees* and mentally slap myself.

"You never told me you were from Vancouver." I change the subject.

She nods. "There was a lot we didn't talk about that night."

"True. Someone got too tired to stay awake."

"It's not my fault I spent an hour crying in some jock's bathroom."

I stiffen at the reminder. "How have you been with that?" She looks at me, confused. "With the breakup, I mean."

Her eyes fall to the ground, making me frown. "It gets easier."

"Has he tried to talk to you at all?"

"He didn't stop trying for a few weeks after we got home. But I think getting the cold shoulder for so long is too harmful to a man's pride to continue trying. Thank God for that."

"Good. Fuck that guy. Are you still sure you don't want to tell me who he is?"

Her eyes go wide. "Yeah. Very sure," she rushes out.

Suspicion licks my spine. "You're acting very suspicious right now, Ava. But I'm feeling generous today, so I'll let it be."

"Wow, thanks." She laughs.

I stretch my legs back out and lean back on my hands, turning my head to stare at her. Our eyes meet as I lean closer to her. Her breath hitches, and a spark of success fills my veins.

The smell of her perfume hits me, and I hold back a groan. Sweet and spicy. Just like her.

I lower my voice. "You should know, though, that I do plan on finding this guy. And when I do, I'll make sure he's sorry for what he did to you. You deserve better."

"O—okay," she breathes, nodding slightly.

Our closeness is alarming, but I push that thought to the back of my head. I smirk. "How's your ass feeling?"

Her eyes bulge as she pulls back and bursts out laughing. "What?"

"You know, from sitting on the ground? Are you wet at all? Because of the grass, of course." I hold back my smile, feigning innocence.

"It's a bit numb. But dry, I think," she sputters.

"That's good. We wouldn't want you getting wet out here." When her cheeks turn a bright apple red, I bark a laugh and nudge her playfully with my shoulder.

"You're a jackass," she groans, tucking her face in her sweatshirt.

I lift a shoulder. "Nah. Just wanted your opinion on my flirting skills. I'm pretty shit, huh?"

"I wouldn't go that far. Maybe rusty, but not terrible. I'm sure there are tons of willing girls that would sell a limb for the chance to help you with your lines and whatever else you wanted." She wiggles her eyebrows.

I wince. "Lucky me."

"You don't have to play coy with me. You've already dragged me out to the middle of the woods with you. The least you can do is be honest."

A muscle in my jaw flutters when I tense it. It's not anger that's clawing my insides. It's disappointment. Ava's perception of me couldn't be more wrong.

"If I wanted an easy lay, I wouldn't be here with you. I would have taken up one of the many offers I've gotten today and slipped my dick inside someone by now. I don't think with my dick, Ava."

Her gulp is audible. "Oh. Okay."

Trying to relax, I heave a breath. "I have too much going on in my life to be chasing girls. I enjoy your company. I did three months ago, and I still do just as much right now. You don't look at me with dollar signs in your eyes. And you don't give a shit about my future and what I might give you in a few years. That's why I'm here with you."

She's so tense I worry she'll break in half. Guilt churns in my stomach, assuming that maybe I said too much. But when she shifts her body toward me and brings her eyes to mine, I know she isn't upset with what I said. She actually looks pleased.

"Okay, I'm sorry I jumped to conclusions."

"Be honest with me for a second," I mumble.

"I'm always honest with you."

I smile at that. "When you first saw me at that party, what was your first impression?"

She sucks in a sharp breath through her mouth before releasing it through her nose. Her blunt, black-painted nails tap against her thigh.

"I wanted to turn around and leave," she admits. "I didn't know who you were, but I mean . . . look at you. I knew you were a hockey player. We've established my opinions there already."

"Look at me?" I tease. She blushes. "Was that a compliment?"

"You would only pay attention to that part." She shakes her head, but I catch her smile.

Before I realize what I'm doing, I have her knee beneath my palm. She tenses in my grip, and I quickly release her. *What the fuck, dude?*

"I think it's safe to assume that I've proven your assumptions wrong, then?" I ask stiffly.

"Why would you say that?"

"You're here."

She releases a slow breath and looks at me softly. "Yeah. I'm here."

IT'S LATE. Too late to be dropping a girlfriend back at her apartment without her roommate asking questions, but I couldn't care less. There was no way that I was bringing Ava home before we were both too exhausted to keep talking. I haven't enjoyed just talking and being with someone this much in a very long time.

"How long have you and Morgan been best friends?" I ask. "Matthew talks about her all the time. He's obsessed with her."

I sneak a glance at her and watch as she smiles, picking the black nail polish off her fingernails.

"About five years. We went to high school together. Morgan loves him, so I'm glad to hear that it goes both ways. I was worried when she first told me about him. You already know how I feel about jocks, so I won't bother explaining the reason why."

I nod, flipping on my blinker and pulling up along the curb in front of the girls' apartment building. The lights are still on in the living room, and I relax a bit knowing she won't be home alone.

Putting the truck in park, I face her. Ava unbuckles her seat belt and shifts in her seat until she faces me. The streetlights cast a faint glow across her face, softening her tense expression. When she slips her bottom lip between her teeth and bites down on it, my cock fills with blood, and I nearly rip off the steering wheel. *Fuck*. Not good.

"Morgan's probably waiting for you," I blurt out, tearing my eyes away from her and squeezing them shut.

The urge to wince is almost unbearable, but I somehow ignore it. I've made a total asshole out of myself, but I'm not about to let myself get hard because of her. That's definitely not a friendly thing to do.

"Yeah. You're right." Her voice has frozen over. "Thanks for tonight."

She's opened her door and hopped out of the truck by the time I say, "I had a lot of fun, Ava. I'll see you around."

Her smile is nothing more than a slight tilt of her mouth, but I soak it up nonetheless.

"See you around, Boy Scout," she says. Then she's gone.

# 7

# Oakley

I WAKE UP WITH A START, A THRASHING PULSE IN MY TEMPLES AND A sheen of sweat across my forehead. A symphony of clashing and banging comes from the other side of my bedroom door, letting me know that one of my roommates is already up and fucking around in the small kitchen we share.

When I was prepping for my move to Vancouver, I met with the Saint's head Coach to go over last-minute details, and he mentioned a couple of the players were looking for a roommate. It was a no brainer decision to reach out to my new teammates and ask for the spot, considering that living off a stipend from a WHL team doesn't exactly leave me with a bulging wallet and a lot of options. After a quick meeting Matt and Braden, it was as close to a match made in Heaven as I was going to get.

The only downside to living with them is Braden and his obsession with getting and keeping his dick wet.

A few curse words bounce off my bedroom door, forcing a rough chuckle up my throat. Squinting, I drag my palm over my face and sit up. Sunlight streaks in through the crack in my curtains, so it must be well into the morning. 9:15, the clock on my bedside table reads. I have an hour until I have to be at the gym for training.

With my eyes half-open, I crawl out of bed and slip on a pair of sweatpants before leaving my room. Like I guessed, Braden's trying to butter a toaster waffle in nothing but his boxers. I don't notice the naked girl sitting on the counter until I reach the fridge.

I don't spare either of them a glance as I open the door and grab the jug of orange juice.

"You're roommates with Oakley Hutton?" the girl asks quietly. Braden makes a pained noise.

"Does it matter? And don't flick me," he grumbles.

Turning from the fridge, I move to the cupboard to grab a glass and say, "I thought we all agreed on not letting your company prance around the apartment naked, Braden."

Once I've poured myself some juice, I turn and face both of them. Braden's leaning a hip against the counter, grinning like the cat who got the cream, while his friend is still splayed out on the counter, her cheeks flushed but not from embarrassment. She seems far too confident in herself to realize placing her bare ass on somebody else's countertop is more gross than it is sexy.

My stare shifts to her, doing a quick sweep of her nakedness when she makes a purr-like sound and plants both hands flat behind her, pushing her chest up and out. "Should I get down?" she asks, tilting her head and smiling.

I lift a brow and bring the glass of juice to my lips, drinking it slowly. Her eyelids droop as her gaze falls to my throat, watching my Adam's apple bob with each swallow. If it weren't for the liquid in my mouth, I would laugh at how easy it is for me to turn her on, considering she was just in bed with a different guy.

"I would prefer it if you did, yes. But I'll leave it up to my roomie to tell you what to do," I say. Setting my now empty glass in the sink, I slant Braden an annoyed look. "If you'll excuse me, I have to get ready to go to the gym, just like you should be doing."

I almost run to the bathroom in my haste to get out of there.

As soon as I shut the bathroom door, I make sure to lock it before stripping out of my pants and starting the shower. The team is supposed to meet at the arena for a workout before lunch, and if either Braden or I are late, I have no doubt Matt will ream our asses.

He might not be captain, but he's one hell of a leader. You might not be able to tell past his normally chill attitude, but he can be a real hard-ass when it comes to hockey.

I bend over the sink and stare into the mirror, scratching at the stubble speckled along my jaw. I've been way too lazy to shave lately, too busy working my ass off at the rink.

When I first got to Vancouver, I wasn't sure entirely what to expect of the Saints, but it only took one practice for me to see first-hand just how good they are. They might not be the best junior team I've ever seen, but they're pretty close. If I'm going to have a chance in hell of standing out to scouts, I have to keep working. *Hard.*

With a shake of my head, I turn and step into the tub, letting the scorching water burn away my thoughts. I shower and brush my teeth quickly. I'm barely back in my room when my mom's ringtone sings from the bed. Her gentle voice flows through the speakers before I've even brought the phone to my ear.

"Good morning, sweetheart," she sings. I grin. "How are you doing? You're still coming home next weekend, right?"

How she manages to be this high energy in the morning is beyond me. I guess it's a mom thing.

"Morning, Ma. I'm good. A little tired, but that's nothing new. And yes, I'm still coming. Is Gracie excited?"

Gracie has been doing ballet since she was seven, and one of her biggest performances is coming up. It's all I've been hearing about during our phone calls for the past month. I wouldn't miss it. I would never hear the end of it if I did.

"You never have been a morning person," she teases as I'm hit with a strong sense of longing. I miss her. "I don't think she can be more excited. It means the world to her that you will be here, honey."

I tuck my phone between my ear and shoulder and slide on a pair of shorts and a T-shirt. After I'm dressed, I grab my gym bag and rush to the front door, pleasantly surprised to see Braden lounging on the couch alone, waiting for me.

"I wouldn't miss it, Ma," I say. Braden looks at me, then points to the door. I nod. "I'll be home Saturday morning."

Braden gets up and grabs his bag from beside the couch before heading out. I follow after him, locking the door.

"Okay, sweetie. I just wanted to check in."

"I'm glad you did. I miss you guys."

Mom sighs heavily. There's a brief pause before she whispers, "We miss you, Oakley. So much."

Slipping my keys into the pocket of my sweatpants, I say, "Don't cry, Mom. I'll be home in no time."

I can almost imagine her hand slicing through the air, waving off my concern.

"Yeah, yeah. Well, I'll let you go. Call your sister this week, please."

"Will do. I'll talk to you later. Love you."

"Love you too."

I take the stairs down two at a time before pushing open the front doors and walking outside. Braden is already waiting for me beside my truck, his thumbs flying across his phone screen. He looks up at me when I round the front and unlock the driver's door. "You're driving. My car's at the shop."

With a nod, I quickly slip inside the truck and reach across to the lock on the passenger door before popping it up.

Braden joins me inside a second later. He's a huge guy—even compared to me—so I'm not surprised when he has to adjust the seat all the way back so that his legs aren't crushed by the dash.

"Everything good?" he asks when I start the engine and pull out onto the street. The arena is only ten minutes away from the house, so we might actually have a shot at making it there on time.

"Yeah. I'm going home next weekend. My mom was just checking in."

"Getting tired of us already?"

"Of you? Absolutely."

He roars a laugh. "Fair enough. I did try to get Vanessa to leave before you got up, by the way, but she said she was starving, and I'm not that much of an asshole to throw her out with an empty stomach."

I roll my eyes. "Right. You big softie. I'm sure it had nothing to do with her nakedness and the hopes of another quick round before training."

"Definitely not," he replies, grinning.

"Where did you meet her, anyway? I didn't even hear you get in last night."

"Remer's party. No clue how we got back to the apartment, though."

"You didn't drive there, right?" My muscles bunch beneath my clothes. Panic seizes me.

"Fuck no," he grunts, eyeing me curiously. "I was horny, not stupid."

I relax slightly and nod. "Okay. Good."

"I wrapped my cock up, too, in case you were curious about that, Dad."

"Fuck off."

His brash laugh pierces the air. With a shake of my head, I turn up the radio and settle into a comfortable silence for the rest of the drive.

# 8

# Oakley

"ABOUT TIME, BRO. I WAS STARTING TO THINK YOU WERE BAILING ON me. Hurry up, I need a spotter!" Matt shouts the minute I walk inside the busy training room.

The Saints logo is painted on the far wall, surrounded by framed pictures of every championship team. A hunger builds inside of me when I imagine our team photo hanging up there.

"Dude, there are four other guys here that can spot you. Don't be needy," Braden says, brushing past me. He drops his bag against a nearby wall, not bothering to shove it inside his locker.

I follow suit but make sure to grab my water bottle from the side pouch. Reaching behind my head, I tug my shirt off and toss it on top of my bag before setting my bottle on the ground and joining Matt at the weight bench.

There are two seventy-pound weights set on his bar, one on each side. I hover my hands beneath it and say, "Come on, then. Let's see how many reps you got in you."

The guy grins up at me before moving into action. He completes thirteen reps before I notice his arms giving out and take the bar from him, setting it back in its place on the rack above him.

"Not bad," Braden notes. He's jumping rope at a pace that makes me wince. His boxing experience makes him one hell of an athlete, hockey aside.

Matt scoffs and sits. He uses the bottom of his shirt to wipe away the sweat on his forehead.

"You stretch before starting that shit?" he asks him.

Braden rolls his eyes. "What's with you guys and your worrying lately?"

"Take it as a compliment, asshole," I throw back.

A gruff laugh comes from the back of the gym before Tyler and Adam come sauntering over from the row of treadmills, both dripping with sweat and breathing heavily.

"What's so funny?" Matt asks.

Tyler throws Adam an annoyed look. "Fuck face over here thinks he has a chance of outscoring me next game."

I cock a brow. Braden snorts. "Not gonna happen."

"Come on, man. What happened to loyalty?" Adam places his hands on his hips.

"If you're so sure you'll win," Braden starts with a smirk, "why wait until Wednesday? We can easily take it to the practice rink after training."

Tyler shrugs. "Works for me. I'm not worried."

"Me neither," Adam says adamantly.

"Let's make it happen." Matt claps his hands on his thighs. "But nobody is leaving this gym until your shit is done. So get to it."

"Aye, aye, Captain," Braden snickers. He tosses his jump rope back on its hook before moving to the bench Matt is occupying. "Get up and let me show you how it's really done."

Matt's eyes light up with the challenge, and he stands from the bench with an easy-going smile. "It's all yours."

Braden slips both weights off the bar before replacing them. I shouldn't be surprised that he can so confidently bench-press a hundred and eighty pounds, but I am. The guy could probably bench me if given the chance.

"You're a cocky asshole," Matt grumbles, his arms crossed. "I can't wait to save each one of your shots after this."

I clap a hand on his shoulder. "It's okay, Matty boy. The guy is a behemoth."

"Can say that again," Tyler grunts.

There's a warm feeling that spreads through my chest as I watch the ego show. These guys are ridiculous, but I think I like them that way.

I'm the first one on the ice, my skates laced, stick quickly taped, and my Warriors practice jersey on. Everyone but Matt skipped the bulky gear, promising to keep it a clean game, and I can only hope that that stays true. We would never hear the end of it if one of us got injured playing shinny.

I slip my left glove on and flex my grip on my stick, smacking it on the ice a few times. Tyler comes onto the ice next, his strides elegant and confident. He nods for me to join him along the boards, and we do one lap around the rink before Adam and Braden join us for a second.

With a smirk, I spin around and face the two stragglers, keeping my speed as I go backward. I fake a yawn, and Braden rolls his eyes.

"Shut it, twinkle toes," he says before picking up his pace and flanking my left side. In a quick movement, he's flipping around and moving backward.

Soon enough, all four of us are skating backward, looks of determination on our faces as we race each other, seeing who can go fastest.

"If you ladies are done, I'm ready for you!" Matt shouts from the far end of the rink. He's leaning back against the goalie net, his helmet pushed up and away from his face.

There is a pile of pucks waiting on the centre line, and Adam is the first to come to a stop and scoop one toward him with his stick. He passes it back and forth to himself before turning to Tyler.

"Who goes first?"

Tyler lifts his stick and moves it between Adam and Matt. "Go for it, pretty boy."

Not needing to be told twice, Adam readies himself and takes off toward Matt. He passes the puck between his legs a few times to show off before opting for a simple wrist shot that hits Matt's shoulder before hitting the post with a loud *ting*.

"Boo! You suck!" Braden hollers.

Adam's grinning when he comes to a stop beside me. He only shrugs and nods to Tyler. "I was warming up."

The defenseman sniffs and mumbles a gruff "Right" before picking a puck and skating toward Matt.

Tyler doesn't try any fancy moves; he just stops at the blue line and winds back before making a slapshot that has me wincing from the sound of it alone. The puck slices through the air and over Matt's right shoulder before it's caught in the net.

"That's it!" I shout, smacking my stick on the ice to mimic a clapping noise as Tyler glides around the back of the net and throws his up in the air.

"Hey!" Adam says. "Don't pick sides. You'll hurt my feelings."

I chuckle. "My bad."

With a new look of determination, Adam collects another puck from the pile and rushes at Matt for a second time. Matt moves just outside of his crease, his eyes trained on Adam and the puck as they get closer and closer.

Adam slows right down and starts playing with the puck like a little shit, shifting it side to side in front of him. Braden starts laughing beside me, and I join in without a second thought. It's when Matt gives his head a shake that Adam takes his shot. The puck slips between Matt's legs, into the net.

With the score tied at one each, the two guys take turns

shooting and scoring, until Tyler misses two shots in a row, and Adam doesn't miss again.

Tyler's scowl is intense when he reaches me and Braden, but I like to think that I've grown to know him well enough to tell he's not really all that upset by the loss.

Braden doesn't hesitate to poke fun at him. "Maybe I need a new linemate, Ty."

"What you need is a working brain and to deflate your damn ego," Tyler replies.

"Ooh, burn," Adam snickers, joining us. His smile is so wide I'm surprised his cheeks haven't split.

Matt is sliding his helmet up and over his face when he reaches us. He looks at Tyler. "Not bad. You still favour your backhand too much."

"That's not technically a bad thing," I say. "I know that I use too many wrist shots. It's all comfort. You only know what we tend to use most because you train with us nearly every day. The other goalies might know what we favour, but there's no way to be able to predict the same shot each time."

Matt nods. "True enough."

Tyler shoots me an appreciative look, and I shrug. A player's confidence is everything. The last thing we need is to risk that over something as harmless as a shooting competition.

"What do you say we play a quick 2V2? I call teaming with Oakley," Braden says, staring at me. I grin in agreement.

"Okay, I can be down for that. But I want something if we win," I say as a lightbulb goes off in my head.

"*When* we win," Braden corrects me.

Matt laughs. "Okay, big shot. What do you want if you win?"

"I want you to tell me more about Ava."

Adam sucks in a sharp breath, but I ignore him, keeping my eyes trained on the goalie that's now scowling at me.

"Any reason why that's what you want as a prize?" he asks tightly. I already knew he was protective of Ava, seeing as she's his girl's best friend, so I was expecting this.

"Call me curious," I reply, careful not to give too much away. In all honesty, I don't have a real reason as to why I feel so inclined to learn more about her. I just do.

"Bro, you could have just asked me. I would have told you everything I know for free," Braden says with a laugh.

"And that would have been a waste of time, considering you know *nothing*," Tyler quips.

Braden says something in defense of himself, but I'm not listening anymore. I'm too focused on the harsh way Matt is watching me, almost like he's trying to dig a hole inside my head with his eyes and take whatever answers he wants himself.

"Fine," he says a breath later. His stare breaks. "Three questions. That's it."

I nod. "Deal."

We move quickly to clear the extra pucks out of the way, leaving one behind on the centreline. Adam and Tyler move to the two face-off zones on the opposite sides of the net while Braden and I get ready to attack.

Matt shouts to begin, and I scoop the puck before taking off. Tyler barrels right for me while Adam goes for Braden. I can't help but laugh at the scowl on Tyler's face when I shoot off the puck to Braden and evade him with a spin.

The puck hits Braden's stick with a clap before he's shoving Adam out of the way and closing the distance between us and Matt. As soon as we reach the blue line, Braden passes me the puck, and I wind back before sending it top shelf.

"Fuck yeah!" Braden shouts. He rushes toward me and slaps me on the back.

Matt collects the puck and passes it off to Tyler. The four of us change sides, and we go again, this time with Braden and me playing defense.

I'm not surprised when Adam scores. He's an incredibly sharp shooter, especially under pressure. I'm even less surprised when each side continues to score until finally, Adam misses a shot and hands my side the win.

It's not until we're all back in the locker room and I finish unlacing my skates when Matt flops down beside me.

"Three questions."

"Here?" I look at Adam cautiously from where he sits onto the bench opposite us.

Matt makes a rough sound in his throat. "Ignore him. He's been massively friend zoned."

I drop my voice. "Has he? 'Cause the guy watches her with damn hearts in his eyes."

"Is that one of your questions?"

"Yeah. Sure."

He laughs but has the decency to lower his voice as he says, "Infinite best friend status. I don't even think she knows he's into her."

I try to pretend like that doesn't help settle me. It shouldn't. If she wants to date the guy, she should.

"Who's the ex?"

"A hockey player."

I sigh heavily. "Not good enough. Is it someone on the team?"

Matt slants me a pointed look. "Last question. Are you sure you wanna use it on that?"

"Yeah, fuck. Whatever. Just tell me."

"David Remer. Third-line right wing," he says.

I blink slowly and then grimace. "The guy who was just bragging at practice about getting his dick sucked behind the rink after last game?"

"The very one."

"Seems he loves having his dick sucked," I grunt.

"You know about that?" Matt asks, his eyes wide.

"Yeah. It's a long story."

"Don't care. Tell me."

I crack my knuckles, nerves buzzing beneath my skin. "The party that Remer cheated on her at? Yeah, that was my going-away party before I moved out here. I met Ava in the backyard that night."

Matt makes a weird noise. "No shit."

Braden drops on the bench on my other side and gives my face a questionable look. "You talking about Remer? I would know that expression anywhere." When I nod, he spares a glance at Tyler and says, "See, I know some shit."

"Everyone knows about Remer, asshole," Tyler grunts.

"Go stand in front of a moving car, Ty," Braden replies grumpily.

"Please, after you."

Adam stands up suddenly and throws his duffel over his shoulder. "I gotta go."

"Alright, man. See you at practice tomorrow," Matt says with a nod.

It doesn't take a genius to know why he's leaving so suddenly. But nobody says anything other than a simple good-bye. We might love picking on each other, but we're not complete assholes.

The four of us share a look that says we're all thinking the same thing.

Nobody says another word on the way out of the arena.

# 9

# Ava

I RELEASE A NOISE THAT SOUNDS LIKE A MIX BETWEEN A HISS AND A growl and click my seat belt into place. Morgan sighs, as if the fight I put up just mere minutes ago has taken five years off her life.

"I can't believe I had to literally drag you out of the house," she grumbles, starting her car.

Her long blonde hair is split down the centre and twisted into two perfect braids. She flings one over her shoulder and fiddles with the touch screen on the dash until a country song floods through the speakers.

I tighten my ponytail and slant her a look. "You wouldn't have had to if you would have just let me be."

There's a stack of school work that damn near wobbles in the wind on my desk at the moment and only so much time to complete it all. Accompanying Morgan to pick her boyfriend up from a shinny game is not at the top of my priority list.

Unfortunately, my best friend doesn't share the same focus when it comes to school as I do, which in turn hinders her ability to understand where I'm coming from most days.

"You were in need of a break."

"I was doing just fine."

"Have you eaten today?" she asks after pulling onto the road.

I roll my eyes. "Yes, Mom. I had just finished off a jar of peanut butter when you barged into my room."

Her nose crinkles. "Is that all you've had?"

"It was the crunchy stuff."

"As if that makes much of a difference." She clicks her tongue. "At least you had something. I won't bug you about it anymore."

I nod and smile gratefully. Morgan's heart is in the right place; it always is. She's a momma bear through and through.

Luckily, she really does drop the topic and chooses to just sing along quietly to music for the rest of the drive. My eyes are droopy by the time we reach the arena, and I'm suddenly feeling extremely bitter at the fact I can't ever seem to sleep in the car. A nap—albeit a short one—would have done wonders for me.

Morgan parks her massive Jeep Gladiator beside a familiar truck that I know belongs to the newest member of the Saints. I twist in my seat, glowering at my soon-to-be ex-best friend.

"You couldn't help yourself, could you?"

She unbuckles her seat belt and grins, completely unbothered by my attitude. "Nope. Now, get out. It's rude not to say hello."

I watch her slip out of the vehicle and disappear but don't make an effort to follow. A shriek builds in my throat when my door is ripped open and I'm being dragged out by my arm.

Stabilizing myself on the concrete, I gasp, "You're absolutely crazy."

Morgan laughs. "And you're stubborn. I'm not asking you to get down on one knee and bow to the guy. Just say hi."

I dig my heels into the ground, but Morgan's love for the gym has made me no match for her when it comes to brute strength. With a set of neon green talons she calls nails biting into my skin, she pulls me hard enough that I stumble out from behind the cover of Oakley's truck and into plain view. A colourful string of curses falls from my mouth when I see the two guys standing a few yards away, their eyes on me and Morgan.

"Hi!" she shouts.

Forcing a smile, I lift my hand in a small wave. I gulp when the guys start walking toward us. Matt rushes to Morgan, but I don't see what happens after. Not when my eyes have become trapped on Oakley's and the warmth that fills them.

Like every time I've seen him, the guy oozes confidence. Not in an overbearing way but in a way that stirs your curiosity, making you want to get closer and learn more about exactly where that confidence comes from. At this point, I'm not sure which is worse.

Two dimples pop in his cheeks when he grins, and my stomach tightens in response. Oh boy, he's *hot*.

I'm relieved when Matt speaks up, his voice cutting through whatever was building between me and his new friend before my nipples got hard enough to cut through my shirt.

"About time, baby. I was worried you got lost or something."

"We would have been here sooner if it wasn't for Ms. 'I'm-not-leaving-the-house' over here," Morgan replies.

Aware that Oakley still hasn't looked away from me, I turn to Morgan and say, "Or you could have just left without me."

"Don't tell me you didn't want to see me," Oakley says, his voice a deep rumble.

"Aw, Boy Scout. Are you happy I'm here?" I ask before I can stop myself.

"Boy Scout?" Matt asks.

Oakley ignores him, his eyes trapping mine. "Yeah, I am."

My breath hitches at the honesty in those words. "Oh." *Oh? Am I for real?*

"That's cute," Morgan says. Matt sputters a laugh.

Oakley pins him with a glare. "Hey, Matt?" Matt stops laughing. "Go home."

"Fuckin' rude, Oakley. I thought we had something good going right now," Matt gasps.

Morgan heaves a sigh at her boyfriend's dramatic ways. "Good Lord, Matthew. Come on. We'll hit that frozen yogurt shop you love on the way home."

"What about you? Do you like frozen yogurt?" Oakley asks. I dart my eyes his way, surprised to find a set of sharp green ones watching me.

"Me?" I ask, as if he were asking anyone else. I want to cringe at how ridiculous I'm being right now. It's like I've never spoken to a guy before.

Oakley chuckles. "Yes."

"Not as much as I do ice cream. Fro-yo is more Morgan and Matt's thing," I answer honestly. Morgan swears up and down it tastes the same as ice cream, but I'm positive that's just a lie she tells herself to feel less sad about missing the real thing.

"Let me take you for ice cream, then."

I ask in a small, quiet voice, "Right now?"

His chin dips. "If you want to. As friends, of course," he clarifies.

"Oh, she wants to," Morgan cuts in. *Bitch.*

With his hands in the back pockets of his dark-washed jeans, Oakley eats up some of the space between us with large strides. He stops a short distance away, close enough that he can see how flushed I am but far enough away that I can barely pick up the hint of his body wash. Suddenly, I want him closer.

I'm aware Matt and Morgan are just a few footsteps away, but they've faded to the background. I tug my lips into a small smile that I hope is enough to convince him that I'm comfortable with the idea.

"I think I would like that."

His grin is blinding. "Let's go."

❄

"Full transparency, I was worried you would turn out to be a plain vanilla ice cream kind of girl," Oakley quips from across the small checkered table.

The ice cream parlour is relatively quiet, with only us and an older couple sitting inside to enjoy our treat instead of out in the sun. I've never been to this place, but when I searched *local ice cream parlour* on Google Maps, this was the first one that popped up.

I dip my red plastic spoon into my paper bowl and scoop up some of my strawberry cheesecake ice cream. My eyes hold his in a silent challenge as I press the spoon to the outside of my sticky lips. "What if I was? Would you have turned and left?"

His eyes flare, zeroed in on my mouth. He looks sinful, and I falter for the briefest second before regaining my composure. Doubt is a prick in my side—doubt that he can possibly be looking at me the way he is.

"Hell no. I would have just encouraged you to try something else. Maybe begged if need be," he states, voice thick with something too dirty for *just friends*.

My muscles lock, and I can't seem to make myself push the spoon into my mouth. I inhale sharply and shiver when a cold drop of melted ice cream falls to my bare thigh. The second my lips part, I'm shoving the spoon between them and licking my lips to rid them of the stickiness left behind.

Oakley looks pained for a moment before he shifts his attention to something behind me, and his expression turns to anger.

"What's wrong?" I ask before twisting in my chair to look over my shoulder. The second I do, my heart squeezes painfully, a knot growing in my belly. I spin back around and try to ignore the way Oakley's curious eyes seek out mine by staring at the empty table behind him.

"Hutton? Hey, man." The overly friendly greeting comes from behind me, and I tense up.

A shadow forms at our table, thanks to the man now hovering over us like a storm cloud that just won't drift away.

My immediate reaction is to punch him in the dick, seeing as his groin is in perfect hitting distance, but instead, I paint on an exaggerated smile and turn to my ex-boyfriend. *Kill them with kindness, Ava.* My mom would be proud.

Oakley clears his throat. "Remer."

David looks exactly as he did when we first met in high school, minus the forehead acne and the shaggy blond hair he cut the week before our first day of university. His eyes are still a sharp, icy blue that I used to fawn over and his nose a bit too straight. He still carries a serious case of daddy issues on his back like a badge of honour and believes his actions reap no consequences.

Both explain why his explanation for cheating on me was that he was simply experimenting, as if that was reasoning enough. "How do I know if I want the lobster if I haven't tried the crab?" he had said in his defense. And that was that.

I refused to ignore the raging alarm in my head at his actions, and we haven't talked since I left him standing outside our hotel room door in Penticton. There was no regret as I watched him walk away ten minutes after I shut the door in his face, just an ache in my chest as I questioned why I wasn't good enough.

It's a terrible feeling to feel disposed of, like you never really mattered. That was the worst part of it all. The part that still stings when I think about the years we spent together.

It was an awful sense of déjà vu. Suddenly, I wasn't a nineteen-year-old woman watching my boyfriend walk away; I was a little girl standing in a room at children's services, wondering why another potential family had decided against adopting me.

I sit up a bit straighter when David finally looks at me, and his grin falters, his facade crumbling at the edges.

"Octavia," he says tightly, painfully.

With my smile still in place, I ignore him and straighten in my chair, effectively brushing him off. Oakley's lips twitch in amusement.

"I heard about your shinny game this morning. Next time,

you should let me know. I would love to join." David is all but beaming at his new teammate. He's never been all that good at reading a room, but this is a new low.

"I don't think so," Oakley replies before shovelling a scoop of ice cream in his mouth.

The blunt statement comes so suddenly that I laugh before I can stop myself. I slap a hand across my mouth to stifle the noise, but it's too late. The damage has already been done.

"Why are you laughing?" David asks me, his blue eyes no longer ice but fire instead. I steel my expression, refusing to look affected by him and the hostility he's showing me. "I never thought you were a puck bunny, but clearly, I was wrong. Hockey dick is the best dick, though. So I'm not surprised."

I wince. *Ouch.*

"Are you talking from experience? Do you get a lot of hockey dick, Remer?" Oakley accuses. His eyes are two angry slits.

"Fuck no! That's not at all what I meant," David defends.

Oakley hums and lifts one hand to gesture to the door. "Well then. If you wouldn't mind, we were in the middle of a conversation when you interrupted us."

"Uh, yeah. Okay. Sorry, man," David stammers. Is that sweat between his eyebrows?

Clearly not wanting to be subjected to any further embarrassment, my ex-boyfriend spins on his heels and walks away, leaving a ding from the bell above the shop door in his wake.

A warm sensation fills my chest in response to Oakley's support, and I find myself staring at him. "Thank you."

He nudges my foot with his beneath the table and flashes his white teeth in a swoon-worthy smile. "Anytime, Ava."

# 10

## Oakley

THE SAINTS LOCKER ROOM IS BUZZING.

It's our first game of the season against the Kelowna Wolves, and although I've never played against them, it's common knowledge they are our biggest rival—making this game one of the most important this season.

I need to show our team and the opposing one that I'm a better hockey player than they already think I am. Just because I'm not captain of this team doesn't mean I don't have to play my best. I thrive best under pressure, and there's no shortage of that tonight.

As I finish putting on all my gear and tie the last knot in my skates, Coach walks in and yells for everyone's attention. We huddle around him, shoulder pads brushing and heavy breaths mixing. You could taste the nerves in the room right now.

Coach Garrison is a big guy—probably the biggest one in the room. With a bald head and stern brown eyes, he's nothing short of intimidating. Playing under him is different than playing for Banner, but I've more than accepted the change.

"Tonight is big, you all know that. We need to show these guys that we're coming out hot this season. Got it? We might have lost our captain, but that doesn't mean we're at a disadvantage. We have the number one goal scorer in the league."

I flash a grin to the team when Coach turns his attention to me.

"Lowry and Bateman, keep Hutton clear. They're going to be on him all night. Stay focused and keep it clean. Don't fall for their shit. Beat them on the scoreboard, not in the penalty box. Now, go kick some Wolf ass."

The team erupts into cheers and howls of excitement. Matt's as serious as ever when I spot him through the crowd and make my way over to him.

"You good?" he asks, bumping my shoulder with his gloved hand.

"Good as ever. You? We need you on your A game tonight."

"Don't worry about me." He falls in line behind me as we weave our way to the exit.

Screams, music, adrenaline.

There is nothing that comes close to this feeling—the one you get when you skate onto the ice on game day and hear your name and number being called into a full arena. It's one of those surreal moments where you want to take a minute just to stand and soak it all in. But you never can. There's never the time to.

As soon as my skates hit the ice, I'm focusing on the game by building a wall between the prospect of winning and any distraction that could possibly take the W from us. But when I finish my final warm-up lap, I feel that wall crumble just enough to spark a sliver of panic in my veins.

My eyes are drawn to her, to Ava and Morgan as they sit in the front row. Ava's lips are spread in a wide grin, her eyes laser focused on me. It messes with me, and I nearly trip over my feet —something that hasn't happened since I was a kid.

But as confusing as these feelings are, I have to admit there's something almost addicting about having a beautiful girl smiling at me in the stands while sporting my team's jersey. *Whose number is she wearing?* Nope. Doesn't matter.

With a flashy wink, I bump my shoulder against the glass as I skate by her seat. That damn smile is branded in my mind as I head for the centreline.

Getting in position to take the first faceoff of the game, I look over at the two wingers beside me, Knoxville and White, and give them both a head nod. My heart pounds as the ref drops the puck on the ice and I scoop it up, taking off.

WITH THIRTEEN MINUTES left to go in the game, we're tied with three points each. Our team is exhausted from playing defense most of the game—thanks to our hotheaded defensemen not taking an ounce of smack talk from the opposing team without losing their calm.

It also doesn't help that I've spent most of my remaining energy maneuvering around their killer blueliners while slapping useless shots at their goalie whenever I have a chance.

My helmet knocks against the boards when a defenseman hits my shoulder. A hiss of pain escapes my lips, and I struggle to regain my balance, shaking off the ache in my shoulder. I turn and give my missing cover man a death glare.

"Fuck sake, Braden," I growl under my breath.

I see Matt in front of me as he stops the puck behind his net and gets ready to pass it off. I slap my stick against the ice to let him know that I'm open. I do a lap around our zone before skating toward the other end of the ice.

Matt passes the puck to me before the other team's centreman reaches him. As soon as I hear it clap against my stick's blade, I push off my feet, speeding up. I only make it a few feet ahead before another Wolves player heads straight in my direction.

Fortunately, this time Braden does his job and watches my back. He throws his body against the player—*hard*.

I skate past the pair and run straight into the second defenseman. Spinning around, I move around them and sneak a quick look behind me to see Braden lose his edge on his player.

It's now or never. I wind up and slap the puck hard, successfully sending it five-hole. The red lamp goes off, and my teammates immediately tackle me in a fit of hugs and punches.

After a few pats on the back, I push myself over the boards and sit down on the bench beside Adam. I spot Ava and Morgan standing in their seats, cheering loudly, and smile to myself.

The game ends quickly after that, with no other goals being scored. We win by one, but that's good enough for me.

"Good game, man," Matt tells me once we reach the locker room.

"Thanks. You kept us in it, though," I reply.

With his helmet already off and put away, he shoots me a grin and pulls off his jersey, throwing it into his bag. Braden brushes past him and throws his arm around me. I crinkle my nose when I get a big whiff of him.

"Get off me. You smell like a donkey's ass," I say, pushing at him. The guy barely moves.

He scowls and smells me obnoxiously. "Like you smell any better."

Tyler collapses on the bench in front of us and snickers. "He's not the one going around groping people."

"Jealous?" Braden smirks and removes his arm from my shoulders, only to move toward Tyler in slow motion. "Come on. Give me a hug."

Tyler's eyes narrow. "Touch me and I'll break your hands."

"Tough love. What a shame," Braden sighs.

"Hit the showers, Braden. I'm sure your fangirls are waiting for you." Matt laughs.

"You make it sound like they're a problem or something," he replies, making quick work of discarding his gear and stripping to his underwear.

If it weren't for our several requests that he doesn't walk around the dressing room butt-ass naked all the time, I'm positive he would have already been tossing his junk in everyone's face by now.

"Not a problem. Just annoying," I grumble, shoving my gear back in my cubby and hanging my jersey on the hook.

"I understand Matt being a bitch about getting bunny pussy, but what's your deal? You a virgin or something?" Braden asks me, his brows lifted.

"The fact you just referred to it as 'getting bunny pussy' is exactly why I'm not discussing this topic with you."

He scoffs. "Oh, come on. Even Tyler sleeps around."

"What is that supposed to mean?" Tyler grunts.

"You're the most introverted person I've ever met. I would have expected you to be the virgin."

Tyler shakes his head and grabs a stack of clothes and a bottle of body wash before disappearing toward the showers.

Braden shrugs. "Was it something I said?

Matt only laughs, and Braden takes that as a signal to shut up and let it drop. At least he knows better than to keep poking. He's a big guy, but I don't doubt I could send him on his ass.

We all make quick work of showering and getting dressed. Afterward, I say my goodbyes to the team and leave the dressing room, hoping to get out of the arena as fast as I can. I'm not only exhausted, but my shoulder aches something fierce.

Unfortunately, I don't make it very far before I'm stopped by a tall, leggy blonde I've seen around the rink a few times.

"Hey, Oakley! You did amazing tonight. Are you going to the after-party?" she asks brightly.

I stop a few feet from her and offer a forced smile. "Hey. Yeah, I was planning on it."

"Exciting! You'll have to save me a dance."

"I'm afraid I'm not much of a dancer . . ." I trail off, coming up with nothing but empty thoughts when it comes to this girl's name.

Her bottom lip juts out. "Cassie. My name is Cassie. You don't know who I am?"

"Should I?" I hope I look more apologetic than I sound. There's no way I've spoken to this girl before.

She looks taken aback, and I'm about to apologize for not knowing who she is when a small arm slips around my waist. The tension in my shoulders evaporates when I breathe in the familiar smell of Ava's perfume.

"Hey, babe. Ready to go? Everyone's waiting," Ava murmurs, peering up at me with mischievous green eyes. She runs her fingers up and down my chest, and my mind blanks. *What is happening? Babe?*

I frantically attempt to collect myself. "Yep, good to go. It was nice to meet you, Cassie."

Grabbing Ava's hand, I drag her out of the arena.

"Thank you," I say once we make it outside. The night is warm, and I'm grateful I brought a change of clothes so I didn't have to slip back into my heavy suit. "That was a bit uncomfortable."

"Just repaying the favour for what you said the other day with David. I figured you probably got swarmed tonight. Being the star of the night and all." She nudges me with her arm and laughs into the light breeze.

"Either way, I appreciate it."

"Hurry up, Ava. Let's go!" Morgan yells from the parking lot, half hanging out the unrolled window of her Jeep.

"That's my cue. I'll see you in a couple of hours, Boy Scout. Unless you bail on us," she teases while spinning on her heels and jogging down the cement stairs toward Morgan.

Shuffling my feet, I smile. I don't think I could ever bail on her.

# 11

## *Ava*

When we arrive at Adam's house, the victory party is already in full swing.

The music is so loud I can feel the bass pulsing at the soles of my feet as we step out of the cab. I look up the winding driveway and release a dreamy sigh. The sight of Adam's parents' mansion never fails to amaze me.

Floor-to-ceiling windows line the dark grey brick walls, and tall, strong arches drape above the exaggerated cobblestone walkway. Elaborately decorated flower boxes that would make any florist's mouth water are perched below each window.

The house is a designer's dream, that's for sure.

Now, my parents' house is by no means "small." Thanks to both of their successful culinary careers, they've been able to provide a comfortable life for me and my brother. But unlike Adam's parents, they've never been obsessed with looks and broadcasting their money in purchases that don't actually have any meaning. To each their own, but I know Adam would love their genuine attention more than another expensive car or a giant flat-screen TV. Their absence wears on him, whether he wants to actually admit that out loud or not.

Morgan and I walk past the countless drunks who are

already throwing up and stumbling around in the well-groomed bushes and cringe at the shirtless frat boys who are playing beer pong on one of the large white tables scattered along the driveway.

"To the kitchen!" I yell over the music as we carefully maneuver around the growing crowd. After a couple of minutes, we enter the full chef's kitchen. Much to my disappointment, it's not any less busy here. If anything, it's worse.

"Finally. I need a drink."

I nod, and Morgan heads off to the drink table while I look around. Relief washes over me when I spot a grinning Adam leaning against the back wall with Matt, Tyler, and a couple of other guys I don't recognize.

Adam is wearing a white hoodie at least one size too small and light-washed, distressed jeans with far too many holes. His dark brown curls are hidden under a tight fitted baseball cap, and when his shining chocolate eyes meet mine, they light up.

Morgan pushes a cup full of what smells like a vodka drink into my hand, and I mumble a quick thank you before we head toward our friends. Matt greets his girlfriend by pulling her into his side and whispering something in her ear that turns her cheeks bright red.

"Damn, baby. What's your name? Do I know you?" Adam murmurs when I reach him. He palms my back before dragging his hand up to cup my nape. I roll my eyes at his antics but decide to go along with whatever game he's playing.

"Oh, my God! Are you Adam White? *The* starting left-winger for the Saints? I just loved you in tonight's game." I twirl a lock of hair around my finger, and his smirk turns into a grin. I reach out and grab his massive bicep, squeezing the hard muscles twice.

He leans in close to me until his cheek brushes mine and whispers his next words in my ear. "Not going to lie, you had me at the beginning. But no puck bunny would know that much about hockey. Solid effort, though."

He pulls back, and I swear I see something warm grow in his stare before he distracts me with a hug. I accept his affection without hesitation.

An hour, five shots of tequila, and two rounds of beer pong later, the group of us has migrated to the massive backyard.

Matthew and Morgan are lying together on a hammock strung from a massive tree, talking to themselves, while Adam and I sit beside the house on a thick blanket. The breeze has a bit of a nip to it now, but it's not uncomfortable yet.

"Should I order pizza? I'm starving," Adam mutters. I look at him, surprised at the random outburst but definitely into the idea. My stomach has been rumbling for a solid half hour.

"Yes, please."

Adam turns to Morgan and Matt. "You guys hungry?"

"Hell yes," Morgan groans, and Matt mumbles his agreement.

"What kind?" he's asking me.

"Anything without pineapple."

"You haven't grown out of this ridiculous phase of yours yet?"

"What do you mean *phase*? You can't honestly tell me that fruit belongs on pizza? With meat?" I scoff. Adam scrunches his nose. "Tomatoes will forever be the only exception."

"That's because tomatoes go on everything, gorgeous," he rebukes, leaning back on his hands and tilting his head to the sky.

"They most definitely do not."

"Prove it."

"You don't always have to be right, you know?"

"What's the fun in being wrong?" he throws back, looking mighty smug.

I shake my head. "Always the smartass."

Adam doesn't respond; he's too busy glaring at something over my shoulder instead. I turn to look at whatever triggered his drastic mood change and feel my face flush.

I trail my eyes up two very long legs and thick thighs and grin up at Oakley. A plain navy blue T-shirt hugs his chest, leaving almost no muscle to the imagination. I stare, mouth hanging open. The ball cap on his head is facing forward for a change, and for some reason, my fingers tingle with the urge to flip it backward.

I hear Adam mumble something about going to talk to one of his friends, his tone surprisingly sharp, but when I turn around to say goodbye, he's already halfway across the yard.

I chew on my lip but decide to shake off his attitude. Shifting my attention back to Oakley, I find him staring at me. I know I'm wearing a huge grin when I push myself off the damp grass and throw my arms around his neck.

If I didn't have an ample amount of alcohol in my system, there would be no way in hell I would jump on a guy that I barely know. Thankfully, he responds almost immediately and wraps me in his arms. He holds me there against him before I can pull away and hide, flushed with embarrassment. I step away from him after a few seconds and smile timidly.

"You came. I was starting to worry you stood me up."

"Wouldn't dream of it. I got a call from my sister on the way here that lasted way longer than I expected."

My gut twists. "Is she okay? Nothing bad, I hope."

He shakes his head and rolls his neck. "That depends on what you consider to be bad. Personally, learning that she has a new boyfriend is disastrous news for me. I called my buddy to check him out for me."

I fight back a smile. "Big brothers. You're all the same."

"What do you mean? It's our job to be protective."

I arch a brow. "It's your job to scare away any person who dares spare us an interested glance?"

"Yes. It is." He says it like it's the most obvious thing in existence.

"There's something loose in your brains. A few missing screws, maybe. I think that's a more acceptable probability."

A smirk tugs at his mouth. "You enjoy picking on me, don't you? I think I like that about you."

"That's good, because I wasn't planning on stopping."

"And there it is, that quick return I've also grown to enjoy."

"Alright. Cool it on the compliments, Hotshot." *I'm too tipsy to hear them without blushing.*

"Hutton! Come over here and play a game of pong!" a slurred voice calls. We both look at the crowd of jocks huddled around a long white table and sigh at the same time.

"Your presence has been requested," I tease, hoping he can't hear the twinge of disappointment in my voice at losing his company so soon.

He stares down at me. "Will you come with me?"

"That looks like a nightmare."

"I agree. But it won't be so bad if you're with me. Please don't make me go over there alone," he pleads. His eyes widen, and his bottom lip juts out ever so slightly.

"Are you seriously giving me a puppy dog face right now?" I choke on a laugh.

He blinks innocently, and I lose it. My loud laugh breaks through the night, but I can't stop. Watching a six-foot-three Hulk of a man pout might be the most ridiculous thing I have ever seen.

"You're ridiculous," I wheeze.

He sobers up and takes a step toward me. My laughter dries up at his closeness. The smell of his cologne makes me woozy in the best way. He smells *so* good.

Tipping my head back, I swallow at the heat in his eyes.

"You're something else, Ava," he mutters, his voice deep and raspy.

"Thanks."

A laugh rumbles in his chest. "You don't take compliments well."

"Was that a compliment?"

"A bad one," he admits with a half-smile. "Look, I promise I'll make it up to you if you come play a quick game with me."

"How are you going to do that?"

Oh God. Am I flirting with him? This feels a whole lot like I'm flirting with him.

His grin is sly, dangerous. "Name your price."

"Anything?"

"Anything."

I roll my lips and try to think of something but come up with nothing but hot air. "Do I have to decide right now, or can I think on it?"

He runs a hand over his jaw. "Think on it. You'll have plenty of time after we whoop some beer pong ass."

Despite how badly I don't want to spend my night with a bunch of random bro-guys, I find myself nodding. "Okay."

My breath skips when Oakley reaches for my hand and flashes me a white-toothed smile. His fingers are long, his palm wide and hot. My hand disappears in his as he holds it and starts to lead me toward the crowd.

I steel my spine when everyone turns to look at us. The group of guys couldn't care less about my presence as they focus on Oakley beside me, and for that, I'm oddly grateful.

A blond-haired guy with a manbun I recognize as Jarod Knoxville, Oakley's linemate, whoops loudly when his pupil-blown grey eyes focus on Oakley. "My man!"

Oakley shifts me slightly behind him when Jarod comes stumbling over and pulls him into a half hug. "Hey, Knox."

Jarod releases him and spins to the two guys on the far end of the pong table and yells, "You're done! Hutton's on that side."

Without hesitation, they quickly place their Ping-Pong balls in an empty red cup and move out of the way. It's creepy how they just do what they're told like that.

Jarod looks at Oakley again. "You need a partner?" Before Oakley answers him, he's already pointing at someone else in the crowd. The guy looks surprised but nods anyway. "You're Hutton's partner now."

Oakley squeezes my hand and pulls me in beside him again before looking at his new "partner" and saying, "I have a partner already. You're good." Then he grips Jarod's shoulder. "Thanks anyway."

Suddenly, everyone's looking at me as if just realizing there was someone beside Oakley the entire time. My skin immediately starts to itch under their stares. Some uncaring, some scrutinizing.

"Avery, right?" Jarod asks, moving his eyes over the length of my body. He smirks.

I clear my throat. "Ava."

"Oh shit. That's right. Adam's Ava. I recognize you now." He says it like it's some revelation. I narrow my eyes on him and open my mouth to tell him that I'm nobody's Ava when Oakley beats me to it.

He grits his teeth. "It's just Ava to you. To *everyone*."

Jarod puts his hands in front of his chest. "You got it, boss. You and Just Ava can go first."

I sense Oakley getting annoyed again and squeeze his fingers to let him know it's okay. It's actually quite funny to watch these people interact with each other. Does Jarod know how douchey he seems, or does he just not care?

"Who are we playing against?" I ask the group.

"Us," says one of the two beefy guys already at the end of the table. I don't know either of them.

Oakley nods at them, and we walk to our side of the table. Someone has replaced all of the cups from the last round with new ones, organizing them in the usual triangle shape. Jarod has taken charge of refilling them all with a pitcher of beer. I cringe.

"That's definitely going to taste like piss," Oakley notes. He reaches up and takes his hat off before quickly running his fingers through his hair and slapping it back on. Backward this time.

*Swoon.*

"Do you want me to drink your cups for you?" I ask softly.

His eyes are warm when they meet mine. He smiles. "Sure. I don't think you'll need to, though. I've never lost a game of beer pong before, and those two look about two drinks away from collapsing."

I peel my eyes away from him and look at our competition. They're taking turns draining the extra beer from the pitcher, swaying every few swallows.

"Good point." I laugh.

Jarod comes over with two plastic, white balls in his hands and holds them out to me. I take them from him with a quick thank you.

Oakley moves quickly, catching Jarod's arm before he slips back into the crowd. He drops his voice. "That beer better be clean, Knoxville. You got me? If she drinks something—"

"She's good, bro. Got the beer from the keg right before I poured it in the cups."

Oakley lets him go. "Great. Let's get started, then."

I hold back my laugh, watching Jarod rush off. Oakley nods encouragingly at me and waves his hand toward the cups.

"Ladies first," he says.

I release a breath before stepping in front of him and lining up my first shot. It's distracting having him behind me, his body heat pulsing against my back and the smell of his cologne swirling in the wind, but I try to pretend he's somewhere else and focus. It turns out to be a lot harder than I was hoping it would be. Especially when he shifts closer, brushing the back of my arm with his.

Gripping the ball, I force myself to concentrate on the middle cup and let it fly. It arches in the air before sinking in the beer. I do the same with the second ball, this time aiming for the cup beside it. It goes in. Two for two.

With matching scowls, our competitors remove the balls from

the cups and drink. Once they're empty, they toss them on the grass.

"Atta girl," Oakley murmurs, his breath brushing the back of my ear.

I look over my shoulder at him, flying high on his praise. He grins at me, green eyes twinkling.

"I've never lost a game either," I admit.

His grin gets bigger somehow. "I knew I chose you as my partner for a reason."

"You mean it wasn't because I wanted to play so badly?"

"Absolutely not." He laughs.

One of the guys across the table clears his throat and yells, "Beginner's luck. Watch and learn."

He uses a shaky hand to push his shaggy brown hair out of his face before narrowing his eyes on our cups and tossing the first ball. He overshoots the cups, and Oakley catches the ball in one hand before it hits the ground.

"Come on, Rex," the thrower's friend grumbles. "Get it in!"

*Rex* spins to face his friend, his face red. "Yeah. I'm trying, dipshit."

Oakley chuckles and cocks his head at the two guys. "You said something about learning?"

Rex throws up his middle finger and throws his second ball. It rims the top of our first cup before bouncing off the side and hitting the table. The crowd makes an *ooh* noise.

Oakley collects that ball with a smug smile. "There's always next time."

I step to the side of the table to make room for Oakley to take his turn. He lifts his arm, lining up his shots, and I watch his biceps bulge and tense with the motion. My hopeless curiosity has me wondering what it would feel like to wrap my hand around all that warm muscle. Would I even be able to touch all of it?

The crowd cheering pulls me from my thoughts. When I zone

back into what's happening, I find Oakley watching me, a spark of what I think is arousal in his eyes.

He quickly looks away and rolls the ball in his palm. "One more to go." Moving into position, he doesn't hesitate before tossing it. My eyes go wide when he misses and it hits the table in front of the first cup.

"Grab it!" Rex yells at his friend.

But it's too late. Oakley stretches that long body over our cups and covers the ball with his hand, grabbing it and standing back before the other guy even gets close.

"Trick shot!" Jarod shouts.

Oakley ignores him, turning to me instead. "Come here." I blink at him. He laughs. "Please, come here. I need your help."

Eying him suspiciously, I slowly close the distance between us.

"Will you stand behind me and cover my eyes?" he asks.

"There's no way I'll reach." Not without a step stool, at least.

He shrugs. "Hop on my back, then."

Flutters bloom in my stomach. "Okay."

Without wasting any more time, Oakley faces the table and crouches down. I stand behind him and carefully drop my hands to his shoulders. He tenses beneath my fingertips.

"Just jump on, Ava. I won't drop you," he says quietly.

*If only that's what I was worried about.* I move slower than a normal, sane woman would given this opportunity, and it's apparently too slow for him. I gasp when he reaches back and grips both of my thighs, pulling me toward him. On instinct, I wrap them around his waist and slip my hands from his shoulders down to clasp in front of his neck. God, I shouldn't fit against him this well.

"There we go," he says, his voice low. "Now, cover my eyes and wish me luck."

I place my hands over his eyes and smile when his eyelashes flutter against my palms. "Good luck," I whisper.

He lets go of one of my legs but keeps his hold on my other

one, even though there's no reason to. They're squeezing his waist tight.

I hand him the ball and watch as he blows on it and then slowly brings it up to where he thinks my lips are.

"Blow, Ava. For double luck."

He's a few inches off, so I push myself higher up his back to reach. I swallow to keep myself from making an embarrassing noise at the sudden pressure between my legs as I move. *Stop it.*

I purse my lips in front of the ball and quickly blow on it before leaning back.

"Good to go," I murmur.

His body vibrates with a quiet laugh before tossing the ball. My jaw drops when it falls in a cup.

"You got it in." I don't hide my surprise.

Oakley barks a loud laugh, and I drop my hands. "I did. And now we can leave."

With those final words, he grabs my thighs again and starts off toward the house, leaving the game and everyone watching like they're not even there.

"The game isn't done!" Rex's friend shouts, but Oakley only waves him off.

My chest floods with something ooey gooey. I rest my chin on his shoulder and let him take us away.

# 12

## Ava

I WAKE WITH A PULSE IN MY SKULL.

My mouth is dry as I attempt to swallow. With my eyes still closed, I push up on my elbows and wince at the tight muscles.

"What the hell happened last night?" I mumble.

A shot of bravery has me opening my eyes and taking in the dark room. My room. Relief rushes through me.

The pile of homework and textbooks is still high on my desk, and my floor-length blackout curtains are pulled tight, keeping the sun out. My alarm clock reads 10:05 a.m.

I'm surprised at the quietness of the apartment for this late in the morning. Morgan is an early riser, but maybe she's as dead to the world as I am.

I kick off the blankets and stand on shaky legs. When I lift my hands to push my hair out of my face, I'm surprised to see two long sleeves swallowing them. Holding my arms out, I stare down at the Saints emblem on the chest and find the name Hutton on the right shoulder.

Flutters awaken in my belly as I furrow my brows, trying to piece together what happened before I ended up at home. The last thing I remember is me and Oakley finding Matt and Morgan in the dining room.

"*My love! I hear you've been showing off again.*" Morgan scoops me up in her arms and kisses my head over and over again. "*I'm proud of you for socializing,*" she whispers before pulling back, grinning.

"*Yeah, well. It seems hiding in the background is not a possibility in the presence of a top NHL prospect after all.*"

"*Not when he wants you with him,*" She winks.

"*It was just beer pong, Mo.*"

She hums. "*Yeah, yeah. I'll take the small win. But now that you're here, it's time to drink up. Matt is as sober as a nun and refuses to drink with me.*"

I scrunch my nose. "*What are you drinking?*"

She lifts a long bottle of red wine in the air. "*Adam busted out his dad's wine from the cellar. He put a bottle in the fridge for you a few minutes ago.*"

"*Not the wine.*" I wince. It's Adam's daily fuck you to his parents.

A warm hand touches my tailbone as Oakley comes to my side again. "*What's wrong with the wine?*"

"*It's grossly expensive. The more we drink, the happier Adam gets,*" Morgan says, her words slurring.

I look up at him. "*There's nothing wrong with it. I just hate that he has to go to these extents to get attention from his father.*"

As an ache grows in my chest, I find myself reaching for the bottle in Morgan's hands and bringing it to my lips. I drink it down like it's water before pulling it away and shivering at the bitterness.

Oakley's touch becomes firmer, the heat of his fingertips seeping through my top.

"*His parents are that bad?*" he asks.

Matt nods. "*Yeah. They're that bad.*"

"*Shit.*"

"*Just don't mention it to Adam. It's best if we leave that topic alone,*" I say.

"*Got it. Should I go get your bottle?*" Oakley asks me.

I smile sheepishly. "*Sure. Thanks.*"

He looks reluctant to remove his hand from my back but eventually *does. As soon as he's headed back inside, I take another gulp of wine before handing it back to Morgan.*

"I hate you for playing the Adam card. Now I'm going to have a terrible hangover."

I shudder at the memory. That would explain the throbbing headache.

Stumbling out of my room, I stare at the empty apartment. The only shoes by the door are the white trainers I wore last night.

If it weren't for the nausea starting to make me sway in the middle of the living room, I would have gone searching for my phone and called my missing roommate, but instead, I head for the couch and collapse on the cushions.

My forehead is sweaty, but my limbs are freezing, so I pull a blanket over me and flip the TV on, not bothering to change the channel from some sports talk show.

The two men drone on and on about the upcoming NHL season, their voices putting me back to sleep. That is until I hear them switch gears.

"I know we haven't really dug into this year's pot of prospects yet on the show, but what better time than the present. Ryan, first thoughts when you look at that list?"

I peel my left eye open and look at the screen. The two men are older, probably mid-forties. One has cropped black hair and a thick, bushy beard, while the other has a shiny bald head and iceberg blue eyes.

The camera zooms in on the bald guy, and a picture of a long list with ten names is placed beside his head. The first five names are highlighted a bright yellow.

My eyes go wide when I see Oakley's name at the top.

"First thoughts? This is going to be a hard year. The skill is unbelievable. The race will be tighter than it has for the past few years."

"Absolutely. I mean, I look at this list and can't confidently say which one of these players will come out on top at the draft.

It's still early in the season, but these are players that have been watched for years now. One for way longer than the others."

The bald guy, Ryan, laughs. "That's the elephant in the room, isn't it? Oakley Hutton has finally entered the draft. I won't lie; I was getting a bit nervous for a while there."

Curiosity rolls over me. Suddenly, Ryan is replaced by a video of a hockey game. I recognize the player at the forefront of the video by the number eleven on his jersey.

"This was the Oakley's last game with the Penticton Storm. Watch as the players swarm him and they battle for the puck, but in a split second, Oakley makes a play, evading both of them and setting up his teammate for the game-winning one-timer. I mean, come on. He's a once-in-a-lifetime playmaker."

"I've seen this replay hundreds of times, and it always gives me shivers."

"Same here, Marcus." He waves at someone behind the camera. "Pull up the replay of the Vancouver Saints' home-opener game."

I roll to my side and prop my head with my hand as I watch the video change. The black-and-red Saints home jerseys flick around the ice. The camera follows the players around until I see Braden get hit from behind and crumple to the ice. I fight back a wince when Oakley grabs the player who delivered the hit and starts to hit him.

"Regardless of the fact that fights like this aren't encouraged in the minors, I can't help but be impressed by number eleven here. If I'm a GM right now, I'm looking at everything Oakley can bring to their team. Not only is he an offensive beast, but he's not afraid to drop the gloves and protect his team," Marcus says, his voice light, almost as if he's in awe. The thought has me smiling.

I lie back down on my back when the hosts start to talk about the guy with the second spot on their list. It's not that I'm not interested; I just don't want to focus on Oakley's competition.

Obviously, I knew Oakley was good. Matt wasn't shy about

sharing how hard their coach had tried to convince him to sign with the Saints, but it's different seeing it so openly on TV. It makes it more real.

Being his friend is even more daunting now than it was before.

I shove that thought to the back of my head and close my eyes. The sooner I can fall back asleep, the quicker my hangover will go away.

I DON'T KNOW how long I sleep for, but I'm woken by the slamming of a door and chatting voices.

"Quiet, Mo. She could still be sleeping." That's Matt.

"If she isn't up yet, I dibs dumping a bucket of water on her head," Morgan says, way too enthusiastically.

I use a tingling hand to swat the top of the couch. "Nobody is dumping water on my head."

"And she's awake." The deep voice has me pushing into a sitting position and looking at the group over the back of the couch.

Oakley has a giant bag of McDonald's in his hand, and my stomach grumbles loudly. He grins and, after kicking off his shoes, joins me on the couch. I pull my legs in to make room for him.

Setting the bag down between us, he starts to pull out a bunch of food, placing it in front of me. "We didn't know what you would want."

"So you got me one of everything?" I tease.

He laughs. "Close enough, yeah."

I pick up a hash brown. "Thank you. I'm starving."

"It's the hangover. I'm telling you, that wine is no good," Morgan whines and sits on the loveseat, dragging Matt behind her.

"How much did I drink?" I ask, finishing my hash brown.

"A bottle and a little bit," Oakley answers.

Morgan clicks her tongue. "You were trying to finish mine off before Oakley convinced you to come home. You should thank him for not letting you sleep in a puddle of your own vomit."

"He drove us back here, and Morgan took you and tucked you in bed. The food was his idea too. Bless his soul," Matt puts in.

I toy with the sleeves of the hoodie I'm wearing. "When did I get this?"

"Before we left the party. You told me you were cold." I look at Oakley and find his cheeks a subtle shade of pink. He meets my stare, and our eyes lock. "You look good in it. Keep it."

I nod and push down how happy that makes me. With a hell of a lot of inner strength, I tear my eyes from his and focus on the TV. This time, there's last night's Vancouver Warriors game playing.

"Is this what you've been doing all morning?" Morgan asks, her mouth half-full so the words are muffled.

Everyone looks at me as I say, "No, I mostly slept."

"Tell me you were at least watching a game better than this one. The VW lost 6 to 1 last night," Oakley says.

Matt sucks air through his teeth. "At least it's only pre-season."

"Still," Oakley grumbles. He hands me a bottle of orange juice, and I take it without hesitation.

"Thank you." I smile. "And this game must have started while I was sleeping. There was some sports interview show on when I first came out here."

That grabs Oakley's attention. His eyebrows shoot up. "Which show?"

"Was it Marcus and Ryan, Ava? I've been trying to get you to watch that show since last season! Marcus is so hot with that scruffy mountain man vibe." Morgan swoons.

Matt scoffs. "You don't like beards."

"Maybe I just don't like them on you. Your jawline is too chiselled to cover it with a beard."

"You're going to give me a complex, Mo."

"As if you don't have one already."

Oakley and I look at each other with the same entertained expression as the couple bickers. He leans toward me, and I follow his lead until we're no more than a breath apart.

His voice is a low rasp. "What do you say we finish breakfast, and then you let me take you somewhere."

My curiosity piques. "Will it be a secret? Is that why we're whispering?"

"You're not a keep as a secret kind of girl, Ava. I just figured you wouldn't want Morgan to force you to come with me if she heard me asking."

There's no stopping my blush once I feel my cheeks begin to warm. This guy keeps finding every single one of the stereotypes I've ever had about hockey players and crushing them in his bare hands.

"I appreciate that," I admit. He smiles. "And my only plans were to veg out in bed, but if you have a better idea, I'm game."

His eyes twinkle. "Challenge accepted."

# 13

## Ava

TWO HOURS AND A SHOWER LATER, I'M SITTING IN THE PASSENGER seat of Oakley's truck as he pulls into the parking lot of the Saints arena.

Skating and me are like oil and water. I'm a baby deer on the ice, but seeing Oakley's eyes light up at the prospect of spending the afternoon teaching me how to skate stole the ability for me to say no. Now, here we are.

The truck's cab is nice and warm compared to the fall chill outside. I wasn't surprised to look outside for the first time this morning to see rain and gloomy skies, but it was a letdown nonetheless. The weather did nothing to help my hangover.

Oakley let me choose the music again on the drive here, and I'm beginning to think that might be because he's nervous I won't like what he normally listens to.

As soon as he puts the truck in park, I twist in my seat to face him. The white hoodie he's wearing makes his green eyes look sharper than usual. I decide to bite the bullet and satisfy my curiosity. "What kind of music do you like?"

He looks taken aback but laughs it off. "I'm not overly picky. Usually whatever gets my blood pumping. We listen to rock during practice and warm-ups. Why?"

Yeah, I can see him listening to rock. Or anything that would make him want to move around.

"You always let me choose the music," I state.

"I do."

"Why?"

He rubs a hand over the back of his neck. "You get excited when you pick it. Your leg starts bouncing, and you smile."

I throw my head back against the headrest and groan. Even without looking at him, I know he's confused.

"Wait . . . is that a bad thing?"

"No. It's a sweet thing. An incredibly sweet thing," I sigh.

He chuckles, but it sounds forced. "Then why do you look like I just pissed in your cereal?"

I open one eye and look at him. "Have you pissed in someone's cereal before?"

This time, his laugh is very real. "Fuck no. I don't know where that one came from. You frazzle me."

Hold up . . . "I frazzle *you*?"

"Yeah. Isn't that obvious?"

"No."

"Well, you do."

I snort. "Yeah, you frazzle me too. It's like you have a point to prove or something by stomping all over everything I think I know about hockey players."

"You're only partially right. I don't care what you think about anyone else, just what you think about me."

I watch as Oakley dumps his hockey bag on a bench in the team locker room and pulls out two sets of hockey skates. His and the old pair Mom got me a few years back. He moves around the room with an easy confidence that shows how at ease he feels in this environment.

My eyes widen at the pair of skates I'm sure Bigfoot could fit into. "No wonder you're a good skater. You have ski-sized feet."

Oakley bellows a laugh. "Thank you?"

"I'm surprised you don't trip over them when you walk."

He shakes his head, grinning. "Sit down and put yours on, funny guy."

I quickly slip them on and attempt to lace them, even though I have no clue in hell what I'm doing. I've always bribed someone else into doing this part for me.

"Here, let me help," he says before stepping in front of me and kneeling on the hard floor. One big hand wraps around my ankle and pulls my skate-covered foot to rest on a thickly muscled thigh.

His fingers quickly and skillfully loop the laces through each hole, and I watch with greedy eyes. My skin heats when he slips his bottom lip between his teeth and chews on it as he concentrates on his task. The scar above his top lip is more obvious to me right now, and I realize it's not as old as I first thought. Not with how raised and pink it is.

I lose my train of thought when he sets my one foot down and grabs the other, repeating the process. His fingers brush the bare skin of my ankle where my sock has slipped, and the buzz that erupts beneath the surface has me hissing.

"Is that too tight?" he asks, eyes flashing with concern.

I shake my head. "They're good. Sorry."

He doesn't push me on it and finishes the laces. Flashing a toothy grin at me, he sets my foot down beside the other and pats his thighs.

"All done. They feel okay?"

I stand up and wiggle my toes in the skates. "They're perfect. Thank you."

He sits down beside me then and puts his skates on, tying them in what seems like one fluid motion. Before I know it, he's standing beside me and motioning to the door.

I'm grateful when he places a hand to my back and helps me wobble out of the locker room and down the hallway that leads to the ice. The tip of my left skate catches on the mushy rubber flooring, and I stumble before he wraps an arm around my waist and steadies me.

"Careful," he says, and I can hear the hint of a laugh in his words.

"Not funny," I mumble.

He squeezes my side. "Right. Not funny at all."

When we reach the rink, we stop by the boards, and I take a long look around. I've never actually seen it empty before. There are no goalie nets, only markings where they should lie. No referees are skating around blowing whistles, trying to calm the players. Gone are the groups of people sitting in the ugly red seats that make up half the arena, filling it with ear-piercing screams.

"Peaceful, isn't it?" He turns to face me. "Don't get me wrong. I love playing hockey, but sometimes it's nice just to skate. There's no pressure when you're just skating."

I look over and see his eyes flash with an emotion I can't decipher. Sadness, maybe? No, that doesn't make sense.

"You ready? I promise I'm a fantastic teacher." He steps onto the ice and holds his hands out for me to take.

Slowly, I make my way toward him and grab his hands. The heat from them beats into my skin as he holds me tight.

Oakley slowly starts to pull me around the ice, laughing every time I start to lose my balance.

"You weren't lying. You're a terrible skater," he teases when I nearly fall on my ass for the second time.

"Not all of us are hockey prodigies." I roll my eyes.

"I'm not so sure about the term 'prodigy.'"

"Isn't that what they call you, though? You're estimated to be drafted first overall; you don't have to be modest. Not with me."

Interest flares in his eyes as he smirks. "Have you been looking me up, Ava?"

My cheeks burn. "I didn't have to. They were talking about you on TV this morning."

"What did you learn?"

"Just that you're a hot commodity. They seemed nervous that you weren't going to enter the draft this year."

He tenses briefly. "Yeah, I dragged my feet for a while. My mom has been trying to convince me to enter since I was seventeen and scouts started paying more attention to me."

I gasp. "Seventeen? That young?"

He shrugs. "There are more young players than you would think getting that kind of recognition. The talent is getting better every year."

"What kept you from entering earlier?" I blurt out before I can stop myself. I wince at the personal question. "You don't have to answer that. It's none of my business."

He squeezes my hands. "It's okay to ask me questions. I trust you."

A weight lifts off my chest. I don't know why it feels so reassuring to know he trusts me. Maybe because I think I trust him with my secrets too.

"I wasn't ready to leave my family yet, and I hadn't finished high school. I didn't want the pressure that would have followed me there if I had entered the draft then. There was also a huge part of me that didn't think I was good enough. This year is my last chance before I'm too old, so I figure it's better late than never."

I want to ask more about his family, like why he never seems to mention his father, but I think better of it before I risk ruining our good day.

"Well, you're definitely good enough now." The best I've seen, but I choose to keep that to myself.

He smiles softly. "Thank you."

I hold my breath as he slips his fingers between mine and uses our joined hands to turn us in a wide circle. When I don't trip over myself and fall to my ass, I release my breath.

"You're getting more comfortable with it," he notes.

"I have a pretty great teacher. Not everyone can say they've had a future NHL star hold their hands and help them glide around a rink. How will I ever recover from this once-in-a-life-time experience?" Sarcasm is thick in my voice, but my grin is as real as it's ever been.

He suddenly starts skating faster, faster than anyone should be able to going backward. A slight wind brushes my cold cheeks, and I shiver.

"You're a little shit."

"You're going to kill us both," I screech when he makes a sharp turn. My grip on his hands is way too tight.

"Live a little, Ava. Let the adrenaline course through you. Soak it up."

"I like to live on the safe side. No adrenaline for this girl," I squeak.

"Too late. There's no way you don't feel it right now. That erratic thumping in your chest? The flames in your blood? That's adrenaline, gorgeous."

"Yeah, that's not adrenaline doing that to me right now," I mumble to myself.

Suddenly, Oakley releases one of my hands, and I wobble. My arm falls to my side like a heavy weight before I immediately toss it into the air and pull on the hand still in Oakley's in an attempt to regain my balance.

"Relax." Oakley slows down to a smooth glide. "Watch my feet. Go slow, small, fluid movements. Imagine you're pushing yourself on a scooter."

I nod along with him and stare at his feet, watching as he takes backward glides. Each one is confident, sure, and steady.

My toes curl when I push off my left foot, attempting to keep up with him instead of continuing to be pulled along. It's way scarier than I was expecting, but after a while, I start to feel more comfortable on my own.

One foot after the other, I get better. As soon as I start gliding by myself, Oakley goes to release my hand. I surprise myself by refusing to let his go.

When he looks at me questioningly, I only shrug. "I don't trust myself yet."

A knowing smile is his reply. In one smooth motion, he moves to my side, skating alongside me.

The quiet of the arena makes each one of our skate strokes more noticeable as we continue doing slow laps around the rink. Usually silence makes me feel awkward, but that's not the case here. It's almost calming.

But after a couple of minutes, Oakley's voice ripples through the quiet.

"I tried to find you after that night."

My head snaps up as I stare at him with wide eyes. He continues looking ahead of us. "You did?"

He nods. "The next day. Nobody knew your name, though. It makes sense now, considering you weren't from Pen, but yeah. I had the entire team looking, but I didn't even know David's name at the time. There was no way of tracking you down."

Flutters erupt in my stomach. I had assumed that our meeting was just a once off. Two people who needed company, even if it came from a complete stranger. Of course, I wondered about him too. But there was no way I was going to track down a guy like Lee. Someone who is so far out of my league, I'm sure I would have been laughed at for asking about him.

"To be fair, we didn't really give a lot about ourselves to go off of," I tease lightly.

"We should have. I should have given you my number. I wanted to."

Would I have taken it?

Yes, I would have.

I swing our linked hands in the air. "We're here now. And I like spending time with you just as much as I did then."

I can feel his happiness rolling off him in waves. It sinks into my skin.

"Good, because I want to spend a lot more time with you. You're pretty great."

And just like that, Oakley Hutton burrows himself in my chest a little bit deeper.

# 14

# Oakley

TODAY, I'M SEEING MY FAMILY FOR THE FIRST TIME IN A MONTH. I'M embarrassingly excited.

I pull up outside the house at noon, having timed my arrival perfectly for lunchtime. I'm starving, and Mom would never turn down the opportunity to feed her baby boy.

Turning off my truck, I collect all my shit and step onto the familiar street. Potholes still litter the road, and the trees still hang over the curbs, dropping leaves on every windshield.

It's home.

A noise at the front door pulls my attention to the house. Gracie is running straight for me, her blonde curls bouncing wildly behind her. I drop my overnight bag down on the sidewalk and catch my sister as she crashes hard into my chest.

Winded, I croak, "I missed you too."

"I never said I missed you," she mumbles into my chest.

"Right."

"We haven't seen you since August. Stop talking and ruining the moment."

I do, and after a few more seconds, she pushes me away. Laughing, I tuck her under my arm and use my fist to mess up the hair at the top of her head.

"Knock it off!" she shrieks, elbowing me in the gut until I let her go.

"Are you gonna help me carry my stuff inside?"

She slants me a glare. "No."

"Talk about shitty service."

"Does this look like a hotel, jackass?" she throws back.

I grin and pick up my bag, slinging it over my shoulder.

"Tell me about the competition tomorrow. Are you feeling ready?" I ask as we walk up the sidewalk.

She opens the front door and surprisingly holds it open for me as I let my bag fall to the floor and head straight into the living room. I flop down on the couch and stretch out my legs, the muscles tight and sore from the long drive. Gracie sits beside me.

"I've spent the past month locked inside the studio. There isn't much more I can do to get ready. I feel good, though."

I take her in and sigh. She looks exhausted, and it doesn't surprise me by any means. Being overcommitted to things we love runs in our family.

Her electric-blue eyes are duller than usual, and the bags under her eyes are more prominent. I immediately feel guilty for not being here to help.

Of course, I don't tell her that. "Yeah, you look rough. I would recommend some sleep."

She gives me a nasty glare, leans forward, and punches my leg.

"You know, you're a real ass sometimes. My boyfriend seems to think that I look just fine." Wearing a smug expression, she crosses her arms. Now it's my turn to glare. She did that on purpose.

"Ah, yes. Your *boyfriend*." The corners of my lips quirk up. I cross my arms and lean back against the armrest. "Jacob Lane. Seventeen years old. He plays for a junior hockey team and drives a fancy BMW. Am I right on the money?"

Her smugness vanishes. It's quickly replaced with blistering rage. "You looked him up? Are you kidding me, Oakley? He's a really nice guy! Mom thought it would be nice to have you both meet him tomorrow at the competition, but now I don't think I even want you to meet him at all."

Okay, maybe I shouldn't have said that. But in my defense, Gracie never gets this mad when it comes to boys. She doesn't usually give them the time of day.

I put my hands up in surrender in an attempt to calm her down. "Is it serious? I just don't want you to get hurt. But I want to meet him. I'll behave."

She stands up, lets out an exasperated sigh, and runs her hand through her long blonde hair. "Yes. I happen to like Jacob. He's not a bad guy." As she takes a deep breath, her face morphs into a look of consideration. "Okay, fine. But the minute that you say anything rude, I'm punching you in the face. I'm serious."

"Have a little faith in me. I can behave when I want to." As long as he isn't a total prick.

"Sure. Anyway, I have rehearsals in an hour, and I need a ride. Wanna get ice cream first?" She grabs her dance bag from the rack by the door and slips on the pair of biker boots I bought her last Christmas.

"Do I have a choice? Where's Mom?" When I talked to her yesterday, she said she'd be here all day.

"Oh, right. I forgot. She got called into work—said she wouldn't be home until dinner. Now, are we going or what?"

I get up and meet her by the door. After putting my beat-up trainers back on, I open the door and hold out my arm in front of me.

"After you, Gray."

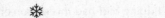

"MY MAN!" Andre shouts from across the football field. The turf is soaked from being rained on for the past few hours.

After we filled up on way too much ice cream and I dropped

my sister off at the dance studio, I asked Andre to meet me at the football field—one of the newer additions to the town—to catch up and toss a football around like we used to back when we had nothing better to do with our free time.

It's been months since I've seen him. There was no way I was missing out on a quick catch-up while I'm here, even if it is just to throw a ball at one another.

"Hey, buddy." We pull each other in for a quick hug. "You did something to your hair. It looks different."

Andre's head of shaggy hockey hair, the colour of the football in his hands, has been cut to a medium length, styled up in a slight swoosh with short shaved sides. For the first time in years, I can see the gold loop hooked through the tip of his ear.

"Figured it was time I stopped looking like a total douche. Got it cut a few days ago." He runs his fingers through the top a few times before spinning the old, faded football in his hands.

"I like it. You look all grown up and shit." I give us a few yards of distance and clap my hands in front of me, signalling for him to throw the ball.

"Nah. That's the hockey pressure. I've aged a decade since you left." He winds his arm back and then lets the ball go.

I position my hands in front of my chest and catch the perfect throw. "I saw the team's photo in the newspaper this morning. It looks like you're doing just fine without me. Four straight wins is fucking amazing."

"Coach has been relentless. I think he wants to prove we have what it takes to win even without you."

I throw the ball back at him and say, "That's because you do."

He has to jog back a few feet to catch the ball. "Tell me about the Saints. I've caught the end of a couple of your games, and you aren't doing half-bad this season either."

"It's good. Surprising, but good."

"That's all you're gonna give me?" He throws the ball harder than usual and winks at me.

I jump in the air to catch it before it hits the ground behind me. "I don't know what else there is to tell you. The competition is way harder, the players are more aggressive, and the media presence is starting to get a bit overwhelming."

"Media presence? You're used to that shit, Lee. Been answering interview questions since we were fifteen."

I shake my head and tighten my grip on the ball, using it like one of the squishy balls Matt squeezes when he gets nervous before a game. They're supposed to calm you down. Maybe I should get one when I go back.

"I know. It's just a lot all of a sudden."

I should have been expecting it, and to some extent, I was. I guess I just wasn't prepared for how curious everyone would be as to why I waited so long to enter the draft. Especially when I've been scouted since I was seventeen.

It's not like I went to university or decided to wait and travel the world on my own before deciding to sign my life away to play professional hockey. I waited for purely selfish reasons. Reasons I haven't shared with anyone besides my family, coaches, and Andre.

The blame for the media's curiosity falls on me. But that doesn't make it any less grating. Especially when our team's social media manager can't even post a simple picture of me playing beer pong with a girl without them ending up on hundreds of Twitter pages.

"You're only human, Lee. Nobody likes to have random people all up in their business."

"It's not like I have a choice, though. I have to get used to it. Preferably before I end up saying something I shouldn't."

I relax my grip on the football before throwing it back to him. He catches it easily, spinning it in his hands.

"You'll figure it out. You always do."

"Your confidence in me is a bit concerning," I tease.

He lets his head hang back as he laughs. "Maybe. But you've earned every bit of that confidence."

"Thanks, man."

Andre nods his head before tossing the ball back at me. "Now, tell me who that hot chick was I saw with you on the Saints' social media pages. You're really out there playing beer pong without me?"

Ava's face floods to the forefront of my mind before I have a chance to stop it. It's been a week since I took her skating, but we've only really seen each other in passing since. I know she's studying like crazy, even so early in the school year, but damn. What I wouldn't give to spend even an hour sitting in the library with her, doing nothing.

I don't notice I'm smiling until Andre does. His lips tug in a no-good grin.

"That good, huh?"

I throw the ball back at him way harder than necessary. "Ow! Did you have to throw it that hard?" Rubbing his belly, he grabs the ball off the grass and launches it back at me. "I never thought that I would live to see the day Oakley Hutton decided a woman was worth his time."

I scowl. "Don't say it like that."

Andre sits down on the grass and pats the spot beside him. I drop beside him and stretch my legs, rolling my ankles.

"You know what I meant," he says.

I do, but for some reason, his words still bug me. "Do you remember that girl I was with at my going-away party?"

His eyes are wide when they meet mine. "The one with the long brown hair and perky tits?" The withering look I give him has him quickly continuing. "I remember. Shit, Lee. You didn't stop talking about her until you took off to Vancouver."

"Yeah, turns out she lives in Van. We've been hanging out a lot the past couple of weeks." Andre's eyes are still bulging, his mouth hanging open. "You're starting to offend me now. I'm not allergic to female attention."

He gives his head a shake, as if he has to actually pull himself out of his shock. "I'm just surprised. I didn't think you'd actually see her again, let alone chase after her if you did."

I glare at him. "What do you mean again? I didn't chase her before."

"Fuck off, Lee. You guarded her like a rabid dog when you finally came in from the backyard and then walked her wherever the hell you guys went in the middle of the night. She could have been trying to get you alone and robbed you or something."

I bark a laugh. "Right. You've been watching too much *True Crime*."

He shrugs me off. "Either way, I know what I saw. You wanted her that night."

"It doesn't matter what I wanted. She was heartbroken over that dumbass who couldn't keep his dick to himself," I grumble.

"Shiiit. That's right. Have you figured out who he is?"

I blow out a long, frustrated breath. "Yeah. He plays on my damn team."

Andre grunts, "Makes it hard to beat the shit out of him, then."

"Yep. Every time I see that guy, I want to break his jaw."

David doesn't notice it either. It's like he purposefully ignores the glares I send him. Like he believes there's no way I could possibly be looking at him with such pure hatred.

He's as delusional as he is a cheating sack of shit.

"I'm sure you could still find a way to rough him up a bit."

"Not in a way that wouldn't risk my reputation and draft odds."

His eyes twinkle with mischief. "You're gonna have to get creative with it." He pats my back. "I know you can think of something."

"Maybe. Thanks."

I should talk to Matt about it. I'm sure he has some ideas in that evil head of his.

"Always. You know I have your back. If you need the team to take a fun little road trip up to meet you in a dark alley, all you have to do is say the word." He winks.

I reach out and push his head, sending him rocking on his ass. "Yeah, I'll keep that in mind."

My chest grows warm at the reminder that my hockey family here still cares about me. God knows I won't ever stop caring about them.

# 15

## Oakley

MOM PULLS ME INTO A BEAR HUG AS SOON AS GRACIE AND I GET back home. It's a gesture I've missed more than I thought I would.

"Oh, sweetheart. I missed you. Gosh! What have they been feeding you out there?" She pulls back, holding me in place in front of her by my forearms.

"I missed you too, Ma."

Gracie pushes by me, laughing. "That's what I said, Mom. He looks like a protein shake junkie. Better hide his collection of shaker cups while he's here so he can detox."

I scowl and yank her ponytail before she can get away. "Shut it."

"Oh, how the house has been too quiet without your pointless bickering," Mom sighs. She makes quick work of pulling me to the kitchen and settling me in one of the dining table chairs before sitting in the one across from me.

Her smile is warm, and her eyes are glowing with excitement. I know I must look the same. In every way that counts, my mom is one of my best friends.

"Catch me up. I want to know *everything*. How's the team?

Have you made any new friends? How's your apartment? Your roommates?" she rambles, her hands folded beneath her chin.

"One question at a time, Mom." I laugh when she waves me off.

"Fine. How's the team been? Have you been keeping your temper at bay? And don't you lie to me!"

"Temper? You make it sound as if I'm some raging idiot," I joke.

She shoots me a look that tells me she isn't in the mood for jokes.

"My temper only flares as much as it usually does when I play. Only a couple of fights so far," I assure her. She raises her eyebrows, skeptical, but I just shrug, sending her an innocent smile. "The team's awesome. The skill is a lot better than the Storm, but we already knew it would be. There have been a few scouts out already, but I'm still waiting for Dougie to call me with updates."

Dougie is my agent and a guy I've been working alongside for the past few years of my hockey career. He's a nice guy, genuine, a straight shooter. Mom likes him, and after the interview from hell she put him through before we hired him, it's safe to say he's perfect for the job.

He's usually great at keeping me updated on the rumours and any talks he's had with potential teams, so it shouldn't be long before he reaches out again.

"They'll come. You're going to be a hot commodity this draft. I saw you on TV, you know? Well, it wasn't really you, but they were talking about you. Can you believe that? My son . . . on TV!" She beams and sits up straighter in her chair. My heart thumps hard in my chest at the sheer amount of pride in her words.

"The Ryan and Marcus show, right? I heard about that. It's still weird for me to see that stuff. I haven't turned on any of the sports networks in months," I admit.

"You never have liked being in the spotlight."

"Makes my skin itch," I grumble.

"I'm afraid you have to get used to it, my love. It doesn't seem like it's going to shine anywhere else for a long while."

The timer on the oven buzzes loudly, making Mom jump out of her chair. She looks up at the clock hanging on the kitchen's far wall. "Oh, no! Is it six already? Go get freshened up before Gracie's boyfriend gets here."

I double blink. "Her boyfriend? I thought we weren't meeting him till tomorrow?"

"You were, yes. *Before* Gracie called me from the studio to let me know she thinks it might be better for you to meet him in more of a private place. With fewer people watching."

"Oh, how lovely. I'll get changed, then!" Patting my hands on my shorts, I give her a sly smile and head toward the stairs. Mom hums in response before cupboards begin to open and close.

Once I get to my room, I close the door behind me and swap my shorts for jeans and my Saints hoodie for a black T-shirt. Mom would have a fit if she saw me sitting down for dinner in baggy shorts.

I grab a baseball hat from the large stack resting on my old dresser before heading back downstairs. Flopping down on the couch, I turn on the TV to find it already playing a Vancouver Warriors game. Muscles I didn't even know were tight instantly relax as I start to watch.

As soon as Vancouver takes the lead just twenty minutes later, the doorbell rings. I move to open it, but Gracie comes barrelling down the stairs before I have the chance. She slants me a sharp glare before taking a long, deep breath, like she needs mental prep before inviting her boyfriend inside. I can smell her fruity perfume from here and wrinkle my nose.

"A little overkill on the perfume, Gray." I cough for good measure.

She flips me the bird. "Behave, Oakley, or I swear to God you won't be able to play hockey ever again after I'm done with you," she hisses before smiling and pulling the door open. I roll my eyes and turn my attention back to the game, trying to focus on it again.

"Hey, babe." I hear from the porch, followed by a girly giggle. "You look beautiful, Gracie."

There's that giggle again. What the hell? Since when does my sister giggle? Cackle like a witch, maybe, but never *giggle*.

The door closes, and feet pad across the wood flooring toward the living room. Gracie coughs loudly, and I take that as my cue.

I tear my eyes away from the game and turn to give the guy a once-over. Slowly squaring my shoulders, I wear an impassive expression and take my time examining him.

The kid's pretty tall, towering over my sister—but not as tall as me. I have a few inches on him. He's dressed in dark jeans and a button-up plaid shirt that looks like he might have even ironed it before coming here. Shaggy blond hair falls carelessly in his face before he reaches up and pushes it back nervously. He looks like a loser.

"Oakley. The big brother." I hold my hand out in front of me and wait to see if he has a weak handshake, the same as the last guy she brought home. Dad always said a handshake is the most crucial first impression you can give.

"Jacob Lane." He nods. "The boyfriend." Much to my surprise, he shakes my hand with a firm grip. "Is that the Warriors game? I only caught the first period before I had to head over. Are they winning?"

Okay, so he's got confidence. He'll need it when it comes to my sister, or she'll eat him alive.

"Yeah, they got two goals in the second period. As soon as they stopped racking up the penalty minutes, they started making moves." Sneaking a glance at my sister, I catch the proud smile she's wearing before she sneaks into the kitchen, leaving us alone. *Risky.* "Make yourself at home. I'm sure our mom will be out soon."

I return to my spot on the couch and risk sending a text to Ava to brag about the fact that I have yet to punch Gracie's boyfriend in the face. What's the worst that can happen? She doesn't answer?

> So I met my sister's boyfriend and he's still breathing. Proud of me?

After sending the text, I slip my phone back into my pocket and turn my attention to the game once more as the Warriors manage to slip another puck into the opposing team's net.

"Yes! Let's go!" Jacob shouts from the opposite end of the couch. My head snaps up in surprise. When he catches me staring at him, mouth slightly agape, his cheeks flush. I get the idea he hadn't meant to say that out loud.

Chuckling, I decide to ease his embarrassment a bit. "Relax, dude. We're a hockey family. If you don't lose your voice by the end of a game, you weren't loud enough."

He lets out a relieved sigh and nods at me. His eyes dart around the room awkwardly. "Um, I just wanted to say that you're a legend in the locker room, man. My buddies were so jealous when I told them I was going to meet you."

I nod at him, but suspicion coils my stomach tight. "Thanks."

"Do you think you could like . . . sign something for me? For once you're in the big leagues?" His face is bright red.

It only deepens in colour when I lean forward and narrow my eyes at him. "Be honest with me here, Jacob. Tell me you're not with my sister so you can get close with a future NHL player. Having the connection would definitely help you out in the long haul, right? Are you planning on entering the draft at some point?"

He visibly swallows. "Shit, no! I care about Gracie. I swear."

"Do you plan on entering the draft?" I ask again.

"Yeah. I was hoping to."

My phone vibrates as I say, "My sister seems to like you

enough, so I'm not going to throw your ass out before you have a chance to prove yourself. But if I find out you've been playing with my sister's feelings, I'm going to shove a hockey stick—"

I swallow the rest of my threat when Mom comes prancing into the room. She does a double take at the view in front of her and watches Jacob's face pale before turning to me with accusations written all over her face. I shake my head at her once, and she lets it go with a tight exhale.

Jacob shoots out of his seat when he notices Mom and goes around the couch to stand in front of her. Holding his hand out in front of him, he introduces himself. "It's a pleasure to meet you, Mrs. Hutton. I'm Jacob."

A huge smile spreads across her face as she pulls him into a hug. I chuckle to myself as he relaxes in her grip. "We're a hugging family. And please, call me Anne."

I choose this minute to grab my phone and grin like a fool when I read Ava's text.

> Woah. Want a trophy?

> > That would be great, actually. It would look great beside all my other ones

> Is that your way of bragging? Should I be impressed?

> > That depends

> On what?

> > Are you impressed?

The three little bubbles appear before they're gone, and when her response still hasn't come through a minute later, I slip my phone back and try to shrug off the mild sting of rejection.

When I slot myself back into the conversation happening around me, I see Gracie clutching Jacob's arm, standing far too close for my liking. Mom, however, just stares at them with hearts in her eyes. The romantic in her has come out in full swing.

I'm about to slip up to my room when my phone buzzes. It's criminal the way my pulse skips when I read the text.

I seem to always be impressed by you.

# 16

## Ava

I USED TO WONDER WHAT IT WOULD BE LIKE TO KNOW MY biological parents. Would I love them simply because we share DNA? Is it an automatic response, or does that type of love have to be earned?

Did they ever love me like I wanted them to?

I know the answers to these questions now. After nineteen years of abandonment, that ache that started as a form of missing the parents I never knew morphed into a hatred for two cowards.

I remember spending countless hours—days even—watching happy families run around outside together and filling the bright yellow jungle gym across the street from one of my several foster homes with high-pitched, heart-tugging laughter. I don't remember which house it was—I lost track somewhere around my tenth placement, but I've never been able to forget the vibrant shade of yellow paint that coated that damn playground.

Every kid licking a perfectly swirled ice cream cone while being pushed on that rickety old swing set brought forward a storm of agony that made me wish I could turn it off. I wanted every tormenting, heartbreaking emotion to disappear. I wanted to feel numb, to be nothing more than an empty shell. I wanted anything, anyone, to stop the pain. But nothing came. Nobody came.

I sat in my makeshift bedroom and stared longingly out the window, day after day, night after night. I relished in my loneliness while pleading that by some wicked chance, my mother would realize I was more important than the feeling of getting high, and my father would suddenly wish that he had stayed to take care of me, knowing that my mother couldn't. But that day never came.

When Mrs. Taylor, my social worker, sat me down at the long, splintered wood dining table in the crowded group home and told me about Lily and Derek, I burst out laughing for the first time in months. I remember telling her not to get her hopes up. That I was going to be eighteen in a couple of years and then I would be able to take care of myself. But despite everything, I had started to trust her, so I agreed to meet them. Thank God I did.

Lily and Derek are the closest thing to biological parents—a real family—that I could have asked for. The minute I walked through the front doors of their large home, I was met with the faint scent of flowers and the peanut butter and chocolate chip cookies Lily was baking in her chef's kitchen.

It makes me sad to remember how shocking it was to smell just common, comforting scents and be so taken aback. But after years of musty clothes and burnt food, my surprise wasn't out of the ordinary.

Lily's son, Ben, took the older-brother responsibilities in huge strides—welcoming me as his little sister the second we met. He protected me from everyone and everything until he went off to university, a year before I did.

Lily and Derek like to keep the subject of my biological parents tucked away, hidden behind lock and key. They know it's still a challenging topic for me. That's probably why I was completely blindsided when Lily called to tell me my biological mother showed up on her doorstep last night.

My phone is against my ear, but all I hear is static. Anger floods my veins and washes up memories I never wanted to think about again. The teasing, the tear tracks and swollen eyes I hid every morning. The abandonment that I haven't been able to shake.

I know Lily must be speaking, but her words are muted, like I have my head underwater and she's shouting for my attention.

Closing my eyes, I turn on my side and tuck my face into my pillow before releasing a breath. The comfort of my bed keeps the walls from completely closing in.

Lily's soft words finally slip through the fog. "Speak to me, baby. Don't shove me out."

"What did she want?" I whisper.

"Your phone number. She wanted to know where to find you."

My chest tightens. "You didn't give her anything."

"No, sweetheart. I didn't. It wasn't my place to interfere. She shouldn't have even known where to find us. Those records should have been sealed."

"I don't want anything to do with that woman."

Rebecca, the no longer nameless woman whose blood runs through my veins, is nothing more than someone who carried me for nine months. She will never be anything more than a surrogate in my eyes.

"And you never have to. I'm going to find out how she found out about us. I promise you that."

I nod even though she can't see me. Maybe I should be crying at this whole situation, but I think I've already run out of tears for that woman.

"Thank you, Mom."

Her breath hitches just slightly before she says, "You're welcome, love bug. You're my girl, right?"

I hiccup a laugh. "I'm your girl."

"Now tell me if you're okay because you know I won't be able to hang up without knowing."

Am I okay? I decide to be honest with both her and myself. "I don't know. I guess I'm more confused than anything. Confused and angry. I'm *so* angry. What gives her the right to just pop up and ask about me after all these years? Doesn't she know she's not wanted?"

"I don't know, sweetheart. I really wish I did so I could put your mind at ease."

"What does she look like?" I blurt out before I can stop myself.

Mom pauses, and the silence is heavy, unsettling. Finally, she says, "Like you. But nowhere near as beautiful."

I swallow a lump of emotion in my throat and suck in a shuddered breath. "Thank you."

"I love you, Ava, and we're both here with you."

"I've been watching quite a lot of *Bones* lately, just saying!" Dad shouts from someone near Mom, his voice muddled.

A smile tugs at my mouth, and I don't fight it. "Did he just hint at his ability to destroy a dead body?"

"Yes, I think he did," Mom confirms with a soft laugh.

"Tell him I say thank you."

She starts to reply when there's a knock on my door. Five of them.

"O, baby! Open the door before I drop our food all over the ground," Adam shouts.

Mom's laugh rings in my ear before she says, "Call me if you need me. I mean it, call anytime."

I get out of bed and head for the front door. "I will. I love you, Mom."

"I love you too. Have a good night."

"Night," I mumble before ending the call. Adam starts knocking again, and I swing open the door with a frown. "You're going to piss off my neighbours."

He grins at me and lifts a massive box of pizza and a shopping bag in the air. "Would be worth it. Let me in, I'm starving."

I step out of the way and let him through before shutting and locking the door. "How did you know I was at home? You could have texted me or something."

He sets all the food on the coffee table and flops down on the couch. With warm brown eyes, he stares at me far too curiously for my liking.

"What's wrong?" he asks.

I don't want to talk about Rebecca, so I avoid his question, flipping the conversation on him instead. "Why are you here?"

"Other than to bring you food because I knew you were planning on studying all night and you never prioritize food when you're in one of those moods?"

Of course, he has to be so damn caring all the time. He makes it impossible to push him away when you don't want to talk about your problems.

"Dammit, Adam," I grumble, sitting beside him on the couch. "What kind did you get?"

"Meat lovers. No pineapple for you."

I flip the lid on the pizza box and hold back a moan at the smell. My stomach growls as I take a slice and start to eat.

"Thank you, Adam. You know me so well," he sings.

I swallow. "Thank you, A. Now, stop gloating."

He stacks two slices before bringing them to his mouth and taking a massive bite. I lift my brows and watch how quickly he scarfs back the pizza. When he notices me watching him, he quickly swallows and smirks.

"You're drooling."

"Oh, please." I scoff. "How do you not choke on your food?"

"I got a big mouth, baby."

"If that isn't the truth," I agree, adjudging myself on the couch until I'm comfortable. Once I have my back to the armrest and my cheek pressed to the back cushions, Adam huffs and pulls my legs over his lap.

He rests his forearms on my thighs. "You're sad."

I sigh. "I'm a lot of things right now."

"Enlighten me. You've told me on more than one occasion that I'm a good listener."

"My birth mom has been asking about me. She found Lily and Derek's house," I mutter.

"Woah. What?"

"Yeah. Messed up, right?"

He frowns. "How is that even possible? I thought the foster system didn't give out that information? Isn't it, like, super creepy for her to even know where to look for you?"

I groan. "Yeah, Lily's trying to figure this whole mess out, considering it was a closed adoption and all records should have been sealed. My parents didn't know who she was until she told them."

Adam brushes his fingers over my shin. "I'm sorry, Ava."

"I just don't know what to do about it. Do I pretend it doesn't matter that she's sniffing around? Or do I let myself get angry and upset? I've spent too long hating her for her to just reappear."

"You can do either. I don't think there's a right or wrong with this kind of thing."

"That doesn't help me," I mumble.

Adam chuckles. "No, it probably doesn't."

I release a long exhale. "I hate her."

"I hate her too."

"The only thing I was ever told about her was that she was a drug addict who couldn't take care of a baby. Not what kind of person she was or why she didn't want to get better so we could be a family."

Adam doesn't say anything; he just reaches toward me and pulls me to his side. I let him hold me as I try not to let loose the sobs wreaking havoc in my chest.

"She shouldn't have this much power over me," I say. Hatred turns my voice into something hard and cold.

"There's nothing wrong with feeling the way you are.

Someone who was supposed to love you betrayed you in the worst way. Who wouldn't carry that with them?"

I know he's right, but I can't get myself to tell him that. It's like if I accept that I'm allowed to feel these feelings, they'll only grow and grow until I can't handle them anymore.

"Talk to me about something else, Adam. Please," I beg.

"Okay, O." He tightens his arm around my shoulders. "My dad's still trying to get me to join the law firm. He set up this fancy dinner with all of the partners for this weekend and hopes that after I meet everyone, I'll have some kind of epiphany and change my mind. It's a last-ditch effort, but you and I both know it won't work."

"Tell him he can shove it. You would be an awful lawyer."

"Oh?"

"You're too much of a joker. You'd end up getting kicked out of the courtroom for making an inappropriate joke or something."

"You know me too well, O. Now, if only you could convince my dad of that."

"I could try."

He scrunches his nose. "I wouldn't want to subject you to being under his beady eyes as he tries to rip you apart for standing up for his rebel son."

"God, he's gross."

He kisses the top of my head. "The grossest."

"Thank you for coming tonight. I don't know how you do it, but you're always here when I need you."

"Call it best friend intuition. I wouldn't want to be anywhere else."

# 17

# Oakley

"GET A MOVE ON, GRAY!" MOM SHOUTS FROM THE BOTTOM OF THE stairs.

I cross my arms over my chest and lean against the wall, watching as Mom taps the face of her watch with bitten nails. She has her hair swept back in a twisty bun that Gracie did for her this morning and the delicate gold chain around her neck that Dad got her on their fifteenth wedding anniversary. I swallow hard.

"She's a perfectionist," I say, forcing a smile.

"I wonder where she gets that from."

"I have *no* idea what you're talking about."

She slants me a look. "Right."

"Don't throw stones, Ma. I haven't forgotten about the time you missed the first and second periods of my biggest game last season because you couldn't find the jersey you wanted to wear."

"That's a low blow. I couldn't very well show up wearing the wrong one and look a fool when my son is *the* Oakley Hutton," she teases.

I drop my chin to my chest and laugh. My parents were always my biggest supporters, and now that it's just Mom, she's taken to support me enough for two people. I'll never be able to repay her for all she's done for me, but making it into the NHL is the first step in the right direction.

"Oh, how the moms would have gossiped about that."

She hits my arm, and I look up to find her smiling wide, the corners of her eyes wrinkled. "Exactly. I wouldn't have been able to show my face in that arena ever again. They would have shunned me."

"Mom! Come here!" Gracie shrieks, sounding about as frantic as I would imagine after being this far behind schedule.

"We should have been there already," I note.

Mom sighs before yelling, "Coming, baby!" With quick steps, she's moving up the stairs and disappearing from sight.

Not having anything better to do, I push off the wall and follow after her. The only thing I want to do to keep myself busy is text Ava again, but she's been radio silent since our last few messages yesterday afternoon.

I don't know if I came on too strong or if she's simply busy, but there's been a knot in my gut since this morning that tells me something is going on. Whatever the cause of it may be, I know I won't be able to fix it from here. Right now, this is about Gracie—

I come to a sudden stop in front of the open bathroom door, and my jaw damn near dislocates on its way to the floor. The smell in the small room is too strong, and as soon as it hits my nose, I'm throwing an arm up in front of my face and sneezing.

"*What the fuck?*" I sputter.

Gracie spins on me from her place in front of the sink, her eyes welling with tears at the same time Mom glares at me.

"Oakley!" she scolds and tries to shield my sister from my view. It doesn't work, and I continue to stare at her over Mom's shoulder.

"Get out!" Gracie shrieks, burying her pink, splotched face in her hands. It looks like she's been stung by bees or rubbed poison ivy all over her skin. *Shit.*

I try to fumble for words. "What did you do to your face? And what is that smell?"

"Lotion! It's lotion," she cries.

"Then why do you look like that?" I feel like an idiot right now. I'm so out of my depth here.

Her watery blue eyes pin me in place when she drops her hands and snaps, "I didn't know it would do this, jackass."

"This is why it's been taking you so long to come down," I mutter, finally piecing everything together.

"What am I supposed to do? I can't go like this."

"Do you want me to beat up anyone who looks at you?" I offer.

A smile teases her mouth before her scowl returns. "No. I want to not have my face feel like someone dumped fire ants on me and left me to die in the ditch."

"We have calamine lotion I can slather on," Mom says. She pulls away from Gray and starts rooting through the cabinets under the sink.

"I hate calamine lotion."

Mom frowns at her. "Too bad. It's this and an antihistamine. We'll have to figure out what's up with that lotion after." With a slim pink bottle in her hand, she turns to me. "Go get two Benadryl's, and stop staring at your sister like she's an alien."

I stifle a laugh and head back downstairs. We keep the common medications in a cupboard in the kitchen, and the Benadryl is easy enough to find. After grabbing a bottle of water from the fridge, I rush back and hand the pills and water to my sister. She takes the pills with a huge swallow of water.

"Did you see any Midol down there? Not only do I look like a giant hemorrhoid, but I'm also bleeding like a carotid injury."

"Jesus, Gracie," I grunt, avoiding eye contact.

She scoffs. "Oh, don't be so sensitive. It's a bit of period blood."

"From what you're saying, it isn't just 'a bit.'" I do finger quotations around the last two words before flicking my gaze to Mom. "Shouldn't she be going to the hospital for that?"

"She's being dramatic, Oakley," Mom says on a long exhale.

"Oh."

"Can you go put your sister's bag in the car? I'm going to try to fix what I can here, and then we'll go before we miss the entire damn thing."

Gracie's eyes flare with annoyance, but she doesn't say anything, just goes about fixing her hair. It's not in the usual slicked-back bun I'm used to seeing and looks more like a back-combed bird's nest.

"On it," I tell Mom before heading downstairs.

If we're lucky, Gracie will still do really well today. If not, it's going to be a *very* long night.

MY SISTER IS A NATURAL-BORN DANCER. Ballet to her is hockey to me.

My grin shows only a sliver of the pride I feel watching her up onstage, twirling and moving her body in such a fluid, precise way. Her features are taut with concentration as she lifts her leg and bends her knee, resting the flat of her foot to her inner thigh as her spin comes to a graceful stop.

She raises her arms above her head and bounces across the stage. Her feet are perfect points as she owns the stage, captivating every set of eyes in the audience. I might be biased, but there's no way she's not winning this competition.

Gracie is a Hutton, and we don't lose. Not even if she's up against some of the best in British Columbia.

"She looks perfect," Mom whispers to me from the seat to my right. She looks at me with a soft gaze and covers my wrist with her hand. "I'm so happy you're here to see this. It means a lot to her, even if she won't admit it to you."

I nod. "Happy to be here, Ma."

She squeezes my hand before turning her attention back to the end of Gracie's dance. The music trickles off as Gray finishes off three consecutive twirls and drops into a bow position.

I'm the first person out of my seat, clapping loudly before shoving two fingers in my mouth and whistling. "Atta girl, Gray!"

She finds me in the crowd and laughs, shaking her head but taking the praise in stride. Mom grabs my hand and waves at Gracie with the other.

We look like the perfect family, and for the most part, I would agree. But I can't ignore the ache that's appeared in my chest at the reminder that we're missing someone who would have been just as embarrassing as I am with his praise for Gracie's performance.

It's been six years since Dad passed away, but sometimes, the wound feels too fresh. The guilt too heavy.

He should have been here today, watching his daughter completely steal the show like she always manages to do. It's unfair, and regardless of how often I remind myself that life isn't meant to be fair, it never gets any easier.

I've begun to wonder if it ever will.

# 18

## Ava

THE TEXT MESSAGE IN FRONT OF ME HAS SNARED MY TIRED EYES. Guilt chews at my subconscious, and I don't bother trying to brush it off.

> Oakley: Just got back. You home?

It popped up two hours ago, but I haven't made any move to reply. After everything that happened yesterday and the awful night's sleep I had with Adam snoring loud enough to be heard in my room from the couch, I don't think I would be the greatest company.

I can admit that I missed Oakley over the past few days, especially after spending so much time with him recently. But that in itself scares me, which does little to give me the push I would need to invite him over.

If he were to show up here today, I would have to explain why my eyes are red and swollen and how my dark circles became so damn pronounced.

Is airing out my dirty laundry the right move here?

I don't think so.

> Me: Yeah. Super tired though. Think I'm going to spend the day napping.

I set my phone down on the kitchen counter and pick up my discarded coffee cup instead. The coffee inside is cold, but I drink it anyway. My stomach twists as it settles.

Morgan has been at her parents with Matt over the weekend for his cousin's wedding, and the apartment feels too quiet.

Shoving Adam out at the crack of dawn was probably a bit premature now that I'm standing here alone, drinking cold coffee and wallowing in self-pity.

A knock on the door has me rolling my eyes. Think of the devil, and he shall appear. Only when I unlock the deadbolt and pull open the door, it's not Adam I see—it's Oakley.

"Oh, shit," I mutter before instinctively shutting the door in his face. My cheeks are on fire as I drop my chin and look at my outfit. The white sleep shorts and thin tank top do little to hide my body, and I'm cursing the lack of heat in the apartment when I spot my nipples trying to cut through my top.

"Ava?" His voice wobbles with what I assume to be humour.

"What are you doing here?"

A throaty laugh. "Open the door and find out."

"I need to change." Before he can answer, I'm rushing to my room and tearing through my drawers in search of something more appropriate to wear in front of the guy I have a seriously embarrassing crush on but am unsure what to do with.

After tugging a baggy grey sweatshirt over my head and slipping on some pyjama pants, I head back.

As soon as I open the door, I watch as Oakley's playful smile drops and twists into a scowl. I lift my brows at the dark twinge to his usual warm eyes. He's glaring at my sweatshirt, and I can't fight back the shiver that tickles my spine at the intensity behind the look.

"You okay?" I ask slowly.

His throat bobs with a heavy swallow. "Yeah."

I nod once before spinning on my heel, set on going to sit on the couch. My lungs seize when a strong hand clasps around my wrist, stopping me. Startled, I look up at him from over my shoulder, and our eyes collide.

"I think I've made a mistake by not being more honest with you," he starts, his voice no more than a husky whisper.

I shudder. "About what?"

"I like you, Ava. Enough that the sight of you wearing another guy's clothes makes me see red."

Suddenly, I'm being spun around, and the door is slamming shut. When my back makes contact with the wood, I gasp. A firm hand curls around my hip as another slips up the side of my throat and holds the back of my head.

Sparks fire beneath my skin as I watch him lose his grasp on control. As soon as his heated stare falls to my mouth, I know I'm a goner.

"I missed you while I was gone. Tell me you missed me too."

"I missed you too."

And that's all it takes.

As if my words had stripped away the last of his self-restraint, he growls two almost inaudible words before bending down and capturing my lips in a rough, possessive kiss.

*Thank fuck.*

I fall prey to his attack and surrender, reaching for him and curling my fingers in his shirt. Using the new leverage, I pull him closer. His tongue traces my bottom lip before I open for him and meet his cautious strokes with confident ones.

A rumbling sound builds in his chest when I nip at his bottom lip and curve into him, forcing us even closer together. He shifts his hips, and I feel the hard, thick outline of him against my lower stomach.

I suck in a heavy breath when he jerkily pulls his lips away, hovering them over mine instead. His fingers toy with the hem of my sweatshirt.

"Is this Adam's sweatshirt?" he asks.

"Yes."

When I look at him, I expect to find the same anger from earlier, but it's not there. It's like our kiss smothered that fire, replacing it with another. One we both feel.

"I'm not the guy to tell you what to do, but please wear mine next time."

I smile coyly. "I wasn't expecting you to have such a possessive side."

"Me either," he admits. "Never have before."

I can't stop the nip of pride in my chest. "Want to move out of the entryway?"

"We should." Instead, he sweeps in for one more kiss. One that doesn't last nearly long enough. "I did come over here for more than to maul you against a door. I swear."

"Mm, right. You'll have to let go of me before we can move."

A dimple pops in his cheek when he smiles at me and takes a generous step back and drops his arms. "After you."

"MY MOM'S BACK," I blurt out once we've made ourselves comfortable on the couch and silence has started to make my skin itch.

Oakley stiffens. "What?"

"I found out yesterday that she's been sniffing around looking for me. I've been wallowing in my feelings since. That's why I didn't text you back."

He fixes his eyes on me and stares intently, like he's trying to slip inside my head and root through it. I'm glad he can't. He would probably run for the hills if he could.

I swallow a groan when he opens his mouth to speak and then closes it, looking sheepish. It would be naive of me to think he doesn't have questions. Especially after we kissed and turned this friendship into something muddled with feelings and attachments.

"Ask what you want to ask," I say, giving him the floor.

He reaches across the sliver of cushion between us and covers my knee with his wide palm. His fingers start to draw circles over my sweatpants.

"Will you tell me if I ask something you don't want to answer?"

"Yes."

He furrows his brows. "How long were you in foster care?"

"Fifteen years. Pretty much from the time I was born until I was adopted."

His fingers flex. "That's too long."

"It is," I agree with him. There's no denying the damage inflicted on children that have spent a massive chunk of their lives without a family. I'm incredibly lucky to have been adopted by such amazing parents. Better late than never. "But it could have been longer. I was fifteen when Lily and Derek adopted me."

"They seem like great people."

I smile softly. "Yeah. Not only did they choose to adopt a teenager, which is pretty rare, but one that was also acting out and a total bitch to everyone."

Oakley barks a laugh. I cock my head as if to ask why he's laughing. "You acted out? I can't see it."

"Of course you can't. I'm a good girl now. But back then? Not at all." He still looks like he doesn't believe me, so I reach over and tug at the hairs curled behind his ear. "It's true! I never did anything outright dangerous, but I did have one of the older kids at my group home pierce my nose with a paper clip, and I made sure to stomp around the house in my muddy boots every time a potential foster family came through the doors.

"My attitude cost the chance of adoption for more than just me. I guess it was my way of getting even with the world, even if now it doesn't make sense."

My eyes fall to the floor. Shame slithers up my spine at the reminder of the person I used to be. The girl full of so much hate and resentment.

"Rebecca was—or I guess, maybe she still is—an addict. That was the only thing I knew about her for years. Not her name or if she still lived in Vancouver. She was a ghost, and I made peace with that. My birth father was most likely an addict too, and he ran off as soon as I was born."

"These people never deserved you, anyway, Ava. Jesus, baby. I'm sorry," Oakley murmurs.

He shifts closer and moves his arm over my shoulders, bringing me close and tucking me into his chest. His arms wrap around me like two protective walls, and I exhale a long breath in his shirt.

"It's okay. I've worked hard to move on from that place in my life. I think that's why Rebecca showing up is having such a toll on me."

I slide my eyes over the quiet apartment before getting them snagged on a black-framed photo hung on the left side of the TV. Emotion collars my throat as I stare at the family picture.

It was taken after my very first Christmas dinner with Lily and Derek. We had only just finished eating—the table was still full of leftover food—but Mom ushered us all out of our chairs and in front of the fireplace. She propped her camera up on the coffee table and set a timer before running over to stand in her spot beside Dad.

I remember how it felt at that moment, looking around at my new family. For the first time in my life, I was completely and utterly happy.

"What was it like for you? To be in foster care."

I blink back the tears that are beginning to cloud my vision before coughing to clear my throat.

"It had its good moments. My experience wasn't anything to write home about, but it wasn't as bad as it's described in movies and television. Not my experience, at least. I spent most of my childhood in all-girl group homes. I only stayed with a few different foster families."

"Were they good to you? If they weren't, tell me and I'll track every single one down and break their legs."

I laugh, despite the seriousness of his threat. There's no doubt in my mind that he would really do that for me, and that makes me far happier than it should.

"They were okay, Boy Scout. I promise."

Peeling my cheek from his shirt, I sit back and look at him. As soon as we lock eyes, I'm searching his for any sign that I've scared him off or changed the way he sees me. I must show my surprise when I come up with nothing because he shuts down all of my negative thoughts in two sentences.

"Nothing you could tell me would change the way I think about you, Ava. That's a promise."

# 19

# Oakley

MY GEAR IS HEAVY ON MY ACHING MUSCLES, BUT I KEEP PUSHING, finishing the rest of my breakaway exercise as if I'm not a few deep breaths away from going into cardiac arrest. I line up my shot and shoot, sending the puck flying off my stick. It rings off the top bar before sinking into the back of the net.

Braden and Tyler fly up beside me before stopping, snow shooting up from where their blades cut the ice. They grumble about how they nearly got me while Matt scoops the puck out and passes it back to me. I kick it to the centreline as Coach starts scolding one of the fourth liners for taking a corner with his head down on the opposite end of the ice. I grimace at the anger in his voice.

Knowing that practice is coming to an end, I skate to the bench and take my helmet and gloves off before grabbing my water bottle and squirting the cold liquid all over my sweat-streaked face. I groan at the feeling before drinking the rest of my water.

"What a dumbass. Rogers couldn't keep his head up on that scrawny neck of his to save his life. How he got a spot on this team is beyond me." David's brash laugh grates against my eardrums from his place amongst a group of our younger players.

Anger bubbles in my blood, but I stay quiet, choosing to continue listening to David run his mouth. My restraint is already hanging by a frayed string after learning about Ava's past last week, and David's only painting a larger target on his back.

I've never put up with anyone who cheats on the person they supposedly care about, but this prick really went above and beyond. He cheated on her, fully knowing about her past with abandonment and everything she's gone through. He doesn't care either. There's no remorse or guilt.

While Ava didn't spell it out for me, it was easy to piece together why she's so cautious when it comes to building connections with people. David is just some pussy-hungry piece of shit who didn't care about her the way she deserved.

"Someone needs to knock him on his ass the next time he skates like he's scared of his own shadow. He ain't got no place on my team," he continues.

"Your team?" I snap, turning to glare at David and the sheep-ish-looking players standing beside him.

His head snaps up in my direction, and his lips part in surprise. "Oh—hi, Hutton. We were just joking around."

"Is that what that was?" I toss my water bottle back over the boards, running my fingers through my wet hair when I shift back toward the group. "It sounded a lot to me like you were talking shit about one of your teammates. Someone less experienced than you, at that."

He blanches. "No way, man. Rogers knows it's all in love. Right, boys?" His attention desperately falls on his friends. All three of them look at me, their mouths opening and closing over and over again.

I ignore them and skate toward their ringleader, stopping a couple of feet away. "We don't talk shit about our teammates. *Ever*. Rogers might need more help than others, but he's on this team for a reason. Maybe you should watch some of our past games and see exactly why that is. I can tell you right now it isn't because he hates passing off potential shots like you or dishing out dirty hits he can't take right back."

Someone around us sucks in a sharp breath, but I really don't care who it was. As far as I'm concerned, it's just me and Remer right now.

"We're a team, Remer. It's wise you remember that." The warning is heavy in my words.

I furrow my brows when suddenly, he's smirking at me. My stomach sinks.

"You almost had me there for a minute," he says, and when I refuse to show any sort of reaction to his words, his poisonous smirk only grows. "This isn't about Rogers at all. This is about Ava."

"You have no idea what you're talking about."

"Oh, I think I do. Green eyes, long, brown hair that wraps around your knuckles just the right way. *Phenomenal* ass."

My laugh is harsh, dark. "You're going to want to stop talking now."

The air between us is tense, too tense for everyone around not to notice. Several sets of eyes prick my skin as my chest rises and falls way too rapidly to continue acting unaffected. My fingers curl, nails biting my palms.

"What's going on?" Matt's voice cuts through the silence. He skates up beside me, staring at David and the players behind him. "Practice is done. Get the fuck to the dressing room," he orders, and they quickly scurry off.

"Hey, Matty boy. Nice of you to join us," David sneers.

"Shut up, Remer. From the looks of things, you're lucky you haven't been concussed yet."

I shrug and look at Matt, ignoring the fuming player in front of me. "He acts brave, like he doesn't turtle every time a hit comes at him. Thoughts?"

Matt meets my stare with a slow smile. It's a sign that we're both thinking the same thing. David deserves to be knocked on his ass, and all of the guys have been wanting an opportunity to be the one to dish out his punishment. But the best payback will be the kind that doesn't require my knuckles to bleed or for any of us to miss our next couple of games.

No, he needs to be the one with bloody knuckles. The best revenge is best served cold, and I want Remer to freeze.

"You're right. It's cute he thinks we haven't all noticed that."

"I'm right fucking here," David snarls.

We continue to ignore him, and I can nearly taste his rage in the air. "I wonder what would happen if we stopped protecting him," Matt says.

As soon as a hand grabs my shoulder and shoves, I let a smile part my lips. Playing dumb, I stare at him blankly and ask, "What? Did you have something to add?"

His lip curls as he snarls, "What happened to never talking shit about our teammates?"

"You're no teammate of mine. You'll never be worthy of that label or a position on this team. If I had it my way, you would never touch another team roster."

It doesn't take long before he's pulling his arm back and throwing a surprisingly strong punch right at me. I grin when his fist connects with my face. The pain is instant, and the skin above my eyebrow busts open. Warm blood drips from my head, hitting the ice.

Voices begin to shout around us, but I keep staring at David, loving the way his jaw ticks with blinding rage.

"Thank you," I tell him, my voice low as Matt steps in and starts to shove David back, away from me.

"For what?" he shouts.

"For proving that the trash is indeed fully capable of taking itself out."

❄

AN HOUR LATER, I'm stitched up and in the passenger side of Matt's car. His phone is plugged into the aux cord, and "My Own Worst Enemy" by Lit fills the silence between us.

Matt refused to let me drive myself home after being on the receiving end of a hard hit to the head, with the promise of returning my truck to me tomorrow.

The drive to our apartment goes quickly, and as we pull into our parking stall, I say, "Thank you for backing me up earlier. I appreciate it."

He puts the car in park and turns it off. "Don't worry about it. You're one of us now, and we take care of each other around here. I've been wanting to beat that asshole's face in for months now, but this is an even bigger win."

"How many games do you think he'll be out for?"

"At least three. Coach has never looked that pissed off. Think he'll give you shit too?"

I reach over my shoulder and grab our bags from the back seat. After dropping his in his lap, I tighten my grip on mine, and we step outside.

Once we start walking up the sidewalk, I say, "Probably. Remer didn't punch me for no reason."

"He won't sit you."

"No, he won't."

Matt pulls open the building door, and we head inside, taking the stairs two at a time. "Not going to lie, man, you looked like a fucking psycho when he hit you. That bloody smile? No, thanks."

"Maybe Remer will see me in his dreams tonight."

"Nightmares, maybe," Matt chokes out.

Our apartment door is already unlocked when I slip my key in, and I give him a questioning look. He simply shrugs and walks right in, not even bothering to take his shoes off before going to his room.

My next breath comes out in a rush when a small body

collides with my chest and wraps around me with a steel grip. The arms that were hanging at my sides slowly wrap around the body when I smell the familiar perfume.

"Are you okay? Morgan called and said Matt told her you were in a fight. What happened?" Ava asks in a rush.

I pull away from her and watch her eyes widen in shock as she reaches up and brushes her fingers around the stitched wound above my left brow.

"It's not as bad as it looks." Covering her hand with mine, I pull it away from my face and link our fingers instead.

"It was David, wasn't it? That prick. Crap, I'm so sorry this happened," she sighs.

Shrugging, I give her a small smile. "It was worth it. Trust me."

"No, it wasn't. He is not worth you being hurt."

"Stop," I murmur, gently pinching her chin and forcing her to look at me. There's far too much sadness in her eyes. "I can't change the past, but I could make sure that he knew he wasn't getting off scot-free for what he did. Trust me when I say I would take a hundred more punches if it meant he would get punished for hurting you."

She smiles softly. "Has anyone ever told you that you have a bleeding heart?"

"Not many people have gotten the chance to figure that out about me."

"I have."

I bend down until our lips brush, her breath mixing with mine. "Yeah, baby. You have."

She stretches on her tiptoes and kisses me, not wasting another second. I groan at the sensation of her mouth on mine again, not caring how desperate it makes me seem.

Ava pushes against me, her chest flush to mine. There's no doubt in my mind that there will never be anything that compares to the feeling of her body against mine and her tiny sounds of pleasure filling my mouth. I continue to take and take from her, utterly obsessed with the way she does the same.

My hands fall to her waist, and I squeeze, digging my fingers into the skin. A heavy sense of possessiveness has me sliding my hands down over her hips and round ass before gripping her thighs and lifting her.

*Mine, mine, mine.*

She wraps her thighs around my waist and whimpers when our bodies line up in a way that has my cock pressing against her legging-clad core.

A ripple of pleasure has a groan hitting her lips. "We need to slow down," I rasp.

"We do," she breathes but slides her mouth to my jaw, kissing all of the skin she can find on her way to my throat.

I walk us to the couch and sit down, keeping her planted on my lap. She cries out when I thrust my hips and my hard length grinds against her.

"Shhh, sweetheart. Matt could hear you." Her eyes flare at that, and I groan. "Does that turn you on? The thought of him hearing how good I want to make you feel?"

Shakily, she nods her head, and my restraint snaps

Holding her stare, I move my hand between us and brush the waistband of her leggings. When she only parts her lips and drops her eyes to watch, I slip my fingers inside and curse when I feel nothing but hot, bare skin.

The first touch of my finger against her wet flesh has my dick throbbing, and for a second, I fear I'm about to shoot my load in my pants like some virgin. Her whimper as I slide one long digit through her slick flesh doesn't help.

"You're so wet." I sound like I've swallowed glass.

She just nods and pushes against my hand, seeking more. I give it to her, dipping a finger inside. Her pussy is tight and so fucking hot, sucking me in and weeping when I slide my finger out before starting to fuck her with it.

Her eyes drift shut as her body shudders. "Yes, Oakley. Please."

"Please what?" I move my finger slowly, and her eyes open, the vulnerability she's feeling hitting me like a hammer to the chest. The tip of my finger circles her wet hole. "Please keep doing this?"

"No." Cheeks a deep pink, she grinds against my palm and begs, "Make me come. Please, I need you to make me come."

"Okay, baby. I'll give you what you want," I whisper, thrusting a second and third finger inside of her alongside the first. She rests her hands on my shoulders and rides my hand, her nails digging deep into my skin.

With quick, desperate movements, I'm shoving her shirt up and over her breasts and pinching her nipple through her sheer beige bra. Her inner walls quiver around my fingers, and I lean toward her, my breath heating her ear.

"Come, Ava. Let me hear what you sound like when you let go. Let everyone know how good it feels."

As I press my palm to her clit and she rocks forward, meeting me, I both feel and see her go off. I watch with a slack jaw as she comes, her head flying back and her body curled in ecstasy. She jerks in my lap, and my fingers keep filling her, even as she flings forward and catches my stare. The sounds that come from the slow movement of my fingers inside of her drenched pussy are beyond dirty, but I can't seem to get enough. Not until she touches my arm and I notice the slight wince that travels across her face when she shifts.

I quickly remove my fingers and slip them between my lips, sucking her taste off them. She shudders against me.

"Are you okay? I wasn't too rough with you, was I?"

She shakes her head and presses a gentle kiss to my lips. "No. I'm more than okay."

"Good." I pull her shirt back down and drag my thumb back and forth over her hip.

She folds in my lap, curling up against my chest. "Are you staying?"

That same vulnerability that I saw earlier is back, this time causing her voice to wobble. It doesn't take a brainiac to realize she's talking about more than just tonight.

"Yeah, sweetheart. I'm staying."

# 20

## Ava

THE BITTER WIND HITS MY SKIN, AND GOOSEBUMPS RISE ALONG MY arms beneath my sweatshirt. The mid-October chill pushes me to walk faster down the sidewalk, the coffee shop where I'm meeting Adam getting closer and closer.

My neck has the mother of all cricks in it from spending all night sprawled over a massive man on a way too small couch.

Oakley and I passed out soon after he made me come so hard I saw stars. And despite the reason behind why I wound up at his house when I should have spent my night at home in my room studying, I woke up with a massive smile on my face. It took some pleading to get him to unwrap his tree trunk arms from around me, but eventually, he relented.

He didn't seem overly thrilled with the idea of me meeting Adam at the coffee shop after my classes today, but he didn't have a choice in the matter. Adam and I have been meeting for coffee every other afternoon for months. I'm not about to change my routine for anyone, even if Oakley did try to convince me by pressing me into his mattress this morning and making me come with his mouth.

I nearly gave in and was left with only twenty minutes to

make it to my morning seminar by the time I managed to shake myself out of my horny haze.

At least Oakley was enough of a graceful loser to give me a hoodie to wear in the cold since, me being me, I left my apartment yesterday in nothing more than a long-sleeve shirt and a pair of thin leggings. The hoodie reaches my knees, and the sleeves hang over my hands, so I snuggle into it.

I reach the coffee shop right on time and look through the front window to see Adam sitting at our usual table with two white cups in front of him. The bell over the door jingles as I step through the door and breathe in the familiar smell of strong coffee.

I reach our table and pull my chair back. The screeching sound as it drags across the floor makes Adam's head snaps up.

He slashes me a toothy smile. "One pumpkin spice latte for the lady." He pushes the cup toward me and takes a sip of his foamy drink.

"Thank you. How was class?" I ask as I sit and settle in.

His smile twists into a scowl. "Long. Boring. You name it."

Adam is majoring in kinesiology—which is a fancy way of saying that he's learning how the human body moves—and minoring in business. His main focus is business, but I'm pretty sure he chose to major in kinesiology as a *giant* fuck you to his dad.

"That bad?" I lift my cup and blow away the steam before taking a careful sip.

"I was too hungover to pay attention to anything other than how painful Rackham's voice ringing in my ears is. That woman's voice is the equivalent of nails on a chalkboard, I swear." He shivers dramatically, and I laugh.

A sharp *shhh* travels to our table, and I twist in my chair to find Beth Winston shushing me from her nearby table. She pushes her round glasses up her nose and shoots me a glare. If looks could kill, that girl would have killed me a long time ago.

I met Beth at the beginning of last year when we were all

fresh meat, in this exact coffee shop. I tripped over my untied shoelace and spilled my cup of fresh, piping hot vanilla latte all over the light pink sweater she was wearing.

Despite apologizing profusely and even offering to buy her a new sweater, she marked me as enemy number one. Her hatred of me has been very clear ever since.

To make matters worse, she's had a crush on Adam since elementary school and hates me even more for being his best friend. According to Adam, they were *somewhat* close in high school. But she never got the hint, and eventually, he completely distanced himself from her.

I narrow my eyes at her and give her a finger-wiggling wave.

"Just ignore her, O," Adam urges. "She'll get over it eventually. It should be water under the bridge by now."

I shrug and turn back to the table. When I look at Adam, he's staring at Beth with a far too curious look in his eyes.

"She *does* seem to have gotten hotter over the summer break, though. In a sexy nerd kind of way, eh?" Adam adds, cocking his head to the side as he boldly stares.

I roll my eyes and glance back over at Beth. He's not totally wrong. The waist-long, unruly brown curls that used to fall in her face have been cut and straightened, left to rest at the base of her neck. Her defined cheekbones and large chest seem. . . *new*— probably courtesy of her rich father. The only thing that seems to have stayed the same is her piercing blue eyes.

"Don't even think about it. You've done enough damage to the girl. Plus, she's pure evil."

He turns back to me, looking completely unbothered. "I was just saying Beth didn't use to be that hot. Anyway, how were your classes today?"

I slink further down in my chair. "It was brutal. This year might kill me. To think I still have two years of this torture makes my head hurt. If that isn't bad enough, I have to start looking for somewhere to do my placement next year."

"Have you decided what you wanna do for your placement?"

"Maybe." I huff, adding, "I think so? Gah, one minute I do, and then the next, I don't know."

He offers a supportive smile. "You still have a while to figure it out. Stop stressing yourself out before you get an ulcer."

"I'm leaning toward a community centre, but I also want to try working alongside a school counsellor. I just want to make sure that I get the spot I want and not procrastinate." I stop to give him a pointed stare, then continue. "Or by my luck, I'll end up with the only one I don't want."

Adam places a hand on his heart as if I've hurt his feelings. "Uncalled for, O. I never procrastinate," he says, and another loud laugh escapes.

Without preamble, Beth shushes me again.

Fed up, I turn and give her the finger. She scowls.

"Your mouth is going to get stuck in a permanent scowl if you don't sometimes smile, Beth," I sing. I can practically *see* clouds of dark grey smoke shooting from her ears.

"I'd rather have a permanent scowl on my face than have to look like you, Octavia," she shoots back.

I bite my cheek when Adam snickers, trying desperately to hold back his laughter.

"Beth, cut it out," he says.

As soon as he's spoken, her anger is replaced by fake glee. She focuses on him. "Oh! Hi, Adam," she gushes. "I didn't see you there. You know there's an empty seat beside me, right? You don't have to sit beside her."

"You do know I got here before you, right? I didn't see you making any move to sit beside me. Lay off of Ava," he snaps, then raises an eyebrow at me, his easygoing attitude quickly spoiled. "Are you ready to go? I don't want to be here anymore."

"Yeah, sure. Let's go." I stand up from the table and place my half-full coffee cup on a cleanup tray by the door on our way out.

Once we get into his sparkling new Lexus—another new apology gift from his parents—he sighs. "I miss you. I miss hanging out all the time like we did before school started."

I double blink, surprised by the admission. "I'm sorry. I've been busy and haven't really made time for anyone—"

"But Oakley?"

I grimace at the hurt in his voice. "Not really. Stuff has just happened that's brought us together."

"Does he know about your mom?"

"He does."

"Right. Of course he does." He makes an angry noise in his throat. I shoot him a glare.

"What is that supposed to mean?"

"Nothing. Just that he seems to know a lot more about you than I originally thought. I mean, come on. You barely even know him."

"I really don't like your attitude right now, Adam."

His nostrils flare. "I'm just trying to protect you, O. We know nothing about the guy other than he's a fantastic hockey player and moved here from Penticton. Or has he opened up to you when he won't to any of his teammates? I don't want you to get hurt again, O, and this reeks of heartbreak."

Adam's words hurt. As much as I don't want to believe them, I can't stop that small trickle of doubt from poisoning my thoughts. Suddenly, the last place I want to be is right here.

"I just want you to be careful, Ava," he whispers.

"I know," I say shortly. "Can you drive me home? I have a lot of homework to finish before your game tonight."

"Yeah, sure. I love you, O." He gives me one last look of concern before turning on the ignition.

"Love you too, A."

❄

"I'M HOME," I say as soon as I get inside the apartment. The smell of food cooking makes my stomach grumble.

"Hey, girlie. How was your day?" Morgan calls from the kitchen. I join her by the stove just as she sticks a wooden mixing spoon into a pot full of something that looks kind of like macaroni but more . . . brown?

"Don't wanna talk about it. What are you cooking? I'm starving." I turn to the fridge and grab a bottle of water before untwisting the cap and taking a long drink.

"Hamburger Helper."

"Good enough." I'm hungry enough to eat just about anything, and despite the look of it, Morgan can make anything taste good. She's like my mom in that way.

"Cool it with the excitement," Morgan teases and continues to mix the noodles and beef around in the pot.

"Let me know when it's ready. I'm just going to put my books away."

She replies with a hum as I speed to my room. As soon as I drop my bookbag on my bed and start pulling out my books and laptop, my phone pings in my back pocket.

Grabbing it, I grin at the message.

> Oakley: On my way to the rink…mind if I stop by? Have something for you.

> Me: Sure. It better be something good *wink emoji*

I'VE JUST FINISHED GETTING ready for the game when there's a knock on the door.

"Ooh! I'll get it," Morgan sings.

"No, I got it," I rush out, speeding through the apartment

and cutting her off on her way to the door. She wiggles her eyebrows at me.

"Expecting someone special?"

I point to her room. "Go. I don't need you eavesdropping on my conversation."

"Me? Eavesdrop?"

I glower at her. "Go, Mo."

She tosses her hands up. "Fine. But hurry up. We do need to leave soon."

"Got it." I wave her off and open the door.

Oakley is waiting in the hallway in all of his towering, amazing-smelling glory. Only there's something different about him. Instead of blue jeans and a T-shirt, he's wearing a goddamn suit.

As soon as it fully registers what he's wearing and how delicious he looks, my panties flood. Literally, they *flood*.

There are a pair of wrinkle-free black slacks fit snug to his thick thighs and a long-sleeve, white button-up stretched over his torso, the top two buttons undone. He's gone without a tie, and for a brief second, I wish there was one I could grab and use to pull him toward me.

"You look beautiful," he murmurs, either unaware of the eye-fucking I was just giving him or choosing not to tease me for it.

"Thank you." I jerk my head toward the couch, hoping to God he can't see how flustered I am. "You wanna sit down for a minute?"

When I don't get a response, I turn to face him again.

"Are the only clothes you own Adam's?" he grumbles, glaring at the jersey like he thinks he might be able to set it on fire with his eyes.

"I'm wearing your sweater underneath! This is the only jersey I have," I explain, fighting back a smile.

"Not anymore." He reaches into a bag I didn't notice he had and pulls out a Saints home jersey. "Now you can wear mine."

My cheeks reignite as I reach out and take it from his hand. "Thank you," I nearly wheeze.

"Promise me you'll wear it. I need my girl wearing my jersey in the stands, or I might lose the game."

I arch a brow. "Your girl?"

His eyes darken as he takes a step toward me and grips my waist. "Yeah, my girl. I thought I made that clear last night."

"Just clarifying," I tease, leaning up on my toes for a kiss. He meets me halfway and captures my lips, stealing my breath.

What was meant to be a quick peck quickly turns into something hot and wanting before I plant my palms on his chest and separate us.

"I promise I'll wear it," I whisper, far too breathlessly.

His lips lift in a grin at the same time his phone chirps with a message. He curses before wrapping me in his arms and squeezing me tight against his chest. "I gotta go before Coach benches me. I'll see you there. Your usual seats tonight?"

"Morgan said something about getting ice-level tickets."

He nods, and I shiver when he steals another long, desperate kiss. "I'll look for you."

"I'll be screaming your name in the stands," I breathe.

His grin is pure sin. "Go crazy, baby. It'll be good practice for later. See you soon." And then he's gone.

# 21

## Ava

MORGAN AND I ARE SITTING THREE ROWS FROM THE ICE, AND WHILE I don't know how Morgan managed to wrangle these seats the morning of a sold-out game, I'm happy she did.

I've only ever sat this close to the ice with my dad when I was a teenager. And I definitely did not have a guy on the team who keeps flashing me winks and blowing kisses every time he skates past back then.

Oakley's attention to me tonight has caught the eye of a few people in the crowd, but I've tried to block out their hushed gossip as best I can. Being in the spotlight has never appealed to me, but for the first time since things with my hockey star have become more serious, I'm starting to realize that I might not be able to avoid it much longer.

When it's time for Oakley to do his final warm-ups, I make sure to stand with my back to him so he can see the name written on the jersey that hangs loosely from my shoulders. The proud smile that lights up his face is enough to have me blowing him a brave kiss that incites a flurry of whispers around me.

There's an unmistakable flush all over my body when I collapse back into my seat and subtly cover half my face with my hand.

"Oh, my God! Did you see his abs when he lifted his jersey? I think I need a fan," says a voice behind me. Being my nosy self, I don't hesitate to listen in on the girly giggles.

"Oh, that's enough out of you. Tyler Bateman is far too old for you." The second voice is far more mature than the first one and has me turning my head in search of the two mystery ladies.

I spot a woman two rows back who looks to be in her mid-forties. She sits comfortably beside a much younger, almost carbon copy of herself. Both women are beautiful, with blue eyes and light blonde hair, the kind of hair that girls like Morgan pay hairdressers hundreds of dollars to have.

The younger girl has the longest eyelashes I think I've ever seen, a small nose that fits her face perfectly, and sleek, sharp cheekbones. Both of them are sporting matching Saints jerseys, although I can't see who they are cheering for from where I'm sitting.

"Whatever, Mom. Just because I have a boyfriend doesn't mean that I can't look at other eye candy."

"Where did I go wrong with you?" her mother sighs, but it's not an annoyed sigh; it's a happy one. It makes my heart clench. I turn back around in my seat in fear of getting caught eavesdropping. However, the woman calls me out before I can escape.

"Oh dear, I am so sorry for my daughter's lack of manners. I hope we didn't disturb you," she says, glaring light at her daughter, who is now texting away, completely unbothered by her surroundings.

"No—no! You weren't. I was just looking for . . . for my friends! They're not here yet," I stammer awkwardly.

"Well, I hope they get here soon. The game's about to start. We just got here a few minutes ago ourselves. I hate missing the warm-ups! I'm Anne, by the way." Her motherlike tone warms my heart. I can't help but smile at her.

"I'm Ava. It's nice to meet you."

Anne's eyes flash with something that looks like realization, but before she can speak on it, her daughter interrupts.

"Mom, stop freaking out the locals." The teenager puts her phone away and glances at me. The same look flashes across her face, and my stomach churns with nerves. The girl blinks and the look is gone, replaced now with a casual stare. "Sorry about her. She doesn't get out much. I'm—"

"Ava, the game's about to start. Tell your new friends that you'll see them some other time," Morgan chides.

The lights in the arena dim as I say, "I hope you guys enjoy the game. It was nice to meet you both."

IT'S HALFWAY through the second period that it happens.

The crowd is screaming so loudly I want to cover my ears when Oakley gains control of the puck and clears the Saints' defensive zone. He's skating full speed down the ice, outmaneuvering every single player on the opposing team with a confidence I've only ever seen him possess.

I see the player before he does. It's almost like it happens in slow motion.

There's no chance of Oakley catching himself when he snaps his head to the side and gets hit from the side. He was going too fast, and as he goes flying across the ice, I stop breathing. He was too focused on making it to the net that he didn't see the defenseman until it was too late.

My heart thrashes in my chest as I stand and watch his shoulder make contact with the ice before he just lies there, not moving. Silence falls on the crowd for the first time tonight.

The team medic blocks my view as he runs onto the ice, carrying a stretcher and a small red bag. My hands shake as I try to move past the fans standing in front of us. I don't even notice Morgan holding my hand until she pulls me through the dozens of bodies. When we finally reach a clearing, my hand flies to my mouth, covering my gasp.

Oakley is lying on his back, clutching his right shoulder and grimacing in pain, but at least he's moving again. He yells at the ref, blood flying from his mouth and splattering the ice around the puddle that rests beside his head.

The medic kneels beside Oakley and looks like he's trying to help him sit up, without much luck. Morgan calls my name, and I wrench my eyes away from Oakley to look at her. She points at the fight now taking place on the ice.

Tyler has the player who hurt Oakley by the throat, punching him again and again. He knocks the opponent's helmet off and kicks it off to the side with his skate. The remaining referees frantically try to rip Tyler off, but he doesn't stop.

I hear the words *ejection* and *suspension* fly from the referee's mouth, but they don't seem to register with Tyler.

"What the hell is happening?" the blonde teen shouts, but nobody has an answer for her.

Adam shouts to get Tyler's attention, and by some miracle, Tyler drops the player so quickly you would think he burned him. He spins around without a second glance at anyone and storms off the ice.

By the time I look back where Oakley was, I find him gone. There's only a deep red puddle left in his place. My stomach churns.

"Go, Ava. He'll be in the medical room. Do you want me to take you?" Morgan rubs her hands up and down my arms.

"No, I got it," I mumble before turning and leaving her there.

With my elbows out, I start shoving my way through the crowds, not caring when I piss someone off and they curse at me. I've made it past the stands and am damn near jogging through the big open area by the concessions when someone grabs me.

I'm almost so shocked I trip when scrawny fingers wrap around my wrist and tug me toward a round, short body.

"Hey! What's going on? You're Oakley Hutton's girlfriend, right? I've seen you in pictures," the stranger says, spittle flying from his mouth. I can't tell if he's curious or angry.

"Let me go," I command, trying my best to keep my voice from shaking with the fear I feel vibrating my bones.

"Take me to see him. I have questions for the paper." His grip tightens when I pull my arm.

"Let. Me. Go."

The man sneers at me, and I swallow my whimper when his grip becomes painful. "Take me to him. This could get me a promotion that's been long overdue."

"The only thing grabbing at her like that will get you is a broken fucking spine."

Dark brown, almost black eyes meet mine over the stranger's shoulder, and I nearly cry at the relief that floods me. Tyler's jaw is clenched so tight I'm sure it aches as he steps between the stranger and me and grasps the hand holding me tight enough the stranger cries out.

My wrist throbs when it's released. I take two giant steps backward behind Tyler as I gulp down air and try to forget this ever happened.

"Tyler Bateman! Care to tell me what happened out there? Your knuckles look broken."

"Broken knuckles or not, if you don't fuck off back to whatever hellhole you came out of, I'm going to do to you what I did to Sullivan back there," Tyler snarls.

"Just one comment," the man pleads, clearly not caring about Tyler's threat.

"Let's go," I say quietly. Somehow, Tyler grows even stiffer. "You can't be seen out here like this, and the team doesn't need bad press from you beating up some low-life reporter."

A quick nod is the only reply I get before I come around to his side and let him lead me away from the reporter. Only when I see the bloody heart tattoo on his hip do I realize he's half-naked.

He chuckles darkly as if sensing the exact moment I notice his lack of clothing. "It was get dressed or find you and bring you to Oakley. He threatened to go find you himself, but the medic popped his shoulder back in before he had the chance to make good on it."

"Is he okay?"

"He will be. That fucker got him good."

"And you? Are you okay? Did you break your knuckles?"

He lifts his right hand in front of him, and I blow out a breath. "Yeah. Not the first time and won't be the last. It was worth it."

I stop walking, and as soon as he follows suit, I'm moving in for a hug. He's as still as a statue as I slip my arms around his waist and press my cheek to his chest. The friendly hug starts out quite awkward, probably because Tyler isn't much of a people person, let alone a hugger. After a few seconds, though, he relaxes and wraps his massive arms around my shoulders. He leans into me, and I smile.

"Thank you. For standing up for Oakley but also scaring that guy away."

"It's not a big deal." His gruff voice cuts through the silence as he pulls away from me. His eyes dart down to the swollen, mangled mess that was once a set of knuckles. "Come on. Oakley's probably driving everyone crazy."

We don't speak for the rest of our walk, and before I know it, we come to a stop in front of a white door with the word *medic* plastered on the front in bold red letters.

"I'll leave you to it. Just go in. I'm sure they're expecting you."

I laugh. Tyler nods once and turns around to make his way back to the locker room before he stops short and looks around awkwardly.

"Oh, and thank you. For the . . . hug . . . earlier. I didn't know I needed that until, you know." He rocks on the balls of his feet, ready to bolt at any moment.

"You don't have to thank me, Tyler. We're friends, and that's what friends do. You don't have to keep your feelings bottled in all the time." I give him a small, reassuring smile and watch as he returns it. He nods and turns around once again, walking away.

With as much confidence as I can muster, I pull the door open and walk into the room. I'm hit with the smell of disinfectant instantly, and my nose scrunches.

Oakley is sitting on a makeshift hospital bed in the middle of the room, scowling at the wall. His gear and jersey have been removed and replaced with a sling holding his shoulder and an ice pack around his lower back. There's red staining the side of his face, making me shudder at the reminder of the bloody puddle on the ice.

I suck in a sharp breath, drawing his attention. The minute our eyes meet, I'm rambling. "Are you okay? What the hell happened out there? You gave me a damn heart attack when you were just lying there, not moving!"

Oakley laughs airily, his lips curling up. I glare at his lack of seriousness. This is not a laughable situation.

"This is not funny. You're in a sling!" I jab my finger in the direction of his injured shoulder.

"Ava, I'd like you to meet my mom and sister, Anne and Gracie," Oakley says, hiding his smile behind his fist.

I go still. *What?*

"Oh my! It's so lovely to see you again. We didn't get much time to chat earlier, let alone properly introduce ourselves."

Slowly, I turn my head and see the mother and daughter from earlier sitting in two chairs pushed up against the wall.

Holy shit, this is not happening right now. Heat creeps up my neck as I give them a beyond awkward wave.

Gracie snickers when Anne jumps up from her seat to greet me. She rushes over and pulls me in for a hug that I cautiously return.

Anne smells like peppermint and fresh linen, reminding me of Lily. A warmth spreads through me as I start to relax. Over Anne's shoulder, I notice Oakley staring at us, his face stark with confusion.

"I didn't get knocked out, did I? How do you know each other already?" he asks.

"You might as well have. How did you not see that guy?" Gracie scolds.

He flips his sister the finger. "I did see him. Just a few seconds too late."

"Don't start, you two. I've just watched my son get absolutely levelled. The last thing I need is more stress."

"Levelled?" Oakley grimaces. "Who taught you to talk like that?"

"I did," Gracie states.

"Well, stop. It sounds weird."

"No, thank you. I like it that Mom's becoming more hip."

Oakley crinkles his nose. "More *hip*?"

"Stop acting like a dick."

Anne groans. "Can we stay on track, please? You were asking how we met your Ava."

Oakley's eyes are soft when they fall on me again. "Right."

"Your sister was being loud and drew Ava's attention in the stands. We barely got a chance to start chatting before the game started. It took me a minute, but I recognized her from those pictures floating around," Anne explains. I flush. *Oh.*

"I was simply telling Mom about how hot Tyler looked. It wasn't as if I was screaming it for all to hear," Gracie adds.

Oakley glares at his sister. "Tyler is *not* hot. He is way too old for you."

"Too old for me right now, maybe. We can revisit this subject in two years."

Gracie is brave, that much is obvious as she continues to go head to toe with her overprotective brother. In all honesty, I don't think Oakley needs to worry about Tyler. I don't know much about his type other than he's not really the dating kind of guy, but I doubt he's into underage, sixteen-year-old girls.

"Do you need to go to the hospital to see a doctor?" I blurt out.

Oakley gives me an appreciative smile for interrupting and holds his good arm out in front of him as if waiting for a hug. I shake my head, cautious of showing PDA in front of his family when we've only just met, but he just rolls his eyes and gets off the bed, heading right for me.

"My body hurts, Ava. Don't make me beg," he whispers once he's standing right in front of me.

Apparently, that's all it takes to change my mind because a second later, I walk right into his chest and wrap my arms around his waist. He can only hold me with one arm, but it doesn't matter. His touch is a comfort that I didn't know I had been missing.

"We're going to take a walk until you're ready to go, Oakley," Anne says softly before footsteps carry to the door, and the door closes with a click.

"Finally." Oakley heaves a sigh, pulling back. "I didn't want to ask them to leave, but I've wanted to do this since the minute you walked in here."

I open my mouth to ask him what he's talking about when he presses his lips to mine and groans deep and low. The vibration of it travels from my mouth to my toes.

After a few moments, I pull back, Oakley's mouth chasing mine. If it weren't for the way his left arm lies between us, against his chest, maybe I would have let him continue to kiss me. But my worry for him is too prominent right now.

"You never answered me when I asked you what happened out there. What's the diagnosis? Do you need to go to the hospital?"

Looking tired and sore, he pulls me over to one of the chairs resting against the wall and sits down, patting his thighs. With slight hesitation, I sit on his lap, as close to his knees as possible. He wraps his good arm tightly around my middle and leans forward, chin resting on my shoulder.

"Don't worry about my pain, Ava. The medic was quick to give me something for it. I have a bruised tailbone and a dislocated collarbone. I could do without the sore tongue from chomping down on it when I fell, but it's nothing serious. I'm lucky."

I nod. "How long are you out for?"

"If the healing goes well, three to four weeks."

"So you should be playing again after the Christmas break."

"Mhm. That's the goal. I still need to go to the hospital to get proper X-rays and make sure there isn't anything else there, but the medic was pretty confident it was a dislocation," he murmurs, slipping his thumb beneath the jersey I'm wearing and sliding it along the band of my pants.

"We should go before you fall asleep in this chair."

"You're coming?" he asks quietly, his cheek pressing against my ear.

"Yeah. Who else is going to make sure you don't get into another fight with your sister?"

His laugh is nothing more than a slow rumble, and I'm relieved when the door opens tentatively and Anne pokes her head in. A look of awe flashes across her face at what she sees before she smiles at me.

"Ready to go?" she asks.

Oakley doesn't answer, and I don't have to look back to know he's dozing off. I pat his thigh. "Yeah. He's ready."

# 22

## Oakley

"THIS FUCKING SUCKS," I GRUMBLE AGAIN. THE BUZZER SOUNDS, signalling the third consecutive Saint's loss in the past two weeks.

Frustration is a pinch in my side that won't go away. The team was off to a damn good start this season, with stats more impressive than half the entire WHL league. We were playing as a real team, and every single player was bringing their best each game. But the team playing right now? They're slow, laggy. The passion, the *drive*, is gone. Just like that.

What was once going to be our best first season opening in years is slipping like sand through our fingers.

"They're playing like they haven't slept all week," Ava sighs.

"Maybe you should go to the dressing room and say something," Morgan suggests. She's staring at Matt with a mix of annoyance and sympathy as he raises his right glove to catch a shot but misses by a long shot. The buzzer goes off again, and the opposing team gets another goal.

I frown. "That's Coach's job."

Ava sets her hand on my thigh. "I don't think that matters. Hearing from you might be what they need to win this."

"She's right," Morgan says. "Matt hasn't missed this many

saves in years. The worst that happens is that they don't play any better after you talk to them. They're already playing like shit. It's not like they can get any worse."

I look at Ava and grow more confident when I find her smiling at me. She nods and squeezes my leg. "Give it a shot. I'll let you know if we leave our seats and wander off."

Morgan has a point. It's not like it can do any harm. Decided, I lean over to kiss Ava's cheek, feeling it warm beneath my lips, and then leave the two girls to watch the mess of a game.

I pull my ball cap further down my face to try and slip out of the stands unseen and nearly scream with joy when I succeed. The walk to the dressing room is quick, and after heading inside, I find it still empty.

The smell of sweat and disappointment is pungent in the air as I sit on one of the benches between the cubbies and wait. At the sight of the clean Hutton jersey hung in my cubby, my stomach rolls.

Feeling guilty right now is unfair to myself, but as I listen to the buzzer ring out on the ice, announcing the end of the second period, I can't help it. The team needs me, and I'm sitting here doing absolutely nothing.

Shouted voices break the silence, and grumpy, pissed-off hockey players come trampling into the dressing room. It takes them a breath to realize I'm there, and once they do, I watch as shame stifles their rage.

Matt is the first to speak up. "Don't waste your breath, Lee. We already know."

Coach enters the room last, disgust twisting his features. The second his eyes meet mine, his scowl digs deeper into his face.

"Who wants to tell Hutton why we're losing by eight goals tonight?" His eyes travel the length of the room, focusing on each and every player for the same amount of time. When nobody speaks up, he asks, "No takers?"

I wince at the seething hot words.

"Fine. I'll do it. We're losing because you're playing like you don't want to be here. You're playing like you don't give a shit about this team or our shot at the championship! I should bench half of you for the rest of the damn season for the shit you've been pulling out there. You're embarrassing yourselves. You're embarrassing the fans and this city. Is that what you wanted?"

The team is silent.

Coach snarls, "Is that what you wanted?"

"No, Coach!"

"Do you want your fans to go home tonight and talk about how disappointed they are in you?"

"No, Coach!"

"Do you want to be disappointed in yourselves?"

"No, Coach!" They scream this time.

"Then pull yourselves together out there. You are not playing like a team stacked with this year's prospect pool. Keep playing like this and you can kiss your chance at the NHL goodbye." Coach turns to me and nods to the empty space beside him. "Hutton. Up here." I don't hesitate to join him. He squeezes the clipboard in his hands in a white-knuckle grip. "Pull them together. I'll be back."

With that, he leaves us alone. Uncomfortable, I rub at the moist skin at the base of my neck. My teammates watch me with an unusual desperation, like they're hoping I can somehow turn their game around. I swallow.

"I didn't come back here to tell you what to do. You're all more than capable of figuring that out on your own," I start nervously. The pressure of expectations weighs on my chest, and my next inhale is shaky. "I guess I just wanted to say that I've never played with a better team. Never. The chemistry we have on that ice is unbeatable, and I'm so grateful to have gotten a chance to play with you guys.

"But the team I'm seeing out there tonight? That's not my team. My goalie doesn't miss glove saves, and my defensemen don't throw dirty hits. My offensemen don't give away the puck on breakaways and trip over their own skates. My team doesn't play without passion and confidence. So, what gives?"

Several sets of eyes drop to the rubber floor while others refuse to look away. I try not to think about David or the arrogant way he's standing there watching me like he couldn't care less about what I'm saying.

"We'll get it together," Adam says. I look at him, surprised that he's the one to answer me. He quickly pushes his matted brown curls out of his eyes. "You're right. This isn't us."

"Good," Coach grunts, suddenly back in the room. He nods at me in approval. "Catch your breath, boys. We're nearly ready to go back."

I give the team another look before heading for the door. A low voice stops me when I grab the door handle.

"Thank you."

I twist around and spot Tyler leaning against the wall, his tired eyes pinning me in place. "Anytime, man. Good luck."

He nods, and I leave.

AVA IS TALKING to someone I don't recognize when I find her by the concession stands after my attempt at getting my team back to themselves. Her laugh hits the air, and I grin, picking up my pace, needing to reach her faster. Morgan has disappeared, most likely giving Ava some time alone with the woman making her laugh that damn laugh.

"If I would have known you were coming, we could have gotten tickets in the same row, Mom!" Ava says.

The short woman across from her flicks a piece of brown-and-silver hair out of her face as she waves off the words. "We wanted it to be a surprise. Ben didn't know if he was really going to get to come home or not until just yes—oh! Hello, there."

I meet the woman's stare as I come up behind Ava and slip

my arm around her waist, palming her side. She doesn't so much as stiffen as I do, and that makes my confidence soar.

"Hello. Sorry to interrupt. I'm Oakley Hutton," I introduce myself and offer the small woman my hand.

She grins and grabs it with both hands, squeezing it twice. "Lily Layton. It's a pleasure to finally meet the star my daughter has told me so much about."

"Mom," Ava scolds lightly.

Lily releases my hand and smiles innocently. "What?"

I chuckle and press my chest to Ava's back, inhaling the scent of vanilla and oranges. "At least I feel less embarrassed about talking about Ava to my family so much now."

Lily nearly melts, and I take that as a crucial win. "Oh, that's so sweet."

"What's so sweet?" a man asks. I quickly place him as a tall, beefy guy coming to Lily's side and not the younger version of him standing on his other side. The two guys narrow their eyes on me.

"Oakley. Ava's boyfriend," Lily tells him.

Ava sputters a cough and shakes her head. "I never said he was my boyfriend, Mom." She looks at me apologetically over her shoulder. "I never told her you were my boyfriend."

I tighten my grip on her waist. "Boyfriend has a nice ring to it."

Lily grins and elbows the man beside her. "Introduce yourself to Oakley."

The surly man does, and the second our hands meet in a tight shake, his smile is pinched and awkward. "Derek Layton. Octavia's dad."

"Great to meet you," I reply.

"And I'm Ben, the big brother," the other guy says, shaking my hand once his dad releases my throbbing fingers.

Ava's brother is not what I was expecting. From how she described him before, I was expecting a guy that looked a lot like her father. Commanding and intimidating with biceps the size of my thighs.

But Ben gives off more of a calculating, quiet vibe. Like he's thinking about the ways he could ruin your life without leaving tracks.

I'm not sure who is more terrifying—her father or brother.

"There. Introductions are done. Now, can everyone go back to their seats so we can watch the rest of the game?" Ava pleads.

She and Lily share a subtle look that I can't decipher before her mom says, "Of course. Don't forget about dinner tomorrow night, okay? Your father is going to grill up some steaks."

"Yeah, that's great. I'll see you there." Ava grabs my hand and starts to pull me away from them before her dad stops us.

"You like steaks, Oakley? I can pick another one up."

Lily squeals. "That's a great idea! Tell us you'll come."

I sneak a glance at Ava, and when she lets out a resigned sigh and nods in approval, I say, "I love steak."

# 23

# *Oakley*

I'M NOT USUALLY SOMEONE WHO GETS NERVOUS, CONSIDERING THAT I thrive under high-pressure situations, but this is not the type of situation I'm used to. Not by a long shot.

Despite my confidence when I met Ava's family at the rink, I feel like I could kneel over and throw up the oatmeal I had for breakfast right on the Laytons' stone driveaway.

I've never had a girlfriend. I've never brought a girl home to meet my family or made the time in my schedule to meet theirs. Dating has never been on my radar, but when it comes to Ava, it's a flashing red light that's impossible to ignore.

I'm falling for this girl, just like I was the first night I saw her with splotchy eyes and a broken heart. As far as I'm concerned, she's mine to date, and I'm going to date the shit out of her. Dinners with her parents come hand in hand with that, just like they do with my family.

A faint tap on the window has me jumping in surprise, smacking the top of my head to the roof of the truck. With a thumping pulse, I focus on Ava as she stands outside the door, watching me with barely stifled humour.

I quickly turn the truck off, grab the flowers my mom insisted

I bring from the passenger seat, lock the doors, and then join my girl outside.

"Were you planning on staying out here all night?" she teases.

The mischievous glint in her eyes seems to intensify as I curse myself. Apparently, I was sitting outside for longer than I thought.

I reach out and grab her by the hips, pulling her toward me. Vibrant green eyes fly up my body before getting caught in my stare. She places her palms flush to my chest and leans into me.

Dropping my voice, I say, "Maybe I was waiting for you to come get me."

Her laugh sets off zips of electricity in my blood. "Ah, is that what you were doing?"

"No. But it makes me look like less of a chickenshit."

"You're not a chickenshit, Boy Scout. You're not the first guy to be intimidated by my dad. But I swear, he's just like a coconut."

"A coconut?"

"You know, hard on the outside, gooey on the inside?"

"Does he know you refer to him as a coconut to the guys he's trying to scare?"

"No. Are you going to tattle on me?" she asks coyly.

"Maybe. We'll see." I wink.

Toying with a loose curl blowing in the cold breeze, I take the opportunity to fully drink her in before we head inside.

She's wearing a pair of loose-fitting blue jeans with rips below both front pockets and over the knees and a tight, mossy-green long-sleeve shirt that makes her eyes pop even more than usual.

The stray curl I can't seem to leave alone isn't one of a kind. It's surrounded by so many more that I ache to wrap around my fist—

"You brought flowers?"

I clear my throat and shift on my feet in an attempt to release the pressure my jeans are creating on my new erection.

"Daisies," I reply.

"Mom loves daisies. Come on." She intertwines our fingers and starts to lead me up the driveway.

The Layton home is relatively large yet homey-looking and sits at the top of the driveway. The light brick and massive floor-to-ceiling windows make it look more modern than most houses in the neighbourhood. The lawn is neatly trimmed, despite the weather and time of year, and the cobblestone is illuminated by garden lights all the way up to the porch.

Once we step up the porch stairs and reach the front door, Ava turns to me. "You ready?"

"Almost." Before she can speak, I'm kissing her. She releases a soft sound into my mouth when she pushes up on her toes and responds just as eagerly.

If I had it my way, I would kiss her every minute of every damn day, but a noise from inside the house reminds me where we are, and I reluctantly pull away.

Ava blinks slowly when she opens her eyes and smiles at me. "What about now?"

"Yeah, I'm ready."

❄

I HAVE FAR TOO much food stacked on my plate, with a steak the size of my hand and more than a hearty selection of different salads. It's not a surprise that Lily and Derek are two world-class chefs, but I think a career in grilling might be in Derek's cards after all.

"This is the best steak I have ever had," I blurt out while slicing through the perfectly cooked meat. It oozes juice, and my mouth waters.

Ava laughs beside me and pops a piece of bun into her

mouth as Derek looks at me across the table and slowly sets down his bottle of beer.

"Thank you," he says.

"You're more than welcome to come for dinner anytime, Oakley," Lily pipes up, flashing me a smile.

Ben shoves a forkful of pasta salad into his mouth before saying, "Yeah. It would be nice to have a guy around more."

"You're barely home as it is, Benjamin," Lily sighs.

"I'm home as much as I can be. Ava knows how hard it is to make time, and she lives in the same province. I'm hours away."

"I know. But I'm still allowed to miss you." Lily starts to fiddle with her napkin, but a breath later, Derek is covering her hand with his and squeezing. His wife smiles lovingly at him.

"I miss you too," Ben replies, and his girlfriend, Sydney, leans toward him and bumps his shoulder in what looks like an act of support.

"Let's switch topics. Ava tells us you're from Penticton. How are you liking Vancouver?" Lily asks me.

"It's big. Bigger and busier than I'm used to, and it rains too much, but I think I actually like it." I take a bite of steak and fight my eyes from rolling back at how good it tastes.

Ben laughs. "You should try living outside of BC sometime. I'm at university in Alberta, and it's dry as hell. I actually miss the rain some days."

"Oh, wow. Why Alberta?"

"Honestly? I picked a province out of a hat. All I knew was that I needed to experience something this place couldn't give me."

"Good for you, man. That takes guts." I have a new appreciation for Ava's brother.

"That's our Benny boy." Lily grins proudly. "Now, hockey is more Ben's cup of tea, but we do watch a game every once in a while in this house. "Is hockey what you want to do for the rest of your life, Oakley?" Lily asks. Her genuine curiosity is refreshing.

"Absolutely. Hockey is something that I want to do professionally for as long as I can," I reply.

"So your plan is the NHL?" Derek asks, his voice harder than I was expecting.

"Yes, sir. Quite a few teams have already approached me. It's been my dream for as long as I remember," I admit.

Derek leans closer to the table, his sharp stare unwavering.

I resist the urge to reach for the back of my neck.

"Have you and Ava discussed what will happen when you're gone? You're serious enough about my daughter to come back for her?"

I turn to look at Ava as her fork clatters on her plate. Flushed, she glares across the table. I rest my hand on her thigh and rub my thumb back and forth in an attempt to soothe her.

"I'm right here, Dad. You don't have to ask about me as if I'm not. I can answer these questions too."

"I can assure you that I'm very serious about your daughter. I wouldn't be here if I weren't." My promise is for Ava just as much as it is for her dad.

Derek flicks his eyes to his angry daughter. "Are you ready for all of that?"

"All of what?" she asks, indignant.

"You know what."

She bristles. "Why don't you tell me and clarify? Because I know you're not about to bring up what I think you are. Oakley's not like that."

I stiffen to stone. *Fuck.*

"That's enough, Derek. Let it go," Lily says gently.

Derek keeps his eyes on me, though, and my skin breaks out in a nervous sweat.

"All athletes are like that. David proved that to me," Derek states.

My eyes fall shut as I sigh. Yeah, I saw that one coming.

"You deserve better than to be left behind while he travels the world doing God knows what. I thought you had already learned that lesson."

When Ava's breath hitches, I cut in, "With all due respect, you don't really know what you're talking about. I am not like David, nor do I have any interest in any woman but Ava. If I didn't respect the hell out of her and her plans for the future, I would ask her to come with me wherever I end up going. Knowing that I'll be away from her once I'm drafted is something that keeps me up at night," I tell him, trying very hard to rein in my rising temper.

"Pretty words, Oakley. But we're just supposed to trust you on that? I can't believe what you say with blind faith," he grunts.

"I'm not asking you to believe what I'm saying. The last thing I want to do is upset anyone, but if I'm being completely honest, I don't care what you think. The only person whose opinion matters to me is Ava's, and if she didn't trust me, I wouldn't be here with all of you right now."

Lily stares at her husband, open-mouthed, as Sydney raises an eyebrow and takes a sip of her drink. Ava simply looks furious.

Derek opens his mouth to no doubt tell me to kiss his ass, but Ben cuts in before he has a chance to fire that final blow.

"Dad, just drop it. This isn't what tonight is about."

"Ben's right. It isn't. But if you'll excuse us, we'll be upstairs," Ava growls.

She shoots up from the table and storms out of the room, dragging me with her and leaving our half-eaten meals behind, my steak included.

Her breaths come out as short, angry puffs as we ascend a grand spiral staircase. I don't say a word the entire time, and neither does she.

I don't blame her dad for asking those questions. Yes, they could have been phrased differently, but he's a father at the end of the day, and I would have asked the same things if I were in his position. David isn't someone I would ever want to be compared to, but Ava's father doesn't know me as more than a guy dating his daughter.

There's no doubt in my mind that I think Ava and I can handle whatever comes after the draft, but does she think the same?

I swipe a hand over the back of my neck to wipe away the perspiration at the same time Ava comes to a stop at the end of the hallway.

"This is my room. Make yourself at home." She pushes the white door in front of us open, and I hesitantly make my way inside.

Her room is exactly the opposite of her bedroom at the apartment. This one is clean and sleek, without a single thing out of place. The walls are painted a cool teal—matching her bedcovers —and every piece of furniture is white. A neat, tidy desk sits under the window, and there are two white doors on the opposite wall that must lead to a closet and bathroom.

My eyes track Ava as she crosses the room and flops onto her bed. With a groan, I sit down beside her on the edge of the bed and slowly rub her calf.

"Are you okay?"

"He's not usually like that. I'm sorry," Ava sighs, staring at the pictures and prize ribbons hanging on her wall, most of which come from elementary school spelling bees. *Cute*. "I don't know what his deal is."

"Don't apologize. I can handle an overprotective father."

She hums and, after a few moments of silence, whispers, "Do you ever worry about what could happen with us?"

My lips part, but I say nothing. The last thing I want is for Ava to start doubting this—to start doubting us.

"What do you mean?"

"You're going to be gone most of the time, and I'm just going to be . . . well, *here*. Hockey is the only thing keeping you in Vancouver. What happens when you aren't here anymore?" The slight wobble in her voice has my chest aching.

"Come here," I plead, my arm held outstretched. Slowly, she sits up and crawls toward me, moving to sit on my lap. She tucks her face into my neck and wraps her arms tightly around me. "You're insane if you think hockey is the only thing I have here."

She draws in a shaky breath and nods as she leans into me, sighing. I rub my arm up and down her back.

"Besides, the odds of me being drafted somewhere really far are slim with how the NHL season is playing out. But I can promise you right now that no amount of distance will change anything for me. I know that already."

Ava nods again, and a sudden feeling of desperation for her to believe everything I've said has me blurting out, "Would it be too presumptuous of me to ask you to come home with me for Christmas?"

Her breath hitches, and I almost tell her to forget I said anything before she kisses my throat and says, "No. Would it be presumptuous of me to say yes?"

"Fuck no." I palm the back of her head and kiss her, hoping that she's half as obsessed with me as I am with her. Because if she is, distance doesn't stand a goddamn chance.

# 24

## Ava

SOMEHOW, OVER THE PAST FEW WEEKS BETWEEN EXAMS AND HOCKEY game after hockey game, Christmas is only a couple of sleeps away.

It's cold and wet. Snow has fallen to cover the ground only to melt and freeze again, leaving the roads slick with ice. It's an absolute nightmare. One that's the culprit of the unexpected extra hour we've had to add to our drive from Van to Oakley's mother's house in Penticton.

Tyler has barely spoken the entire drive so far, not after I denied his pleas to drive. I think his sullen mood might have more to do with his nerves regarding even coming to this dinner in the first place, but when Anne Hutton invites you to dinner, according to Oakley, you go. No questions asked.

In all the years I've known Tyler, he's kept his personal life pretty close to his chest, and I can admit that makes me sad. It doesn't take a rocket scientist to piece together that family isn't a term he's accustomed to, not when he's never once spoken about his or left to visit them to anyone's knowledge.

Anne picked up on it too, if her suddenly inviting him to Christmas dinner is anything to go off. To say he was surprised by the invitation would be putting it lightly, but there was no way he could resist that pleading smile of hers.

I drum my fingers on the steering wheel and stare at the sheet of white in front of me. The wind has picked up over the last hour and blows the snow over the road, making it even harder to see where we're going.

"How close are we?" I ask my surly co-pilot.

He looks at the GPS on his phone. "Ten minutes now. Take a left once you see the stoplight."

Right. If I can see anything in this storm at all.

"At this rate, I won't see it, and we'll end up in a ditch."

"You can pull over and let me drive."

I huff, wanting to glare at him but not wanting to risk looking away from the road. "No. I'm a great driver."

"I would prefer being in control if we wound up spinning out of control."

"Luckily for you, we won't be doing any spinning," I reply. Tyler makes an annoyed grumbling noise but doesn't speak. "You're upset about something other than this stupid storm. Wanna talk about it?"

"Do I want to? No."

"Will you? It might help, you know. Let it off your chest."

A pause. "Is it weird for me to come today?"

My brows tug together. "Why would it be weird?"

"I'm not a part of their family. It feels weird to go."

"I'm not family either."

From the corner of my eye, I catch Tyler looking at me curiously. "You're Oakley's family."

"Oh," I breathe, my stomach suddenly a mess of fluttering wings. "I guess so."

"It's different for you. I'm just . . . what? A pity invite?"

The flutters are gone as fast as they appeared. An ache grows in their place. *Oh, Tyler.* "No. I don't think it was pity at all."

His laugh is dark. "Really? Then what was it?"

"Anne is very similar to my mom. All she wants is for people to feel loved. You can look at that as pity, or you can look at it from a place of love. You deserve to spend Christmas with people who care about you instead of alone."

Another pause, this one longer and heavier than the previous one. When Tyler responds, his voice sounds almost . . . uncomfortable? "Oakley's sister will be there. She always stares at me like she's trying to undress me."

I laugh, so damn loudly. "Go easy on her, Ty. She's a teen with a crush. One wrong word and you might as well rip her heart out and run it over with a semi-truck."

"That's dramatic," he grunts.

"That's a teenage girl for you. Dramatic and stubborn as hell."

"Right."

I narrow my eyes and see a brief flash of red break through the snow ahead. Slowly pressing the brake and flipping on the signal light, I bring us to a sliding stop in front of the traffic light.

"Finally," I mutter.

Tyler clears his throat, and for the first time in hours, I turn to look at him instead of the windshield. His hair is beyond messy, sticking up in all sorts of directions and looking like he's spent hours with his fingers tangling it up. When I twist my mouth in a nervous smile, he looks as shy as I think I've ever seen him.

"Got a bit anxious there for a bit," he says.

I nod and turn back to the road just as the light turns green, and I make a cautious turn when oncoming traffic clears. "I think there are nail punctures in the steering wheel from how tight I was squeezing it."

"Turn right at the school, and then the house is the second one from the corner."

I just nod, not surprised when he changes the subject. We don't speak again until I pull along the curb in front of an adorable bungalow decked out in multicoloured Christmas lights and inflatable lawn decorations.

"Oh," Tyler says, his face strained like he's trying not to show how much he hates the decorations.

"Me and Anne have more in common than I thought."

Christmas has been my favourite holiday for as long as I can remember. Even in foster care, where we never really celebrated, I would cut out snowflakes from paper and string them up over my bed every single year. It was hardly a Christmas decoration, but for me, it was everything I needed. Cutting paper snowflakes is a tradition now, one all of my friends have taken part in over the last few years.

Without replying, Tyler's undoing his seat belt and tugging his hood over his head before pushing open the door and getting a face full of snow. I stifle a laugh and watch him fight against the wind and move to the back seat, making quick work of grabbing our bags and throwing them over his shoulder.

As soon as I zip my jacket up all the way and pull my mittens on, I'm following after him, trying not to shiver when rogue pieces of snow slip beneath the top of my jacket and stick to my skin.

"Ava! Jesus Christ, do you not know how to answer your phone?" I hear Oakley shouting from somewhere ahead of us, but the howling wind doesn't give me much to go off. Tyler reaches back for me and clasps a hand around my forearm, continuing up the sidewalk toward where I hope the house is.

It looks like the sidewalk has been shovelled recently, but with how the snow just keeps falling in piles, I really have no idea.

"I'm going to kick your ass, Tyler! Did you want to give me a fucking heart attack?"

I wince at the anger in Oakley's voice. I told Tyler to text Oakley and let him know we would be late, but we were so focused on the road and the GPS that clearly, we could have done a better job of keeping him updated.

Tyler stumbles back a step, in turn making himself yank on my arm and forcing me to lose my footing. I'm squeezing my eyes shut and preparing to eat snow when I'm being caught mid-fall.

Storming green eyes snare mine when I look up and find Oakley standing over me. He tightens his grip on my arms and pulls me up and into his chest. I barely have time to appreciate the comfort his presence gives me before he's moving us through the snow and up a set of freshly cleared stairs.

He whips a door open, and a wall of heat smacks right into me. Instantly, I sigh and let my body soften.

"Oh, my God! Look at you two! Come, come. Oakley, shut that door." Anne brushes her son off me, wraps her arm around my back, and hurries me through the living room, parking me in front of a brick-walled fireplace.

My hands fly out toward the flames on their own. I release a long breath and shiver at the sudden change in temperature.

"I should have driven you," Oakley states gruffly behind me before I'm being tugged back toward his chest. His arms wrap around my front, and he presses his palms to the top of my hands, keeping them in front of the fire.

"You got here two days ago, Oakley. Plus, I'm fine. We're all in one piece. Just cold, and that has nothing to do with the drive."

His stubbled jaw brushes my ear as he holds me. "I was worried."

"I told Tyler to tell you we would be late."

"He did. But my other texts went unanswered. I was close to going out and looking for you."

Warmth beats at my cheeks. "Well, I'm here now."

"Yes, you are," he murmurs. "I'm going to bring your bag to my room. Stay here and warm up."

He slowly backs away, and I look over my shoulder, catching his eye before he turns away. "Your room?"

Oakley arches a bushy brow. "You think you would stay anywhere else? Over my dead body."

I laugh. "Right. My bad."

"Be right back, baby." He tosses me a wink and walks away.

# 25

## *Ava*

A COUPLE OF HOURS LATER, ALL OF MY TOES ARE BACK TO A LESS purply hue, and the house smells delicious, like turkey and potatoes and every other kind of dish you could possibly find at a holiday dinner.

Anne kicked Gracie and me out of the kitchen a few minutes ago after we finished mashing the potatoes, and we've been sitting in the living room with the guys ever since.

Oakley's fingers draw slow circles on my arm as Gracie anxiously taps her fingers on her thigh. She's trying not to stare at Tyler from where he sits in an armchair across the room but is failing miserably. Every time I look away from the *Elf* movie playing on the TV, I find her looking at him with a blooming attraction in her eyes.

Reaching toward her, I poke the outside of her thigh. She whips her head to the side and lifts her eyebrows at me. I dart my eyes between her and Tyler.

I lean as far as I can without drawing Oakley's attention and whisper, "Stop staring."

A red hue slithers up her cheeks. "Right," she whispers back.

The last thing any of us needs tonight is for Oakley to beat up

Tyler because his sister has a crush on him. Not to mention that Gracie's boyfriend, Jacob, should be here any minute.

*Talk about awkward.*

"It makes me jealous that you and my sister have secrets already. Why don't we have any secrets that only you and I know about?" Oakley murmurs into my hair.

I shiver as his breath slides down the back of my neck. "We could always make some."

He kisses my head. "I'd like that."

"What are you two whispering about over there? You're making me feel excluded." Gracie clucks her tongue to the roof of her mouth.

"It's a secret," Oakley tells her, and I feel his lips parting into a smile in my hair.

"Of course it is," Gracie groans.

"I think I hear another guest!" Anne exclaims, bustling into the living room. An apron is tied around her neck and over a dress she must have just recently changed into. Written across the front of the apron is *World's Best Mom*. It fits her perfectly.

I grin at her. "You look beautiful, Anne."

The black dress comes to a stop a few inches above her ankles, and beautiful yellow daisies are splattered across the silky material.

"Oh, no need to flatter me. I already like you." She grins. There's a set of four knocks on the front door, and Anne hurries toward it. A rush of wind bucks into the house when she pulls open the door and urges the new person inside.

"What's up with the storm out there? Shit's insane," a low voice says, sounding like the owner swallowed gravel.

"It came out of nowhere! I'm glad you got here okay," Anne sighs.

"I would drive through a tornado for your turkey, Anne."

"Oh, knock off the flattery, Andre. There will be plenty of left-overs for you without you kissing my ass."

"I would never. It's all the truth."

Oakley places one more kiss to my head before standing up and heading toward the new arrival. I can't see the guy until Anne mumbles something about the turkey and leaves the room, exposing the two friends.

"So glad you could make it." Oakley fist pumps his friend and pulls him in for a quick yet tight hug.

Andre is maybe an inch or two shorter than Oakley and truly does live up to the hype appearance-wise. He reeks of playboy, which is no surprise from what I've heard.

Oakley has only told me a handful of things about Andre over the past few months, but he seems to have been a good friend to him in the past, and that's good enough for me.

"You heard me. I came for Anne." The two guys laugh before pulling apart and facing the rest of us.

Oakley gestures to me, and I smile. "Ava, this ass kisser is Andre. Andre, this is my girlfriend, Ava."

Andre slowly looks me up and down before smirking. "You forgot to mention that she's a fucking smoke show, bro."

"Don't call my girl a smoke show," Oakley growls.

"Yuck, Andre." Gracie pretends to retch.

Andre blows her a kiss. "Merry Christmas, Gravy."

Tyler makes a choking noise, drawing everyone's attention. "Gravy? That's terrible."

"Little G here loves it. Ain't that right, Gracie?"

Gracie's face looks like it's on fire. I feel bad for her. "I hate you."

"Whatever you say," Andre sings before turning to me again, not bothering to hide his attraction. "You know, Ava, if you eve—"

"No." Oakley scowls.

Andre's chest shakes with silent laughter. "No what?"

"Don't say it unless you want your ass in the snow. Ava's not someone for you to razz." Oakley moves back to me and, with a gentle touch, reaches his arm across his body and pulls at my fingers, shifting me so I'm at his side. He plays with the fingers on my right hand as I press the other to his lower back and fiddle with the loops on his jeans.

Andre looks genuinely shocked by the display of affection. On the other hand, it doesn't seem like anyone else is. Oakley hasn't been able to keep his hands off me since Tyler and I got here.

"Damn. Seems like you've found the one after all. Now, who's going to be the one to break it to all the fangirls? I've already seen some of the comments on the photos of you playing beer pong, and even I would have been feeling pretty scalped after that."

Silence.

It's so quiet I start to worry if everyone can hear the sound of my stomach falling between my knees. I feel like I could take a play from Gracie's book and start retching, for real this time.

Social media has been a no go for me since the night Oakley and I were photographed together at that party and it was posted online. There weren't many comments at the time, but because I wasn't suspecting it, each one hit deep, at my weakest points.

I've never put much value into the opinions of others, so it was an easy decision for me to put my accounts on private and avoid checking in if possible. But hearing one of Oakley's closest friends bring it up feels like sandpaper on a scabbed wound.

Those photos are old news; I thought they would be forgotten by now.

"Andre," Oakley snaps. His fingers tighten their hold, but I can't tell if it's to calm himself or support me. Either way, I easily return the squeeze.

"I'd stop when you're ahead, if I were you," Tyler grunts.

Andre scoffs and tries to defend himself. "I'm not being a dick, guys. I'm just curious."

"Those people have nothing better to do. Their opinions mean nothing and stem from a place of jealousy. Oakley hasn't brought a girl home ever, and that says it all to me. Stop causing drama," Gracie reprimands Andre.

Warmth fills me at her words. My lips curl into a smile. "Thank you," I mouth to her. She nods and mouths, "Anytime," before turning up the volume on the TV, filling the silence with Will Ferrell's voice.

My appreciation for Oakley's little sister grows tenfold. I've never really gotten along with people younger than me, but I'm happy to know she's an exception.

As everyone starts to go back to their own thoughts, Oakley releases my hand and steps toward Andre. His back muscles are taut, and his lips are turned down instead of up like they usually are.

He speaks to his best friend in a low, frigid voice, and I barely catch the words.

"Consider that your one free pass. Bring up any of that shit to Ava or myself again and you'll be playing the rest of the season without your front teeth. Best friend or not."

"THAT WAS DELICIOUS, Anne. I guarantee my mom would be gushing about your caramelized carrots if she were here," I say once we've all finished eating.

My stomach is trying to pop open the button on my jeans, regardless of how hard I try to suck it in. Oakley's hand warms my knee as he holds it beneath the table and carries on a conversation about hockey with Tyler.

The awkward tension from earlier dissipated as soon as we started piling our plates with food. I can finally breathe again.

"Thank you, sweetheart. Will you help me with the dishes?" Anne's eyes shine with happiness.

I nod eagerly and start to collect the plates, giggling when Oakley pinches the underside of my ass when I grab his plate. Once all the dishes are gathered, we start washing. Anne fills the sink with warm soapy water, a light hum filling the peaceful space as I start loading the dishwasher.

"I'm so happy you could make it today," Anne says.

"I'm happy to be here. You're a fabulous cook." I place a glass bowl on the top rack.

"Coming from the daughter of two professional chefs, I'll take that compliment." We both laugh while she starts to scrub a gravy dish.

"I'm sure Mom would love to share recipes. If she could talk about food for all hours of the day, she would."

"Well, I would happily let her."

I slide two forks into the dishwasher. "I could give her your number if you want. If not, that's totally okay. It's not like you need to talk to a chef about your cooking—you're really amazing. Okay, now I'm rambling." Am I sweating? Why am I suddenly so nervous?

A warm hand touches my shoulder as Anne laughs softly. "You don't need to be nervous with me, sweetie. You could have walked through my door with a third eye or pastel green skin and I would have still adored you simply because you make my son happy and he loves you."

That makes me pause, turning to a statue.

"That surprises you?" she asks.

"We haven't really said that to each other yet," I wheeze.

"That's okay. You're both so young. It'll come."

"You sound so sure."

She hums thoughtfully. "I know my son well, Ava. There's no way he would have brought you to meet me if he didn't see a future with you, and the way he watches you when he thinks nobody is looking? He couldn't hide those feelings from me."

"Can I ask you something?" I blurt out, her words sinking deep and scaring me far more than I want to admit.

Anne turns to me with a gentle smile and pulls her hands out of the sink, wiping them on a dishtowel. "Always, honey."

"Do you ever worry about when he'll be gone?"

She raises a now dry hand to her neck and grasps the locket dangling on a chain in a tight fist. "Of course I do. But I know he'll always be here when we need him. Oakley has been taking care of Gracie and me ever since his father passed away. He needs this chance to move on."

My breath skips, and Anne curses under her breath. I'm sure I look like a maniac as I stare at her, my lips parted in surprise. A sudden pain ricochets through me, one that has me wanting to run toward my boyfriend and wrap him in my arms.

"Is there any chance you already knew that and I didn't just completely stick my foot in my mouth?" she asks, her features crinkled. I just shake my head. "Oh, shit."

"It's okay. I can't pretend I never wondered why he never talks about his dad." Or why he's not here spending Christmas with them. "You didn't know."

"Please, let me finish these dishes while you go talk to him. I don't want to be the one to tell you anything more that he should have the chance to." She sniffles before rushing to the roll of paper towel on the counter. Tearing one off, she hides her face and sniffs again. "Oh, Lord. Here I go."

Something has me moving around her and wrapping the tiny, hunched woman in my arms, hugging her tight. She lets me hold her for a few seconds before returning the gesture and wetting the corner of my shirt with tears I'm happy I can't see.

"Tell him that I'm sorry for blurting this all out before he had the chance to tell you. Please, Ava."

"Of course."

She sniffles one final time before stepping back. Besides a light red ring around her eyes, you would never know she had been crying.

"Thank you. For this, but also for being you. I can see why Oakley has fallen for you." The sincerity in her eyes is a bit overwhelming. Thankfully, she just gifts me one more smile and then turns back to the sink, resuming her washing.

With that, I steel my spine and walk back out to the dining room, coming face to face with the only person left at the table.

I can't even try to pretend I didn't just learn about his father when Oakley stares up at me with a pain in his eyes that says he heard everything.

# 26

# Oakley

AVA STARES AT ME LIKE A DEER IN HEADLIGHTS. A WINCE CROSSES her features, and I shake my head once, as if to reassure her she hasn't done anything wrong.

"I should have told you."

"You would have," she states, sounding so sure.

"He's not a secret," I defend.

"No, he's not."

I blow out a breath and drop my eyes. My dad isn't a secret, but I feel shame as if I made his death into one. Sure, it's not anything I spew out to a lot of people, but that's not because I'm trying to hide it from them. I just like my privacy.

But Ava? Ava isn't just anyone, and I should have told her before she found out from someone else.

"Can we talk in my room?" I ask.

She reaches toward me and grabs my hands from where they lie clenched together on my lap. I stand. "Of course we can."

We head upstairs to my room in silence, and as soon as we walk inside, I shut the door and lock it incase someone tries to come in and be snoopy while Ava looks around. She hasn't had a chance to be in here yet with how busy today has been.

"It's very you," she says softly.

I turn my back to the door and glance around the room. "It's cluttered. Mom refuses to let me pack up some of my stuff."

Ava steps up to the shelf above my dresser that's sagging with trophies, ribbons, and photos. She lifts a finger and brushes the bottom edge of a frame housing a photo of my father and me when I was in co-ed hockey.

"You look like him."

My throat swells. "We used to get that all the time. I still do. Gracie is Mom's carbon copy, and I'm his."

"I'm so sorry, Oakley."

I look at her and let the love in her eyes fall over me. I'm greedy for more of it, and before I can register what I'm doing, I'm scooping her into my arms and bringing us to my bed. She settles on my lap once I sit with my back to the bed frame. I tighten my hold on her.

"Tell me about him," she whispers.

"His name was Jamie," I blurt out. Ava gently squeezes my shoulder.

"*Is*," Ava murmurs. I meet her gaze, confused. "His name *is* Jamie. He never left. Not really," she explains. It's a simple statement, yet the words make my head spin.

I'm suddenly hyperaware of how fast and hard my heart is thumping against my rib cage as I stare into her eyes. Emotion overwhelms me.

It's now that I know the words are there on the tip of my tongue.

*I love you.*

It shouldn't be this hard to let them slip past my lips, to tell her that what we have isn't something that can be forgotten once I'm drafted. To ensure that she knows this is a forever type of thing for me. I'm never letting her go. Not now, not ever.

But instead of doing exactly that, I swallow the words, keeping them for another time.

"He was my hero," I whisper before taking a deep breath. "He was a contractor for a small construction company in town. His job came in handy whenever there was work to do around the house, which happened often. Mom would make him tear down almost every wall in the house just to paint the new ones every ugly colour you can think of. She always felt like the house needed a *change*, but I never heard him complain. Not once."

Ava chuckles and brushes her nose along mine. "It sounds like he loved her a lot."

I let myself smile at her comment. "Even as a kid, I could feel the love radiating off of them. Once he was gone, though, that's when I realized how much they loved each other. He was her whole world, and she was his." My eyes burn, but I swallow back the tears and speak again.

"Mom struggled. It was hard watching her hurt the way she did. I would wake up in the middle of the night and hear her crying in their room. After the first few nights, I started getting up when I heard her cry. I would just hug her until she eventually fell asleep."

"What happened to him?" she asks softly, so damn softly.

"He was hit by a drunk driver when I was nine. The paramedics said he died at the scene. The driver was just a stupid teenager who should have called someone for a ride home from a party and wound up running a red light."

It's not until Ava wipes her thumb beneath my eyes that I realize tears are streaming down my cheeks. I try to get them to stop falling, but when I feel the tightening in my throat, I know it's too late. My shoulders drop, and Ava threads her fingers in the hair at the back of my head and pulls me toward her, pressing my face to her chest.

The tears only fall faster as every ache and pain that I've shoved down over the years comes tearing through me.

"I'm here. You don't have to bottle this up anymore," Ava whispers, continuing to run her fingers through my hair in a soothing motion.

My body shakes as I let out gentle sobs, finally giving in to all the built-up emotions that I've held in for so long. We sit there in silence for a while as I let it go, until the last of my tears run free and I can breathe properly again.

"I want to show you something," I say, pulling back from her and wiping at my wet face. In one swift motion, I reach behind my head and pull my shirt over my head, dropping it on the bed beside us.

Ava's lips part as she stares down at my bare torso, desire sparking in her eyes before she's blinking it back. "You're stripping."

A smile tugs at my mouth. "Let me turn around."

She scootches off my lap, and I give her my back, showing her the ink etched deep in my skin. Her fingers start to trace the tattoo, and I shudder.

"I got it for my dad. You're now the only person besides Mom and Gray that know the meaning behind it."

Ava sucks in a breath and kisses my right shoulder and then my left.

"I remember being so pumped the day my mom agreed to sign off on me getting it. It was my sixteenth birthday, and after two years of nagging every day for her to let me get the damn thing, she finally caved.

"The tattoo artist and I had spent hours redrawing the design until I decided it was good enough. I'll never forget Mom's face when I showed her. Her eyes welled up the second they landed on the paper."

The tattoo is a scene of sorts—a memory. It's set in the middle of winter, with piles of fluffy, white snow and tall, bare trees sitting along the bank of a frozen lake. A young boy dressed in full hockey gear is winding up his hockey stick, ready to shoot the puck into the nearby net. Hutton is written across the back of the boy's jersey, above the number eleven. My dad's lucky number and now mine.

Yet the most meaningful part of the tattoo is the cross hidden between the trees and behind the snowbank. It's hidden because written on the cross is the date my father passed away.

"It's beautiful."

"It is," I agree.

"You know he's proud of you, right?" Ava murmurs.

Is he? I like to think so. I've tried to be the best man I can, not wanting to let him down. All I can do now is hope he's happy with what he sees.

Turning back around, I hover my face a breath from Ava's and slide a hand around the back of her neck, palming her nape. I tilt her head back and kiss her so suddenly I'm swallowing her gasp of surprise.

It doesn't take her long to snap back, and once she does, her hot palms crash against my bare chest as she starts to explore the hard-earned muscles and ridges there. Nails scratch along the trail of hair leading below my jeans, and I groan at the pleasure that sparks.

"You mean so much to me," I breathe against her wet, swollen lips. With steady hands, I grab her hips and pull her back to my lap, chomping on my lower lip when her core slides along the growing bulge in my pants.

"You mean the world to me," she sighs, her head lolling forward, forehead hitting my chest. A shiver shakes her body. "God, that feels good."

I slowly guide her back and forth over me, and she whimpers, making me throb and seep precum into my boxers. "I'm so hard for you, Ava. So fucking hard."

"I'm ready." She moves her head, and I drop my eyes, finding her staring up at me. The air is charged around us, our desire so thick and heavy it's hard to breathe.

I swallow my groan. "I didn't tell you about my dad to sleep with you, baby."

She holds my face in her hands and drifts her thumbs over my cheekbones. "I know. I'm ready because I love you."

*That's all it takes.* The dam holding me back from devouring her comes crashing down, and I flounder with the new emotions humming in my veins.

She moans when I take her mouth and part her lips with my tongue, taking and taking from her.

"I love you too," I rasp, dragging my lips over her chin and to the underside of her jaw. "I want to show you how much." Thrusting up against her, I suck at the pulsing skin of her throat and move my hands up her sides, beneath her shirt. She's covered in goosebumps.

"Yes—do that, please."

In one quick motion, I toss her back on the bed and crawl over her. She parts her legs for me, and I settle between them, grinning down at her in appreciation.

"I've thought about this moment way too much. Fuck, look at you—so beautiful." It scrapes up my throat. The way her eyes flare at the compliment urges me to push back to my knees and really take her in.

Well-kissed pink lips, flushed skin, and a rapidly rising chest as she tries to catch her breath. What a vision. And it's all mine.

I swallow heavily and finger the hem of her shirt, slowly pushing it up her stomach, revealing sliver upon sliver of freckled, pale skin. She watches me with laser focus the entire time, and when I stop with the green material bunched beneath her breasts, she just smiles coyly and pushes it up and over them, exposing her black bra and the two nipples trying to poke through the cups.

"Shit," I hiss. With two hands, I quickly pull the cups down and pull a hard peak into my mouth, nipping at it before flicking away the sting. Ava bucks off the bed and pushes more of her breast into my mouth. I gently bite down on her nipple again before switching sides and giving it the same attention.

"Good, baby?" I release the peak with a pop.

Her fingers find my hair, and she scratches at my scalp. "I need more."

I hum low in my throat but don't make her beg. Her jeans are easy to undo, and she lifts her hips to help me pull them down before I toss them to the side. Again, she lets her legs part, but this time, it's to find her wet and slick, her pretty pussy stuck to the scrap of material keeping me from seeing her bare.

"*Jesus Christ*. Can I get rid of them? I need to taste you."

She nods eagerly. "Yes. Please."

With that, I'm reaching for her panties and pulling them down her legs and flinging them across the room.

I groan at the sight of her. Pink and slick just for me. Licking my lower lip, I palm her thighs and push her knees up toward her, opening her up for me.

"Hold them there, baby." I release her legs and make a noise of appreciation when she does as I said. Gently, I run my finger over her slit, feeling how wet she is before sinking it deep.

Her pussy grips me so tight my cock jerks, wanting its turn. Ava opens her mouth, but no sound comes out, and for some reason, I need to hear her. That's what drives me to add a second finger and put my mouth on her, giving her glistening pussy a soft kiss.

"Ah," she whispers, reaching for me and grabbing my head. I grin and slip my tongue over her, running it over her slit and up to her clit. It's so swollen I find it instantly, and she cries out. *Fuck yes*. Much better.

I suck on it, and she bucks up before I pull back and lick my lips. "Not too loud—you don't want everyone to hear, do you?" She shakes her head, watching me, hungry with desire. "Good girl. Now, let me eat."

I dive back in, this time flattening my tongue and swiping from top to bottom, drinking her in, desperate for more. With my fingers still inside, I curl them and lightly tap the spongy wall I find.

"Oakley—right there. Right there," she whimpers, and I press on it harder at the same I bite gently on her clit.

"That's it. Come for me, baby. Be a good girl and let me taste you," I growl.

I sound like a wild animal, but it only seems to make me harder.

I'm desperate for her, and I want her to damn well know it.

Like magic, her walls quiver around my fingers. My scalp starts to burn when she pulls at my hair, but it only urges me on. I pull my fingers out as soon as her back curls and replace them with my tongue, fucking her with it as she comes.

I lick her through her orgasm before placing more gentle kisses on her pussy, over her thighs, and up her stomach. Swirling my tongue around her belly button, I memorize the sound of her content sighs.

By the time I'm sucking at her throat, she's a wiggling mess beneath me. Her hands are all over my body, scratching at my skin and pulling me as close as she can get me. Knowing I make her feel like this does things to me that, if I'm not careful, will go right to my head.

"Get your clothes off," she urges, lifting her legs and pushing at my jeans with the heels of her feet. I pull back and smirk at the marked skin of her neck. Her eyes go wide. "You didn't just give me a hickey."

I start to unbutton my jeans. "I've just eaten your pussy and you're worried about a hickey?"

"Your mom and sister will see a hickey. Nobody has to know you ate me out."

Standing up, I shove my jeans and boxers down my legs in one go before kicking them off. "I'm about to do a lot more than just lick your pussy, baby."

Her eyes fall to my cock as I grip it in a tight fist and give it a slow pump. There's a bead of precum on the tip that I spread around with my thumb.

"Let me," Ava whispers, crawling across the bed. She stares up at me with blazing green eyes, and I curse when her tongue darts out from between her lips and slides across the head. A strangled noise burns my throat when she suddenly takes me in her mouth.

Her tongue dances across the underside as she takes as much of me into her mouth as she can before pulling back, focusing on the tip. When she licks the slit, I bury my hands in her hair, threading it through my fingers and trying not to rip it out as pleasure builds and builds.

"*Fuck.* Just like that," I groan, breathless.

Tentatively, her fingers find my balls, cupping and rolling them, and that's when I pull out of her mouth and toss her back on the bed.

"Later," I tell her when she blinks at me, confused. Before she can say anything else, I've grabbed a condom from my bag and joined her on the bed. "Is this what you want? We only do this if you're sure."

She nods. "God, yes. I want this."

I grin and rip open the foil, settling between her legs before rolling the condom on.

Her eyes meet mine, and they hold, locking together as I line us up and drag my length through her wet flesh, getting it slick before pressing inside. She's so tight, and I move slowly, not wanting to hurt her. Fuck, the idea of hurting her makes my stomach roll.

"I love you," I croak when I get halfway before pulling back and pressing in again. This time, I sink deep, bottoming out. Her breath hitches as she stretches around me, her pussy sucking me in like it wants to keep me there forever.

"Are you okay?" I rasp, hating the way she winces when I hold in place, too worried to move.

Ava cups my cheeks and pulls my face to hers before kissing me softly, softer than I was expecting. My eyes flutter shut as I drop to my forearms beside her and trace her jaw with my thumb.

"I love you too," she breathes. "Now, please move. You're huge, and I haven't had sex in a long time. I just needed to adjust; you weren't hurting me."

I drop my forehead to hers and watch the pleasure and relief flick across her face as I pull out and thrust back in, rolling my hips before doing it again and again.

Ava's lips part in a silent cry when I lean back and toss her legs over my shoulders, pressing deeper, moving harder. My jaw aches from how hard I've been clenching it, the pleasure too good, too fucking intense.

Somewhere in my mind, I'm reminded that we should be quieter, softer, but I shove it all away. The only thing I can focus on is Ava. On the love in her eyes and the near suffocating feeling of obsession I feel for her.

This isn't soft or gentle. It's intense and overwhelmingly intoxicating. She's giving everything to me, and I'm taking just as much as I'm giving back. This girl is my world, my sun and fucking stars. She has me—all of me—in the palm of her hands, and I don't think she even realizes it.

"You're mine, Ava," I hiss through my teeth. She clenches around me, and a growl rumbles in my chest.

Her eyes are glossy, dazed as she stares at me and grips my bicep. "I'm so yours.

I turn my head and nip at her ankle before dropping my hand between her legs and finding her clit. Her lips part on a moan, and I know she's close. The sounds that fill the room are obscene, but I'm too far past caring if anyone hears. I need my girl to come.

"Come, Ava." She fights to keep her eyes open as I flick her clit back and forth. "Milk this cock, baby. Fucking drain me."

It's like a trigger. As if I just flicked a switch, she's clenching around me and crying out so loud I have to cover her mouth with my hand. I'm right there beside her, fucking her through her orgasm before stilling, buried to the hilt.

"I feel like I can't move," she wheezes as soon as I pull out and collapse on top of her.

"I'm not that heavy."

Her laugh is heaven. "Not because of that. Because you just screwed me boneless."

I kiss all over her chest and neck before finally reaching her pink lips. "Good. Now, let me clean you up, and then get in this bed with me. I'm not letting go of you again today." *If ever.*

She softly rubs our noses together. "I like that plan."

# 27

## Ava

I'M SMILING. LIKE I HAVE BEEN SINCE LAST NIGHT. I DON'T THINK I've stopped once. Not even when Oakley walked me to my car this afternoon and kissed me goodbye or when I sat in the passenger seat and listened to Tyler's endless playlist of rock music for four hours.

My head is light, and my heart is soaring.

I should feel nervous being this happy, but I just can't. Not yet. I'm going to live in this bubble of bliss for as long as I can.

The soreness between my legs is a reminder of why I'm so high in the clouds, but it isn't the sole reason. Oakley is. God, the way that man makes me feel is something I certainly wasn't ready for. Not by a long shot.

I wasn't supposed to fall for a hockey player, let alone one with a future ahead of him that has a high probability of pulling us apart. But I can't find it in myself to regret it. Not when Oakley is that guy. The guy with the wild heart that he wears on his sleeve and a protectiveness so fierce it's almost lung seizing.

He makes me feel safe and loved, and I trust him more than I think I've ever trusted someone before. That's probably ridiculous—it feels ridiculous to admit to myself—but it's the truth. One hundred percent of it.

The apartment door is locked when I try to turn the knob, but before I can find my key, it's being unlocked and whipped open.

"Thank God! I thought you would never get home," Morgan squeals, ushering me inside.

"I was gone for one night." I laugh. Shrugging off my jacket, I watch Morgan curiously. She's bouncing in place, staring at me. "Did you do something bad while I was gone? You look weird."

"Wow, thanks." Her lips form a straight line.

"Oh, stop. You know what I meant."

"Maybe I just missed you."

I lift a brow. "Did you?"

"Of course I did. You want to hang out today?"

I laugh again. "See, you're being weird. Since when do you ask me to hang out and not just demand it?"

She scowls. "You're really out for blood today. Luckily, I'm in the mood for some gossip, and since I know you're just brimming to your lid with it, I'll forgive you for being so mean."

Suddenly, it all clicks into place. "You want to know what happened at Oakley's."

"Well, obviously. You stayed the night."

"I did."

She huffs. "So? Are you down to hang out and spill the beans? We can go last-minute Christmas shopping like we love so much."

I hang up my coat and drag my overnight bag to my room. Morgan is hot on my tail. "It's Christmas Eve. Is anything even open?"

"The mall is open for a few more hours. Just drop the damn bag, and let's go."

I toss it on my bed instead and cringe when all of my clothes spill out the top. "Guess I forgot to zip it."

Morgan turns to me, her eyebrows waggling. "Nice panties. Real sexy."

"Shut up." I haphazardly start pushing the clothes off my bed and into a makeshift pile on the floor. "And stop looking at my panties."

"Okay, okay. It's not like I've helped you pick out half of your sexy collection or anything."

Ignoring her, I gather the pile of clothes in my arms and deposit them in my closet. Then, I swivel on my heels and leave Morgan laughing to herself in my room.

"Okay, I'm sorry. Sheesh, maybe you didn't get laid like I thought."

I roll my eyes. "Oh, I definitely got laid." As if summoned, the pain between my legs flares. "Great, now I'm sore again. Thanks."

"You're sore? Oh my God. Tell me everything!" she shrieks from behind me.

"I thought you wanted to go shopping?" I glance at her over my shoulder as I tug my mittens back on and laugh at the look of desperation on her face. "Come on, you're driving."

"Deal! I'm right behind you."

*Ah, it's good to be home.*

❄

"HAVE you gotten Matt's gift yet?" I ask when we enter the busy mall. There are so many people here my skin prickles with discomfort, but I suck it up.

As much as I didn't really want to have to go to an over-crowded mall right after a four-hour road trip, I do need a gift for Oakley. I pushed it too far, but it wasn't until yesterday that I knew what I was going to get him.

"Yeah. I got him some new sneakers and a framed photo of us from his cousin's wedding because I'm that girlfriend. There aren't nearly enough photos of us in that apartment of theirs. I think Braden has been hiding them so his one-night stands don't see anything womanlike when he ends up shagging them on the couch or something."

"You're probably right. Matt loves having pictures of you all over the place, so it isn't him hiding them."

"I can't wait for the day Braden finds a girlfriend. Good luck to her," Morgan grumbles.

"Do you really think he'll ever settle down? He's like Tyler but worse."

"Speaking of Tyler," Morgan sings, and I groan. *Walked right into that one.* "Did he behave at Anne's? Or better yet, did you?"

"He was very well-mannered and respectful, yes."

She pinches my hip. "You damn well know I don't really care how he behaved."

I gasp. "Really?"

"I literally hate you."

"No you don't. Now, come out and ask what you want to know. You already know I slept with Oakley."

She grabs my arm and pulls me to a quieter section of the mall. She stares at me with stars in her eyes. "But how *was* it? Do you love him?" I bite my lower lip, but my smile is hard to contain. It spreads of its own will. "You do. Oh my God. You love that guy."

"I do."

Her grin is wide enough to rival mine. "And? Did you tell him?"

"I did."

"Stop with the blunt answers! I'm losing my cool over here, and you're acting all relaxed and put together. Gah!"

I giggle. "I'm sorry. I guess I'm still getting used to it. It's like an out-of-body experience."

"Did he tell you it back? Please tell me he did." She clasps her hands beneath her chin.

"He did. Isn't that crazy?"

"What do you mean? You're fucking amazing. How could he not love you?"

"That's not what I meant." I frown.

"Good. Because if anyone is lucky here, it's *him*. He gets to be loved by you. The girl who loves with her entire fucking soul."

My eyes mist with the heavy emotion swelling in my chest. This is my best friend right here. My ride or die.

"Thank you, Mo."

She rolls her eyes, but her smile says everything she doesn't. *You're welcome.* "Now, let's stop standing around and get to work."

Arm in arm, we head down one of the wings of the mall and come to a stop in front of a sports store. Morgan makes an excited noise while I fiddle with my purse strap, nerves stroking my spine. The sales associate is using one of those long pokers to hang Boston jerseys on a tall hook but quickly flashes us a smile when he sees us gawking in the store.

"Wanna head in and get a good long look at what a hockey store looks like before your man's name is all over everything? It might be your last chance to browse without being mauled," Morgan suggests with a shrug.

I twist my mouth. "Not exactly selling me on the idea. But I do need to go in to get his gift."

"I'm just saying. It's not a far-fetched idea, Ava—it more than likely will be a reality. Especially now that you're serious."

"I know. Trust me, *I know*."

She gives me an analyzing look before leading us into the store. Without so much as sparing a glance at the basketball and baseball merchandise that's only maybe a third of the store, she pulls me to the much larger hockey section before finally releasing my arm.

I find the Vancouver Warriors jerseys without player names on the backs and start riffling through the first row of them.

"What is it you're getting Oakley, anyway? Doesn't he already have a thousand hockey jerseys?"

"What size do you think he is?" I ask, ignoring her previous question.

She starts to look through the racks closest to her. "Giant size?"

I snort. "Thanks. That narrows it down."

"Can I help you ladies find anything? Are you looking to customize a jersey?"

My head snaps up, and I find the same sales associate from when we first entered the shop standing a few steps behind Morgan. He looks around our age, with a very symmetrical facial structure and blond hair cut close to his scalp. His lips tug in a grin.

"Yeah. What size jersey do you buy for a six-foot-three, two-hundred-and-twenty-three-pound hockey player?" Morgan asks, spouting off the numbers like it's nothing. When I stare at her in disbelief, she shrugs. "I know his stats. Sue me."

The guy is quiet for a minute, seemingly as shocked as I am, before he recovers. "Is this for just daily wear or like over gear for shinny games or whatever?"

They both look at me, and I splutter, "Uh, it's not really for him to wear."

"What?" they ask at the same time.

"It will be more of a keepsake, I guess. I don't know what exactly he'll do with it."

"That's an expensive keepsake," the guy mumbles, looking at me weird. I chew on the inside of my cheek to keep from biting back. "Anyway, in that case, I would suggest ordering a size down from what he usually wears. They fit big, and if he's not going to be wearing it over any gear, you shouldn't need a bigger size."

"Okay, and what size is that?" Morgan asks.

The guy furrows his brows, seemingly frustrated with our lack of knowledge. "You guys don't know his regular size? Like his everyday sweaters or anything?"

"Well, neither of us are his mother, so no," Morgan grinds out.

I swallow my laugh. "What would a large look like? I should

be able to eyeball I if I see it." *Maybe if they didn't have such weird sizing for hockey jerseys and instead just used the regular sizing system, this never would have been a problem.*

He picks one off the rack and holds it in the air. It looks pretty big, but I'll keep the receipt in case.

"Looks great. Thanks," I say. He hands it to me. "How long will it take to get a name stitched on the back?"

"I can have it done on Boxing Day."

Morgan comes to stand at my side. "When does he get back?"

"Late on Boxing Day." Another two days, and I *already* miss him. Great. Turning to the sales associate, I say, "That works. Let's do it."

MORGAN DIDN'T END up buying anything at the mall despite being the one to suggest last-minute shopping, but I sort of suspected that it was all a ruse to get info out of me.

She seems sated now, bobbing her head to an Ariana Grande song as she drives us home. The roads have been plowed and salted in the aftermath of the storm, but as I found out the minute Tyler and I got back into town, the storm was much calmer here than where we were.

The drive goes quickly, and soon we're pulling up to the curb and I'm stepping back into the cold. The sun sets too early in the winter, and it's dark on the sidewalk, only a few streetlamps casting a light. With careful steps, I head up the sidewalk, focusing on not slipping on any ice, when I notice Morgan isn't behind me.

Looking over my shoulder, I spot her still in the car. I roll my eyes and stand there with my hands on my hips until she looks up and pulls her phone from her ear, showing it to me. She waves for me to head inside, so I do.

As soon as I get inside the building, I take the stairs two at a time until reaching our floor. When I see a woman leaning against the wall opposite my apartment, I quicken my pace down the hallway, curiosity nipping at me.

If this is one of Adam's one-night stands here to ask me for information, I swear I'll kill him.

As I get closer, I realize she's way too old to be a one-night stand. Or at least I would hope so.

The woman's hair is thin, and a dark shade of brown—nearly black—that highlights just how pale her skin is. Her green eyes are bloodshot as they move to stare back at me, hauntingly vacant.

"Hello? Do you need something?" I ask when I realize she's standing directly in front of my apartment.

She pushes away from the wall and straightens herself, brushing her hands across her torn clothing. The sweatshirt she's wearing isn't exactly the most eye-pleasing piece of clothing I've ever seen. It's stained and faded, and the yellow material hangs loosely on her thin frame.

"You're beautiful," she whispers, her voice rough and faraway. I raise my eyebrows and take a cautious step back from her, gripping my keys tight in my hand.

"Do I know you?" I murmur, panicked and unsure of what to say. The woman flinches back at my question. I want to ask her more but decide against it.

"You don't know who I am?" she asks in disbelief, which only confuses me more.

The sound of the stairwell door slamming shut makes her jump. She steadies herself against the wall and looks in the direction of the noise.

I take my gaze off the woman to see Morgan making her way down the hall, her hands rubbing together due to her lack of mittens. Her eyes bulge when she notices our visitor. Glancing between the two of us, she mouths something at me that I don't understand before pulling back her shoulders and walking right for the woman.

"Who the hell are you?" Morgan asks. She gets no response from her, just an emotionless expression. "Well?"

Still, the woman doesn't speak. She just stares at me like she's waiting for me to suddenly recognize her. I begin to feel even more uncomfortable when she bravely places her hand on my forearm.

I cringe and pull my arm back. "Can you just tell us who you are?"

"I want to talk to you alone. Without her," she adds in a sneer, not hiding her dislike for Morgan.

"Yeah, right. Not happening." Morgan laughs and points her house key at her. "I suggest you scurry away back to whatever hole you crawled out of. I'll call my friends if I have to. My friend's boyfriend here is quite the fighter, and you really wouldn't want to be on the opposing side of his anger. Or mine, for that matter."

I catch what looks like a flash of interest in her eyes before she blinks it away and steps back. She regards Morgan with cautious eyes before turning her gaze back to me.

"Is that what you want, Octavia?"

How does she know my name? My heart pounds in fear, hands beginning to tremble.

"Who are you talking about? We don't even know an Octavia, you wack job," Morgan lies smoothly. She steps in front of me as if to shield me and pulls her phone out of her coat pocket. "Last chance. All I have to do is send one message, and you'll be in for a whole world of trouble."

"Just five minutes. That's all I want," the woman pleads.

"For what?" I ask cautiously.

"I don't want to talk about it here. Can we meet for coffee sometime?"

Morgan's laugh is dark. "No. You can't meet my best friend for coffee sometime. We don't even know who the hell you are."

The woman just continues to look at me, and my stomach rolls when I finally make out flecks of brown and dark blue circling her pupils. They're too similar to the ones in my eyes, but also not enough to be completely positive.

That doesn't stop my skin from flushing cold, though. Or the bile from creeping up my throat.

"Sure. Give me your number and I'll call you," I rush out. She needs to leave right now, and I know this is the only way to make sure she does.

"What are you doing?" Morgan asks me in a hushed tone. I ignore her.

The woman in front of me quickly rambles off a number, and I type it into my phone. When she finishes and I look up from the screen, I nearly keel over.

*Leave, leave, leave.*

"I'll text you. I have to get inside now," I mumble before I'm shoving my key in the lock and stumbling my way inside the apartment. Not even the familiar smell of home can soothe my stomach.

I don't stop moving until I reach the bathroom. Dropping to my knees in front of the toilet, I retch and retch until the only thing coming up is memories of my broken childhood.

# 28

## Oakley

CHRISTMAS MAY HAVE COME AND GONE, BUT THAT ISN'T STOPPING our group of misfits from celebrating together, like our own little family. Even if it is a week late.

It's a supposed tradition for everyone to get together before Christmas break ends to exchange gifts and run a movie marathon. This year, they're doing it at the girls' apartment.

My friends back home never did anything like this. Sure, we would go out to eat after games, and Andre and I would hang out at my place more often than not, but the dynamic of my new friends here is surprising. In a good way.

They care about each other in a way that surpasses just friends. In every way that counts, they're a family. And I think I'm a part of that family now. Or at least, I hope I am. I want to be.

Ava is rushing around the apartment when I get back from stopping at the grocery store. With two full bags of food in my hands, I watch her switch on each set of Christmas lights strung over nearly every surface. The edge of the island, the tops of the kitchen cabinets, hell, even the TV has been decorated with multicoloured lights.

It's nice to see her smile like this again. Rebecca's drop-in outside of the girls' apartment tore Ava right up. She left my house on cloud nine, and I found her two days later, hurt and betrayed.

My first instinct was to track down the woman who thought it was okay to blindside my girl like that, but I knew that would only make it worse. So I held her as she cried over someone who was far from deserving of her tears, and then she woke up the next morning with that happy gleam in her eyes again.

I'm still worried, but I've laid off. Ava is strong, and I know this won't break her.

"You look like a Christmas elf," I say, dropping the bags on the counter before walking over to her as she moves on to the tree, fiddling with the candy canes hanging from the branches.

"A cute one, I hope."

I gather her in my arms and pull her to my chest, kissing the top of her head. She smells like peppermint, and I take a long inhale. "Damn right. The cutest."

She relaxes in my hold. "I debated wearing a cute little elf hat, but I figured it would be a bit much."

"Do you have one?"

"Of course I do," she guffaws.

I smirk. "Wear it tonight. I've also wanted to bang an elf."

She spins in my arms, staring at me in disbelief. "Really?"

"No. But I still want you to wear it."

"You're a goof." She giggles and slips out of my arms, going to the Bluetooth speaker on the coffee table and turning it on. It rings out, saying that it's connected to her phone, before Mariah Carey's "All I Want For Christmas Is You" starts to play.

I cock a brow. "Really?"

Ava's eyes twinkle, the flecks in her eyes nearly glowing. "It's a classic."

"Would it be cheesy if I said that all I want for Christmas is you?" I ask, my voice low. Feeling incredibly sentimental, I close the distance between us and plant my hands on her hips, pulling her flush against me.

She glances up at me and smiles softly. "Yes. But it seems that I like cheesy when it comes to you."

"I missed you."

It was only a couple of days, but I did. The moment she left, the only thing I wanted was to bring her right back and never let her leave my side again.

"We're helpless," she whispers.

"I can't find it in me to care."

I bend down, and she pushes up on her toes, our lips meeting in a slow kiss. Her fingers slide up my chest and tangle in the hair curling behind my ear, toying with it. It makes me shiver, pressing harder against her, bringing her even closer.

Someone knocks at the front door, but I trace her bottom lip with my tongue, refusing to let her go. As soon as she parts those soft lips for me, I'm diving in, sucking on her tongue and swirling, drowning in her taste but refusing to come up for air.

The knocking starts again, this time harder.

Ava's hands drift down the sides of my neck, pressing into my shoulder muscles before lying flat on my pecs. Slowly, she starts to push herself back.

I chase her mouth with short kisses until she starts to laugh and softly swats at my chest. "I need to answer that."

"Go answer it, then." I smirk, pressing my fingertips into her waist, loving the way she turns to putty in my hands. I'm able to steal another kiss before she breaks away.

The silver bells hanging from the doorknob jingle as she pulls open the front door. She beams at the guests waiting on the other side. "Merry Christmas!"

"Merry Christmas, beautiful," I hear Adam say. The compliment grates my nerves.

I move fast, coming up behind Ava and pulling her back to my chest, lacing my fingers across her stomach. "Merry Christmas, guys."

"Merry Ho-Ho, Lee. Where should I put these?" Matt steps forward, holding a massive Santa sack out in front of him.

"Are those presents?" Ava squeals. Matt nods and starts to look around the apartment.

"He almost forgot them. We were halfway here when we had to turn back around," Tyler puts in from behind him.

"Hey, way to throw me under the bus. I got them here, didn't I?" Matt rolls his eyes, and the guys come inside.

He drops the bag beneath the tree, beside the expertly wrapped gifts already there. As the living room starts to fill with everyone, I make sure to snag a seat at the end of the couch, beside Matt.

"Did I hear something about presents?" Morgan comes strolling out of her bedroom. Finally.

Matt smirks, eyeing his girl up like his next meal. I wonder if that's what I look like when I check Ava out. *Probably.*

"Not for you. You didn't help get this ready at all," Ava says from beside the couch, a tray of cookies in her hands.

"Like you would have let me help, anyways." Morgan swipes a cookie off the plate and moves over to sit down on Matt's lap. Ava rolls her eyes, sets the cookies down on the coffee table, and sits down next to Adam on the other side.

*Yeah, right.*

I stand from the couch and pick her up, carefully placing her in my lap once I've sat again. She lifts her brows at me over her shoulder. "What?"

She hums, disbelieving.

"The PDA is fucking gross," Tyler grunts, sitting down on the floor in front of Adam.

"You just need to get laid," Matt says, taking his attention away from Morgan for the first time since she plopped down in his lap.

"I do get laid."

"Are we talking in terms of your hand or a living, breathing woman?" Adam chuckles.

"I'm not talking about this with you," Tyler snaps.

Matt roars a laugh. "Your hand, then."

"I'll kick your ass, Matthew."

"Ooh, I love it when you say my full name."

I press my face to Ava's back and laugh, a warmth spreading through me. These guys are complete idiots, but they're my idiots.

"Look on the bright side, Ty. Oakley's little sis is more than ready to move mountains for you. Give it a few years and I'm sure you could reach out and ask for a coffee date," Matt teases, his eyebrows dancing. Morgan smacks his arm.

I take back my previous sentiment. "Tyler's not going to touch Gracie. Now or *ever*," I grind out. "She'll snap out of her fascination soon enough. She's a smart girl."

"Underage girls aren't really my type, Oakley," Tyler snips.

The thought of my sister even thinking about one of my friends in a romantic way makes my skin crawl. No way in hell would I ever let that happen. Not in this lifetime.

"It's just a cute, harmless crush, so don't go teasing her about it. Any of you," Ava threatens, pointing an accusing finger at the guys.

"I agree. I had a crush on Ava's brother for like two years," Morgan admits with a shrug.

"You *what*? Why didn't I know about this?" Matt demands, his eyes narrowed.

Ava laughs, covering for Morgan while she stumbles for an explanation. "I think all of my friends liked Ben. Don't worry, Matt." Ava pats Matt on the arm. "Plus, I think he's going to propose to his girlfriend soon."

"Eep! A wedding is on the horizon," Morgan sighs dreamily.

Adam laughs. "Hear that, Matty boy? Morgan wants to get married soon."

"She didn't say that," he sputters.

"Read between the lines, bro," Adam chides.

Matt spins Morgan in his arms, his expression completely open. He bares his soul to her like it's no big deal. "You want to get married soon?"

His girlfriend just laughs, fussing with his hair. "That depends. Are you going to propose to me soon?" Matt's lips part, but no words come out. "I would marry you any day. But maybe let's graduate first, yeah?"

Ava stares at me over her shoulder, and I pull her close. She rests against my chest and sighs, content.

Yeah, these are my people.

EXHAUSTED, I sigh as soon as the door shuts behind Adam and Tyler, and the nearly engaged couple heads off to Morgan's room.

"I think I'm in a food coma," Ava moans.

I shift my gaze from the glimmering lights hung over the front door to Ava's outstretched body on the couch. Her eyelashes flutter as she tries to keep her eyes open.

"You want to go to bed?" I ask softly.

She hums and pushes up on her arms. "Are you staying?"

"If that's okay?"

"Of course. Merry Christmas to me." She winks.

I shake my head, the ghost of a smile tugging at my mouth. In a few strides, I'm in front of her. I bend over the couch, slide one arm under her knees, and cradle her back with the other as I lift her and walk us to her room.

"You don't have to carry me. You were just injured," she protests.

"I was. But I'm fine now, and I want to carry you."

"Fine."

I chuckle when she goes lax and snuggles her face into the spot where my neck and shoulder connect. "Did you have a good Christmas?"

"The best."

The bracelet I got her dangles from her wrist, the charms making a soft jingle noise when they hit each other: a Converse sneaker, an old truck that I had to custom order from the lady in the store, and a star with her birthstone in the centre.

When we all exchanged presents, I wasn't expecting everyone to get such elaborate, thought-out gifts. It shouldn't have surprised me, seeing as how well everyone knows each other, but it was a good surprise.

"I have something else for you," Ava whispers when I set her on the bed.

She doesn't look at me as she gets off the bed and drops to the floor, digging around beneath the frame. When she pulls her hands back, they're holding a large brown box.

"Morgan used the rest of the wrapping paper before I could get to this."

"I don't care about wrapping. You already got me a present, sweetheart." A damn nice black-and-red hockey stick. It was both thoughtful and useful, considering I go through them like crazy.

She shrugs. "I got you two."

There's a shake in her hands when she stands and hands over the box. She's nervous, and for some reason, that makes me nervous. And excited.

I sit on the edge of the bed and pat the spot beside me. Only after she's sitting, her thigh brushing mine, do I open the box.

After I lift the lid, I peel back the snowflake-printed tissue paper and freeze. My swallow is audible.

"If you hate it, I can return it," Ava rambles.

I will my fingers to move, and they brush the green jersey, over the letters stitched on the back. My lungs burn, but I swear I'm breathing. My eyes sting, but I blink away the feeling, keeping the name and number in front of me clear, visible.

*Jamie #11*

Ava touches my arm. "Are you okay?"

My laugh is wet, heavy with emotion. "Yeah, baby. I'm okay. Better than."

"But you're crying. I didn't mean to make you cry."

"This is the best gift I've ever gotten."

She sighs, relieved. "You should have something that reminds you of all the good memories. He may be gone, but he'll always be with you."

This girl. *This damn girl.*

"I don't think I could be any more in love with you if I tried," I admit bluntly. I'm completely down for this girl. There's nothing keeping me from her—no guard at the gates of my heart, no fears or secrets. I'm completely hers, and I feel so goddamn free. "There aren't words to explain it. Fuck, I would drop my heart at your feet if I thought that would work."

She leans her head on my shoulder and laughs, the sound shaky. "Don't do that. I have no use for it on the ground."

I turn to her, my gaze unguarded. Fucking soul baring. "This isn't something I ever want to let go of."

"So don't let go. Please."

Her words stroke something inside of me, something unfamiliar but reassuring. It turns me curious, hopeful even.

"Humour me for a second," I say before I lose my edge and chicken out.

She nods, and I rest my cheek against her head. "Okay."

"Once you finish school, do you want to stay in Vancouver?"

"I'm not sure. I don't see why I would have to."

"Not *have* to, Ava. *Want* to."

A pause. "Where are you in this hypothetical situation?" she asks softly.

"Not in Vancouver."

She blows out a breath. "Then no. I wouldn't want to be here."

A slow smile parts my lips as I turn my face into her hair. Hope rushes through me. Her words hold a promise that I couldn't miss if I tried.

"I'm never going to dye my hair blonde, though," she adds.

I pull back and snort a laugh. "Why would you do that?"

Her eyes glimmer with humour. "I've been looking, and almost every NHL player has a blonde girlfriend."

I laugh and slide my arm over her shoulders, pulling her close. "Consider me the odd one out, then."

There isn't a damn thing I would change about Ava. Not one.

# 29

## Ava

AFTER CHRISTMAS BREAK, LIFE CONTINUES ON LIKE NORMAL. Students are back at school, and everyone else has gone back to work. New Year's brought in exciting resolutions for everyone to commit to until February, when they begin to neglect them. Christmas trees were shoved into their boxes and hidden somewhere until next year. No more joyful music plays in coffee shops.

By February, everything has gone back to the norm.

The hockey season is now in full swing, and the Saints are playing better than ever now that Oakley is back. Playoffs are approaching at an alarming rate, and tensions are at an all-time high. The Saints are holding the top spot in the league, but with that, it's brought a ton of pressure. Oakley is handling it all really well, but I've begun to worry that he's piling too much on his shoulders.

We've spent every spare moment together, learning everything there is to know about one another, even things I wish I didn't know about him. Like what his gym bag smells like at the end of the week and that he puts raw eggs in his preworkout smoothie. I'm sure he wishes he didn't know that I only drink juice out of the carton, but it's too late for that.

He left on a last-minute trip to St. Paul, Minnesota, to meet with the general manager of the Woodmen this morning. His agent told him that while it's a bit unethical to be flown out to meet with a team, it would be a waste to refuse the offer of not only a first-class round trip but also a full arena tour and a team meet-and-greet, so Oakley agreed, even though he won't be home until the morning of their game this weekend.

It's also been two weeks since I've seen Adam, and I've decided to finally put a stop to the distance he's put between us. That's why I'm storming up his driveway right now, trying not to slip on compacted, slick snow that looks to have been driven over but not shovelled for quite a while.

My stomach twists at the realization that Adam's father never would have let it get this bad had he been home recently.

I stand in front of the door and will myself to knock. I take a few deep breaths, desperately trying to relax. I'm not sure why I'm so nervous; Adam is my best friend, not a stranger, even if that's what he's felt like lately.

The door swings open, exposing a dishevelled Adam before I get a chance to pull my big-girl panties on. His eyes widen at the sight of me on his parents' doorstep unannounced.

I raise my eyebrows pointedly at his appearance. He's only in a pair of plaid boxers and white socks—quite the getup. His chest is sweaty, and I crinkle my nose.

"Who is it, babe?" a vaguely familiar voice squeaks from somewhere in the huge house.

Adam pushes past me, closing the door behind him. With a hand ghosting my back, he starts to lead me away from the door. "What are you doing here?"

I smirk, wiggling my eyebrows suggestively. "Who was that?"

"Nobody. Just some girl from the bar," he stammers, avoiding eye contact. "Why are you here? We don't have plans, do we?"

"No, I came here to talk. If it's a bad time, I can come back," I offer. His dismissal is surprising and, honestly, a bit wounding.

"No, it's fine. Just let me change, and we can go get coffee or something. Stay here. I'll be right back." He rushes inside, leaving me standing here, utterly confused.

What the hell just happened? He's never had a problem parading his conquests around me before. Why is he being so dismissive and secretive?

The door swings open again, and I have to suppress a gasp when I see a pair of narrowed blue eyes.

"You," the girl sneers, stepping outside.

Beth Winston is the last person on Earth I expected to come out of Adam's house wearing nothing but a baggy T-shirt. One with the Saints logo on the front in bold letters.

I scowl. "Beth Winston, what a pleasant surprise. I thought I recognized your squeal."

"You should have been here last night, then. You couldn't have missed it."

"That's disgusting," I say, popping my hip. "If you wouldn't mind, I have something important to talk to Adam about. If you could scurry off, I would appreciate it."

"If Adam wants me to leave, he can tell me himself."

"Beth, leave. I'll call you later," Adam sighs from the doorway. He's fully dressed now—in his usual jeans and T-shirt combo.

I stifle a laugh when she flushes.

"Please. I'll call you tonight," he promises, sincerity colouring his tone. *Huh?*

"This isn't over, Octavia." She glares at me and stalks off toward her car, still wearing only Adam's shirt.

"You have a lot of explaining to do," I huff and push past him through the open door.

He doesn't argue, just walks inside without a word. "Want anything to drink? We have ginger ale."

"Ginger ale will only get you so far," I say, my mouth watering at the mention of my favourite drink.

I trudge behind Adam into the industrial-style chef's kitchen and sit down on one of the leather bar stools in front of the marble island. A can is placed in front of me, and I crack it open, drinking it quickly despite the burn from the bubbles.

"She's not that bad, O," he says casually, like it's nothing.

"You're kidding, right? She's the child of Satan."

"I think I could like her." He scratches the back of his neck. "She's different when you get to know her."

I am undeniably having trouble grasping what he's saying. Different when you get to know her? This coming from the guy who completely cut her out of his life years ago?

"Isn't there a best friend code for not fraternizing with the enemy or something? She's rude."

"She's . . . sharp-tongued and isn't afraid to say what's on her mind."

I shake my head in disbelief. "You're actually defending her."

"Yeah, I am. I don't see how this is your business, anyway."

"You're kidding," I splutter. "She's going to end up hurting you. And when somebody hurts you, that is automatically my business. You're my best friend, Adam."

"I'm not a fragile little boy, Ava. For God's sake, I'm a grown man fully capable of making my own decisions. If you're my best friend, then just support me here."

I snap my head up and narrow my eyes. "Supportive? Like you've been so supportive of *my* relationship?"

"I don't know what you're talking about," he snaps.

I shoot up off the stool, and the legs screech against the expensive tile floor. Adam glares at me, his cheeks flushed.

"Don't play dumb. I'm not a stranger. I know when something's up with you. So, spill it. Let it out and tell me what the hell your problem is with Oakley. Is my relationship why you've been ignoring me lately?"

"I'm not having this conversation right now."

He turns to leave, but I grab his arm before he can. "We *are* having this conversation now. You're scaring me. I can't lose you."

His eyes fall to the hand wrapped around his arm, and a look I know too well flicks across his face. As soon as I drop my hand, our eyes meet. The longing in his deep brown eyes is enough to make my heart curl up in a ball.

"Adam." My voice breaks.

He shakes his head. "Don't. Please don't look at me like that."

I dart my eyes around the kitchen and worry my bottom lip. At this rate, I'll bite a hole right through the damn thing.

"Don't put this on your shoulders, O," he says.

"How long?"

"What?"

I can't look at him. "How long have you had feelings for me?"

"Honestly? I don't know. I thought I was content with just being your best friend until Oakley came along. Seeing you with him fucked with my head."

Words escape me. I can't find the right thing to say, if there even is a right thing.

"Do you love him?" Adam asks cautiously, like he's scared of the question. Or my answer.

"I never wanted to hurt you. I didn't know you felt like that." I try to change the subject. The last thing I want to do is hurt him more than I already have.

"Do you? I know he loves you. It's obvious."

"I do. I love him," I breathe.

"Does he make you happy?"

My voice shakes. "Very."

"Then that's all that matters. If you're happy, I'll be happy."

Panic steals my breath. "Am I going to lose you? I don't want to lose you," I whisper. My heart aches at the thought of not having Adam in my life.

"You're not going to lose me," he says without hesitation. "But I need time."

I nod, not knowing what to say.

"I should probably get some training in. With the playoffs coming up and all," he blurts out, dismissing me. I flinch before I can stop myself.

"Right. Okay. I'll see you at the game tomorrow."

"Yeah, of course," he says, wearing a tight smile.

"Oh, okay. Bye, then, I guess," I stammer, wringing my hands in front of me.

"I'll walk you out."

"Great, thanks." I follow him to the door, making sure to keep my distance. Not like it would matter—he's miles away from me right now.

As soon as I slip on my shoes and walk outside, we say a quick goodbye, and I walk to my car, the closing of the front door ringing in my ears.

MY LAPTOP SCREEN goes in and out of focus as I continue to stare at it, my pulse thumping in my head.

I've spent hours in front of this screen, staring at an essay that hasn't grown in word length over the past thirty minutes. The headache is new, only just now blazing in and making my night even worse than it already was.

Morgan is at dinner with her parents, and Oakley landed in St. Paul this afternoon. I flip my phone right side up on my desk and pull up our text conversation. A smile blooms on my face when I reread the messages we sent after he was picked up at the airport by a driver in some luxury SUV and driven off to a hotel with a nightly cost that probably equals my monthly rent.

**Oakley**: *Which state has the smallest drinks?*

**Me**: *Hello to you too*

**Oakley**: *Hey, baby. Now answer my question.*

**Me**: *Okay…Arkan-small?*
**Oakley**: *LOL. Close*
**Me**: *Tell me what it is!*
**Oakley**: *Mini-soda*

He continued to send me Minnesota-themed jokes until he was dropped off at the hotel and switched topics to how he wasn't sure if he would ever be able to fly commercial ever again after experiencing first class.

I know he doesn't want to end up in Minnesota—his dream is to play for the Vancouver Warriors—but the reality of it is that we won't have a choice in where he ends up. It's the luck of the draw, literally.

I've avoided thinking about the draft too much, mostly because it scares the crap out of me but also because it's the start of a new future I still haven't prepared myself for. The fame, the women, the travelling. Sometimes I feel like I'm stuck in a whirlpool of decisions completely out of my control. Like ever since I met Oakley, my future has been taken from my hands and placed in the set of another.

Oakley would never force me to abandon my goals and follow him, but that means another few years of me stuck here and him everywhere else. The thought is enough to have me dropping the topic. But as soon as I hover my fingertips over the keyboard, a knock on the front door startles me.

Confused as to who it could be, I get up and walk to the door. My stomach drops when I look out the peephole and see probably the worst person that could show up here tonight.

*As if I needed anything else to go wrong today.*

Rebecca fiddles with her hands and stares down at her clothes as she waits. She's dressed well, proper, like she's dropped a hefty penny on her wardrobe since the last time she was here.

Maybe she's decided to drop the act. It was clear when I left her standing alone in the hallway of my apartment that day that

I knew exactly who she was. There was no hiding our similarities then, nor is there now.

It's easier to notice now that she isn't covered in grime and whatever else was all over her. Not only do we have the exact same eyes, but also identical high cheekbones and similar swoops at the tips of our noses.

*It doesn't matter*, I remind myself. *It doesn't matter how similar we look, she is no mother of mine.* I take a deep breath and unlock the deadbolt before opening the door.

She's glowing. That's the first thing I notice when we're face to face. She looks healthy. Her hair *shines*, for God's sake.

A few moments of stunned silence pass before she speaks. Even her voice sounds better, clear and steady.

"Hello, Octavia."

"To what do I owe the pleasure, Rebecca?" I deadpan, leaning against the doorframe with my arms crossed. "Why are you here? I told you I would call." It was clearly a lie; I don't think I was ever going to end up calling her. But that should have spoken for itself.

She bows her head. "You didn't call."

"No. I didn't."

She winces but recovers quickly with a warm smile. "Can I come in?"

My immediate reaction is to tell her no and to leave and never come back, but a small voice is pushing me to give it a shot and at least listen to what she has to say. It's not like she deserves my time—far from it—but would it help me finally get over her once and for all? Maybe. Or maybe it will only make it worse.

"For a few minutes. My roommate will be home soon." I take a step back and let her pass through the doorway.

She smells like expensive perfume, the kind you test at the mall but never pull the trigger and buy. I shut the door behind us and watch her kick off her shoes before lining them up against the closet door.

"It's a beautiful apartment," she notes, walking inside.

My skin itches, and I fight off the urge to scratch at my arms. It feels wrong having this woman here. Like I've just invited a predator into my home.

"Thanks. Lily and Derek helped us pick it out."

She stiffens but keeps walking further inside. "They have good taste, then."

I tap the outsides of my thighs. "Do you want something to drink? We can sit on the couch and talk."

"No, thank you. I'm not thirsty," she's quick to say, like it's second nature to deny people when they offer something. I don't push her on it as I sit on the far end of the couch and she sits on the other.

"Are you in school now?" she asks, staring at the pile of discarded textbooks on the coffee table.

"Yeah."

She glances at me. "What are you taking?"

I almost laugh. "Social work."

"Oh," she whispers.

"I want to help kids like me. The ones without families and a trash bag filled with all of their belongings." My molars grind when I shut myself up before the anger inside of me comes barrelling at the woman who abandoned me.

Rebecca swallows before slipping a fake smile across her face. "That's very selfless of you."

"Selfless? Not really. The system is overrun, and children are the ones suffering. If people would just stop giving their children up in the first place once they realize they don't want them—never mind. Sorry."

I can remind myself as many times as I like that it's not always that easy, that sometimes it's the only option and placing judgment isn't right, but my parents left a pit in my chest that's filled with resentment and bitterness.

I hate how it's so easy for them to cloud my judgment. It

won't do me any good once I graduate if I'm assuming the worst of every parent.

Rebecca is as still as a statue, her eyes fixed on a loose piece of stitching on the arm of the couch. Discomfort wraps around my lungs, squeezing tight.

"Don't apologize. You live through your experiences. Yours was a bad one."

A bad one? A *bad* one? This time, I do laugh. "Why are you here, Rebecca? This conversation is about nineteen years too late."

"I don't know why I'm here. I guess . . . I guess I was curious. It's been so long, and I wanted to see what you looked like now. How you're doing."

I shoot up off the couch and face her, my hands clenched. She avoids my stare as I look at her with the same hatred that turns my blood to lava. I can't sit here and pretend that this isn't too little too late. She wants to know how I am? What I look like? *No.*

"You don't get to know how I am or what I look like. You abandoned me. Nobody should have even told you where I am, and trust me, my parents already have a lawyer working on finding out who the hell told you that information. You're the one who requested a closed adoption. It was easier to dump me onto someone else knowing I couldn't ever come find you, right?"

She blinks fast, biting at the inside of her lip. I search her face for any sign of guilt but come up short of anything but embarrassment. Maybe a little shame. That only stokes the flames.

"You don't feel guilt at all, do you?"

Finally, she turns to me, those same green eyes that I stare at every morning when I brush my teeth making my stomach ache as I look into them, like I've spent too long on a spinning ride at an amusement park.

*Whatever this ride is, I need off of it ASAP.*

"Give me a chance, Octavia. Just one."

"It's Ava," I snap. "It's always been just Ava."

She nods. "Okay. Please, just listen, Ava. My boyfriend, he's a good guy. I've moved in with him, and I'm clean—really clean. I haven't touched any drugs in a couple of months. I'm here now, and I want to try and make it up to you."

"I don't think I want that. You still haven't told me how you got my information."

With one large step, she's right in front of me. "I will. I'll tell you everything the next time we meet. Please. Just give me a chance to get to know you. That's it."

I back up. "I need to think about it."

"Okay, yes. Think about it. But you will call me, right?"

"Sure."

She looks wary at my blunt answer. "*Please* call me. I need to see you again."

I dip my chin in a barely there nod. "Yeah. I'll call." *Even if it's just to tell you to get lost.*

"Okay. Okay, good. Great. You'll call," she rambles, smiling now as I gesture to the door. "I'll go, and we'll talk again soon."

"Yeah."

I open the door and watch as she starts to quickly put her high heels back on. There's something about her frantic movements that has me unsettled, but I shove the unwanted feeling back.

She pauses halfway through the doorway. "It was nice to talk to you, Ava."

"Get home safe," I reply before shutting the door and locking the deadbolt again.

Spinning around, I rest my back against the door and close my eyes, hoping that when I open them again, the past few minutes will have all been a figment of my imagination.

# 30

## *Oakley*

THIS WEEKEND HAS COME WITH A LOT OF FIRSTS.

My first trip on a plane not sitting in economy, my first time being picked up at an airport by a man dressed in an expensive suit driving a blacked-out Escalade, and my first time being wined and dined by someone who could potentially offer me a chance to live my dream.

It almost seems backward being schmoozed by those who could give me everything I've ever wanted instead of the other way around. I feel like I should be the one taking Harvey Anderson, the general manager of the Minnesota Woodmen, out for dinner and pulling tricks out of a bag in hopes of impressing *him*.

Harvey is only one of several GMs that my agent and I have agreed to meeting with before the draft, but he is also the only one who has flown me out to *him* instead of coming to Vancouver to see *me*.

Dougie is more than just my agent. He's also my friend, and I trust him as well as I really can, I think. He warned me that this meeting isn't of the usual variety, which could make it a ploy of some type. Seeing as how his wife just gave birth to their third child, he couldn't come with me like he wants to. That's why he wants me to stay sharp tonight, and I plan on doing exactly that.

This morning, I woke up nervous, and as the day went on and I was paraded around the Woodmen arena and locker room like a show pony, I only grew more antsy. There's a feeling nipping at me that I just can't shake, like something isn't right. It's probably ridiculous—it feels ridiculous—but I've always trusted my gut, and right now, it's telling me that something bad could happen tonight. It has me in knots.

I check the time on my phone before firing off a text to my mom, letting her know that I'm going to dinner in an hour and to wish me luck. In half that time, I'm showered, my hair is gelled back for the first time in forever, and my face is shaved bare.

My phone starts to ring from the mattress, and I rush to grab it, not caring anymore how desperate that makes me.

"Hello?"

Ava's laugh feels like coming home as it flows through the speakers and sinks deep in my chest. "One ring. That's got to be a new record."

I sit on the edge of the bed and grin. "You just caught me at the right time. Don't get cocky."

"Never. That doesn't sound like me at all."

"Riiight. I've got you all wrong," I tease.

"It's got me thinking that you haven't really been paying attention." I would bet money that she's smirking right now. Her eyes are probably glimmering the way they do when she's trying to rile me up.

"Oh, baby. I pay attention. Probably too much."

She blows out a long breath like she's annoyed, and it makes me smile. "You can't say stuff like that to me when I'm not there to kiss you."

"Shit, my bad."

"How are you feeling about dinner?"

I fall back on the bed with a sigh. "Nervous. Dougie's put all these things in my head that are messing with my aura or something. I've felt uncomfortably wary all day."

"They're trying to impress you, Boy Scout. Let them pull out the big guns and woo you. What's the worst thing that can happen? They force you to eat salmon and drink draft beer?"

I shudder. The two worst things to exist. "You have a good point."

"What are the odds of Minnesota picking top three in the draft?"

"High, but it's impossible to know."

The Woodmen might look like they'll finish the season at the bottom of the league, but the draft lottery hardly ever goes to plan. They could end up picking in the middle of the pack for all we know.

"So try not to overthink this meeting. Have dinner, and then come back home. Everyone misses you."

"And you?" I ask, needing to hear her say it.

"And me what?"

"Do you miss me?"

"Yeah. I really miss you," she murmurs, and for the first time tonight, I feel ready to do this.

Fifteen minutes later, my driver is pulling up in front of a restaurant with a glowing white sign and a lineup from the door, all the way to the crosswalk at the end of the way.

My suit feels scratchy, even though I've worn it so often I'm sure it's molded to my body. I step out of the SUV and give a quick thank you to the driver before my dress shoes hit the pavement. The door of the restaurant is opened for me by a young-looking guy in a pair of wrinkled slacks and a white button-up. I flash him a smile as I walk inside.

The hostess is already on her way to greet me by the time the smell of garlic and wine hits me. Her high heels tap the floor at a hurried pace, the long skirt of her sunflower-yellow dress smacking her ankles. I pull my shoulders back and shake out my hands.

"Oakley Hutton, please, follow me to the table. Everyone is already waiting," she says in a rush.

"Great, thanks," I reply, my voice too stiff. *Knock it off.*

She leads me to a table at the back of the restaurant, sectioned off from the rest of the customers by a massive fish tank full of colourful fish and a snail suction cupped to the glass. As soon as we round the tank, three sets of eyes zone in on me.

I recognize Harvey straight away. He's an older guy at fifty-three years old, with a receding hairline and a scar across his right cheek from his time in the NHL. He was hit by a puck in his third season—it split that fucker right open and cost him most of his teeth on his right side.

He was a decent, solid defenseman through most of his career but was known for throwing around some questionable hits whenever he felt like the time was right. It's been over a decade since he played.

"Oakley Hutton! I'm so excited to meet you in person. I apologize for my absence earlier today—a meeting popped up I couldn't get away from." Harvey moves around the table with an easy confidence and a sly smile. I shoot my hand out in front of me when he offers me his, and we shake quickly.

"It's nice to meet you, sir. Thank you for taking the time and for flying me out here," I say. My voice is strong now, confident. *Thank fuck.*

Approval flicks across his face before he grabs my shoulder and starts to introduce me to the other two people at the table.

"You've already met our head coach, Jonathon Laredo. He had nothing bad to say about you after showing you around today." The coach smiles at me and lifts his crystal glass in the air before Harvey turns me to face the opposite end of the table, where a woman is sitting beside an empty chair. "And this is my daughter, Ronnie. She's working for the organization alongside me as I prepare her to take over after my retirement. The Woodmen owner wanted to be here, but he's out of the country at the moment."

The woman—Ronnie—parts her lips on a coy smile when I nod my head in greeting. She's tall, dressed in a deep red dress that swoops down far enough I refuse to find out where it ends. I shift on my feet when she wraps long fingers around her wineglass and stares at me with swooped eyelids as she tips it back and drinks the red wine.

"Nice to meet you," I say, looking away.

"You too, Oakley. My father hasn't stopped talking about you for weeks."

Harvey squeezes my shoulder, *hard*. "What can I say? It's not every day we have the chance to meet a future franchise player. Especially one of your calibre."

Ronnie sets her glass down on the table and twirls her finger around the rim. She waves a hand over the empty chair beside her. "Sit, Oakley. You're making everyone nervous."

Jonathon laughs, the sound gruff. "What do you drink? Beer?"

I shake my head and stiffly lower myself into the empty chair. "I don't drink."

"You're not twenty-one, but they won't ask here," Harvey says, sitting in his chair across the table.

"It's not my age, sir. I don't drink at all."

His eyes narrow slightly. "Call me Harvey, please."

I nod.

"Water it is, then," Jonathon grunts and waves his hand in the air for the server.

My eyebrows knit together at the slur in his words, but I don't touch on it. I don't even have the chance to before a server scurries over and Harvey starts spouting off dinner orders. It doesn't bother me much to have my food ordered for me as long as it's not salmon, which, gratefully, it's not. I wouldn't know what to order in a place like this, anyway.

Once the server leaves, Harvey looks at me. "So, how has your stay been?"

"Good, si—Harvey. Thank you again."

"Oh, it's nothing. My pleasure, really. The Woodmen organization wants you to stay in luxury while you're here. Have you gotten a chance to explore the city yet?"

There's a water already sitting in front of me, and I grab it, taking an eager gulp. "Not yet. I hope to do that tomorrow before I leave." I don't plan on exploring because I don't plan on playing here in my entire career unless I'm given no other choice.

"Good, good. What did you think of the team? I know we haven't been a playoff contender in a few seasons, but we can see the light at the end of the rebuild. You would be the missing piece."

Ronnie laughs lowly. "Dad, don't overwhelm him."

"From what I've seen, he doesn't get overwhelmed easily. Do you, Oakley?" Harvey asks, his expression open. I swallow at how obvious his interest in me is.

"No, I don't. I thrive under pressure." It's the truth.

Ronnie shifts her body slightly, just enough for our arms to brush. I inch further away.

"Your agent tells me you favour going to Vancouver or somewhere in Alberta. Is that right?" Harvey asks.

There's something in his voice that sounds off, like me wanting to stay close to home is more of an annoyance to him than anything else.

"Yes. I would prefer to stay close to home if possible."

"Vancouver is doing well this season. It's not looking like they'll pick very high," Jonathon says, his words slurring worse than just minutes before.

I stare at him, unblinking. "I'm aware."

Ronnie leans toward me and purrs, "Vancouver is having a surprising year, but who's to say it isn't a fluke?"

Harvey makes a noise of agreement before clasping his hands in front of him and leaning forward. His eyes are intense as they keep me locked in their sights. It's borderline uncomfortable.

He taps his hands on the table. "I'm going to be honest with you, Oakley. Wherever you land in the draft, you have options. I'm sure your agent has done a good job of letting you know that, but when it comes to Minnesota, nothing is off the table. I mean that. There are no chips we wouldn't move in order to see you in green and red. Absolutely nothing."

I stiffen. Yeah, Dougie has told me what my options are after the draft, but I also know there could be repercussions that follow the decisions I make.

No player has to sign with the team that drafts him. But if you don't? That's a grey area—or more like a murky black one. Not signing with your draft team makes you look stuck-up, like you're too good for whoever chose to take a chance on you. That's not the kind of player I want to be known as. That's not who I am.

Having a team's general manager hint at me not signing with my draft team and coming to Minnesota instead? Gracie would tell me that's an obvious red flag. Not to mention if I were to risk turning away my draft team for any other, it sure wouldn't be the Woodmen I chose.

A hand on my knee has me popping out of my seat. There's a flash from somewhere behind the fish tank, but when I spin around to see where it came from, Ronnie grabs my hand, pulling at me to sit back down.

"What's wrong, Oakley?" Harvey asks tensely. He glances at his daughter with a scowl before looking back at me with a phony smile.

"I have to use the bathroom." It comes out in a rush.

My hands are sweaty, and I use that to my advantage as I pull away from Ronnie and head for the bathroom. Eyes and voices follow me, but I don't focus on that.

Maybe I should have.

I collide with someone and fumble backward, trying to shake it off. Another flash and I rub at my eyes from the close range.

"Oakley Hutton! Are you here for business or pleasure?" The question is shouted at me, and I blink rapidly to try and push the stars out of my eyes from the flash. "Are you dating Veronica Anderson?"

"No." I glare at the human shape in front of me and start back for the bathroom. My elbow makes contact with the reporter's stomach, and he groans.

"Ouch! Are you a violent guy, Oakley?" he asks, still following me as I swerve through the tables, my vision finally clear. His fingers latch around my arm, and I stop, spinning around to face him.

"I will be in about five seconds if you don't get your hands off of me," I spit through gritted teeth.

The reporter's shitty brown eyes widen. "Can you say that again?"

"No."

The bathroom is close, so I hightail it through the rest of the restaurant, the reporter still on my heels. I don't recognize him from around Van, so he has to be from here. If he works for someone, he's done a great job of hiding his badge.

My phone vibrates in my pocket, but I let it go to voicemail. A shaky exhale slips between my lips when I quickly open the bathroom door and move inside before locking it. Only then do I try to calm my racing pulse.

The first thought I have is to call Ava and ask her to talk to me and calm me down, but it's illogical. Dougie is the only one who would know what to do right now, so I slip my shaking fingers into the front pocket of my slacks and pull out my phone.

He answers on the fourth ring, his voice thick with sleep. Right, the baby. *Shit.*

"Lee?" he mumbles. The reporter bangs his fist on the door, and I gulp.

"God, man. What the fuck is this place? I need your help. Shit, I think I'm losing it right now."

Whatever it is he hears in my voice wakes him up. His next words are more alert, sharp. "What happened?"

I put the call on speakerphone and explain to him everything that's happened tonight while listening as he curses words I've never even heard before. He's angry, and his anger only adds to mine, helping dull the feelings of dread and anxiety that are running wild inside of me.

"Who's the reporter? Is he still there?"

"I don't know. He's stopped banging on the door."

"Okay. Stay in there while I call Harvey. For the love of God, please tell me you didn't agree to any of the shit he was selling you."

I shake my head even though he can't see me. "No."

"Good. I'm going to call you back in a few minutes, yeah?"

"Okay."

I stand in front of the sink and turn on the cold water. Once it's had a minute to run, I set my phone down on the counter and use my hands to cup the stream in my palms before throwing it at my face.

*Man up, Oakley. It's going to get a lot worse than this once you're drafted*, I try to remind myself. *One reporter won't compare to what you'll face then*. But if that were the case, why does this feel so different?

I need to get out of here before I lose my mind.

"Be right back," Dougie says before hanging up.

Tipping my head back, I close my eyes and grip the countertop with wet hands. I want to kick myself in the ass for coming to this dinner and ignoring my gut when it told me something bad was going to happen.

Glancing down at my hands, I grimace at the memory of Ronnie's touch on them. I quickly wash them, scrubbing and scrubbing until they burn beneath the cold water. My pants need to be torched, too, as soon as I'm out of this hellhole.

If only I could torch this entire trip from my memory, too. But of course, that would be way too easy.

# 31

## Ava

"TELL ME WHY WE HAVE TO WATCH THIS MOVIE AGAIN?" TYLER grumbles. He's sitting on the couch beside me with his arms crossed and his head tilted back against the back cushion.

The four of us—Tyler, Morgan, Matt, and I—are all huddled in front of the TV as the first Captain America movie plays. It was Matt's choice, and although Tyler isn't a superhero fan, Morgan and I would never turn down spending a night with a shirtless Chris Evans.

I rest my elbow on the armrest and set my chin in my hand, watching as a newly Super-Soldiered Steve Rogers lifts a motorcycle weighed down by several women above his head onstage. I've seen this movie more than enough times to have a good chunk of the dialogue stored in my memory bank, so when my thoughts start to drift elsewhere, I don't care.

I haven't heard from Oakley since our call this afternoon. Much to my displeasure, I've begun to worry, but I've kept that to myself.

I know it's ridiculous to be antsy, after only one missed call and a few unanswered texts, especially when I know he's busy, but something feels wrong. It has all day.

There was no way I was going to tell Oakley that I shared his feeling of dread during our phone call, not when he was already so nervous, but that worry is still here, festering. If my mom were here, she would tell me I was going to give myself an ulcer, but I just can't seem to shake this.

My fingers tap at my thigh as I begin to bounce my leg. I check my phone, turning down the brightness so that I don't blind us all in the dark room as I scroll through the notifications.

*Nothing.* I scowl.

Tyler's head swivels my way when I shove my phone back into my hoodie pocket. "Why are you so antsy? You're acting weird."

"I'm fine."

He arches a thick brow and continues to stare at me, unbothered. Maybe that's why I give in so easily. Because he's not pressuring me.

"I just have a bad feeling. Haven't been able to shake it," I admit in a hushed tone.

A noise of what I assume to be understanding escapes him as he turns back to the movie. I'm about to do the same when he— still watching the movie—leans to the side and says, "Would offer you a smoke to clear your head, but you'd just turn me down."

"You really should stop smoking. You're an athlete, y'know? Don't want to damage those money-making lungs of yours."

He chuckles lowly. "It's not my lungs that will make me money. It's my fists."

I shrug. "If you say so."

"Besides, I can't stop. Tried and failed too many times already."

"When did you start?"

I should stop asking questions before he hits *the end* on this conversation and freezes me out, but digging around inside Tyler's head for a few minutes is a pretty appealing distraction from all the worrying.

"Before I stopped caring about what others thought of me," he answers.

"That's not a real answer," I push.

The corner of his mouth twitches. "It's the only one you're getting, Snoopy."

I grin. "A nickname. I'm honoured."

"Can you two stop talking? You're worse than a bunch of middle schoolers in the back of a theatre," Morgan hisses, bending over and glaring at us over Matt's lap.

Tyler gives her the finger before standing up and heading toward the balcony. His fingers dig into the front pocket of his black jeans before he pulls out a white box of cigarettes.

"Where are you going, man? This is the best part," Matt says.

Tyler ignores him and steps outside.

"Stop talking and watch the movie," Morgan whispers to Matt.

He does, and just like I knew it would, the lack of distraction makes my head go into overdrive again. I pinch my lips between my fingers and roll them, dragging my eyes across the room and to the brooding man on my balcony. Tyler's leaning forward, his forearms resting on the balcony, a lit cigarette hanging from his lips. I let out a sigh and move to join him outside.

The quiet click of the patio door closing behind me catches Tyler's attention. He glances at me and tips his chin.

"You really, really shouldn't smoke." I join him by the railing and look down at the traffic that, despite the time, still hasn't slowed down. Vehicles honk, brakes squeak, people yell.

We live downtown, fitted between apartment after apartment. There's no view of the ocean here, just brick and windows. One day, I want to live somewhere secluded, somewhere away from the hustle and bustle of the city. If I'm only minutes from the water, I want to be able to see it.

Tyler takes another drag of his cigarette and blows smoke out in front of him. "I know."

I frown. "You have a story."

He flicks the embers from the end of his cigarette into an empty pop can Morgan put out here earlier. "So do you."

"Everyone does."

It takes him a few seconds to respond. "Your mom's back, right?" He flicks the end of his smoke again.

"Yeah. Suddenly, she wants to get to know me, or so she says."

"She's probably lying."

I wince at his bluntness. "Don't hold back on my account."

I'm not surprised when he doesn't apologize for his harsh words but simply moves on instead. He stares out at the city with a blank expression and says, "I don't mean it like that. Just be careful. People don't abandon those they care about and then decide one day to come back. My biological dad pissed off sometime before I was born. The guy never even knew my mom was pregnant. If he came back now, I would tell him to kiss my ass."

"I didn't know your dad wasn't in the picture."

"It's not exactly something I lead into conversation with. My mom's a junkie, and my stepdad loves to hit anything that breathes. I don't talk about them. Don't like to."

My exhale is heavy, full of a thousand words that I don't think I could ever form into anything worth saying, so I choose something simple. "I'm sorry."

He takes a final drag from his smoke and stamps it out on the railing. Once the butt is in the can, he wipes his hands on his jeans before running them through his hair. "Me too. You're worth more than being a second thought, Octavia."

My chest is tight, achy. God, I wasn't expecting this tonight. "So are you. You're going to do great things with your life, Ty. I know it."

Quietly, he pushes himself off the railing and awkwardly pats my shoulder. "We should go back in before Morgan guilts us for skipping on her movie."

I nod. "I'll be right in. I just want to check something first."

He dips his chin and heads inside. As soon as the balcony

door closes, I pull out my phone and open my call history with Oakley. I'll call once more, and if he doesn't pick up, I'll leave it and wait until tomorrow.

I suck in a deep breath and then make the call. Lifting it to my ear, I worry my lip and wait for the familiar ring. Once, twice . . .

"You have reached the voicemail box of—"

The voice cuts off when I hang up.

Two rings. He sent me to voicemail.

What does that mean? Oh, my God. I sound like a psycho. A full-blown psycho stalker. Good grief, Ava.

I shove the phone back into my pocket and straighten my shoulders. So what if he sent me to voicemail? Maybe he's still eating dinner. Sure, it's past nine . . . but maybe it went long, or his phone died?

*Enough.*

I pull open the balcony door and step back inside. The lights are on now, and the movie is paused. A feeling of dread fills my veins.

"Why is the movie off?" I ask, and all at once, three heads snap my way. My stomach twists when I lock eyes with Morgan. There's no mistaking the sympathy on her face. "What?"

"What were you doing out there?" she asks slowly.

"Uh, calling Oakley again. He put me right through to voicemail. What the hell, right?"

Tyler sets his jaw and stares at Morgan. "You or me?"

"You or Morgan what?"

"Honey, maybe you should come sit down," she murmurs.

Despite the fact I know it's going to hurt when I do, I sit between her and Tyler. She's warm while he's unnaturally cold. I fight back a shiver.

"Before I show you, I really want you to promise me that you will at least hear him out first. Oakley isn't this type of gu—"

"Show me," I order, tone cold. The walls around my heart are already building back up again at hyperspeed. All I can think about is that I've been here before. Right. Here.

Silently, Morgan pulls her phone out from where she must have shoved it beneath her leg when I came inside. As soon as she unlocks the screen, a series of photos is already up, above a caption that I wish I wouldn't have read.

*Is Oakley Hutton already tethered to Minnesota? According to these photos, it seems like we might have all been kept in the dark when it comes to his plans after the draft. Yikes.*

*Veronica Anderson is the daughter of Harvey Anderson, the Minnesota Woodmen general manager. It's no secret that Minnesota has gone to extreme lengths to secure a chance at success, but this doesn't look good. With Veronica set to take over for her father in the coming years, is it a coincidence that she's found herself up close and personal with this year's top prospect?*

*We've reached out to Oakley Hutton's agent, Douglas Trelix, for a comment but have not been successful.*

Acid burns my stomach. I grip my knees when the world dares to tilt on its axis. The photos are enough to make my eyes gloss over.

In the first photo, Oakley's front and centre, his handsome face shining below the bright lights hung above the dining table. He's dressed in a suit, with the top two buttons of his navy dress shirt undone like always. No tie. Yet I can't concentrate on him like I usually would. Not when he's sitting shoulder to shoulder with a bombshell in a risky dress I could never pull off.

The blonde woman I assume to be Veronica Anderson stares unabashedly at my boyfriend, her lids lowered to half-mast, long, thick black lashes teasing the smooth skin beneath. The long red nails on her right hand are wrapped around a wineglass, but her left hand is out of view.

"Next photo," I snap. Morgan slides to the next.

Veronica's left hand is on Oakley's knee as he stands at the table. My brows furrow at the expression on his face. He looks genuinely uncomfortable.

"He looks like he's about to piss himself," Matt notes.

I ignore him, and Morgan swipes to the last photo. Veronica is grabbing his hand, her fingers halfway intertwined with his. He's twisted away from the table, and his eyes are narrowed the slightest bit.

I feel sick. My head is thumping with too many thoughts to sort through. Part of me feels betrayed, like my automatic response to this is to see the obvious and believe he's interested in this woman. That he's been ignoring me for her and lied about why he's there. But another part knows he wouldn't do this to me—to us. Maybe I would have believed the worst of him months ago, but this man loves me. He wouldn't do this.

I bite down on the inside of my cheek when one reoccurring thought thumps harder than all the others.

Is this life for me after all?

Morgan locks her phone and tosses it to Matt. Then, she's wrapping me in her arms and tugging me to her side. She expects me to cry—I think they all do—but I don't want to.

"I need to talk to him when he gets home," I mutter.

"Oakley loves you," she says.

"Do you think he's okay?" I close my eyes, remembering how distraught and upset he looked in those photos.

Morgan tightens her hold. "I think he will be when he gets home and sees you."

I nod. That makes one of us.

# 32

# Oakley

VANCOUVER SPORTS REPORTERS ARE WAITING FOR ME AT THE airport. The moment I grab my luggage, they swarm, shouting and taking pictures. My grip on my bag tightens as I toss it over my shoulder and head for the exit. The questions follow me, but just like Dougie told me to before I got on the plane, I ignore them all.

"Can you confirm your relationship with the Minnesota Woodmen?"

"Harvey Anderson told *The Hockey Catch-up* show in an interview this morning that you were considering all of your options, is that true?"

"Who is Octavia Layton?"

My head snaps up at her name. I find the reporter at the front of the pack, a tiny recorder in his fingers held out in my direction. My jaw pops.

"She's not your concern," I grit out, picking up my pace.

"How does she feel about your blooming relationship with Veronica?" he shouts.

My tongue burns as I bite down on it, hating that I can't say anything yet without seeing Dougie face to face and creating an official statement. My silence feels like a confirmation for every asshole out there who has taken the time to spiel bullshit about my relationship, and it looks like it, too. Twitter has had too much to say about the entire situation. Some bad, some alright, and some downright awful. I fell down the rabbit hole this morning while waiting to board my plane, and I saw a side of social media that made me sick to my stomach.

Sellout, spoiled brat, arrogant prick. I know they're all untrue and that it's mostly the fans' way of expressing their frustration, but it's a hard pill to swallow, feeling like you're public enemy number one over a scheme you had no part in.

I don't know how everything got so goddamn messy, but I'm struggling to stumble my way to clear ground. For the thousandth time today, my chest tightens.

Ava's sudden silence told me everything I needed to know once I finally got back to my hotel room last night. Seeing her missed calls and unanswered text when I plugged my dead phone into the charger was alcohol on a fresh wound, but her denying my calls since? *Fuck.*

I don't blame her for taking space, but it still feels wrong. This entire situation does. It only frustrates me more knowing that Dougie is waiting for me outside to take me home and that she can't be my first stop, regardless of how badly I want to run to her.

For the first time in my life, I don't think my future in the NHL is my top priority, and I'm not as terrified of that as I thought I would be.

*Fuck it.*

I bump shoulders with someone as I quicken my pace and start to slip through the travellers hanging around the airport. The hurried footsteps behind me have dulled a bit, which I hope means I've lost some of my entourage.

Relief washes over me when I see Dougie waiting by the sliding doors. He's sliding an arm across my back and pulling me outside as soon as I reach him.

"Bad?" he asks gruffly, not sparing a backward glance.

"Define bad."

"Right. Never mind. Just get in the car."

His new Audi sparkles beneath the sun as he unlocks the doors and jogs to the driver's side. I toss my bag into the back seat before slipping into the passenger side and finally letting the tension leak from my muscles.

I run a hand over my face as he peels away from the pickup lane and takes off. The GPS on the dash is set for his penthouse, and panic runs through me.

"I need to go somewhere before we start to figure this mess out," I tell him.

His laugh is rough. "No. This is top priority. I know you want to see your girl, but your career comes first."

"Does it?"

He whips his head in my direction long enough to show his surprise before saying, "It always has."

"Things changed."

He scoffs a laugh. "Apparently. I didn't know it was that serious."

"I love her. Have for a long time. Probably since the second I saw her." I tap my fingers on my knee. "Having a chance to explain this mess to her right now, before anything, that feels right. Everything else can wait."

He nods slowly. "You're sure? The longer you take to nip this in the bud, the worse it's going to get and the more rumours are going to pop up. This shit will spread like weeds in the wind if you don't put out a statement."

I know I've made the right decision when I still don't waver. "You want my girl's address now?"

Dougie shakes his head and laughs incredulously. "Yeah, now's good."

❄

# Ava

REBECCA IS SUPPOSED to meet me at a coffee shop I've never been to before in twenty minutes. Maybe it's petty, but when I decided on a whim this morning to see her and called to invite her to coffee, the last thing I wanted was to taint one of my favourite places with her memory. My coffee shop is a sacred space for Adam and me. It's not for her.

Meeting her now in the mindset that I've been in since last night probably isn't the best idea, but it's now or never. She wants me to hear her out, and I plan to, but my mind is pretty much made up. I need to lay this to rest and move on with my life.

Tyler was right. I'm not someone who can just be thrown away and picked back up again at any time. I'm worth more than that.

I make it to the coffee shop with ten minutes to spare, so I take my time ordering a black coffee and then find a table in a more secluded area to wait.

An older couple sits at the table across from me, sipping their giant, steaming white cups while staring at each other with warm eyes. The man sets down his drink and takes his wife's hands in his before raising them to his lips, a sight that makes me think about all of the times Oakley has done the same.

The invisible hands around my heart squeeze. I should text him back, even just to say I'm happy he made it home safely, but I decide against it just like I have every single time I've thought about doing the same thing.

I just need some space. Some breathing room to find my bearings. Oakley is a man who has the world at his fingertips, and I'm a woman who knows exactly what my future should look like. Or I did, before we met.

I was supposed to focus on my schooling, graduate with great grades, and then find my dream job. Finding someone along the way wasn't the plan. But that's not how it worked out, and now I have to navigate a road that I didn't imagine driving. One that seems to be scarier than all the others.

I don't doubt Oakley's devotion to me and to our relationship. He would do anything it takes for us to succeed, but I'm stuck between wanting to let him and telling him that he's better off without the stress of it.

The screech of a chair being pulled across the hardwood floor snaps me out of my thoughts.

"Hello, Ava. You look beautiful," Rebecca says as she drops into the seat across from me. She sets her designer handbag on the table and smiles.

"Thanks. So do you." It's true. She looks like a million dollars.

Her long brown hair is twisted into a neat knot at the back of her head, and her makeup is glowy, looking almost airbrushed. The tight jeans cupping her narrow hips are tucked inside a pair of ankle-height brown boots with little gold charms dangling from the zippers.

She looks surprised by my compliment but hides it well. I gulp my coffee. Questions nip at me, one after the other until my head is swelling with them.

I tap the rim of my coffee cup and decide to get on with it. There's no point in small talk. "Did you ever leave Vancouver, or have you been here this entire time?"

She doesn't hesitate. "Well, after your father left, everything is a bit of a blur. Shortly after I . . . well, I moved from place to place for a few years. I had a few boyfriends before I found Link, the man I've been with for a while. He has a house here in Vancouver that I've been staying at."

Ah, *Link*. The rich guy she's taking advantage of has a name.

I nod. "How long have you been clean?"

"Since I came to see you for the first time."

Her blazing green eyes burn into mine, and for a moment, I vaguely wonder what features I get from my birth father.

"Why come back now?"

She fights off a shiver, but I see it. The way her gaze flits around the room has my gut screaming at me to get up and leave.

"Can't a mother just want to see her daughter?" Her voice cracks, shakes.

"Daughter?" I echo incredulously. "I'm not sure who you think you are, but you are not my mom. You're nothing more than the woman who dumped me in the system before I was out of diapers," I hiss through my teeth, and I take a deep breath before continuing. "Do you have *any* idea what my life was like growing up? Do you ever think of the damage you've done? Do you even *care*?"

"Ava, can we please go—"

"Outside? Sure." I make a beeline for the door. Her heeled boots click against the tiled floor as she tries to keep up with me. I rush out to the side of the building and whirl on her.

"You have to understand, Ava. I wasn't ready to be a mom back then."

I laugh humourlessly and cross my arms. "And that was my fault? Because I was the one who was punished. Not you."

She flinches, her mouth agape.

I take a breath, grappling with the hold I have on my anger as it starts to slip away. "Look, if you came here with hopes of being a parent, you're too late. I already have a mom—a mom who took me in and loved me when you abandoned me. Lily and David gave me everything I always wanted. They cleaned up your mess for you. You're too late."

A wall of guilt hits me. I shouldn't even have spent a minute of my time on this woman. Especially not when I have a family of my own, one who has done so much for me over the years. It feels like a slap in the face to them now.

"I know. But I'm here now, and even if you can't give me that place in your life, I want to at least have something. We're family, and I really want you to meet Link. Both you and your boyfriend. We can have dinner together or something!"

"I don't want to meet your boyfriend. I don't want to have dinners together as if we're some kind of family when we're the furthest thing from it. You might be happy with your life now, Rebecca, and I'm happy for you, I really am. But I don't want to be a part of it."

It's like she's not listening because she reaches for my hands as if to cradle them in hers, but I pull them back before she can.

"Please just give it a chance. What does Oakley think about this? Wouldn't he want you to give me a shot? Don't be hasty here, Ava, please."

I freeze, my muscles turning to lead. Pain flares in my chest as I take a step back and stare at the woman in front of me. She swallows hard, guilt sparking in her eyes.

"I've never told you Oakley's name before" is all I say.

"Now, honey—"

I throw a hand in the air, cutting her off. "When did you find out I was with Oakley?"

The pictures of us broke only a few weeks before Rebecca showed up at my mom's house . . . *oh, God*. I grab at my chest, wishing I could reach inside and feel for myself the cracks in my heart as they spread.

"Let me guess, you saw the photos of us and figured my relationship with this year's top NHL prospect would secure you a nice payday?"

Silence.

"How did you realize it was me? I'm not a baby anymore."

More silence.

"Answer me! Tell me how you got my records from the system and how you even knew I was your daughter in the first place. Tell me what you want from me before I turn around and leave. Because once I do, you'll never see me again."

Finally, she parts her lips on a sigh and reaches for me once more. But just like I did the first time, I flinch away.

"Link, my boyfriend . . . he's a new agent. I met him after he had just signed his first client, some forty-something guy looking for someone cheap. He's had trouble finding new players for a couple years, but he has money—he grew up with it. He's been taking care of me, but I was starting to feel like a freeloader, you know? I wanted to pull my weight."

She pauses, staring at me like she's hoping I'll tell her to stop and apologize for demanding answers. *Slim chance of that happening.* I lift my brows and nod for her to continue, keeping my walls high, impenetrable.

"Link had been talking about Oakley for a while. Said he was going to be a career maker for any agent out there—"

"Oakley already has an agent. He's been with Dougie for years," I snap.

"That doesn't matter, Ava. Not to guys who are as hungry as Link is."

I ignore that and nod again.

She sighs. "He saw the photos of you online. At first, he didn't know who you were, but I did. As soon as I saw you, I recognized those eyes. *My* eyes. And then Link told me your name, and I was sure it wasn't just a coincidence. So I told him that I knew who you were, and the next day, he was dropping me off in front of a small office building with a purse full of cash. It was easy to get your records then. Everything is easier with money, Ava. You'll learn that soon."

I recoil, my lip curling. "You bribed a worker for my records? What the hell is wrong with you?"

She looks surprised by my disgust, and that only makes it worse. "I couldn't risk not knowing for sure. But what does it matter now? Look at us, baby. We can be a family."

"What are you talking about? No, we can't. Do you really have no idea what you've done? You were trying to deceive me into letting you back into my life under the pretense of love and family when you only wanted a connection to Oakley. This was all about money to you. Not me. It's never been about me."

I'm crying now, and I furiously wipe them away as they cascade down my cheeks. Anger, hurt, betrayal. God, I feel like a cocktail of them all. What was I thinking, letting her back into my life for even a second?

*What an idiot.*

"It might not have started that way, but once we started talking and I saw you in person, I decided I wanted a chance. A real chance. Oakley potentially meeting with Link and taking him on as his agent was just a bonus," she defends.

I double blink, genuinely shocked at how ridiculous this entire situation is. "Every single thing coming out of your mouth is disgusting. You don't even see what you've done wrong, and that's enough for me. Oakley would never, *ever* leave Dougie to sign with a rookie agent who's never worked with someone of his calibre before. You wasted your time, Rebecca. It was all for nothing."

"Ava? Baby? What's going on?"

Heat hits my back at the same time an arm wraps around me from behind, the hold tight. Relief has my muscles turning to goo as I relax against Oakley's chest. His breath tickles the back of my ear when he asks, "Are you okay?"

I nod, but it's a tired effort. "What are you doing here?"

"I came by the apartment, and Morgan said you were here."

Flutters fill my stomach, and I let them stay. I didn't know how much I wanted him here with me for this until now. It's like I can finally take a real breath.

"I want to go home."

"Soon." He kisses the side of my head and pulls me closer. "What are you doing with Ava?" he asks the woman watching us with wide, eager eyes.

"Oakley Hutton," Rebecca gasps, extending her hand out in front of her. "I'm Ava's mother."

Oakley stiffens behind me and makes no move to shake her

hand. Once she slowly brings it back to her side, he asks, "What did you do?"

"Leave it. It's not worth it," I tell him.

"But she hurt you."

I smile softly, unable to hold it back. He's so protective. I've never felt safer with anyone.

Turning to tuck my face into his chest, I feel him shiver before palming the back of my head and pressing careful fingers into my scalp.

"She did. But she won't ever hurt me again. Now, please take me home," I whisper.

"Oakley, we need to go. There's a fucking reporter over there." It's a man. His voice comes from somewhere behind us.

Oakley's fingers pause their comforting movements as he growls, "Did you call someone here?"

He's not asking me, which means the question is meant for Rebecca. Bitterness turns my stomach as I let that sink in.

"You called someone here to take pictures of us? Wow. This entire thing was a ploy, wasn't it?" I ask, spinning out of Oakley's embrace and pinning Rebecca with my glare.

She drops her eyes to her boots. "Link did."

"Who the fuck is Link?" Oakley snaps.

"Oakley!" the man calls for a second time. "Now!"

A flash comes from behind a lineup of parked cars along the curb before Oakley sets his arm on my shoulders and pulls me into his side as we turn around and start heading away from Rebecca.

I pick up my pace, trying to keep up with Oakley.

Not once do I turn back to see if she's still there. Even after I'm ushered into a black car and driven away from the coffee shop, I don't look back.

# 33

## *Oakley*

ONCE I GET AVA IN MY ARMS, IT'S GAME OVER. IT DOESN'T MATTER that things between us are on shaky ground or that the past few days have been an absolute nightmare. As soon as I feel her against me and inhale her perfume, everything is okay again.

For as long as we're in the back seat of Dougie's car, touching each other and breathing the same air, we're okay.

I continue to stroke Ava's arm as we sit in the car, her cheek against my chest and my chin on her head. I stare down at her clasped hands in her lap and force myself not to grab them and place them on my body. It's only been days without feeling her touch, but that doesn't seem to matter to me anymore. The memory of her tucking her face into my chest on that sidewalk just minutes ago is enough to give me some reprieve.

She's being reserved right now, but the least I can do is try to understand what she's thinking and let her take this space. I threw myself into that situation with her mother before she was ready to see me, and I'm lucky she didn't outright refuse to come with me.

"Ava, I'm sure this is the last thing you want to talk about right now, but I do need to know who that woman was. Oakley's stuck his foot in this mess now, and with the pictures—"

"I know. Damage control," she says flatly. I set my hand on her thigh and meet Dougie's eyes in the rear-view mirror. He offers an apologetic smile.

"You don't have to go into detail, baby," I whisper.

"It's fine." She clears her throat. "Rebecca, that woman back there, is my mother. She gave me up when I was a baby and only came back into my life a couple of months ago. Turns out it was all just to get to Oakley."

"What do you mean?" I gnash my teeth together.

"She's dating some lacklustre hockey agent, and they saw photos of us together. They got this idea that if we became one big happy family, you would drop your agent and take on her boyfriend. Because you love me and all that."

Dougie bursts out laughing. I see red. I fucking *feel* it.

"She said that to you?" I grit out. She nods. "Turn the car around, D. We're going back."

He doesn't turn the car around. "So you can do what? Shout at her? Kick a few walls? Sorry, kid. Not happening."

"Now, Dougie. I'm not asking."

"I don't care if you're asking or not. We're not going back there."

"Fuck, man. Stop thinking about my reputation for one goddamn minute!"

I tense for the briefest second when Ava covers my hand with hers. My stare softens as it falls to look at our joined hands. "We're not going back. I was already planning on telling her a relationship wouldn't work between us, and what just happened only makes me more confident in my decision," she says.

"Are you sure? Shit, Ava. What she did was awful. You don't have to be okay with it."

She shrugs, but it's weighted. "I've already grieved her. Yeah, it hurts to know that even after all this time, nothing has changed, but the bar was already on the ground. All she did was dig a hole beneath it and let it drop."

"Right into hell, it would seem," Dougie mumbles, and I feel

Ava shake with a silent laugh. "Have you met this Link guy, Ava?"

"No. She's only brought him up a few times."

"I'll look into it. What I need you two to do now is go home and stay home until I can figure out a plan. I'll call in the morning."

I stare in the mirror and wait for him to glance back. "I thought you wanted me to write a statement tonight."

"Tonight or tomorrow morning, it won't matter if we don't have a plan. Let me make some calls and figure it out," he says.

I nod and kiss the top of Ava's head again. She's so stiff, and fear grows as I start to make sense of the shift in her emotions.

We'll fix this. We have to, because I'm not letting her go.

THE AIR IS tense as we sit on Ava's bed, neither one of us wanting to be the first to speak. It was easier in the car, our adrenaline pumping and our hearts doing more speaking than our heads.

Ava's stiff, her closed-off body language doing a great job of letting me know how she's feeling. Gone are the cuddling and reassuring touches. There's a rift between us a mile wide, and I'm struggling to get around it.

"You're not dating Vernonia Anderson," she states.

"No, I'm not."

"You've never touched her or kissed her. You didn't lie to me about why you were in Minnesota."

"I had no idea who she was until I got to that restaurant," I say, although it seems Ava already knows all of this. Her trust has me feeling more confident and secure. I want to yell with how happy it makes me until she speaks again.

"But it didn't matter what the truth is because that's what it looked like to everyone else. It was so easy for one simple dinner to spin into such a mess. One wrong move and I was that girl again. The one who was made out to look like a fool by a man."

My throat tightens, and I turn my body so I can look at her properly. She has her head hung, her long brown hair creating a dark curtain around her face. Small hands are clasped in her lap, and just like before, I want to peel them apart and hold them, but I don't. I keep my hands to myself.

"You didn't do anything wrong, Oakley. None of this was your fault. This is just your life. It's your future, and I just don't know if I can handle it. I love you, and I won't ever fault you for doing what you love. God, you've earned this opportunity. You deserve it. But I just—I don't know if I'm that girl."

My words rush out like the worst case of word vomit. "You're not that girl. You're *my* girl. The worst possible thing that could have happened, happened. But I'm going to take care of it. I'm going to fix it, and it won't happen again. Shitty people will be shitty no matter what you do, but I won't let them hurt you again. It doesn't matter what I have to do to keep it that way. I'd do anything to protect you, Ava."

"I know you'll take care of it, and I know you'll do anything to protect me. But how often are you going to have to put yourself in harm's way to ensure that happens? You're not even drafted yet and this happened. What happens once you are?"

"It doesn't matter because this won't happen again. You think you're not the girl to be able to deal with this shit, but I'm not that guy either. The drama, the headlines, the people that get hurt along the way. It's not for me. Hockey might be my passion, but I won't put us in this situation again."

There's no hint of a lie in my words, and that's because it's all truth. Hockey isn't everything. Not when it could cost me everything else. Ava, my own mental health, my love of the game. Maybe a few months ago, I would have thought differently, but we aren't back there. We're here, in this moment, and I'm as sure about this as I've been about anything in my entire life.

I suck in a breath and take a risk, reaching for Ava's hands. When she doesn't pull them away, I move them to my lap and hold them there. They're cold, so I hold them tighter.

"I don't have a plan B, baby. I'm going to need you here beside me in case I need your help creating one."

Ava lifts her head, and I'm quick to brush her hair back out of her face. My fingertips skim her jaw along the way, and her green eyes shimmer as they meet mine, keeping them locked in place.

"Are you just saying that? Because you were meant to play hockey. It's your future. I don't want you to give that up just because you think you'll lose me if you don't. That's not the case here."

I shake my head. "Hockey has been my dream for as long as I can remember. It's so close I can almost taste it. And I'm going to make sure I get a taste. It's what I've spent my entire life working toward. I just want you to know that this drama and heartbreak, it isn't our future. But everything else? That is. My dreams can fit right alongside yours. Just give me a chance to prove it."

She sighs, her eyes closed. I swallow when she leans closer and bumps her nose against mine, our mouths so close we could hold a piece of paper between them.

"I'm scared of getting hurt again, and you have the power to destroy me," she whispers.

"I would do anything for you, Ava. Including breaking myself before I would ever risk seeing you get hurt again."

Suddenly, her lips press to mine in a searing kiss. It's rough, commanding, *hungry*. I taste her desperation and, fuck, her love for me. It's like we've reached our boiling point. The moment when everything becomes too much to keep inside, and the only way we can move on and accept what's happened is by doing this. By devouring each other in a way only two people completely in love with each other can experience.

Her tongue parts my lips as I suck on it, taking control of the kiss. She places her hands on my shoulders and swings her leg over mine before settling in my lap. I nip at her lower lip and rasp, "I love you, Octavia Layton."

Her eyes blaze. "I love you, Oakley Hutton."

I push her head back with my nose as I start to suck on the underside of her jaw, making sure to replace the marks that have disappeared over the past few days. She can scold me for it later, after I've spent the night reacquainting myself with the way she screams for me when she comes.

"I'm going to marry you someday," I murmur, biting down gently on the side of her throat. She gasps, grinding down on me.

Carefully, I push my hands through her hair, collecting it in my fists before pulling her head back. She stares at me, pupils blown, puffy pink lips parted.

"I'm going to give you my last name, and we're going to have a life together. A family. You and me and however many kids you want."

Her tongue wets her lips, and I track it the entire time, groaning when it slips back into her mouth. She palms my cheek, bringing me close.

"However many I want?" Her hips shift as she slides up and down my lap.

I tighten my grip on her hair and thrust up, letting her cry of pleasure wash over me. "Yeah, baby. However many you want."

She hums before bringing our mouths back together. I respond eagerly, my hands drifting down her back and to her ass. With one cheek in each hand, I squeeze and use my grip to pull her closer.

"Take off your clothes for me, Ava. I need to see you before I come in my fucking pants."

She pulls back, and her eyes twinkle like the sky the night we met. My heart tries to fly right out of my chest when she steps out of my lap and lifts her sweater over her head. I skip a breath or two as I watch her strip for me, one article of clothing at a time.

By the time she's standing in front of me in nothing but a pair of thin pink panties, I'm harder than I've ever been. She smiles knowingly as she tucks her fingers into the waistband and shimmies them down her legs, leaving them to pool at her feet.

"Get up here," I order, the sound pained and stressed. "Sit on my face and let me fuck you with my tongue." She gasps, but I simply lie down on the bed, staring up at the ceiling. "Now, Ava. I'm fucking starving."

Finally, the bed dips on both sides of me before she starts to crawl over me. I swat at her ass when her bare, wet pussy slides up my chest, and she stops.

She sucks in a sharp breath at the sudden sting, her cheeks flushing a deep pink. "Did you just spank me?"

I rub her ass before massaging it. "I told you to sit on my face. That's my chest."

"Right, silly me," she breathes.

I hum low in my throat when I finally come face to face with her swollen flesh. Her scent alone is enough to have precum seeping from my cock, but I nearly go off at the first touch of my tongue to her slit.

"Such a pretty little pussy, baby. So soft and pink," I whisper before diving in.

She moans as I use the flat of my tongue to lap at her, groaning like a damn animal. I guess that's exactly what I am, because I'm completely transfixed on my task, everything but Ava fading to nothing.

I groan when she starts to ride my face, her clit brushing my nose with each upstroke. She tastes like fucking heaven, and as I finally drag my tongue up through her folds and find her swollen clit, her thighs bracket my face.

"Oakley," she cries out, her fingers curling in my hair. "Holy fuck. I'm close."

I suck her clit into my mouth and get rewarded with another cry, this one forming my name. Her hips buck up harder than before, and I slip my tongue inside of her weeping hole, fucking her with it for a few seconds before moving back up to her clit.

Nails dig into my scalp, and pain ricochets down my neck,

but it's all an afterthought when she starts to come. I drink her pleasure, refusing to miss a fucking drop of it.

As soon as she falls from the clouds, I grip her hips and pull her down my body. Her eyes are dazed, her limbs heavy, but she knows what to do as she leans up on her knees and lines me up before sinking down, her wet heat enveloping my cock.

"Oh," she coos, her eyes rolling back as her head falls forward. It's a tight fit, and her breath hitches when she takes all of me.

I press my fingers into her hips and drag her forward, rubbing her clit across my pelvis. "Ride me, Ava."

She does, and I chomp down on my bottom lips when her breasts swing forward as she sets her palms on my chest and starts to find a rhythm. Her eyes hold mine as she adjusts, suddenly tucking her feet against my sides and reaching behind her to grab my thighs. My curiosity dies when she lifts, sliding off my cock until just the head is tucked inside before falling back down.

"*Fuck yes*," I grit out, forcing myself not to thrust up as she lifts again. "That's so good, baby. So good."

Her chest heaves as she starts to bounce in my lap, taking me like she knows just what to do with every inch. I reach up and grab her chest, squeezing the soft skin before pinching her nipples and twisting, cautiously at first. I curse when she arches into my touch and cries out when I twist again, this time harder.

"You look so beautiful like this, Ava. So needy for me." I stop holding back and thrust the next time she starts to sink down on me. She moans as I fill her up, but it's her slow, dirty smile that has me thrusting again, and again and again until I'm the one fucking her.

"Oakley!" she screams when I thrust so deep she goes lax in my lap. I watch with surprise as clear liquid pours from her pussy, hitting my stomach and dripping down onto the bed.

"Holy fuck," I groan as my orgasm crashes into me, the sight of Ava squirting sending me toppling over the edge. "I'm coming, baby. You're so perfect."

My ears fill with white noise as I come, filling her up with it until it leaks out, mixing with the mess she made on my pelvis.

Ava collapses on top of me, and I instantly wrap my arms around her, holding her to my chest, not caring that we're both covered in sweat and cum.

"Wow," she whispers, shaking with a soft laugh.

I hum low in my throat and press kisses to the side of her head and over her cheeks. "Wow is right. I don't think I've ever had sex like that."

"Me neither. I kinda want to do it again."

"Already? You're insatiable."

Her giggle is music to my ears. "Proudly."

I draw circles along her spine, letting the calmness of the moment cover us in warmth. "I'm going to fix this, Ava. I promise."

"I know you will."

# 34

## *Ava*

I PRESS THE DOORBELL AND LAUGH AT THE CHIME I HEAR TRICKLE through the house. It's such a specific song, so extravagant and unnecessary. But my mom loves to tweak little things to make a space hers. It's one of her cutest quirks.

Just as that thought trickles away, my dad pulls open the front door. He grins at me instantly, pulling back the door and inviting me inside.

"Why, hello, sweetheart. I didn't know you were coming today."

I step inside as he wipes the back of his hand across his forehead, smearing what looks like engine oil across his skin. "Surprise!"

"Hey, I'm not complaining. We always miss you over here." He shuts the door behind us and pulls me in for a hug.

I hold him a bit tighter than usual, taking advantage of the moment. He chuckles when I refuse to let him back away.

"You gonna let me go anytime soon?" he teases, his tone light and airy.

Reluctantly, I pull away and smile sheepishly. "Sorry."

He ruffles the hair at the top of my head and leads us

through the house and to the living room. The fireplace is lit, crackling and filling the air with a smoky scent.

"Is that my baby? What a surprise!" Mom comes rushing in from the kitchen, flour smudged across her cheeks. She throws her arms around me instantly, and I melt into her embrace.

"Why are you both so damn dirty? First Dad with the oil and now you and flour."

An onslaught of emotions trickles through me as I stand in the arms of the woman who took me in when I thought I would never mean anything to anyone and turned absolutely everything I thought I knew about love and family completely upside down.

I promised myself that I wasn't going to cry today, but I should have known better. Lily is my mom, and moms have this weird ability to make you cry when you least expect it. It's like they have a radar that beeps at them when they sense some sort of inner turmoil in those they love, and their hugs get tighter, more comforting.

Blinking back the tears trying to escape, I sniffle, and Mom starts to rub my back.

"Oh, baby. I'm right here," she murmurs.

"I didn't want to cry today." I laugh, my shoulders shaking despite the tear that slips down my cheek.

Mom pulls away long enough to lead me over to the couch placed in front of her reading chair. I sit down beside her and pull my legs up into my chest as I lean into her side.

"What happened, Ava?" Her tone is warm and gentle but also inquisitive.

"You can stop your hunt for whoever blabbed to Rebecca. They were paid to do it with a thick wad of cash. It isn't important to me anymore, anyway."

The couch sinks beside me as Dad sits, his shoulder softly knocking mine. "Now, how'd you figure this out, kiddo?"

I haven't hidden anything from my parents regarding

Rebecca, but I wasn't going to tell them about my meeting with her yesterday until after. Obviously, things went a bit off course.

"I met with her yesterday for coffee with the intention of telling her that I didn't think spending time together anymore was what I wanted, but it turned into a total mess. Turns out she didn't come back for me—she came back because her boyfriend wanted Oakley." The words are bitter, but they don't hurt.

"She has some nerve. Oh, I'm so sorry, honey. I was afraid she was going to hurt you, but I wanted you to feel this out on your own. That woman never deserved you, Ava. Never," Mom says firmly. She tightens her arm around me.

"I know she didn't. I guess I just hoped for a second that she missed me, you know? That maybe she had thought about me like I used to think about her. It was stupid."

Dad releases an angry-sounding noise before grunting, "Hold on a minute. It was not stupid. Ava, you spent fifteen years in the system. You hoping that the woman who birthed you missed you and seeing everything you've become is the furthest thing from stupid."

Guilt nips at me, even when I try to fight it off. "I shouldn't have even entertained the idea. I feel like I've hurt you guys, after everything you've done for me. Rebecca showing up shouldn't have even fazed me. You're my family now. You have been for years. I love you guys so much." My voice cracks, and I swallow a growl.

"Octavia Layton, that is the biggest load of shit I have ever heard," Mom scolds, her tone sharp. "I hate that you have been thinking this way. You haven't hurt us, my love. If anything, you've shown us how much you've grown over the past few years. The fifteen-year-old girl we first met, the one who was so, so angry with the world, never would have taken the risk of putting herself out there for that woman. Sure, it didn't have the most ideal of outcomes, but at least you don't have to wonder anymore. It's done. You can lay it all to rest now, baby girl."

"Even if things had gone differently and you had chosen to

have a relationship with Rebecca, we would have supported you through that," Dad adds, sliding his arm around both Mom and me, pulling us close.

My brows furrow. "But you guys wanted a closed adoption. That's why you chose me, isn't it? Me having a relationship with my birth mother kind of ruins that whole idea."

"We didn't choose you because you were a closed adoption, Ava. We wanted you to be a part of our family because we had grown to love you. Even with those horrid biker boots and your rough-around-the-edges attitude," Mom murmurs, emotion thickening her words.

"Those boots were the worst." I choke on a laugh while wiping at my wet cheeks. "I love you two so much. I'm really happy you chose me."

"We love you more," Dad says, kissing one side of my head while Mom kisses the other. I smile, feeling like I'm right where I'm supposed to be.

"Now, tell us about Oakley. I've been hearing about the drama from your brother but not from you, and that just won't do." Mom clacks her tongue.

Dad stiffens, moves his arm from around us, and sets it in his lap, closing himself off. It hurts me to know that he's still so on the fence about Oakley and me. Especially after everything that's happened as of late. Stuff that I will never, ever tell my parents.

"I don't know if Dad wants to hear this stuff," I mumble.

Mom sighs, sounding exhausted. "That's too bad, then. Because I want to hear about it."

I risk a look at Dad and find him frowning, deep lines set in his forehead. He's staring at the floor, but once he feels me watching him, he glances up. "I love him, Dad. Like really, really love him. And he loves me. Even after everything we've just gone through together, that hasn't changed. It's only made my feelings ten times stronger."

"What did he do to you that made everything that much stronger? What happened between you?" he asks.

I release a tight breath and sink back into the couch. "His life is complicated. He's always going to be in the public eye, whether that be on the ice or on the street. Things got messy, and I was faced with the reality of that quicker than I was expecting."

"Explain," Mom urges, her fingers tapping on her leg.

I don't have a chance to before a loud, very male voice shouts from upstairs. "Mom!" Footsteps pound above us before descending the stairs. "Call Ava! She's not answering my calls, and she needs to see this!"

Mom jerks in surprise, and I look over the back of the couch just in time to see Ben come blundering into the living room. As soon as he spots me, his jaw drops, and his phone hits the floor.

"You're here! You need to see this. Dad, pull up YouTube," he orders.

Dad seems to recover from his surprise much faster than Mom and I can because he does just as Ben says, not wasting any time. The sound is low when an image of what looks like a podcast studio comes on the TV, and I grab the remote from Dad, turning it up.

"Is this a podcast?" I ask Ben, confused. He nods, waving at the screen.

"Yes. One of the biggest sports shows in the world right now," he says.

As soon as I focus on the screen, I gasp. "What the hell is he doing?"

Oakley is sitting across from two guys, all of them fully equipped with a microphone in front of them and glasses of water that look like they haven't been touched.

He's the image of perfection, all six feet of him. His hair—the same curls that I spent hours with threaded between my fingers last night and this morning—is shoved inside of a backward hat with stray pieces peeking out from beneath the elastic rim. His smile is sinful, as if he knows something nobody else does.

"You're not an easy guy to get a hold of, Oakley, that's for damn sure. We were shocked to get an email from your agent this morning requesting you get a spot on the show today," a guy with shaggy blond hair and a creepy-looking goatee says.

His partner, a bulky man covered in tattoos, laughs beside him, wrapping a hand around his mic stand. "What he means to say is that we're honoured you chose to speak on our show."

Oakley's voice brings goosebumps to my skin. "The honour is mine. I've been watching this podcast for a few years now. You tell it how it is. I like that."

"We don't usually do live episodes anymore, not with how Mav likes to run his mouth over there, but this was an opportunity we couldn't turn down," Goatee guy says.

The man I assume to be Mav laughs. "Right. It's my mouth that runs. Anyway, we should get right to it, I suppose. Tim, where do you want to start?"

"I think it's pretty self-explanatory. Tell us if Harvey Anderson is as off his rocker as we all think he is. There's no way a guy like you would be making slimy moves just months before the draft, but alas, there are some who think so."

Oakley leans forward in his chair, not showing even a hint of how this entire thing has made him feel. He looks cool, calm, and oh so collected.

"I won't confirm or deny whether Harvey is off his rocker, but I will say that it has never been my intention to turn down my draft team. This has been my dream for most of my life. There's no way I would risk that for even a second. I met with Harvey in Minnesota as I've met with other teams who are looking like they'll pick high in the draft, as most of the prospects have, but it never even crossed my mind to make the moves Harvey has hinted at in the press."

Mav claps his hands loudly. "Good man. Between us, we've heard the whisperings about why the guy is being replaced."

"I'm not sure replacing him with his daughter will help clean up the mess that is the Minnesota management team, but that's for us to find out, I suppose," Tim adds. I hum in agreement.

"Speaking of Veronica Anderson, I'm guessing you aren't dating her either?" Mav asks.

"Never even met her until dinner that night. It was a night of unfortunate coincidences that could have cost me my girl back home," Oakley says, his eyes finding the camera for the first time since I tuned in. My lungs seize.

Tim makes an *ooh* sound before saying, "Right. Octavia Layton, right?"

Oakley nods before a photo of us comes up on the small screen behind him. He swivels in his seat and grins. "Yeah, that's her. That's my Ava."

The photo they chose of us isn't from the party in the backyard like I expected but from outside of the coffee shop yesterday. Oakley is wrapped around me from behind, his hand holding the back of my head, fingers splayed in my hair. My face is tucked in his chest, hidden from the view of the camera.

Despite how perfect we look together, I focus on the way he's staring down at me, like he's ready to flay himself open and bleed for me. Butterflies erupt in my stomach.

*That's my Ava.*

"Well, damn. Ava, if you're watching right now, know you got this guy in all kinds of knots over you," Mav hollers, winking at Oakley.

"And apparently, we've now turned into a messed-up version of a romance podcast. Way to go, Mav—I can already hear the subs dropping."

Oakley chuckles. "I love her, what can I say?"

Feeling eyes on me, I glance over at Dad. His eyes shine, and a ball builds in my throat. A nod is all it takes for me to realize the emotion in his eyes is acceptance.

My laugh is more of a croak than anything else, but nobody seems to care. As I stare at Oakley on that damn podcast, telling anyone who will listen that he loves me, suddenly everything that's happened doesn't seem so bad anymore.

# 35

## *Ava*

Today is the final game of the regular season. How the Saints play now will either send them to the WHL playoffs or end their season early.

Despite having an absolutely amazing first half of the season, the Saints hit a rough patch two months ago that dropped them significantly in the standings, creating the opening for the Edmonton Wranglers to close the gap between them.

He doesn't try to, but I know Oakley blames himself for their drastic drop.

After the mess in Minnesota and then his surprise appearance on that podcast, the team was a bit stunted. Distracted, they just . . . lost their momentum. It wasn't Oakley's fault, not when the team shouldn't have taken their eyes off the prize for something as useless as a bit of drama, but to my sweet, sweet man, that didn't matter.

Today, it's winner takes all. The pressure is on, but still, somehow, Oakley isn't showing it.

For what feels like the hundredth time since I've sat in my seat, the projected first overall pick of the NHL draft shoots a puck in the opposing team's net and points his stick right at me as he stands on centre ice. Oh, boy. My stomach is a fluttering mess.

His teammates create a circle around him, congratulating him on the goal, but his eyes never leave mine. That damn beaming smile tugs at my chest, threatening to pull my heart right through the cage around it.

"That's my guy!" I shout, not caring about the eager eyes watching each of our interactions.

The attention has become a regular occurrence, but each day it gets easier to ignore. I've even taken one of my social media accounts off private, although I've made sure the comments are turned off. It might be completely ridiculous, but I just like to post photos of us together. We look too good to be kept hidden.

Oakley purses his lips and blows me a kiss with his glove. I throw caution to the wind and lift my hand in the air to grab it, not caring that it's probably the cheesiest thing I have ever done.

"I might throw up," Morgan groans from beside me. She's looking at me with a mix of curiosity and surprise. "I'm going to have to pretend I don't know the cheeseball beside me now."

"You love it. I know you do," I tease.

"Maybe deep, deep down."

I knock her shoulder with mine as the teams set back up for a faceoff in the middle of the ice. "Matt has never blown you a kiss during a game?"

Her mouth twitches. "Maybe once or twice."

"Exactly. Zip it."

"You're different, you know?"

I look at her, confused. "What do you mean?"

She shrugs. "It's a good different. You're happy, more open. I've never seen you this way. Like you genuinely couldn't imagine your life any better."

"I'm so happy, Mo."

She hit the nail on the head. I wouldn't change a single thing about my life. Not anymore.

Between my mama drama and everything else, I think I've

finally found a sense of peace that I was living without for far too long. It's like finally feeling the sun on my skin after years of cloud cover.

The crowd goes crazy when Adam scores the next goal, a quick top-shelf shot—his specialty. In a breath, I'm on my feet again, joining in the screams, and as if he can feel how desperately I've been missing him, he looks at me and smiles. It hits like a blow to the chest, and I worry I could actually cry from something so simple.

My feelings only grow more erratic when Oakley throws his arms around Adam from behind and congratulates him, lifting him in the air. As soon as his blades touch the ice again, Adam spins and hits Oakley on the back, grinning and saying something that I wish I could hear.

"Woah," Morgan says. I nod. "That's something I didn't see coming."

My mouth tugs. "I did. Sooner or later, they were going to come together. They're both important parts of my life."

"Good riddance, I say. Think Adam's gotten rid of Beth yet?"

"I don't know. We haven't really talked a lot recently. But I hope he did. Who knows what trouble she could bring if he continues to play with her."

Morgan shudders. "I always pictured him with an athlete. Not sure why, but I'm barely wrong about these things."

"You just want all of us to date athletes, you puck bunny," I poke.

"Hey, I wear that name with pride. Do you see my man out there?" She grins slyly.

I laugh and watch Oakley swing his legs over the boards and collapse on the bench. A familiar zap of energy flows through me when our eyes crash and hold. Lifting my hand, I wiggle my fingers in a wave, my heart thrashing when he pulls off his glove and wiggles his.

My voice is strong when I say, "You know what? I think I will too."

❄

# Oakley

WE LOST, but the locker room still buzzes. Maybe it's the adrenaline still thumping through us or the excitement of such an electric home crowd, but not a single player wears anything but a smile.

"We played a good game, guys!" I shout, slapping both Adam and Tyler on the back. "Six damn goals. That's fucking wild."

The team hoots and hollers, and even Coach walks in with a grin. "That was my team out there today. Regardless of the outcome, you played like champions."

"Damn rights!" Matt boasts.

"I'm incredibly proud of all of you. And even though it's Oakley's one and only season with us, I know we're going to come back next year and not only make it to the playoffs but go the entire way to the championship. We'll come back stronger." Coach's voice is strong, commanding, and I nod in agreement.

My friends will still be here next year, and they'll make sure the Saints take home nothing less than a championship win. I do wish that Tyler had entered the draft before he hit the age limit, but there's no doubt in my mind that he'll find himself in the NHL someday regardless. He's the best defenseman I have ever played with.

"I just want to say that it's been amazing playing with all of you this season. No team would have been a better fit for me," I say after the yelling has calmed.

A flurry of pats, hugs, and handshakes come at me before everyone is ditching their hockey gear and dressing back in their clothes. The locker room empties after a few minutes, leaving only Adam and me.

Awkwardness settles over us as I start shoving my jersey into my duffle bag. Whoever orchestrated leaving us alone is going to get it when we're done here. Apparently after seeing us hug it out on the ice earlier, the team decided we need to talk too.

Adam pulls a sweatshirt over his chest and runs his fingers through his damp hair. It's shaggy, looking like he hasn't cut it in a few too many weeks. As if feeling me staring at him, he looks up and offers me a brief smile.

"They're a bunch of pains in the ass," he says.

I snort a laugh. "Yeah, they are."

He blows out a long breath and sits on the bench, his legs spread, hands clasped between them. "I miss her."

"She misses you too."

"I didn't mean to hurt her. I just couldn't be around her until I figured out what the fuck was going on with me."

I drop to the bench beside him. "She knows that."

"I nearly ruined our friendship over feelings that I didn't understand and wrongfully labelled. What I felt for her wasn't romantic—I just thought it was. My mommy and daddy issues are probably the cause of that."

"Your parents suck, Adam." I belt out a laugh. He joins soon after, our shoulders shaking.

"I don't want to miss out on any more time with her, man. It's only a matter of time before she moves to be with you."

"I'm not going to force her to follow me anywhere, Adam."

"I didn't mean it that way," he clarifies. "I just mean that she won't want to stay here alone while you're somewhere else. She'll go to you on her own, and then she'll be gone. I don't want to miss out on the time I have."

Understanding hits me. His worry is almost comforting. He loves her in the exact way she needs him to, and that's what I want for her.

"You need to tell her that. Explain this all to her because she's been worrying about you nonstop."

More than anything, she just wants her best friend back. They have a connection that I won't ever be able to understand, but for the first time since I laid eyes on them together, I want her to continue to have that relationship.

"Thanks, man. You're damn good for her, you know? You make her happy."

"She makes me happy too. Real fucking happy."

He grabs my shoulder and squeezes before standing and grabbing his bag. "We should go see her before she comes tearing into the dressing room."

I laugh and nod, grabbing my bag before following after him. Loud voices hit me when we get into the hallway and come face to face with a massive crowd.

"Is this a 'congratulations on losing' parade?" Adam asks, shoving through the crowd.

Ava pops her head around one of the other players and sends me a toothy grin as she heads right for me. She jumps and I catch her without difficulty, bringing her close and kissing her in front of everyone. Suddenly, I feel something light brush my face and look up to see her dropping confetti over us.

"You played amazing out there. Win or lose, you'll always be a star," she murmurs before pressing her lips to mine, stealing my breath.

I tighten my grip on her thighs and pull back, bumping our noses. "Your star, Ava. I'll always be yours."

# EPILOGUE 1

## Oakley

"Morning." Ava yawns, lifting her cheek from its place on my chest. I bury my face in her hair, not ready for either of us to get up and face the world yet.

I've been up for a few hours now, but she doesn't need to know that. It was nearly impossible for me to sleep last night with how important today is.

"Good morning, beautiful," I rumble.

"Mmm, what time do we need to leave by?" she asks, stretching her legs out beneath the silky hotel sheets.

"Mom wants to have brunch in an hour. Then we should have a few hours before we have to head to the arena."

The draft is being held in Chicago this year, and since neither of us has ever been here before, we spent yesterday acting like two overexcited tourists. Mom and Gray got here last night after their flight was delayed, and they're both a bit bitter they won't have time to explore the Windy City.

"She's probably freaking out right now. Remember how she was at dinner?"

I shiver. "Oh, God. I really can't take any more tears. I'm already anxious enough."

"She's just proud of you. Her son is about to be drafted into the NHL. How many parents can say that?" Ava smiles up at me and kisses me above the beard she refuses to let me shave. "We need to get in the shower."

"Together? You're feeling risky today. What are the odds we don't make it on time?" I reach behind her and grab a handful of her ass. She lets out a squeak of surprise and leaps out of bed. Her smile fills the room with light as she laughs, sticking her arms out in front of her.

"Is that a no?" I wiggle my eyebrows and throw my legs off the bed, stretching my arms above my head. I catch her eyeing my hardened abdomen muscles and groan. "Don't look at me like that unless you're okay with me ravishing you in that damn shower."

"Well, when you say it like that," she says slyly before pulling the T-shirt she wore to bed over her head and tossing it across the room.

In two quick movements, I'm off the bed and lifting her in my arms. She hooks her legs around my waist and kisses me as I move us into the bathroom and make love to her in the shower.

I finish buttoning my dress shirt and pick up my pink tie from the bed. "How do I look?"

Spinning on my heel, I find Ava coating her lips with gloss in front of the dresser mirror. The wind is knocked out of me with one glance, leaving me standing behind her, slack-jawed. I soak in the image of her as she meets my gaze in the mirror, and her lips quirk in a daring smile.

The dress she chose fits her body like a glove. The white material goes well with my navy suit, and I find my eyes snagged at the smooth, pale leg peeking through the slit at her thigh. Her shoulders are only covered by two thick straps, and she's showing the perfect amount of cleavage, or so she told me.

"And you're my date? Fuck, am I ever a lucky guy," I mutter.

She giggles and grabs my suit jacket from the bed. I track her as she moves around the room, and when she bends down to pick her heels up off the floor, her ass straining the tight material of her dress, I have to adjust my hard-on.

"You have the stamina of a horse, I swear," she says when she catches me moving my cock around.

"You've never complained before."

"Hell no I haven't." Her phone dings from the side table, and she tosses me my suit jacket before looking at the text.

"Your mom and sister are outside. Gracie told me to warn you that your mom is crying again," Ava tells me.

My stomach rolls. "Can't you just tell them I left early? I really can't afford to get any more nervous."

Something about seeing my mom and Gracie triggers my nerves, and I am already far too tightly wound. This is it, and I'm terrified I'm going to wake up and it'll have all been in my head.

"Like they would believe you left me alone looking like this," she scoffs.

I narrow my eyes on her. "You're right. You're not leaving my side once we get down there."

She waves me off, but I see the hint of a smile on her lips before I go to the door.

After taking a deep breath, I open it and get attacked with a hug before I have a chance to speak. Mom's soft cries make my heart ache, and I quickly wrap her in my arms.

"I swear, Mom, I am not redoing your makeup *again*," Gracie scolds. She shoves past us and heads into the room. "Where's my future sister-in-law?"

Girly giggles ring through the room as I pull out of Mom's hug. "Hold your horses, pipsqueak. You'll scare her away."

"If she can handle looking at you every day, I don't think it's possible to scare her away," Gracie shoots back and rushes over to Ava. "That reminds me! Your new apartment is beautiful. I'm so staying over again as soon as possible. I'm still shocked you were willing to live with that ogre, though," she adds as they hurry into the bathroom.

"Is she trying to steal Ava for herself or something?" I grumble. Gray stays at Ava's and my new apartment once and thinks she can have my girl.

"Who knows with your sister." Mom shrugs and reaches into her purse. Pulling out a Kleenex, she wipes away the remnants of her tears. "Your dad would be so proud of you, baby." She balls up the Kleenex and looks over at me with wet eyes.

My vision blurs when she says that, and I have to look away from her. All I ever wanted was to make my dad proud, and I know wherever he is, he's looking down at me with a grin on his face.

"Thanks, Ma," I whisper, kissing her cheek.

"If you guys are done with your sobfest, I have hot hockey player ass to look at," Gracie announces as she and Ava rejoin us.

"You aren't going to be looking at anything. Don't think I haven't noticed what you're wearing. Would it have hurt you to cover up a little?" I glare at the mini dress she's wearing.

"I think you look beautiful, Gracie. Ignore grandpa over here," Ava jumps in, wrapping her arms around me from behind. She kisses the back of my neck, and all of my negative thoughts disappear.

My phone buzzes in my pocket, and just like that, my nerves come barrelling back.

"Shit. We need to leave. Dougie has interviews set up for me, and we're already behind."

"C'mon, then. Time to watch my baby become the newest face of the NHL!" Mom claps excitedly.

I look at Ava as she laces her fingers with mine. I can't help but be blown away by the face she's here, doing this with me. We really did make it.

❋

"Holy shit! That was exhilarating!" Gracie shouts once we find our allocated seats in the arena.

I can't help but nod in agreement. I've never had that many cameras in my face before. When Dougie and I spent hours last week prepping for these interviews, I highly misjudged just how exhausting they would be. It was a completely different experience than the Minnesota fiasco, but still overwhelming.

"Gracie," Mom scolds from her spot on my left. My sister just waves her off and continues to eye every breathing male in the vicinity.

As the lights dim and everyone starts to take the stage, I rest my hand on Ava's exposed thigh and squeeze. She looks up at me with a comforting smile and wraps her hand around my arm, leaning her head against my shoulder. Mom takes my free hand and squeezes it in her own.

My stomach is in knots as I fight off the static that's trying to fill my ears. We've known which team is picking first for months now, but even as the Seattle GM steps up onstage and moves behind the podium, I feel like I can't breathe.

My name is called, and the world starts to move in slow motion. Both of my arms are pulled as the three most important women in my life stare up at me with tear-filled, proud eyes.

I make it to my feet and let myself get wrapped in my mom's arms, giving her this moment. I squeeze her back just as tight and whisper an "I love you" in her ear before the deafening sound of clapping snaps me back into reality. I pull back from her and turn around to lift Ava off her feet.

"I love you," she whispers in my ear as I spin her around.

"I love you, baby." I steal a quick kiss before setting her down to hug Gracie, who squeezes me tightly.

My body goes into autopilot as soon as I start making my way to the stage. Voices congratulate me, and I manage to give some of them a thankful wave before reaching the stage.

The stairs disappear beneath my feet as I eat up the distance between me and the Seattle GM. My grin gets even bigger when I reach the line of management and shake their hands.

Words are exchanged, and I drift off on cloud nine.

Suddenly, a jersey is held out in front of me, and my chest puffs out proudly as I take it with shaky hands. *Hutton* is written in white on the back, contrasting well with the navy blue and bright green silky material.

I instantly pull it over my head and grab the Seals baseball cap from another team member. Beaming, I move to the middle of the line and smile for the camera in front of us.

I spot my family across the arena, and my grin grows tenfold at the pride written across their faces.

I finally did it.

*I made it.*

# EPILOGUE 2
## TWO YEARS LATER

# Oakley

"THAT'S THE LAST OF IT." AVA WIPES HER HANDS ON HER SEATTLE Seal sweatpants as she sets the last of the food down on the glistening marble countertops in our newly purchased home.

"Are you planning on feeding an entire city, my love?" I tease, flicking my eyes over the hefty array of food spread across the kitchen.

"Seems like it, doesn't it? It's been too long since we've had everyone together."

Three months, to be exact. Not since the weekend before the season started. September marked our first hockey season living together, and it's already ten times better than being apart.

The past two years have been a bitch. Between flying to games and then back to BC to see my family, it was a lot. The airport was practically my second—*third*—home, if you count my old apartment in Seattle. And all the late-night calls made Skype my best friend.

Being in Seattle alone quickly became a gigantic pain in my ass. Of course, that doesn't mean it was all negative. I'm living my dream. I was just living it without my other half.

"I still can't believe this is ours. I don't even know what to do with all this space," Ava murmurs.

I walk up behind her and link my fingers around her middle. "Believe it, sweetheart. It's ours for as long as you want it."

She stares out the window above the sink at the big backyard and snow-covered patio. We're a bit of a drive away from town, which gives us the quiet we both need. I push her shirt down her shoulder and kiss the warm skin I reveal.

When Ava graduated this past school year, I did everything in my power to convince her to move to Seattle. I had been living in the same two-bedroom apartment since shortly after I was drafted, and with a new contract with the Seals looming in the distance, it was only a matter of time before a decision needed to be made.

I quickly adapted to my new team. Although it was a lot more difficult adjusting to the higher level of hockey than I would like to admit, I am proud to say that I am doing exceptionally well now. I guess that's the main reason why I don't want to sign with any other team. I've grown to love it here.

I won't lie and say the move to a new country, let alone one where she's still waiting for permission to work, was easy on her. She had to figure out how to say goodbye to her family and friends and her job at the youth home which she'd grown to love. I know leaving everything behind was hard on her. Hell, it was torture for me to leave too. It still is torture to be away from my family—even if we're only a few hours away—but the spam of texts I receive each day from my mother helps put my mind at ease.

"Shoot! It's almost seven. I can't let them see me like this!" Ava shrieks. She pecks my lips and bolts upstairs to get ready. I shake my head, a ghost of a smile on my lips.

She still has no idea how breathtaking she is.

It's been an intense, busy few months, but our housewarming party is finally here, and the house looks amazing.

The doorbell rings a few minutes later, and I hear Ava swear from our bedroom something about not being ready yet as I make my way to the front door.

Peeling it open, the cold nips at my sock-covered feet. It snowed last night but melted pretty quickly this morning, leaving the sidewalk wet as Adam, Tyler, and Gracie make their way up to the house, bags in tow.

Adam has stuck himself between the other two, his arms thrown over their shoulders. He's laughing about something, and the sound is so damn contagious that I laugh along with him, even without knowing what's so damn funny.

"Oakley, we're home, dear," he sings loudly.

Tyler scowls at his friend, and Gracie giggles.

"Is he drunk?" I ask.

Gracie snorts a laugh. "Nope. That's just Adam."

"He's been like this since we got off the plane. Fucking annoying," Tyler grunts and adjusts the two bags in his right hand.

Adam tries to kiss him on the cheek, but he rips his arm off his shoulder and flips him the finger. "Denial has never hurt so bad."

"Right," I chortle. Gracie wiggles out of his grasp when they reach the doorway, and the two guys bust their way inside, leaving her trailing behind. "I missed you, Gray. Hug me before Ava comes and takes you."

"I missed you too," she says softly, stepping into my open arms.

Kissing the top of her head, I give her a squeeze before stepping back. "Flight was good? Those two assholes didn't give you too much grief, did they?"

"Yeah, right."

"Good. Where's your bag?" I ask, noticing she didn't carry one in. Her cheeks flush, and I don't miss the way her eyes track Tyler, as if they have a mind of their own. I scowl. "Right."

Recovering, she blinks a few too many times. "It was too heavy for me. You know how much I love to overpack."

Memories of our trip to Mexico last year come trickling in,

and I nod. "You made me pay for an extra carry-on when your suitcase was already far too heavy."

"I'm merely a dance teacher, Lee. But it was so very generous of you to pick up the bill." She smiles slyly.

"You're a little shit, Gray."

"And proud of it." She curtsies before walking off, leaving me by the open door.

I close it and join the others in the living room just as Ava comes rushing downstairs. She's switched into a pair of skinny jeans and a loose tank top, opting to leave her hair down, curls hanging off her shoulder. It's a challenge in self-control when I don't immediately reach out and grab her, wanting her by my side.

"Look at you all!" she squeals, throwing herself into Adam's arms. Luckily, he was ready for it and catches her easily. "You have a beard!" As soon as they part, she's pulling at the short hairs that have grown out along his jawline.

He swats at her hand. "Don't pull at them, O. Ow."

"Sorry. It's just different seeing you all rugged like," she defends.

"Took a few tips from Oakley. Mountain man over here can grow a beard like no other."

"You're starting to sound like a fan, Adam." Tyler laughs gruffly. "Wanna ask for an autograph while we're all here?"

"Don't be a hater because you can't grow a beard," Adam refutes.

Ava claps her hands together to gather everyone's attention. "Children, children, let's not fight before dinner. Now, come eat before everything gets cold and tastes like ass."

"Great. I'm starving." Adam pats his stomach and groans.

"You ate at McDonald's on the way here." Tyler rolls his eyes.

"And? Little H wanted chicken nuggets, so I obliged. It's not my fault you're not allowed Micky D's."

I clap my hand hard across Adam's back. He winces as I say,

"Stop talking about food unless it's the stuff in my kitchen. Ava spent way too long getting this shit ready for you."

He nods. "Right."

One by one, we all file into the open-concept, brightly lit kitchen. The dining table is on the far end of the room, decked out with fancy placemats and silverware. Ava went all in for this dinner, and I will drag anyone out in the snow who doesn't scarf down as much as they can possibly take to make her feel good.

"Smells damn good, O," Adam notes, eyeing me warily. I nod at him in approval. *Sucker.*

"Thank you, A. You know, the last time we all had dinner together was in Mexico? I say this is long overdue."

Tyler leans against the counter and toys with the handle of a serving fork Ava has stuck in the giant ham waiting to be brought to the table. I grab the heavy silver platter and bring it over to the table, glancing at Tyler as I pass him.

I would have missed the tensing of his muscles had I not been watching him so closely. Suspicion scratches at me, just like it has been since that damn trip.

Once I've set down the ham, I start to bring everything else over to the table. Gracie picks up the bottles of wine I picked up earlier and follows behind me.

"Hey, you're not allowed to drink in the States yet, Gracie. Maybe you should let someone else carry that." Adam stifles a laugh.

My sister pins him in place with a nasty glare. "Keep picking on me and I might just shove one of these up your a—"

"Okaaay," Ava sings, humour thick in her voice. "Everyone, sit down and stop picking on each other. Gracie can drink in this house because she's nineteen and I said she can. Lord knows she's been drinking since she was sixteen."

"She has?" I ask, narrowing my eyes at Gracie.

She only waves me off and flops down in the seat beside Tyler. He turns to a statue, his eyes wide, but she doesn't care. It looks like he's about to burst a blood vessel when she reaches across his lap to grab a scoop of pasta salad from the other side of the table, completely unbothered.

"Earlier than that. You might have forgotten since you moved here, but we're Canadian. We're bred different," she says casually, dropping the salad on her plate.

"Fourteen for me," Adam pipes in, sitting across from Gray. I glare at him, and he laughs. "Right. That was very irresponsible, Gracie. You know the legal age in BC is nineteen."

"Oh, that's right. My bad. Please forgive me." She giggles, and I watch through curious eyes as Tyler starts to fill her plate for her each time he grabs something for himself. It looks like a subconscious effort, and I find a lump building in my throat before I tear my eyes away.

I'm not going there today. It took me months to ditch the suspicions that had grown after spending a week in Mexico watching something unfurling between those two, and I don't want to go there again.

Ava sits on one end of the table, and I finally sit across from her. Our eyes meet, and she smiles at me softly, telling me just how happy she is in this moment without having to speak the words.

Suddenly, the ring in my pocket—the same one I've been carrying around with me for the better part of a year—feels heavier, harder to ignore. But just like I always do, I remind myself that if it were the right time, I would know it.

So for now, I wait. I wait and focus on how happy we are and how perfect our lives are. How goddamn lucky I am. And as I look around the table, at our unconventional family, I feel completely at peace.

### THE END.

# BONUS EPILOGUE
## A FEW MONTHS AFTER EPILOGUE 1

*Ava*

"WHERE ARE WE GOING? YOU KNOW HOW I FEEL ABOUT SURPRISES."
My knees bounce up and down in the passenger seat of Oakley's truck as I stare across the cab at him, brows tugged together.

"I do. But you're just going to have to suck it up this time."

"You're playing hardball tonight, I see."

The hand over my insulated, legging-covered thigh squeezes as Oakley chuckles. "It'll be worth it, I promise."

I hum in reluctant agreement and slip my fingers through his.

The wipers slide over the windshield at a quick pace as the snow continues to fall. The warm air from the heater blows beneath it, causing it to melt almost instantly. It's Christmas Eve, and until today, Vancouver has got away with only a few mild snowfalls this year. It's not uncommon for us to get a limited amount of snow being so close to the ocean, but like always, the minute snow falls, everyone turns into a rookie driver.

The highway is packed, backed up to the nines. Cars sit in the ditch, hazards flashing as they wait for tow trucks, while others slip and slide all over the road.

When Oakley showed up at my apartment an hour ago, he said our destination wasn't far, so I think it's safe to say that it's the ridiculous traffic that's pushed what should have been a quick drive into one well over an hour.

"Okay, can I at least have a hint about where we're going?" Apparently, patience is not a term in my vocabulary tonight.

All I've gathered so far is that since we don't seem to be on a time crunch, we have to be doing something that doesn't require a reservation.

"Ava," he groans.

"Please?"

"No."

"Pretty please?" I try again.

"If you ask me again, we won't go at all." His following grin tells me otherwise, but I decide to let it go.

"Fine." I hold my hands up in surrender and lean back against the headrest. "But are we close?"

He gives me a pointed look, groaning softly.

"What? Are we?"

"Yes. As soon as we can take this exit, it should be on the right."

"If we can ever take the exit," I say, looking forward at the line of cars creeping along the road ahead.

"Are you that desperate to get out of the truck and away from me?"

"Is it that obvious?" I ask through a teasing smile.

He pinches the inside of my thigh. "I can always tell Morgan to send everyone home."

That makes me straighten in my seat. "Morgan is there? You're not helping settle my anticipation, Boy Scout."

"Oops."

"That's just cruel."

"That'll teach you to keep pushing your luck."

I shift my body, facing him as best I can with my seatbelt still on. His hair is longer than usual, and his beard is bushier than he keeps it outside of playoff season. I don't blame him for not keeping up with it. Not with how busy his first season in the

NHL has been. Most of the time, I'm impressed when he so much as remembers to brush his teeth some mornings.

The slight break in the season has brought him back home, and I'm so damn happy to have him here beside me again, even if it's just for a couple of days. I've missed him so much.

He quickly looks away from the windshield and at me, questions in his eyes as if he has sensed my sudden change in thought. "You okay, baby?"

I smile. "Yeah. I'm just happy you're home. Even if it's only for a couple of days."

He hikes the corner of his mouth and his green eyes warm with an inferno of emotions. "Me too, sweet girl. Me too."

The rest of the drive goes by in comfortable silence, with just the drone of soft Christmas music to fill the truck. When it's just the two of us, we don't need to speak to enjoy each other's company. Just being beside him is more than enough.

It's not ten minutes later when we get off the exit ramp and turn onto a white sprinkled gravel road. I gape at the scene before me, eyes drifting wildly over the array of lights and giant blow up's dancing in the wind.

The further down the road we drive, the more of the scene comes into view. It's a field, I think. A massive one decorated for Christmas.

Shimmering lights are draped from tall, frosted trees and wrapped around tall fencing. Countless rows of reindeer and other Christmas decorations fill the field beyond the fence, marking off the crowded parking lot cleared in snow just off the road. It's hard not to lose myself in the beauty of it all as I stare dreamily out the window.

This is a winter paradise.

As soon as Oakley parks the truck, I'm grabbing my toque and mittens and tossing open the door, jumping out. The sudden change in temperature is jarring, but once I'm all bundled up in my gear, I hardly notice it. I'm too excited to care about the cold.

"It's so beautiful here. Hurry your fine ass up!" I shout, grinning when Oakley rounds the hood and settles beside me.

Sweeping my eyes over him, I hold back a sigh of appreciation. He's so handsome, it's honestly a little ridiculous. Even bundled up in a toque, scarf, and a long, heavy wool jacket, he doesn't look the least bit bulky. Instead, he looks like he belongs in a winter apparel magazine. And when he smiles at me, knowingly catching my hungry stare, I fight back a swoon.

"Let's spend a couple of hours here and then we can go home and you can ravish me. Sound good?" he asks with a swift wink.

"Sounds good to me."

Laughing, he throws an arm around my shoulders, pulling me into his side. He rubs his hand up and down my arm as if trying to keep me warm. I lean my cheek against his side.

"How did you find this place?" I ask once we turn down one of the many marked pathways leading to the entrance.

"Matt told me about it. I figured with how much you love everything Christmas, that you would enjoy it.

"It's beautiful," I note, eyes finding the Santa Claus statue marking the entrance a few feet ahead. He's holding a sign that says Vancouver Country Lights in one hand and a plate full of cookies in the other.

"The others should be around here soon. They got lucky and beat the traffic."

Suddenly, a mix of very colourful words reaches us, and I grin. Adam is the first to notice us. He makes quick work of shoving his elbow into Matt's stomach and pointing at Oakley and me.

As soon as I notice the group lingering beside a display of all Santa's reindeer and a big red sleigh, there's no way I could lose sight of them again. Not only are they loud, but somehow, they've convinced Tyler to wear a necklace of big flashing red and green Christmas lights over his jacket. His scowl is obvious, and it makes me laugh like a total idiot.

"About time, O!" Adam says.

I roll my eyes. "Take it up with the traffic."

Everyone makes quick work of collecting their hugs before falling into step with each other and heading through the entrance arch.

"Nice jewelry, Ty," Oakley teases, pulling back just enough to reach across my body and pluck at the string around the grump's neck.

Tyler grumbles something beside me but makes no move to take his necklace off, just swats Oakley's hand away.

"It was my idea. I figured he needed a bit of Christmas spirit. Maybe we'll be able to convince Santa not to fill his stocking with coal this year," Adam pokes, peaking over his shoulder at the three of us behind him, Morgan, and Matt.

Matt slips his arm around Morgan's waist and my heart warms as I watch her stick herself to his side. I don't even want to think about how single I would have felt right about now if I didn't have Oakley with me.

Everyone knows it's only a matter of time before Matt makes her his wife, and I, for one, cannot wait for that day.

Those two are as forever as Oakley and I are.

"Aw, Tyler, you still believe in Santa? That is just precious," Oakley sings.

Adam roars a laugh and Tyler purposefully steps on the heel of his sneaker. It makes Adam stumble and swiftly give him the finger as he catches himself. I roll my lips to keep from laughing.

"You'll be asking Santa for a pair of crutches if you don't shut up," Tyler warns, leaning past me to glare at Oakley.

I shake my head and let a soft laugh escape. The bickering and empty threats continue as we walk through the pathways in the field. The lights seem never-ending in the best way. With every turn, there's a new display of bright lights, designs, and displays. I've never seen anything like it.

"We should get someone to take our picture before we leave," Morgan says once the exit comes into view a few minutes later.

There's a collecting hum of agreement before we're pulling

off toward a fence with dripping blue lights and letting Morgan go on the hunt for someone willing to take a few photos of us.

The cold nips at my cheeks and my breath comes out in big white puffs, but I wouldn't rush this experience for anything. With Oakley's arms slipping around me from behind and his chest at my back, I'm exactly where I want to be.

It only takes my extroverted best friend a couple of minutes to find a willing participant, and after quickly positioning us all how she thinks looks best, she rushes toward the group.

Adam is on my right, Tyler on my left, and Oakley is behind me with his hands clasped on my stomach, refusing to be moved from how he was holding me just seconds prior. Morgan and Matt are cuddled up at Adam's side.

I melt back into Oakley's embrace and shiver when he sets his chin on my shoulder, nuzzling his cheek into my neck. A strong wave of bliss swells inside me as I smile at the camera.

"I love you," Oakley whispers, the tip of his nose brushing my earlobe. "So fucking much."

Covering his gloved hands with my own, I squeeze and reply, "I love you too."

And I can't wait to for the rest of my life.

Thank you for reading *Lucky Hit!* If you enjoyed it, please leave a review on Amazon and Goodreads.

This is only the beginning of the Swift Hat-Trick world. Join the group on their trip to Mexico in *Between Periods*, before diving into Tyler and Gracie's grumpy sunshine romance in *Blissful Hook*.

To be kept up to date on all my releases, check out my website!

www.hannahcowanauthor.com

## Curious where to go next?

Between Periods – Swift Hat-Trick #1.5 (5 POV Novella)

Blissful Hook – Swift Hat-Trick #2 (Tyler + Gracie)

Craving The Player –Amateurs In Love #1 (Braden + Sierra)

Taming The Player – Amateurs In Love #2 (Braden + Sierra)

Vital Blindside – Swift Hat-Trick #3 (Adam + Scarlett)

**Second Generation is here! For more information, sign up for my newsletter and follow me on my social media pages.**

Her Greatest Mistake, a fake dating romance – Maddox Hutton and Braxton Heights

Her Greatest Adventure, a forbidden romance – Adalyn Hutton and Cooper White

His Greatest Muse, a dark themed romance – Noah Hutton and Tinsley Lowry

Book 4 – (TBA)

Book 5 – (TBA)

## BETWEEN PERIODS

**Five friends, one tropical vacation.**

It's been a year since Oakley was drafted into the professional hockey league. Life has gotten a lot more complicated, not only for him and Ava, but also for his younger sister, Gracie, and their two closest friends.

Tyler is about to make his professional hockey debut and is still in Gracie's sights. But things are different now that she's older, and it's becoming harder for him to convince himself that she's *just* his best friend's little sister.

Adam is closing in on his university graduation, and more than ready to completely let loose on this much-needed trip. But what happens when he lets himself get *too* loose and finds himself in a situation that he might not be able to sweet-talk himself out of?

Follow the Swift Hat-Trick group as they invoke on a paradise vacation away from the pressures of the real world and grow impossibly closer along the way.

*Keep reading for a look at the first chapter!*

*BLISSFUL HOOK*

EVERYONE KNEW THE RULES.
GRACIE HUTTON WAS OFF-LIMITS.
BUT TYLER'S NEVER BEEN ONE TO FOLLOW THE RULES.
AND NOW SHE'S ABOUT TO BECOME HIS ULTIMATE SIN.

Tyler Bateman doesn't know what easy is. He's never had an easy day in his damn life. Everything he has he's worked for. Blood, sweat, and tears.

Hockey is his escape, the passion he never knew he could have. He wants to succeed. He wants to prove that he's worth something.

He wasn't expecting her to matter. He didn't want her to. But she had other plans, and now his best friend's sister is about to ruin his life. And he might just let her.

Read on for a taster.

# PROLOGUE

## SIX YEARS AGO

*Tyler*

"GET YOUR SORRY ASS BACK HERE, TYLER. I'M NOT DONE TALKING to you." The gruff slurs echo around the barren room as I walk away from him.

"You haven't been able to tell me what to do since I was twelve, Allen. Stop trying."

I notice a pair of headlights shining through the cracked living room window and pick up my pace.

"Show me some damn respect, you ungrateful waste of skin," he growls from behind me. "Don't turn your back to me."

The old, torn-up, reclining chair smacks against the wall with a thud as he jumps up. My eyes roll back into my head. I come to a stop just mere inches from the front door and turn around to face the old drunk.

Allen's long, dirty black hair is slicked back, his thin scalp emphasizing the bald spot near the peak of his round head. The baggy sweatshirt that hangs loosely off his torso is a deep red colour, similar to the bloodshot eyes that stare back at me. The stench of whiskey seeps from his breath and arouses a gag from my throat.

"You seem to have forgotten your place here. You are *not* my dad," I spit through clenched teeth, broadening my shoulders in front of my stepfather.

"I think it's you that's forgotten your place here, boy. As long as your momma has me here, under this roof, this is my place." Allen seethes the words, his lips stretched back to expose his decaying yellow teeth.

I almost laugh. "The only reason you're here is because I haven't thrown your scum ass out on the street. If I knew she wouldn't follow after your deadbeat ass, you would be long gone."

The same frightening chuckle I used to hear from behind my bedroom door years ago escapes him, sending vicious shivers up my spine. The menacing smirk that dances on his lips used to be enough to send me running away, locking myself in my room from fear. But things change.

"If you have such a problem with how I run things in my house, then why don't you go find somewhere else to live?"

"If *only*. I'm too busy being the only one paying to keep this house from being seized by the bank to focus on finding somewhere else to live. Not all of us can rely on our drug dealing buddies to pay our bills." I throw the words with a force I wish I had when I was younger. It would have saved me a lot of agony if I hadn't been such a pussy back then.

Furious, he closes the distance between us and shoves a long, shaking finger into my chest. "That smart mouth of yours is going to get you into trouble one day. Mark my words."

"I'll be waiting anxiously for that day to come. Now, if you'll excuse me, Allen, my rides here." I flash him an arrogant grin and take a large step back, watching his hand fall to his side. Anger radiates off of him as I dismiss his threat.

Raising my hand, I give him a small wave before walking through the front door. The sticky heat hits me like a brick to the balls as I move down the sidewalk and to the blacked-out car waiting for me beside a busted light post. Pulling out the pack of cigarettes in the pocket of my jeans, I peel it open and grab one, lighting it and bringing it to my lips.

The car honks impatiently, and I throw up my middle finger in their direction before inhaling deeply. With a sigh, I drop the cigarette and stomp it out with my boot.

I reach over and open the car door, breathing in the strong smell of weed. I shake my head and slide into the passenger seat. I hear the other passengers greet me, only to get a lazy, two-finger wave in return before the car takes off down the black tar road.

Here's to another night I can't wait to forget.

# 1

PRESENT

## *Tyler*

"Are you sure you want to leave already? We're still booked in for a few more days and your brother has already paid for the room. You don't want to waste his money. This trip couldn't have been cheap."

My mom's scolding is as consistent as ever as I shove the rest of my stuff into my open suitcase. No shit, the trip wasn't cheap. Brother dearest got married in Mykonos. How else was he supposed to flaunt his wealth to everyone he knows?

"I never asked for River to pay for my room. If I remember correctly, I didn't even want him to *book* me one." I scoff. "I told him not to. He's the one that wasted his money."

"Can't you just be happy for a few days?" Her eyes shut slowly and her shoulders drop like the weight of her disappointment is too much to bear. "You've been bringing everybody down since the moment you stepped off of the plane," she replies with a weighty sigh.

It's odd hearing her speak in complete sentences. Usually, she's too high to hold a conversation—babbling to herself as if she's the speaker of the house and itching at the skin on her forearms until they're raw and bloody.

"My bad." I push the top of my suitcase down over the

clothes I just threw inside and zip it up. Gripping the handle in a tight fist, I pull it to my side and stretch my neck when the wheels slam against the expensive-looking tile floor. "I already changed my flight. There's nothing I can do."

Mom closes her eyes and inhales a deep breath through her nose and places a hand on a jutted hip bone. The dramatic action nearly makes me laugh in disbelief: Nora Bateman almost looks like a disappointed mother.

What a goddamn sight to behold. It only took twenty-three years.

"Alright, Tyler. Whatever you want to do. You've never been one to listen."

Yeah, it's almost like I had no one to teach me how. "Alright. I'll talk to you later, then."

"Say goodbye to River before you leave. I'm sure he would appreciate the effort."

"I'm sure he would." I snort louder than I intend to and drag my suitcase behind me on my way to the door. A huff echoes behind me as I pull it open and step into the empty hallway. I don't bother looking back when the door clicks shut behind me.

She can enjoy the rest of her vacation drinking bottle after endless fucking bottle from the limitless bar until she crawls to River's room, begging for the toilet bowl. When he flounders at the task of having to take care of his alcoholic mother for once in his life, maybe, just maybe, she'll realize I'm the one that takes care of her, and that she's been taking me for granted.

I shove my palm against the elevator buttons, wincing as the metal cuts into my skin. The doors open, and I all but throw my suitcase inside, grinding my jaw. I didn't plan on coming to this fucking wedding for a reason. My older brother and I detest each other. I can barely remember a time when I didn't want to knock him on his ass and leave him bleeding on the floor.

When it comes to showing our hatred, though, that's where me and River differ. If I don't like somebody, they know it.

There's no point in playing games. It's a waste of time. But River likes to plan—to scheme.

He didn't want me here; I knew that. This was all a power move for him. To show me how much better he was than me. The success, the wealth, and now the wife. A wife who looked like a prisoner at that altar, staring at my brother with eyes vacant of anything but greed. I knew the wedding meant nothing, that it was probably for some sort of money-making plan they were both in on.

I guess it just shows how little my big brother knows about me. I may not run a fortune five-hundred company or have my name on a tower, but I have enough money to retire now and never run out, and my name is stitched on the backs of thousands of hockey jerseys and sold worldwide.

As far as the wife charade goes, if he was trying to make me jealous, he couldn't have been farther off.

*Euphoria*: A feeling you get from a good fuck, or from stepping off of an airplane after spending almost an entire day strapped into a seat so tiny only your left ass cheek fits. Then there are the crying kids and the old guys with sweaty armpits that won't stop snoring in your fucking ear. Even the deafening music in my headphones wasn't enough to tune it all out. Maybe if I wasn't already on edge from my trip, it wouldn't have bothered me as much. Nah, who am I kidding? Yes, it would have.

My phone hasn't stopped vibrating since I switched it back on. As message after message flashes across the screen, I watch Mom guilt me for leaving. I scold myself for getting her an international phone plan for the trip. I could have at least avoided this for a few days if I wasn't so damn eager to please her. I know it's not worth it—the hurt, anger, and betrayal. It doesn't matter what I do, she will always choose River.

I'm about to turn my phone back off when a different number

pops up on the screen. "Yeah?" I grumble, answering the call. I spot my Uber from the front doors of the airport and drag my suitcase to the car.

"Just wanted to make sure you landed safely. The flight that bad?" Matt jokes, a quiet giggle sounding behind him.

"Well, clearly I'm alive. You can rest easy now." I pull open the back door of the black SUV and crawl into the backseat, dumping my shit down on the seat behind me. "The flight was brutal. I'm dead tired."

I buckle my seatbelt and we start moving. *Almost home.*

"You didn't sleep on the flight? Come on! That's the only way to fly. If I don't sleep, I puke."

The only tolerable way to fly, yeah. But in the rush of packing and hauling ass out of Mykonos, I forgot my insomnia meds on the bathroom counter, so that wasn't happening.

"Overshare, Matt."

He laughs loudly. "Get some sleep, Ty. Text me sometime this week and we can make plans."

I nod my head even though Matt can't see me and close my eyes. "Sounds good. Thanks for checking in."

"Anytime. See ya," he says before hanging up. I shove my phone into my duffle bag before I become dead to the world.

Once I get home, I sleep straight through until the following afternoon. And after reintroducing myself to the living world, I spend the next two weeks on the ice.

I never take breaks from hockey—not unless I have no other choice—so I guess pushing myself to get back into my routine so quickly is my punishment for leaving town. I can't afford to lose focus, I've already made it so far, way further than I could have dreamed. Hockey is all I have. I can't fuck it up. I don't have a backup plan.

So, every morning, I wake up before the sun rises, drink a

mixture of raw eggs and protein powder, then spend the rest of the day with blades under my feet and the taste of metal in my mouth.

This morning, I showed up at the arena hours before practice was supposed to start. Usually, the arena is empty, but a deep, thundering voice echoes down the hallway as the Vancouver Warrior's new hopeful star player, and my best friend, rips into whoever was lucky enough to be on the receiving end of that call.

My eyes widen the second I hear him yell his younger sister's name. *Shit.*

"You're way too young to be doing this, Gracie!"

"I'm old enough for you to talk to me like an adult, Oakley!"

I stop dead in my tracks as the familiar female voice screams back at him, probably unknown to the fact that the call is on speakerphone.

"You want me to talk to you like an adult? That's rich considering you still act like you're sixteen! What would Mom think?"

"Don't bring up Mom right now. And stop trying to micromanage me! You're not my dad."

My teeth touch and I wince at the harshly thrown insult. The call is immediately taken off of speaker phone. As the blades of my skates dig into the scratched-up cement floor, I debate whether I should save myself the trouble of dealing with the aftermath of Gracie Hutton's erratic behaviour on the ice with her brother or spend the next hour listening to him rant about their conversation in hopes of lightening him up before practice.

"Fuck me," I huff, and proceed to the dressing room.

The door is open when I get there. Oakley sits hunched over on a wooden bench, fingers tangled in his wet, shaggy hair and breaths coming out in pants. He looks up briefly when he notices my presence. He nods once and lowers his eyes back to the floor between his bent knees.

"Hey," he mutters.

"You good?"

"Family drama. I'm fine."

"Ripping your hair out is something you do regularly then? Shit."

His fingers fall from his hair and into his lap. Leaning his back against the wall, he lets his head fall back against the blue brick. "You know the girl that Grant was bragging about? The one he took on the houseboat for three days back in June?" he asks, now staring at me with his lips peeled back in outrage.

"The one with the elastic back?" I recall, my brows furrowed.

"Jesus Christ, Tyler," he hisses. His shoulders shudder as he gags.

*Oh.* Rage is a familiar feeling as it taints my mind. I fight to keep my expression blank. "I mean, she was a dancer."

A sharp pain shoots through my shoulder when he hits it with his, a pointed warning written across his tightened features.

"I'm joking."

"You're not funny."

I keep my voice level. "You don't have to worry about Grant, Oakley."

Nobody should worry about that fucking dweeb. Of all the hockey players on the team, Grant Westen wasn't one I expected her to fool around with. He barely even makes it off the bench and has the maturity of a twelve-year-old.

Her standards must have dropped since the group of us: Oakley, Ava, Gracie, Adam and I, got back from Mexico last year. After everything that happened between the two of us on that resort, the thought of Gracie with Grant has my molars grinding to dust.

"You don't get it. You don't have a sister."

"Just a bastard of a brother instead." I collapse on the bench beside him.

"True," Oakley laughs while raising his arms above his head in a stretch. "It's just not a topic I want to be brought up around me. I don't give a shit who any of you sleep with as long as it isn't my damn sister."

Guilt paints my insides. I can't say who Gracie does and doesn't sleep with is a topic I want brought up either. Not when I spent a week last year inside of her, hearing her cry my name and learning the different ways to make her soak her panties.

I swallow. That entire trip was a mistake, which is why I've barely seen Gracie since then. I'm already up to my eyebrows in guilt from the last time. Any more and I'll end up choking on it. Whatever happened between us is done. It was the right decision to cut contact.

"Duly noted," I mutter.

"As much as I want to sign with this team, I'm not going to if it means that I'll have to hear about more of that."

I scoff. "Yeah right. You'll sign with this team no matter what."

His laugh is a sign that I'm right on the money. Oakley would do anything to play in Vancouver again. He wouldn't throw that opportunity away for anything.

"Don't tell that to Seattle. They still think they have a shot in the dark."

"They'll have to go through me and the entire VW team to get to you."

Oakley throws his arm around my shoulder as he nods and murmurs dreamily, "Don't make me blush, Ty."

# Acknowledgements

Books have always been my passion. And to now say that I have a copy of my very own book sitting on my bookshelf is such an amazing accomplishment. But I know that without a group of very amazing people, my dream would still be that—a dream.

To my fiancé, I am forever grateful for your constant love and for the countless late nights spent listening to me go on and on about Avley's story. We both know that without your hockey expertise, I couldn't have pulled this off.

A special thank you to my amazing group of alpha readers. I love you all so much.

To my editor, thank you for helping turn this absolute mess into something I'm not afraid to publish. You're always a dream.

A big thank you to booksnmoods for creating such stunning covers for this series. Muah!

To Hannah Smith at Penguin Random House…thank you for making my dreams come true.

And to my readers, you have been here supporting me always, and that means more than I could ever express to you.
Thank you.

# He just wanted a decent book to read ...

Not too much to ask, is it? It was in 1935 when Allen Lane, Managing Director of Bodley Head Publishers, stood on a platform at Exeter railway station looking for something good to read on his journey back to London. His choice was limited to popular magazines and poor-quality paperbacks – the same choice faced every day by the vast majority of readers, few of whom could afford hardbacks. Lane's disappointment and subsequent anger at the range of books generally available led him to found a company – and change the world.

*'We believed in the existence in this country of a vast reading public for intelligent books at a low price, and staked everything on it'*
**Sir Allen Lane, 1902–1970, founder of Penguin Books**

The quality paperback had arrived – and not just in bookshops. Lane was adamant that his Penguins should appear in chain stores and tobacconists, and should cost no more than a packet of cigarettes.

Reading habits (and cigarette prices) have changed since 1935, but Penguin still believes in publishing the best books for everybody to enjoy. We still believe that good design costs no more than bad design, and we still believe that quality books published passionately and responsibly make the world a better place.

So wherever you see the little bird – whether it's on a piece of prize-winning literary fiction or a celebrity autobiography, political tour de force or historical masterpiece, a serial-killer thriller, reference book, world classic or a piece of pure escapism – you can bet that it represents the very best that the genre has to offer.

**Whatever you like to read – trust Penguin.**